CANNONBALL

ALSO BY JOSEPH MCELROY

A Smuggler's Bible
Hind's Kidnap: A Pastoral on Familiar Airs
Ancient History: A Paraphase
Lookout Cartridge
Plus
Ship Rock. A Place
Women and Men
The Letter Left To Me
Exponential (Essays – in Italian translation)
Actress in the House
Preparations for Search (Novella)
Night Soul and Other Stories

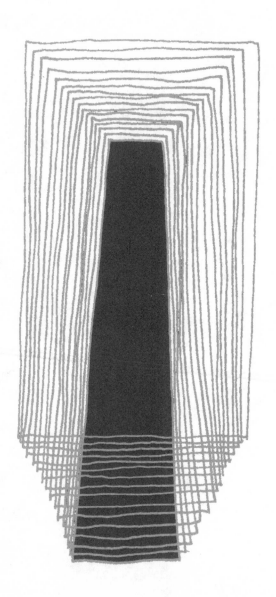

CANNONBALL

JOSEPH McELROY

DZANC
BOOKS

My thanks to three readers: Matt Bell,
Mike Heppner, and Robert Walsh.
J.M.
2013

DZANC
BOOKS

1334 Woodbourne Street
Westland, MI 48186
www.dzancbooks.org

CANNONBALL

"to meet the water," an excerpt from *Cannonball* in slightly different form, appeared in *J&L Illustrated* #3, ed. Paul Maliszewski, J&L Books, 2012, pp. 245-55.

Brief quotations from *The Complete Poems of Emily Dickinson* (ed. Thomas H. Johnson, Boston: Little Brown, 1960) appear in the body of the narrative—specifically from #488, 712, 754, 986, 1129, 1398, 1428, 1553, 1556, and 1642.

Published 2013 by Dzanc Books
Design by Steven Seighman
Cover art by G. Davis Cathcart

ISBN: 978-1-938604-21-8
Second edition: December 2013

This project is supported in part by awards from the National Endowment for the Arts and Michigan Council for Arts and Cultural Affairs.

Printed in the United States of America

10   9   8   7   6   5   4   3   2

1   to meet the water

It is my brother I would speak of — I will call him that —
though I begin with the Scrolls. How they made it through
by water, as our people, a sect of them, said they would who
reportedly at their peril had slid them like rolled-up maps into
a capsule and sent them on their way underground secured
from those who would have misused them. A great find, it was
said, a weapon in the war — for in a way they *were* "maps"
(though all Legend). Yet the Scrolls floating hundreds of miles
under the deserts from En Gedi, even Gaza, eastward along
a web of roughly horizontal wells, like missives arriving then
with such long-range accuracy of time and place, proved
less stunning on that day I record than the apparition on a
diving board himself all too solid and familiar as the pool
was notorious and strange. Suddenly here was my friend, *my*
find — my borderline Chinese so far from our home — in
the depths of a Middle Eastern palace standing immense and
unlikely above waters put there once for a tyrant to swim, dive
into, own, withhold, and worse.

It is my friend I frame, *my* find, found and lost, from the neighborhood of another desert himself not Mesopotamian or American (though he wished). Border Chinese large enough of body and of heart for three potentates or persons, quite recently a vagabond teen in the public pools of a Southern California city who, ineligible to serve, still went to war, tracked me to that palace or was lured, large soul.

Speak of what you know, it's said. Because you were there. With a company piece of junk, an Army videocam not neutral but more yours than your hand holding it, expected to catch the scene as if your job is all you need to do. At one level, the arrival of the Scrolls I had been told to keep to myself. As if that were doing something. Yet at the now crucial moment a dive exploding off a sixteen-foot-long American-made springboard, someone I knew — a friend, I trust. Which largely escapes those at poolside — the nearly naked at their humid, echoing recreation, civilian, brass, in that still intact showplace of the capital's outskirts, among them one set of eyes I thought I recognized if I could only recall his job — faintly like a teacher long ago? biology in the eyes, calculus in the heart, face, chin? — and a few plain-vanilla American women and men in camouflage fatigues (one in an old collector's-item flak vest, at least didn't probably have to share it) back near the pool's walls garlanded with mosaic scenes and Arabic codes, fingering grainy butts of holstered .45s or packing M4 carbines ideal for close-quarter potshots 'case something happens. Which was surely not the dive, left somehow above the deposed tyrant's pool as if it might end there, a second thought, though electrifying.

Though I, a house-to-house Specialist (slow on the uptake, I've been told) armed with what you see plus an equipment bag, fall back now on some other slowness of the diver, my friend midair twenty feet above the water and more than that above what was to happen, feeling it like a wound in my chest. While time, of which there seems so little between springboard and water, instant and instant, all but ignores this unlikely diver huge as a Sumo wrestler in my depth of field, only I knew how young up there coming off the old-fashioned cocoa-matting.

Why the diver came to make that dive in that place, a palace pool, I would know before I'm done. You know already, you *always* knew, I think he says (he could be right), this matchless, often absent friend, my bond, my shadow enlarged — a grandly begun, almost incomplete dive or aiming to meet the sounds the increasing Rock music temblors rising from under this pool. An unidentified arrival up there on the board other armed watchers see the diver as this heavy out of nowhere, Asian or GI — how did he get in? through the ceiling painted with lyrebirds and Egyptian vultures, arabesques of paradise with magenta wings? — hailing from up there this witness his friend it seemed seeing me who aims a standard videocam automatically hurriedly from the hip, the chest, heart, history, keeping in my pocket in reserve the world's neatest mini able to take stills too. The long desert day behind him, my friend launches like a game bird from the onetime marshes his upward dive (convertible at will we always recall back home into a tsunami of a cannonball) which ends still in shock, hope, the mind of an unknowing spy, forgetting his own language. My friend appearing in that palace pool nine thousand miles give or take a country from where I stand eighteen months later, an emerging professional or getting there, California veteran with a deal, to say what I saw, or show what I saved, really I see now suspend that dive, and maybe all it is is why I enlisted.

How fine a fool to be a spy and not know it — witness, but to what? For spies the art of war will avoid it, though more to war than spies we learn from Sun Tzu, obvious if you ask strategists in Taiwan or, week in week out, subtle for the football coach who ascribes his success partly to *The Art of War*. Yet what is new about our ignorance of those who would own us? How do we speak in the midst of what we're ignorant of? Nothing to it, let me tell you. What we're made for on this good earth. Plotting an arc of motions that plotted me. A dive that would swallow up the pool, while history saw it differently, this pleasure place of the lately apprehended tyrant tiled with the vineyards of a vision, minaret, turret, once rich ceramic alcoves, cellars, and arched halls, surprising gardens, erotic resting rooms you might want to renovate, private mosque, and kitchens once red with lamb and trampled vintage, dark levels below even the strangely gamy waters of this pool — detainment quarters we'd erroneously heard housed even their captive leader, his bunker (ours now in the absence of our own bunker busters), and, most, the very wells or one that had been waiting to receive a weapon of critical instruction, long on its way encapsuled, sought for its own sake and to prove the rightness of the war if not even pay for it. A scroll or Scrolls it was said; and, recalling the Dead Sea discoveries, the Gnostic manuscripts at Nag Hammadi, a scroll for a scroll, some strict-constructionist archaeologists say. And now I suspected maybe the thing I had been sent to shoot was under the very waters beside which I found myself, under the pool itself, another level down.

That one of our own specialists, so far from being dug in out among potshard and skull-sown hills, should have been instead wisely waiting for the find to come to *him* (his team), deep in the foundations of a conquered palace and by water along the wells and ruined sewers below pool level — seemed a feat — an Olympic-homing *How* shrouding the ancient *What* of the Scrolls themselves, their said-to-be-Roman/Syriac phrases and good news, ancient stuff of revelation itself. Yet revolutionary, we learn, in their firsthand word this time of the man from Nazareth, a fighter and free trader in ideas, economist, this Jesus the Scrolls would profile in a rare interview, no less than a man who, having the experience to disappear and reappear, might later be one of us attending California Hearings on Competition and who'd somehow always known that to him who hath shall be given. Why did the thought seem familiar? That an undeniable weapon of instruction in the war of thoughts which is history should have turned up as predicted by our people seemed unprecedented because of this seldom piloted network of wells that had survived the mines parachuted in evidently, garden-variety bombs from other wars, our top-loaded quake littering "their backyard" with burnt-out vehicles, roadside attractions, barbecued faces, and "headless horsemen," as a tabloid back home had put evidently it, this "fertile croissant" where agriculture began, this cradle of civilization, of wine-growing, to say nothing of infrastructural casualties of the military war by now winding down, a clock stopped but ticking.

The late Hearings bring back the reasons for the war and, as if he was one, the full figure of my friend Umo. Elusive, illegal, happily homeless we would think here and in Baja at going on fourteen (when we first knew him but wouldn't have guessed his age), going off a high board into one of our outdoor pools, he was later to find his moment in that other pool nine thousand miles east. Biographers say "was to" (or "would") as if they could have known what their man would do. We know better still. Make history our own. Or conceive what we could not know about my friend, a disappearing act competing with me as the worst but best friends will, had we been never so christened with hindsight and what appeared to be the will to win for our city the site of these so-called "postwar" Hearings, their announced Spring Theme Competition. Which, like the Scrolls, was good for anybody grounded, or trying to be, in gain and growth, gifts grounded but not to be hidden away. Even, as I found, in the Goals split up by the Conference organizers into panels and days of far-flung questions, in the later Hearings embracing the Scrolls themselves, what remained of them, for they were Scrolls, and how belief in competition might eclipse belief-based competition itself, to say nothing of faith in your own time management business, the very fragrance you're marketing, and the newfound Master's ancient assurance that "if you give alms it is evil you will do to the beggar and your own spirit." For I had rethought spirit coming home from my war. Where I overshoot is where I still am. Trying for this.

It was the summer of 2001 that word of Umo spread among us. Enterprising stray, giant waif, *What will he do?* this upstart and mysterious truant. A newly opened public pool I myself was told of — *why?* I later asked myself. A bright seacoast day, a population, everyone there. *Two* pools, two blue-floored freshly chlorined oblongs, seen by the recruiting blimp above us, tiles of real estate passing beautiful, squares of California, square 2, square 1.

Suddenly this. What would he do, this massive person at home up there on the high board? Big boy and then some; "big" the smallest word for what this was. Torso, shoulders, legs, long black hair, cheeks puffy about the eyes, the spread of face presiding Asian over three hundred and some pounds you would understand, ready to go, in command. Of what? He looks sixteen, seventeen, this sure-footed newcomer of a scale majestically slower along the durable acrylic surface rough as a bearded lizard's back. His first go off the board.

It would take a beating, if that is even true of boards? He padded out to the end, bent his knees to snap his springboard and let its give lift him jumping straight up. To come back down and bounce again toes pointed and again. And in midair turned immensely and landed and bounced and — the confidence also of a kid — landed now as if he would go off backward but, settling the board, walked to where he'd started, and about-faced.

What could have prepared you, though, for the jump which was first that high, prancing approach hop onto the almost end of the board to depress its laminated wood-and-fiberglass core so deep — don't I myself know — it might have thrown Umo out into the street had he not landed straight up and let the board lift him — like a tool you should let do its work, as my father, a somewhat unfinished carpenter and craftsperson, in the garage would sometimes say of plane or hoe or knife or tinkering with his stopwatches that would one day time Umo — upward stretched leaping like a crane to the wind rising at first eternally only at the top to become a thing compressed like a spring but turned into like a rock in space or something inevitable: and this was the cannonball later discussed, as we liked to say, the mother and brother of all cannonballs to target a pool in our city: that where he hit you'd have said the water parted six feet down and within four of the turquoise-tiled bottom, indicating in the flushed pit of its absence with strange exactness the concave point of the drain that marked the graded low point of the deep end.

It was like one of our patented earthquakes, but from the air. You wondered the excellent homegrown tiles did not crack their grouting.

A pregnant soul well back of the brink got drenched and stood her ground leaning back on her hips, gray-haired. Two deck chairs almost waterborne I seemed to make look back at me, on one a newborn uncomplaining till saved from drowning.

The sound of the impact like something being permanently fixed blots out of my slow mind for a second the future war, its meaning, and Umo's eventual link to the Scrolls. For what do we need if not distraction from the burdens of our nation, our responsibilities, as my mother put it?

Now kids give the high board ladder space. Umo's feat is something else, that day of the first cannonball. No one wants to go and there's a murmur. A path is parted for him back to the ladder. Someone said, "That's Umo." So somebody knew him. "Changsta," someone called. You felt the awe, the silence, the bias. His broad back, bull neck, his confident arms, his hands climbing the silver rungs, holding on, had I seen that back before? Rung by rung, a race apart, brute prophecy was it? A prophecy not easy for me. Someone said, "Cannonball!" Someone older, "He's going again."

A parent near me, something in how he held himself, T-shirt, a camouflage vest, and you didn't know what else to be inventoried under it because when the man hollered to the big boy to get down off that board, I knew him for an Old Town cop off-duty with children here, hand over his heart maybe. I thought he would do something, it's a free country, you can try: stop the engulfing wave sure to arise from Umo's more than weight that threatened with a second cannonball to evacuate half the water at his end of the pool: a strange but (the kids

knew) worthwhile risk, Umo bouncing and bouncing on City
equipment. "Big buck, yellow tail," the off-duty cop-parent said
to his little girl — which wasn't the "style" we hoped in our
award-winning port city with its melting-pot neighborhoods,
its opportunity, its Christian lenders, its Gaslamp Quarter,
pink sidewalks, Fashion Valley, and Pacific Beach. The little girl
said, "He's Chinese." "Monkey outa nowhere," said the man
who yelled to Fatso not to go again. "Nobody's out of *no*where,"
came a woman's voice, an old party in a hat.

What could have prepared you for what came next? The
approach, a surplus some might say or vastness of flowing flesh
— secret weapon, yay, but a target surely, the sun itself marking
the glimmering, drying shoulders up there, the slick hair. Off-
duty cop, his hand inside his vest. A cannonball again? Until
it hits the water a dive is not a dive, we know, so swift but
sometimes a slowness so divided it might never finish in your
mind; and the swan — or *front* dive — that arched upward now
from a board bent not to breaking but to some force unforeseen
by "the maker," as we trace performance to the factory, carried
Umo up arms at full stretch for all to see, or see from his vista
— the city out beyond the Presidio and the Marine Lab and out
to shark land and whale country, unknown sea, high it could
seem as our much traveled Assemblyman's hang glider riding
a broomstick thermal sliding out of the sky it seemed like for
a few feet above the sacred peak in Rio harbor: a cannonball
to maybe blast us all out this time, but no: for suddenly the
diver, that human bulk, its arms now at its sides, axled a great
diameter impossibly greater than the diver himself and wheeled
over into a layout somersault-and-a-half, not tuck, not even
jackknife-pike position but layout more distinguished than any
stunt for which mysteriously (if you measure it) there could not

9

have been time but, in the gasp of silence or gratitude through which we heard two car horns like another question off the I-8, wheeled the huge spoke of this person's body, its flesh, surplus and all, a devoted unit aiming to meet the water hands first, bring somehow legs and toes following the rest of him to snap upright like a tail — and no less a cannonball, it came to me — hands, head, shoulders, belly, hips into the water — for no real splash at all I must be understood to say, but a perfectly small spurt fountaining a foot high at most and a muffled thud like when you fire a smooth stone end over end out into Otay Lake over the head of an outboard troller and it slips in with scarcely a gulp.

2 I have died

How did he do it? Were we amazed? A spreading faith afoot among the watchers. A vanishing, a death almost, but wait. I saw the cop ship his personal pistol back under his arm. It looked something like the .22 semi-auto my aunt and uncle use, like the old German model. A crowd gathered at the pool ladder looking down there for this alien who seemed to hang under water for the longest time before he took hold of a rung and shot up like a penguin.

"Pouring like a waterfall," said the old person, thin in a bikini and a down-under bush hat, a light like candle power in her face, an accent sort of English. "He's an animal," said the off-duty. "Just some of us are better at it," the old person's reply and then, oddly, "He's on our team," she adds. And thirty yards away across a corner of pool, Umo looked in our direction, mine. *What did you* think *you were doing here?* The old dame looking my way too, not quite in my eyes but below them, her skin all over spots or like some body painting trade you get in our city, her sandals and a flash of Moroccan gold on the toenails supportive somehow, her hat that of someone you'd visit, an old bird of a person.

And indeed I *had* seen the diver somewhere. Swimming? Swimming away from me, that was it. Slow motion muscled in folds and rolls of flesh, that back — its rolling bulk. His weight not what was said, but a rumor. But it was something you could see.

"Next stop, Olympic trials!" it was I who called out.

"Who'm I swimmin' for?" he shouted over his shoulder — he was sparring with three seniors from my school who needed to push him in and took to shoving and one missed and fell and his brother got mad and lunged and missed and magically fell in like a wrestler who can't help stepping outside the ring. The off-duty parent-cop looked at me: "Who you think you're talking to?" "East Hill," I called out to Umo.

"East Hill, they got a coach there," Umo called back again, he knew where I was, it seemed. And this was some days before Umo knew me, I had to think, though it was my father the coach of East Hill Club he had in mind, a USA Swimming affiliate club especially well known to me.

"Got no business up there, keep the fat boy off the board, that's what we need to do," said the off-duty. Three girls grabbing at Umo's orange backpack, blocked his way, bathing suit gigglers manhandling his friendly flesh. But what *was* his "way"? Would he go again? People wanted it. "A coach, all right," again he called, "but we need *you*." Just talk, but why that difference?

Me? Was it me? How old was he? Old for his age. It was the two entries into the water, one exploding, the second silent, or even *im*ploding, we say so familiarly; first, the cannonball, but then that overflowing bulk layered below the armpits slipping through water it seemed to make quiet, to anticipate. It was shock and it was vanishing. What did the diver mean, *We need you?* Nothing, to tell the truth. The sun I realized was behind me. Time itself splits up and is at me from all directions, I was nobody. I needed to get home. But why?

I tried to get around the corner of the pool through the crowd to ask Umo what he had meant. My father's job in mind now, if I could bring him some talent. Help him. "… take over the world, those people," said my neighbor the cop, not so off-duty after all. "He has a right," someone said; I turned to see an undernourished guy with an earring and a beard nod to me, "Maybe he has, maybe he don't. See you in court."

Umo had gone. How had he gotten away?

I have dived, but am only a swimmer now, and often know what it is I am seeing. Or I know what I can do — I thought I did — and can tell a rumor flying a mile away. *Thirteen going on fourteen* was hard to credit, and somehow true. By the Fall of my junior year I had again spotted Umo — swimming at Ballast Circle on the south side and at Balboa Knoll on the east. That huge flip turn at the far end, and he comes up in a sweeping breaststroke only now, mid-lap, to medley into a freestyle rolling to swamp neighboring lanes at will, yet somehow not entirely *in* the water, riding it, his broad back rolling not all that much; a skimmer, too, was how you remembered him, a force if he felt like it, puffy eyes slit straight across, not "slant" (as immigrant watchers even in our Pacific city will term them), but concentrating and relaxed the citizen lap-swimmer with limited time, a purpose, a timeless habit I realized was what had made me notice in the first place months before I saw him go off a board. And *not* notice (if that is possible).

What did Umo bring, so free, though homeless it was said?

He made me want to speak.

As I do.

You want to do something with the rumors they cook up, anyone from family to the highest levels as you must know. But was that it? Speak for yourself is more it. I wondered if from his people or country, his years equaled half again as many of ours, somewhat as we reckon the human age of the African osprey we learned about so long as it avoids being pulled under by big fish it preys on from the air: so Umo's thirteen, our twenty, the way we do with dogs or space-naut relatives who come back ten years younger, is more like it, or those very old Tibetans once upon a time. Already he was said to be Mongol Manchurian (was that Chinese?), rumored older — in his twenties — even Muslim, and encountered one day on a corner near my school, the first Fall month of my junior year — then gone. Where did he get to? Water his medium that first summer, Mexico-based, Baja trucking; but from the other side of the world was where he "was originally from," as my mother likes to say, and "illegal as all get out"; mystery man (and kid); joker not quite, for my money. Young crook we heard.

I saw him throw his legs out and sit down on the end of a high board in August that gave so far he might have slipped off. Only to rebound onto his feet, sit down again and go higher now. Maybe well-over-three-hundred-pound teen, his greatness a specialty, was how others saw him and were moved by him, not his everyday life, like me. The diver we'd been maybe waiting for. In our public pools. It wasn't me, certainly. Swan, back one and a half, and my once-upon-a-time favorite, the half gainer that launched you out into a forward-flying back dive, Coach yelling, "Out too far!" as if I didn't hear.

Later, twists were the secret — and now I thought as if in our ancient sea life we had come out of the water exposing all of our body plane by plane, elbow by elbow. A plain full twist, arm across chest first pointing the way, like a sworn loyalty, a beauty. As I was in the end called upon to explain at the Hearings in front of another audience, maybe hungry for competition and the failure of others where they imagined I was telling all I knew about competition. For Umo comes up and what might have been his last dive and, it was thought, the insurgent enemy's last-minute targeting of the suddenly important Scrolls and their early first-century witness to Christ's work ethic to go with all the other witnessing to whoever. His food-fasting vision and good sense, never losing your cool with a rival or over-broadcasting your edge to a pretty woman come to a well with her bucket, experience you don't just have but learn from. Nine thousand miles away in that other seamy, medium toxic though chlorine-rich pool, deep within a deposed leader's palace or very vitals, Umo makes his approach along the board. The double cluck of a chamber at the ready behind me I hear and forget the Scrolls, catch gun oil on the humid air, a hint of burn, a scent of black manganese phosphate I would swear if I could believe the user had found the means to re-rustproof her barrel like back home, or was it a smell of salted raw flesh that haunted my bowel, my balls? We were awaiting momentarily the Scrolls, my orders said, rumor rife in Administration circles already of early first-century Christian, by all reports either a young Roman or Jesus's brother, who, on a friendly footing, had interviewed him on a range of issues, sustainable risk prediction, wind, water, capital punishment within reason, turning always back to the talent that begins as a small-case seed but placed in good earth cannot but grow great, can't miss. Why was I at pool level shooting a dive and not down below at Scroll reception-point among the archaeologists et al?

And why out of nowhere this diver who'd stood before me many times back home? His *own person* another foreigner had said of Umo when he was fourteen (which sometimes means, I see, *Look out*, or *Trouble*). Whose home, though? I ask, like a *why* or a *how* I would put together to understand for myself this Competition our at first not quite postwar Hearings are about. The dive, once up and happening, will be thoughtless, opening, closing — what my father meant by "character" — you just do it. It speaks for itself. Is what it is — which seemed to say, *is*, not *what*. To me, though, retired from diving at sixteen, now home-from-the-war sports psychologist-in-the-making at almost twenty-one as it happened (years after quitting diving), the instants of the dive, infinitely little, half-known to intent derived from all the little I know, and reckoned in your chin and armpits, arching back and calves, as I have so far worked it out (helped by a struggling eleventh-grade teacher who was an assistant coach but more) from increments of flight infinitely slowing and small — like interruption, my sister said (but what of? she said) and you don't mean they're real like snapshots or (she also said one night when I came home from my own enlistment party) *what was it in you* close as the person so close up you can't see her or say what it is, a double-talk narrowing really the thought down, even if Dad cut you short, or a fine, sometimes puzzled, wild teacher taking your speeds to show you where you were at one instant, till years later you cared.

A math that I later linked with life — or slowing down, or reliving, even the lunch hour between morning and afternoon sessions on a day of the Hearings reserved in part for me, careless with figures, honestly. And my own memorial for Umo in particular this big person's entry into the waters of a onetime luxury pool in the basement of an appropriated palace during the war which came up to meet him though that was not the end of it: which recalled all over again a future of my own not that descried by my mother through her daily windshield missing nothing at the wheel or by my father, Reservist big-time who the Spring I graduated high school had made his peace with the coming war across the board (meaning little to me as he reported it except to place on me some curious decision unless he was salting me up), and he would have to reconcile himself *and* my mother (he said) to *my* serving, though maybe not her. What did it matter? It was the last thing he said about it to me at any rate. A father is a father.

My teammate Milt wouldn't think of going, and if elected would not serve. He often quoted his dad, North-side Lutheran minister, whom I photographed bowling once, right arm out-thrust in follow-through so long ago with Milt in the foreground and blurred but his diagonally slanting, almost converging eyebrows visible, as my sister pointed out, and the minister's very own black-and-white "DNA ball" we called it bending down the alley ambushing the head pin to bring them all down, a first strike — a father for you — and once, surprising him when I took a picture of him in his living room his hands clasped together talking to Milt and me, there would be no Draft and if there was had we heard of civil disobedience? A father for you.

For have I begun really with mine, my dad I will call him (and not after all with my friend and with the Scrolls sent under the Mesopotamian desert by water)? — a father who because everyone needs a hobby, not knowing it should be your life, taught me, when I was so young it was still The Dark, how to make a darkroom with a sheet of plywood half covering the bathtub: work slow then fast, change the whole look, the take, lifting a picture with your tongs, agitating it in its bath sometimes diluted (not by me) of TD3 turning its (no telling what) … *spirit* I could now not then say to my testy teacher aware that I would soon get back to working on Lego castles and precarious balconies with my sister, "E," who was willing to follow with her delicate hand (though not as my father taught me) and would join me in our improvised darkroom for experiments parenthetical and blurry she had thought up so we ran out of printing paper and had to ask Dad to get us some more though how it curled up at the edges killed him — whose *face* itself would have been something to work with, my sister said, a crowd in itself, teaching me important things about crowds, I saw, as well as our father, though she was younger, and giggling in the middle of something in the dark remembering how our mother was the one who … who … who said the word "spirit."

How to swim as well, I was willing to believe our father taught me, though I began with more there; and had less of him because my father belonged to hundreds of others in the tile-hard, watery fields (yes) of two unforgiving swimming pools in particular — a somewhat well-known coach at our club targeting Zone meets and always Olympic shortlists but at my high school too, though there, at the risk of getting fired he relied on our cherished assistant, Wick, it is always coming to a head long ago and then recently at the Hearings, it comes up at the Hearings, my dad trained with the Reserve every year and went to meetings, though I see he was away a lot Umo's second summer among us. There were postponements and, putting it all together (but what?), I recall as a habit my father's trips to Sacramento on swimming business and a week's East Coast "DC junket," announced by my mother after he was gone. Travel helped him "blow off steam." These trips added up, stopping off at Colorado Springs, an Olympics meeting, on the way home. Wick was polite about it. Get into that loop it's endless. What loop? "Zone business."

My father sometimes knew exactly what the score was, and sometimes it was about him. He had the latest news, named names who were for him and was still close-lipped, boiled things down; though who for? Maybe in the end someone, but who would know? Me? Though complained that he had been "pigeonholed" as a backstroke specialist curiously soon after I, his son, quit competitive diving. Our historically AAU-affiliated club in its own small way a fixture here like the Marine Lab (which as I pointed out to a father not amused is also "an independent swimming club sometimes"), kept a weather eye on the Olympics, the now "USA Swimming" affiliates (since-just-after-Vietnam, my dad once said), the authentication of meet times, alliances read sometimes as if between the lines of directives coming out of Colorado Springs — but within and beyond, where the money came from. This was what was really going on. And to be placed, if not by me, in the overall scales.

(A father is not an older brother either.)

East Hill had sent three freestylers to the early Zone trials the year before, and a 400 butterfly; but not really our coach, his status that of a provisional backstroke backup coach. The funding was quite real to me, I see now, the money, if I never seemed to think about it, and why would I? It often seemed to come from people, and to be private by some smart, even brilliant stroke like a signature or a voice. I heard Colorado Springs — somewhere where a committee "sat" — and Washington, DC. And a Sacramento-based speechwriter my mother said Dad had glommed onto or the other way around, who worked both coasts.

On a shelf in my father's office at East Hill stood my grandfather's copy of *God Is My Co-Pilot*, about the overage Flying Tiger in World War II China. On the wall among many informative photos one outdoor shot, somewhat boring, from 1968 of a Vietnam correspondent he had known standing with an older guy who had on a seemingly white suit and a dark tie and a dark hat, not looking at the camera, the head of the World Bank, hands on his hips, and the difference in the way the two men stood a giveaway, and contrasts of dark and light, it seemed to me, whatever the World Bank was. Well, my father was an expert on government support for true enterprise; on water, which trusts us and is to be trusted; on the body's forces and vectoring diagonals to a point where, with the will and practice (and team desire), you might *become* a hydrofoil; expert on a trick with the abs, a kind of hike with the muscles, to get the extra stroke on the man in the next lane (yet keeping it all "seamless"). A difficult man (my own father) — nothing personal, perhaps — who knew the way to lift the elbow just so far to swing the wrist through. The body this thing or raft with side paddles ("let the tool do the work," he said in his shop in the garage) and a kick motor that never stops, while, face down except to breathe (like a religion with him), the pool floor glimmering below like the ground, you were a bird on the wing, the planes of air your depth.

Did he love science more than the stopwatch — or team chemistry? If you had to ask, he couldn't explain it to you. Why do I recall here the very rare photo my dad found of mine in the school paper that made him mad enough to anyway shove me: an underexposed overcrowded shot on slow film like a botched time delay of three and a half girls jogging. Nice, my sister had said, eyes and heads everywhere; which set Dad off. Photography was photography. It's a matter of getting it — no more than that, he said with a contempt that disowned me, so once again I thought maybe forget it, a wick waiting for a match. Yet he came back and talked some more, like an unhappy eccentric. A camera could remember a face and catch a criminal, he pointed out (as I recall the pad of bare feet past my room in the middle of the night and my sister's). And I heard him say still photos were an eyewitness record to show a swimmer his habits, his "shape" better than video any day. Some swimmers, he said, "mature ridiculously young" and "the embrace" of the water reminds them of "when they were a fish or nothing and they shouldn't forget they might still wind up nothing."

So long as the competitive drive is there, roughly what he said, awash with echoes, and more than roughly.

Coach's unpredictable kindness — asking you, coaxing you like there was no God to find your form, your "shape": Was that how he did it, co-axing you? E replied, she was on the floor below me charming the floor itself stacking magazines she would clip from, science, home carpentry, garden, fish and game, electrical merchandising, that fell to her before being thrown out. She chuckled (exactly the word) from her cocoon, my pretty sister, to mine and couldn't stop, yet joined me with a word wherever I was going when I was going to stop to be surprised by her: "Coaxing to find ... what?" she said — " ... like a faith and a better one for his money if he could let you alone" — what other profit was there than the competitive beat of your life? "His 'competitive' could make you choke, "E said, remembering.

Because nobody knew what shape he meant for you, or beat — like breathing, if you didn't think about it — words we all including the team joked about, but for him just so, but one day I heard myself think them — *zone, water trust, take inventory, character* (just do it), *reach* (from the shoulder not the hand, whether swimming or at the pistol firing range) — think those words like my own far from home, even why I had enlisted; and knowing not quite empty-handed who and what I might be looking at up there approaching the end of the imported Maharajah cocoa matting suddenly of a dictator's U.S.-imported three-meter board in that palace of a wartime Green Zone outskirt. A payoff, was it? — of all the talk, rumors, interesting spite voiced against Umo to turn him into a notorious delinquent enticed on another business trip — or intervention, as it turned out — into the war itself, was it?

3 water trusts

Umo didn't go to school. I had learned this from the genius who tried to push him into the pool. How did *he* know? One morning first thing my older brother who hadn't addressed me in almost years told me my "Chinese friend" was a hoodlum, a bad guy, a crook, and a smuggler. That would be the day, I said; at fourteen? I said — not even. My mother on the phone shook her head eyeing me: I always knew too much.

In truth, too little, I said with *my* eyes. For *was* this Umo my friend, I thought? If illegal and Chinese, where could he settle? Not the first time people knew things I didn't. I had run into him at three pools. He had lived in Chula Vista on the street working for the Sanitation Department as a night engineer's helper, in fact seen near Otay Park at midnight under the streetlight heading a salvaged soccer ball into the garbage truck's cruncher too late for another kid to rescue it.

Part Manchurian, if one cared, it turned out, though there was more — this kid, this stranger who knew of East Hill swimming club and my father the coach and was friendly with the old woman in the hat at the pool and the free blood pressure nurse on Market Street and Station. Had he known me that first day? Because the proprietor of an out-of-the-way store that I and Milt visited religiously every other weekend who knew foreign languages had asked me how I had liked Umo on the springboard and I told him, never thinking how The Inventor — the name we knew him by — knew I'd been there for that first double-barreled launch.

How had I forgotten? Yet how good, it came to me, to forget that The Inventor himself had told us to be there.

For some unusual activ*eety*, I thought he'd said. Told not me but Milt in the middle of some argument The Inventor was having over the phone with a customer, a model of a canoe at issue, and I was clear across the room flipping through the business envelopes in a shoebox. Yet when I remembered later, it seemed to have been for me, across that distance — Be there for some diving activ*eety* (how The Inventor spoke) of a highly unusual nature. It was natural to show up for the opening of a pool in this city where we have almost everything you need — even this cluttered, how-did-he-make-a-living store not by any means all junk, owned by a man with skin like night who said things and having spoken might think a moment and write it down in a book he had. Such that you were willing to pay now and then for an envelope that came out of a shoebox full of envelopes at the back of the store.

For *a message*, the man had said; but he would say things like that. And his foreign command of the language — no less so for being foreign it came to me — that left its sometimes weirder words potential or a message in me like sediment in me a waterperson or not worth the work to share with anyone but my sister, for he would once in a blue moon crash land in an awkward or, better still, dirty word which he thought merely vivid.

Though show up at the new pool for as good as *a message*? That's what The Inventor had said and I'd forgotten in the middle of Milt attacking Hindu views. (Of what? my sister asked that night. Anything alive, I said. Anything? she said.) Indiscriminate valuing of anything alive, it seemed.

My sister I cherished for things only she said: dumb things, my father thought. But that you thought about then — the way you might oversleep or not take an insult seriously. My girlfriend wondered too about my sister E. Didn't think her dumb, but what's the fuss? (*No* fuss, Liz.) And what's so great about forgetting? she went on, . I do it all the time. (Liz, that's what I — forget it, Liz.) But I did say I couldn't explain it but if no one asks me why my sister affects me, I know, it's how she surprises you with something next to you you could fall into, or how she rearranges her room or uses her hands, or knows you like a sister, and sounds like I'd never had one before.

One evening she and her little boyfriend and his older sister with the driver's license had seen Umo at the risk of his life hitch a southbound truck on the Interchange with Baja plates. "Don't belittle him; you should have seen him just before he hopped in, standing there an inch from the traffic." Belittle Umo? He was in the workforce, I said, recalling then that Umo, only thirteen supposedly, had called out to me that first time at the new pool that I was "needed." One night in a darkened movie theater, a crisis of global countdown there in front of us on the screen, Liz whispered that "the President" reminded her of Umo. "Couldn't get elected," I said, "couldn't get nominated." Liz's eyes aglint upon my lips aroused by holocaust on screen or having been out of town all day and come home, someone muttered behind us, and I said, "You never met him," looking over my shoulder. "Don't have to," was her answer — some truth there.

Seen on the corner of Friar's Boulevard in conversation with Umo, I was later asked by my father's Reserve friend, the motel manager, Corona, if I knew who I'd been talking to — a fella with no papers, Baja, the border, the other side of the world — he'd been told by a mutual friend who "stays with us when he's in town, sells power-lifting equipment, y'dad knows him from the Reserve" but my father said Corona had played fast and loose with the building code though does that mean he doesn't have something interesting to tell us? This I asked Milt one day we visited The Inventor, though Milt got mad, while my sister, when I asked her, kissed me for it.

Milt and I were approaching The Inventor's out in North Wash one day, and a sixteen-foot truck pulled away from the curb, all marked over with graffiti. But a block and a half up the driver got out and it was Umo and he went in a bungalow as we waited staring till The Inventor's old door painted purple on the top half and saffron orange on the bottom opened. Milt, too tall and starved-appearing, was arguing with The Inventor almost before we got inside — his stark skeleton towering over the unthinkably-dark or Dravidian Indian (or part "Paki" it was said he might be) who always welcomed us as his "collectors," his "discoveries," his "fellow citizenry," and made a little speech which would irritate Milt, who I think really understood The Inventor but was nervous for some reason; and when I looked out the shop's side window facing north the truck up the street was gone. But then Umo came out onto the porch of the bungalow and looked up and down the street, turning only his head, and looked in this direction and went back in.

Almost everything at The Inventor's was secondhand, yet each visit we found something new. New for us. Third-hand, fourth-hand, sixth-, it occurs to me. A Watchman comic from way back when we were twelve, an action figure of the President to maybe tickle even my father; yet now among toys, curios, weird Peruvian crafts — Brazilian gods, Mexican animals, two Sumatran buffalos squaring off on a pedestal of polished wood — there were surprises in the back room and, of recent months, yellow and amber gum-stuffs the smells of which The Inventor could name — Pacific pine, woman hair, foot-sweet, gold, rank — and especially now these white business envelopes you had to buy without knowing what they held, and a slanting reference to current events and an old-world turn of phrase as when some Sacramento name I thought I recognized was said to be "close to the loins of the Administration," meaning I assumed Washington.

The Inventor showed Milt a model fishing canoe made by a blind child and Milt was shaking his head this time with awe. "That's ill." The Inventor said he was giving it to Milt. I asked him later what it was that blew him away. He said The Inventor had had a daughter but had lost her. I envied Milt that he knew such a thing, for did not The Inventor confide in me as well? Umo's truck had left; without Umo, I was certain. Suspicious especially when receiving a gift, Milt picked an argument with me when The Inventor went to find a box, Milt suddenly wondering why in our discussion of a cousin of his somewhat blinded by this awful foreign mainly skin disease erysipelas I mentioned a Korean chick I'd met at the high school track one Saturday morning who saw me spit on the ground of the long-jump approach run-up and told me to save my spit, Jesus had spat in the eyes of a blind man in Saint Mark and he could see.

Why had I made up that nonsense, Milt wanted to know. No such thing, I said, she had grinned at me so maybe she was kidding. She was cute. Which was why I went home and looked it up in the Bible in my sister's room and my mom found me there and I tried to explain the miracle to her, the truth behind it, Jesus at work, but my mom shut me up though not till she had heard enough. (Well, I had added a bit to it.) It wasn't a happy moment though it sounds funny. No, it doesn't, said my sister when she came home that night. There it was in the 8th chapter anyway, and when I saw Milt at the pool I had told him and he went ballistic, he was a minister's son (was he ashamed of that?) and here at The Inventor's he came back to it because he was amazed The Inventor was giving him the canoe. I could understand all this. And it was only then that Milt asked if Umo in that truck had unloaded something at The Inventor's.

Oh Umo was around. Seldom out of work. The work there if you could find it. He'd had to learn fast — what his grandfather had warned him. (Did my grandfather live with me? Nope.) Umo had been waiting to be picked up for work just the other day, as it happened near my school. He was always like, Hey I been waiting for you. It might be so. He was hard to find, but then easy, I said. Did I do the crossword puzzle? Was the Mexican who ran the Beatrice Motel a frienda mine? You know Baja? You go fishing? You ever shoot a gun? With my father once. Once? At the range. He was in the Reserve. Oh yeah? You know diving, right? Suddenly then in confidence asking me, What *hap*pened? The question possibly a real friend's. Why did it hit home? We hardly knew each other. Or Umo had already checked it out. Diving? I mentioned *his*. How did he do that? An entry like that.

"Me?" (For I had changed the subject.) "Yeah, no splash, less than no. Someone as big as you." (My "someone" sounds strange.)

"*That's* how." (That was a good answer, I said.) He laughed. "*Less* than no. That's it, we are friends," said Umo, each eye housed by an arch of bone. The face not really fat, just big. "But what happened? he changed the subject to where *I'd* changed it.

"In the air diver lose weight, he weigh gravity," I would recall Umo telling the Marines at the recruiting table few weeks later. Told what? That he could lose weight diving — in midair, he said. A little more than a year he'd been over here. He wasn't going to bus tables or help out at a roadside stand or lose it on the beach. Never never never. He was doing better, staying sometimes with the old lady from that day at the pool who boarded people, transients and kids and Umo said cooked them into pies, he laughed suddenly harshly — an Inner Mongolian laugh? Accidental meetings, though he knew where he could find me. What he didn't know, an illegal immigrant kid, amid what he did.

So he was back and forth across the border on business. He said he would take me some time. Me? I said (this kid).

"You follow up," he said — "I *guess*," I seemed to interrupt him. He cocked his head toward my school. I saw my science teacher leaning out the window. They teach history there? That's right. Geography, maths? Umo had this respect for me.

That's right, I used to be good in math, I said. Umo's laugh was sudden and awful, older and childish. You have to pay attention, he said to me like I wasn't. Did I know Sierra Madre mountains?

Mexico?

"Correct! Orien*tal*. You know Teziutlán?" "Sure," I joked. "I got three paira these in maquiladora — see?" (Umo hooked a finger in a belt-loop of his jeans.) "Special for me, they're gon' outa business." (Umo shook his finger at me.) "You got wood working, photography?" He pointed to the school buildings I never had really looked at till then. I had carpentry in my garage, I said, myself at issue here, tested, puzzled, wrought-up somewhere, God!

"You drive?" Umo said. I knew how. He pointed to my school. He had something on his mind. "Ask kids who is their Senator" — he burst into laughter — "they say, '*Who?*' No: I ask *you*! Ha ha ha!"

"You know photography," Umo said, a friendly demand, he had something for me, I thought. My father had taught me maybe the basics. I had done nothing with it. No? After he taught you? That's right. "Speaks for itself," Umo and his English. "Why?" "Why!" That burst of neutral, harsh thought made laughter. "Nothing does that," I said, "nothing speaks for itself," and wondered if I was right. "You could be wrong." "Always." "Why always?" "I hope not." Justice for all? said my friend. Sooner or later, Umo.

"Photography." Umo pointed at the school. "Yes, with a friend." "You have a friend?" "A teacher here. Coaches swimming. Assistant coach. He's gonna show us calculus."

"Got a pool?" "Of course. An old one." "How big?" "Twenty-five yards." "A team?" "A coach, an assistant coach, a science teacher who — " (I drew a notebook from my bag and leafed to some equations) "who … —" (but found something else). "I know," said Umo, from a weight of experience as if the situation might be someone's fault. "Assistant," he said. "To my father," I said. I indicated the building. He asked what grade would he go into? Did he want to go there? (I meant enroll.) "Well, I am fourteen … (?)." Maybe they counted life credits, I didn't know. How could he have been fourteen? I thought. "Life credits?" He was dead serious. "You speak for me, OK?" "You can speak for yourself," I said. "What have you lived through, Umo?" "Through?"

Did I have a dog? he wanted to know, he's looking at my notebook, some writing of my sister's — it said, *pointed chin, maybe short life, too soon to know* (a face belonging to someone she knew) and then Umo read out loud, "*Blue spots on nose, imprisonment.* I heard that." "You did? Where? My brother says the Chinese eat dog," I said. Umo laughed. Brother, eh? Even the dogs they ate where Umo came from were family friends. "Meat makes you grow up fast," he said, "you gotta sister?" He showed me a snapshot. It was of the upper part of him, coming down a gangplank, blurred faces at the rail. Who took this? Some friend. From the boat, I said. "No. Cheeky took it." Snapshot on the occasion of Umo's entry at the port of Vera Cruz. He had come here on his own when he was twelve, a "regular Boy Scout," he joked.

A boy with a Native American handshake and a secret in his voice I knew even if sometimes it might be me. He answered you back. You did the same. Umo made you want to speak. "You gotta sister?" "Sure." "You say 'Sure.' You know Teziutlán?" "Grew up there." Umo gave me a look. He looked down the street.

This Umo is about *me,* I think. He was and wasn't enlisting my help. You don't have a picture in your head of exactly where Vera Cruz is, but maybe it doesn't matter. His English. His jobs. His age. Occasional work for The Inventor — epoxied a fender, painted a wall. "You have a sister?" "Yes, I do," I said in a certain way. A truck came down the street right at us almost. Umo waved it over. "Home is where the heart is." "Sooner or later."

Adopting a saying like that, his mind already on the move away from where we stood on the street corner near my school, he had a purpose.

A friend should.

Doesn't everyone if they only knew it?

You knew he had a reason for happening to meet me here. "Vera Cruz," I said. "Mexico, my Grampa," Umo said. "Your grandfather!" "Wanted to get there but never did. Never never." The truck pulled over, Umo stood there broad as a Chargers linebacker. "Silverwork …" he said. I didn't understand all this but here he was, my friend maybe, or I could help him. The truck waiting, he showed me a little silver cup that had belonged to his Mukden grandfather whom he'd never known. My dad had a Mexican friend in the Reserve, I said, as if that was something, but Umo right back at me, "With wife much taller," he laughed (like a bark, a harsh I *know*), his hand on the door handle of the passenger side. "And she's going out for pole vault," I said, "I could really help her, but she…" "I *know*," Umo grinned over his shoulder. He got up into the passenger seat. He worked for The Inventor sometimes, knew him in some way closer than Milt and I, who had known The Inventor years before Umo had appeared in our city. Some kids alone in the world just take over, looking ahead. And lose out? "I'll find that place on the map," I called. The truck was pulling out. *Sooner not later*, I thought I heard.

God helps those who help themselves, my mother had said, which is true except about God helping. "Where does it say that?" I said, picking up and twirling her blue Christian Lender ballpoint, but I knew it had made her angry. As if I didn't believe it. "It's in the Bible, wise guy," she said after me, "you don't trifle with the Holy Spirit." It was like a favorite word of hers — *spirit* I will give her. "God's matching grant," I said and was sure it wasn't in the Bible, it sounded closer to home, a web site, I'd definitely seen it, Ben Franklin on some poster maybe. Umo forgetting me as the truck rolled forward, later I couldn't remember seeing anyone in the driver's seat, a vacancy due to him himself. But who was Cheeky? It was no secret, I had concluded as the black exhaust from the truck's tail pipe made me a promise.

I thought, *I'm going to enlist.* Me?

"Hey, you're good with the water," came the voice another day, "you understand it." "I do?" "So do I. I grow up in desert." There was Umo seen upside down standing on the tiles above me, I was near the end of a backstroke lap, chancy in a public pool somebody coming the other way. "Water," Umo began, he lifted an arm over his head, I knew what he meant. "Hey why not we start a backstroke heat with a back *dive* off the platform!" Umo looked down at me like something weird he just noticed. He pointed — I knew at what: "Whatdjoo do?" "Accident." "You still got a vein there." He laughed that nasty, explosive laugh. I hadn't seen him and here he was. "Your sister come here?" No she didn't. I said he would fit in OK here, the race was to the swift.

"The *race*?" Umo said. He got it. "The *race* is," he said, "but …" He really paid attention even when he didn't, and he pretty much knew what I meant, because I at least know that the Bible or Benjamin Franklin, maybe both, say the race is not to the swift. I might be competing with Umo, for all I knew. He asked why I'd stopped diving. I would tell him about the accident some time, I said. I'd just had an idea or memory as you sometimes do swimming backstroke — shadow, though, of someone else's memory, not mine — and here he was, here was Umo noticing the scar from when I had hit the board and could have been killed — and when he had said, "Water," I had remembered, *Water trusts the backstroker.*

Here was Liz, too, my girlfriend body-wading across two active lanes, and when I stood up in mine and looked, Umo was gone, but not what he'd left. It was late August, senior year starting.

"Where'd he go?" "He's over there," Liz said (like, *why?*); she kissed my shoulder, I felt her; "*now* he's gone." "No he's not." A passing lap swimmer kicked a toe hard against the back of my hand and caught the nerve that runs clear up the arm and over the shoulder. "Independent," Liz said, sort of out of sight out of mind. "He wants ….," I began.

Liz palmed my chest and kissed me there, as she often did to remind me, as if I'd had surgery there. Which maybe I had, as my sister had said late that terrible night when I was sore as hell whatever she meant. My idea I almost — (Liz was talking to me) — kept to myself. What would it mean to Liz — what not even Milt knew or my sister — that it was Mexico Umo had come to because it had been his grandfather's dream? "*Mex*ico!"

Liz puckered up, she made a beautiful face. "Why do we do that?" I said. "Other people's dreams," I said, in momentary possession of someone *else's* private *memory* but only from outside — Liz would never to her credit just say, *Yeah.* "It's not Mexico he wants," said my girlfriend. I got a kiss on the shoulder. How're you doing? was one of her thoughts said softly now standing hip-deep in my lane, afternoon tiny bubbles racing up from somewhere, her clear dreamy thigh, an escaped coil of hair at the seam of flesh and suit, whichever came first.

If she wanted to know, though I wasn't about to say, it had been two years ago and three days after the accident, standing in the water here with Liz, I felt again before I'd even known her, the Goldthread herbs I had crushed and boiled and quite secretly with my sister applied the terrible night in her room when the door was flung open upon us like a snapshot by our father though we were the flash, yet time after time in mere memory another place of that time I was in a sweat arguing about nothing with Milt at The Inventor's, and to the third person nearby could it have sounded set off by some For Sale thing on a shelf ? — I was injured — not just injured — ill, sick, I had realized at that moment or changed (how the word has changed, was it a war to make "ill" mean "wonderful"?) — and the angry track the accident had raised on my chest only days ago was mine alone. Milt had hold of the early west Bengali biplane, swooping it this way and that, the fuselage orange and crimson, the top wing pocked with tiny dark marks as of anti-aircraft bursts The Inventor had said were drawings of sea pencils in fact that thrive on the marine reefs to the south off Sri Lanka, the plane designed and built by an oceanographer from Calcutta and these very tweezers lying on the shelf were the ones used to place and glue the balsa struts. ("Let the tool do the work," I said. Milt flicked his finger at a poster of a woman looking at you over her shoulder showing a beautiful ass and just visible the thong top of her underwear, it was odd but I didn't know how much if any experience Milt had had). Brought back from a mysterious unannounced trip abroad of The Inventor's months before, the plane model cost only twenty-five dollars, but who had that kind of money? It was Milt's sixteenth birthday, not enough to make me agree with everything he said today. "You'll get over it, you'll dive," he'd said. "Why should I get over it? I can hardly breathe." The injury to my chest was mine, and The Inventor was puttering in the far room, listening. I heard Milt talking to himself or to the plane behind me, for then I was standing in front of The Inventor counting my money and put it back in my pocket and lifted my sweatshirt to show him. "They said I was lucky." "It needs to heal, then you will *be* better than never *you* knew," he said.

"Than ever?"

The right words will do more had been nonetheless what The Inventor had said when I told him what had happened and that I couldn't breathe, and when he laughed learnedly, sketchy, even forlorn, and asked *how* it had happened, the full twist that came too close to the board, I couldn't breathe again and he lowered his voice and he said that *worrds* had caused the hurt and would do more than the herb to fix it but try the herb, and it made me mad but it was scary, this very dark man — had he been at the pool when it happened? He had a total outsider's hunch — that was it — or weird melting-pot foreign knowledge, yet no, it was some fine-line or species tenderness; for, well, words of criticism had greeted my injury, surfacing, half unconscious or barely conscious or obeying the angry seed he did say somewhere near the very place in me, my heart channels, that had borne abrasion, but how could he know *what* had been shouted at me — could he? — in mid-dive *before* the accident? Of course not.

Remember (he said) what you have always known, the vein you can't see running through the wound, and he handed me an envelope with something in it — the Goldthread — and then another that seemed empty though sealed and I knew Milt was in the other room trying to hear us and I had a grand total of twenty-six fifty in my pocket along with my keys knowing what Milt wanted for his birthday and I had a plunging feeling then hearing the jingle of the till ringing up the sale and knew that sometimes he should grow up, though, and that on the bus he wouldn't be satisfied with loving the plane and would have to know what was in my envelopes but would have to settle for just one of them.

4   in return for what

Independent, Liz called Umo, sounding more a woman than I had heard her. She hauled herself lightly out of the pool. Water streamed down her thighs, no stopping it, and she fingered downward the butt line of her swimsuit. Why travel when we lived in a city like this? was one of her thoughts, I knew. How're you doing? was another, said softly with no slant even now standing in my lane.

But *had* Umo grown up? And so fast. Had he? And illegal, for crying out tears! He gave to the bereft old sun-grained California drifter at the bus stop a couple of bills. Where did the dollars come from? What they call a silent offering at church, where pastor and sheep are not silent about, in our city, begging if you're able to work, which my aunt years ago now called a sin of sloth (an animal I knew from a picture) but Milt's minister father a violation of the very idea of brotherly love, according to someone with whom my mother agreed without knowing who it was and I passed all this on to Umo one day on a city bus. In his great frame and flesh unveined and smooth among its folds a declaration, a friendly force, a citizen of the world on the move. Mexico, anyway. Though maybe no place, and illegal, though maybe a place itself can acquire that status.

My idea had been to bring Umo to East Hill. Make a splash with the coach, his search for regional or even national attention. It might not cross my dad's mind that we were after it together, whatever *it* was. Yet in some more interesting thought that I hadn't learned to follow up, I was soon to be in *another* "it" with my surprising and sometimes embarrassing sister, who had described unforgettably Umo's entry into the water one summer night in 2002. I beside her shot on film or tried to his dive but she just as she'd been interrupted passing on to me a weird family yet neighborhood question Corona's Italian wife Bea had put to her as they had biked home the night *before* through rain divided and gathered and caressed by trees now tonight saw him pull off a two-and-a-half at a public pool under the lights that went out totally for a moment, a breaker fluke that went unexplained, as he left the board plunging us if not my camera into nowhere and came back to reveal him just passing the crest of the as yet undisclosed dive now crunched into tuck — as I became aware of the old woman of a year ago with the spotted skin and the veins materialized now as if by the power glitch itself beside me seeming to say hello with a word: for Umo's dive was so busy a somersaulting that when he just came out of it he's someone unaware of you headed somewhere else gone forever, my sister said, or *ex*ecuted, it came to me she had murmured to herself or me, I thought if anything a sucked-downward tongue or perfect loss. Which like my sister's own, night-inspired remarks I recall, but, hoping for *her* success at least in life (for she dreamed of supporting herself while attending college far away "somewheres" if they would let her go), I'm struck by her thought that Dad was looking to get out of the Reserve "if we weren't careful," for Corona's long-legged wife narrowly avoiding a bike collision with a parked car's door opening had asked last night if it was true he had managed to swing it already, a friend of her husband's told her. And my sister told me she had asked of Bea, "In return for *what*?" Yet what stayed with me wasn't Dad finessing the Reserve, if it was even true, but the seeming slowness of the dive (caught by sheer luck in my snapshot on the back of which one day I found a few printed words of my sister's), and so I recalled for months my sister's I thought unanswered retort bicycling behind Bea, "In return for WHAT?"

That palace dive answers her nine thousand miles and counting months and months later though what had I for answer wrecked at the brink of a now wartime palace pool, too slow to get the micro out for a still, though v-c recorded from the hip? For a spy without knowing it, of what wretched use am I it comes to me like my body itself during the later Hearings? And he this once upon a time huge figure yet not quite of fun, a gigantic kid you could trifle with not at all at your peril, unless privately in your heart and his; a promise at the edge of my neighborhoods so unforgettable I couldn't always hang with it, like my sister's word for his entry, "farewell" (then "frequent farewell," this being my sister) — he was an untouchable diver I only later far away at my own paid picture-taking understood — too late? — and had been a sort of friend before even the cannonball beginning. For what else could I make of the word Cheeky (her name) said to me at the moment of the breaker going by the old woman in blue jeans and the Australian hat, who perhaps a year and a half before had taken the snapshot of

Umo on the gangway in Vera Cruz with his enlarged hand out in welcome or arrest?

How long had they all known me even two weeks before Thanksgiving when I all but ran into Umo, how could I not have seen him stepping down out of the Heartmobile? — and it was as if we knew each other pretty well even then. It was my birthday, I'd bought one of The Inventor's special envelopes and, recalling the potency of an earlier one, I'd been quite absorbed in whether or not to open it and I'd wound up downtown across from the Coaster train station. But now Umo must stop at the recruiters table, flag-deco clipboard, pamphlets of the future spread out where music stampeded blindly somewhere under the table and the two Marines speechless behind grim smiling teeth; Umo asking if this would get him citizenship. You could take him for seventeen. An unusual person maybe. Was it experience? He would need to lose some pounds, said the corporal, not really answering Umo's question. "Shed some weight," said the sergeant. Umo pointed under the table at the pint-size speaker. "That's what they gonna listen to over there." Later I grasped the quality Umo gave to his speech when he opened his mouth — or it could feel like it was coming true anyhow and I was on home ground but it made me mad. "Over there?" said the sergeant, alarmed. "Rock," said the corporal "It's not going to be 'Onward Christian Soldiers,'" I said. "Not on a daily basis," said the sergeant frowning, smiling, pushing a piece of paper toward me. "Help 'em shoot straight," said the corporal. "He's with you guys, though," I said. "All the way," the corporal said. "A peacemaker," I said. "Hey, He was a Marine," said corporal.

I asked him what would happen and he said it wasn't up to him but we were always ready. "*Who's* a Marine?" said Umo so quick always though never what you would *call* quick (though I wished he would pick these guys up and throw them like end-over-end grenades into the middle of the lake, a dumb thought of mine that brought with it Jesus out on the water for the day — prepared was what he was — marine Jesus had come to me). "Well, Jesus," I said, "he's our C.O." "C.O.?" "C.*E*.O.," I added.

"C*E*O?" What did Umo miss? Not much in my voice. "He gives us a hundred and ten percent," I said. The Marines stared. What made me unreal, these words? Why would any kid need to enlist? My foresight weighed me in, shutting me down. The sergeant, extremely low-body-fat, looked over his shoulder at three kids behind him. ("They high school?" he said.)

"He had something going for him," I said. "Those fishermen just left their nets and followed him. Talk about miracles." "Secret weapon," I remember Umo said.

It was my birthday sort of self-anointed, though I kept it to myself when I said I would take him to the East Lake club to a practice. Umo looked at his watch. He understood I now think as much as I, or anyway he was seriously touched, but was ready. "CEO?" I said. Chief Executive Officer, though the Jesus may have lost him. "I like to see what we talk about." That meant, we talked. I got us onto the East Lake bus. I saw something out the bus window. The three (I was pretty sure) middle-schoolers were collecting literature from the recruiters and it looked like ballpoints to sign their names with to and to keep. I was taking Umo over to East Hill to have a look at a practice and get his feet wet. "About Jesus," I began again — "It is not what we believe," Umo said. " — some say he was pro-active," I said, "that was the thing about him, getting things done on all fronts." "That is your business," I recall Umo said.

42

"You get it," I said, "and if you don't get it yourself you can't tell someone else."

"So what are you doing?" Umo laughed like he might not agree, and the bus driver had us in his mirror. I was sorry for Umo and it came out wrong. I said my sister would agree with Umo. It was my birthday, I said. "Hey, your birthday, what's up?" "East Hill." "What else?" Well, my sister was cooking dinner.

I feared I had invited Umo but he said, East Hill, good. Or did he think we lived there? "Your sister," he said, and nodded with enthusiasm or formality. I was sorry for him maybe.

Did I have a look on my face? Jesus had meant business, I said, he had capitalized on what he had going for him, he had a job to do, I said. Umo gave me a look. Not did I believe all that, but. I let my face not say to him Yes *or* No, I think.

"You so ..." Umo, pausing to not find the word, was momentarily older. He knew it was something to not quite find the word you wanted. He was learning. Even kids, I said wryly, should enlist with Jesus, that's what *he* said, "come unto me," as I recalled. It was almost new to me, what I found myself saying, as if my sister and I were up in her room kidding around and talking in our private little family way a job within a job and treating each other right.

"I'm so ... so what?" I said, wondering again what was the secret weapon.

"So plenty," Umo said, and laughed, and the bus driver had us in his mirror. And listen, the old cowboy Umo'd given a dollar to (he hitched his thumb) that's not begging. He was doing his job. "Two dollars," I said. We sort of laughed. "You knew about East Lake and my father," I said. "Yeh, I don't say I know someone already when I meet them. They don't like it." That was right, I said, thinking my sister would have something great to say and then I imagined she got *on* our bus, her hair tied back, just before the doors unfolded shut; and I smelt the aqueous echoing of the pool we were traveling to, and felt an elbow lifting out of the water we hadn't arrived at yet and someone's arm reaching. Umo was looking past me, which he didn't do, but not out the window at the girls with little backpacks, but somewhere; and I remembered the envelope I had given The Inventor ten dollars for for my discounted birthday.

Umo, maybe he wasn't used to the city by bus, a system the envy of L.A. He was a trucker, with or without a license, a kid also. On the spur of the moment deciding to mention The Inventor by his surname, I said he knew all these languages. Had Umo known him long? The bus came to a stop and Umo looked around him and I thought he would get off. We were getting near our stop and Umo was looking out for it like he knew where it was. Inventor knew many languages, I said, that's what we called him, The Inventor. Umo said, Oh yeah. He was paying attention to me somehow.

"Urdu for one (which really says it all)," I said, a bait Umo didn't take (and who was to say The Inventor was Pakistani because he knew Pakistani jokes?) — "and because of Urdu some Middle Eastern. And French." Had Umo known The Inventor long? Yes: long time — and Parsee he knows, I said, distracted. (But how long *could* he have known him? I thought.) "And he knows Hindi, some of those Indian languages — Dravidian, I think." I didn't know what I was talking about, I said.

"That's right," Umo laughed. He was looking out the bus window, somehow occupying only his one seat. He said, "You don't know if you do or you don't. But you do, if you can find out." We had a strange chuckle about that, I thought. What kind of birthday present was this, my bringing him to East Lake, when it was my birthday? I had to open the envelope purchased from The Inventor but had to wait. It was all taking a long time today.

"You like you sister?"

Surprised by the question (feeling still the door and what it had brought), "We do a lot together," I said.

"And Father?"

Soon we were there. At the threshold of the locker room I went looking for towels. I heard Umo shout like an overjoyed kid. Where was he? He was changed ahead of me. I hadn't thought about a swimsuit for him; he must have had it on. Where was he? I had brought him to show my father, but Umo might have been the one enlisting me in the activities of the pool. Yet it was practice time yet discipline is doing what you really want, isn't it? An eight-lane 50-meter pool, a regular palace sometimes almost too big for us. Umo jumped in, arms over head, sinking like a ship you might have thought very slowly and drawing the water to him with scarcely a ripple, and it was magnetic. He had found a lost domain.

Before anyone could get acquainted he swam a sample medley, freestyle and so easy backstroke up like he's on a current, easy breast and volcanic butterfly back, and in the middle my father as if he hadn't noticed from the moment this broad, great-bellied figure had come out of the shower in his camo bikini, yelled, "Get him out of the water" and turned back to following a swimmer along the far side. He was yakking like a crow to "SHAPE it," it was Milt, and my dad could shout so the sound didn't spread but struck like a karate chop upon a stack of pine squares. The water echoes through me, the tile, the volume of the water and the air above it swaying also, a future I would have to do something about, an invader among us. Some people had given our city this club and subsidized it, maintained it, whatever, the pool and the two-board-and-platform diving well, people my father had once told me he knew and didn't know.

Umo standing in front of him a minute later, "What's he doing here?" my father said, arms hanging a little out from his body. Umo grinned, "What did you think, sir?" "That's correct," said my father. "I'm the one you ask."

So you could say I introduced them, two actual black-haired people, one large with a vast field of balance all around him sort of; one wiry, a nervous darter and preoccupied or concentrated strider or occasional staggerer thrown forward by something *in* him, his thoughts, as if he were his own weapon; Umo, mind you, without a really deeply valid driver's license; Dad with his military haircut a relentless driver too. "You don't swim in this Olympic pool without checking in with me." "Zach brought me." "He *brought* you?" "I was hoping to show you something, Coach." "You showed me you are with my son, so what?" "I meant, show *you* — " "*Meant.*" "Correct." "'Correct,' you say to *me*?" "What we could learn from each other." "You and him? Everything he knows he learned from me." "No, you and me, sir." My father turned and gestured to Milt, who was standing up tall in the water, and to others who had approached.

"You gonna sign up," Umo said, looking me up and down, question or prophecy you couldn't tell. My father in profile almost turned. "The music they were playing," Umo burst out with that harsh laugh. My father gave us a look, blinking like he had something in his eye. "At the recruiters table in Old Town," I said, and my father heard something in my voice. "Under the table," Umo said. "You could hardly hear it," I said; "it was 'Stairway to Heaven'." "You had to scratch your head to hear it," Umo said, jovial. "Not Led Zeppelin," I said, "some other band, I was surprised." "You enlisting," said Umo. "Not the Marines," I said. My father shouted at someone sprinting a middle lane; it was shaved-head Oral with the enormous hands and he didn't hear. Dad had forgotten us but, his back to us, his streamlined ears dishing his surroundings, breaking a stroke up into I can imagine what, his brain on all the time, I and on short acquaintance Umo saw him as he was, I believe — *teachin' you what you got to do for yourself sooner or later, not rely on coach tell you what to do*, he was heard to say, I now think in spite of himself.

He walked around the corner of the pool and yelled at Milt.

I wanted to see what was going on over there, I said. "But enlist?" said Umo.

"For God and country, to bring democracy to the heathen."

"You always saying … something; you always so …" the words or word he needed for me or didn't know, I could guess, it came to me, probably. "Take a few real pictures," I said then, as if I'd been thinking of it but I hadn't been, and Umo knew I meant it. Why didn't I correct the impression Umo might have given my father impossible as my father was?

Umo was in the water. Then somehow he was in the far lane and up out of the water and got my father's attention and he said something and my father slapped him hard in the ribs like walrus meat, they actually laughed, and my father had me in his peripheral vision, nothing special about that, it was something no one I ever met was better at, yet not look your way. Sure enough him and Umo — I don't know, they were conversing on the far side of the pool when Coach's cell as if it could hear to interrupt went, and he was irritated, sour, hard for a second; then agreeable to whoever it was suddenly, and laughed (more than he ever did) and frowned sideways at Umo for listening and Umo looked at me and nodded as if hopefully, like when he said whatever he said the first time at the outdoor pool. And then my dad looked at me and was done so quick he had obviously paid attention to what had been said at the other end and then he looked at his phone as if it was the odd thing and shut it, and said something to Umo that was not about swimming and said something else; and more than once now there was something Dad was about to do. Then at last he did it, looked over at me, back at Umo, listening to this water person as big as two Hawaiians, though Dad's patience was to be reckoned not maybe in minutes but in space, and here not just laps — a listener now to the foreign visitor. You notice what you don't get sometimes, and this knowing and not knowing wasn't exactly what I had seen through the bus window, sergeant handing out literature to the middle-school kids and the kids looking at the literature but it brought it back. Umo was speaking to my father about, I was certain, me. I had brought Umo to the pool and introduced him, a bit of iron in my soul said.

5 cutting rhizomes

My term paper that had some science in it I should hope, my sister kept in a scrapbook, a lipsticked impression marking the first page.

Dad went away more, and came home. What had I done while he was gone? he asked. Learned to speak Spanish. That all? I needed to take control of my time, my father said. Break it down. I do, I said. *And* I read some of *this*. (I held up a paperback classic that my sister had gotten out of the library.). Old stuff, my father said. Ancient, Dad. Yeah, why would you read that — or him for that matter (as if you could "rue the day," as he liked to say, that I read a few pages of some Roman on the way things are). Talked to the *Daily Transcript*, I said. They should start you on headlines, you can't write a straight sentence. Mrs. Browning never realized what she had, said my sister, writing in a homework notebook at the dining room table wearing dark glasses for some reason, drawing *and* writing. Mrs. Browning would have given him B minus for a complete thought, said my dad, all he needed to do was —

Talked to Marine Lab, I said. About? said Dad A job. You what? said Dad. Phoned U. Hawaii. Pre-Business. You call that a — ?

I said *Pre*, Dad.

And Pre-Med advice, I added, from a personal trainer who got a callback interview with the Chargers. With *your* Chem — get real. Talked to the Coast Guard, Dad. *Coast* Guard! (The retired bosun's mate down at the boatyard who did not vote had taken me out in his retired USCG 38-foot picket boat, and hanging next to the binnacle were his old running spikes that had been bronzed by his high school in memory of a hard-to-believe-if-you-looked-at-him-now State Championship 880, worth a snapshot.) There's a war on, my father said. There is? said my sister.

"Elizabeth …," my father said. He used her given name (with almost a weird and distant respect) though she had dropped it years ago even at her age. In favor, first, of "E" and later of "E-m," or "M" (for the "m" in "family," she said), though E-Z, I heard occasionally during the summer like a toll pass or, with my first initial, some married name of ours, was the Z a nod back to her given name, and had E to begin with just set her apart from my girlfriend Liz, though it began before Liz's time.

Sometimes I gathered all this together and would think ahead, though it was already happening. "What are you wearing, pyjamas at this hour?" Dad said, but she was at work on her homework notebook. "Pyjama bottoms," I said. We laughed, E and I.

"The dog's tail, you gotta cut it off in one chop they say," my father said, hanging in there on the war and my occupational future, but family-mad. "They'll have a mission statement," said my sister. "I was saying," my father continued as if from what had just been said, "if you could just finish a sentence, forget an idea."

"Well, they have to take this guy out," I said, meaning the war. "Right. Nothing fancy about ..." my father began but oddly didn't finish. "That's what I understand, keep things simple," I said but at a slant probably. "You're so — " my father began as the front door shook the house — "You *don't* apologize," he said, I believe of America. Business as usual about everything, I think I said. "Business as usual," my mother called out, recyclable paper bags crackling with forethought, fresh home from the Presidio Farmer's and her particular friend, the butcher, it came to me and to my sister catching my eye. My father muttered something. They'll find it somewhere, I said. Find what? my father said. Their mission statement, I said. Where? he said curiously.

Division of labor, I said. Someone had said — I stopped — *Some*one? my dad said — that the value of a fixed calling gave us a warrant for it. For what? The division of labor, I laughed. Dad more than didn't like the conversation. *My* job will be ... (I thought a moment). *You two*, he said.

"We'll get it in writing," I said. "A mission statement," my sister said. "Setting out our way of life," I said. "You people are never wrong but you don't have a plan and you never will have," my father said. "You people have a privileged life, time to give something back. In *writing* did you say?" I humored my dad, I said I didn't want to be doing work with no point to it, Mrs. Browning had figured that out, though she didn't know where I'd borrowed the guy endlessly pushing the stone from who knew the secrets of the gods. "Enough of that old stuff," my father said. "You should know," I said. My sister, on my side, said, "She thought Zach made it up, veins in the earth, and she didn't like that." But we couldn't get a laugh out of Dad, who had never perhaps had the full experience of working in the dark. He was less a loose gun than … a loaded gun (E said). And where did they say that about cutting off the dog's tail? she wanted to know. "Chile, of course," a place my dad wanted to visit. Dad had been known to go camping alone when a mood came over him. My sister told her librarian friend things I said — she always answered me and it was she really who said the things. What did he mean *You don't apologize* — you mean me or … ? "You just don't," said my sister. That summer she was "E-Z," incorporating my first letter. (She played softball and had a great free uninhibited left-handed swing.) When did she seem to change her name? You didn't know when exactly it would happen. It wasn't advertised.

Time twisting, braiding, stumbling, for me to see my way out — time to leave. I put off going to see Wick, the teacher I trusted. My home had been escaping me. About this I didn't tell my sister; or didn't need to, it was so old and impenetrably understood, leaning toward her or she toward me, hands, no hands, who could tell the difference? "What you get might always seem less than you should but it's fate," she said of me, the stony gray light of her eyes warming mine but to see more than just the future.

Which I'd espied just yesterday upon leaving The Inventor's: the truck, clean of graffiti, parked up by the bungalow. Most of all, for it was she in her hat and skimpy sunsuit, the old woman picking weed-like greens by the porch whom my sister would have known from the pool.

I hoped for success for my father. What exactly was it about life that was hell for him? He was serious as a person. What a coach he was, hoping to be tapped for Olympic trials. With his unique method yet willing to use whatever came to hand. He knew. And at a glance he could tell watching you in the water. "Wait, wait," he shouted, your elbow too high, arm extended up, shoulder over too far, too high, stroke, reach, turn, and fingers (*that's* right) more like a close grid than a diver's sealed hand. Explain, if you could be bothered, what you thought you had been doing, and he's with you — "That's correct," or, "No, that's incorrect." Another remark heard more than once after I gave up diving was, *You don't know how to compete.* Did he think it was true? It wasn't as if I was against the man, I told my sister. Just be prepared, she said — *Semper paratus.* He was flying far and near. Why? I read where the President himself had intercepted a letter authenticated as written by the insurgent Manadel Marouf-al-Saddam Booshawa prophesying that America would be made to run, as in Vietnam, when it was the big picture this terrorist feared. Well, I wasn't the President yet.

It was true enough of our seriously award-winning city that we had everything here, Liz thought. Why leave? Liz wasn't interested in travel; an hour's trip up to Oceanside on the Coaster to fish off the public pier with her aunt who was married to a veteran who worked at a big kind of men's or bachelor's club just behind the beach, and back by seven the same day, was it. Why go to war? Liz had taken Umo for Hawaiian. My sister said he wasn't old enough, which contained some truth: they had been there so long before they became a state. Liz thought Umo's accent Hawaiian the once they met. She was way off. Liz with a much older Navy pen pal in Ewa who conducted tours of a Pearl Harbor battleship. It was not she who brought Umo up, or when I did she had little to say but liked something about him. It was his body. He was a traveler, she said of his trips back and forth across the border.

"Travel!" I exploded — Umo'd been halfway around the world, and it was pretty much on his own. It probably was, Liz said, he's independent. "A wanderer, " I said, and felt it was a word, a better one, and, as I sometimes would backstroking, I had a thought that the one I really loved was my sister, and lap after lap, my dad was, what? — pretty distant, and Umo, fat, but not mainly fat, but huge, but a kid, which expanded my narrow world of family and all that, though then I thought, Was he really a wanderer?

No surprises for Liz, even if Umo was twenty, which he wasn't. China doesn't let you travel just like that, I said. She said she wasn't surprised even considering they had lots of people there. She seemed to take for granted what I told her of Umo, that is the circumstances noted or unmentioned that called forth his family (if any were left), his reports of them, even the gathering of these upon me tightened by my motive for (though I hadn't announced it) enlisting: Umo's mother taking him to see a leopard in a forest, her fear of water, her winters keeping sheep along the desert borderlands of the steppes before his part-Manchu father one spring delivering a porcelain pot made with his own hands, met her in a village and ran off with her and brought her home to his family's astonishment if not horror. The woman followed the man for some reason of love.

Liz didn't think that happened in China. She was hardly someone you'd say you couldn't keep up with, yet I would listen always.

Was it indifference in her to something? It didn't seem so, moist, her eyes weighty as bees on the hunt or mysteriously bright, everything instinctively regulated, tender, infinitely slow her touch, the cocoa-mat-imprinted troughs of scar upon my chest less angry than a while ago. What did she think of me

beyond love? She didn't like my father. She had even told him so
one night, and everyone laughed. Liz had dropped in for a piece
of my mother's Thursday chocolate mud. She had an evil look
in her eye, my mother said — though that was next morning.
She *liked* Liz. Which said it all, my sister said, with that slant of
hers. Which you can't explain to people who don't understand
it, any more than I could achieve anything by sharing with Liz
all the sometimes mysterious encounters with The Inventor
and his store of work. (I loved her, but.) A drawing sketch he
had brought back long ago for a dam porous enough that it
wouldn't destroy downstream silt. His new type of oven made
of local earth and porous stone encouraging interconnecting
ovens, easing the division of labor and multiplying the product
a hundredfold (like a thought of mine dreamed up for a Global
paper); his ice-skating rink shrine of Five Triangles for the
Descendant (*Which* "descendant"? "Thomas." "Which rink?"
"Oh far away in China, somewhere like that." "'Thomas'?"
"Forget I ever said it," The Inventor guided me to another
object. A Thomas in China? I murmured, persisting. "Very
ancient," said The Inventor. "You know Chinese?" I asked.
Inventor acted modest; he had once had to translate a page of
English into Chinese.)

It must have been when I was still diving, because one of our
every other Saturdays or Sundays the Inventor's door was locked
and nobody home. Milt pounded on the door a little too long
and rapped with the knocker so it sounded up and down the
deserted street. We went away, it was like the future — was that
it? Milt and I had an argument, I forget what about. In fact, a
rich customer who worked for the City had paid to send The
Inventor on a trip to bring back the Bengali plane but then did
not buy it. Other goods he brought back — from Bangalore —

included an antique pinhole camera found on an island in one of those garden lakes; the camera had been used to draw a huge bull as well as a great droog, that subtle topographical eminence, a fortified hill, and the camera was said to even contain the subject matter it had been used to help the artist to draw. It was less than two weeks The Inventor was gone, it was when I was still diving because he changed the subject to that, when I asked where he had gone; because I had only been to Mexico, and only Baja with my dad and when I told my sister, who was up in her room and had never been to The Inventor's, she said, "He went to find his wife." "What would he need with a wife?" I said, and she, "Don't ask me." "What would you say if I did?" "He brought her back because —" "He did?" "—because a temple would have been too big to bring, and we build them here," my sister said, her head now on my shoulder, for I knew we were on the same plane whether I understood her perfectly or not.

He did bring her back?

First I'd heard. Maybe I didn't know him in that way, or rather, he me. Not his house either, apart from the main floor...

Quite a while ago, it seems, some Indian gadgets and models you could find in The Inventor's stock if you looked to outdate fission or poison weaponry — these would have seemed the material side of concepts contained often in his familial backroom envelopes like facts a spy might pass on to outwit war itself if one could only tell the idea to invent the invention. (Were there spies who didn't know it?) So that when I felt Umo hear me say something that would help him prosper, I felt myself unknowingly a part of a real job or even war effort, yet kept from a danger that would help me. I asked what goods my friend Umo had trucked north for The Inventor from Mexico,

who, not the least surprised that I knew Umo, pointed to
minute Christmas mangers made by convicts out of nuts, and
an ancient Chinese (though Mexican-made) tool for cutting
rhizomes from the Goldthread plant, imitation antique knives
— had there been three blind women traveling in the back of
that truck as we heard? If so why were they not apprehended?
As if what you didn't see would not trouble you.

I didn't ask, finding myself confronted one afternoon where
I had expected ancient Nature by several small depictions of
murder grouped around a colorful Mesopotamian picture of
men in headgear, a Muslim embassy kneeling before the throne
of an Abyssinian "king of kings" seeking the extradition of
certain Islam converts I learned (but could never have guessed
— nor the Chinese part of it), and this plus the scene of a
beloved's funeral flanked by mourning leopards and antelopes
and delicate, bending trees Liz would not have cared to know
about, no more than the full range of The Inventor's wares. A
"Book of Brothers" he took from my hand with a shake of his
head, objects for sale that were not for sale, a tiny white China
dog like no mutt I'd ever seen in my neighborhood, long snout
pointed like a turnip, short legs I imagined to be powerful for
fast running, I took it up in both hands all two inches of it, and
turned it to see if it had a dick and found its eyes to be minute
dots of shiny black, and became aware of The Inventor shaking
his head but in some prophetic apology I later surmised — Not
for Sale — Don't Touch. *But if it was for sale how much would
it go for?* I thought, letting it go from my fingers only. Not of
interest to Liz, I felt sure, but definitely to my sister, also the
pained (sometimes) cast of his face, unable to speak at length
of something when speaking at length was what he was good
at. Except that if I had ever brought Liz here her niceness or

whatever it was and casual intuitions which she herself would have forgotten a day later would have interested our host.

The things there. Why were they so important? Maybe they weren't. A small painting of two women blind you could tell from how they were led *by* a blind, hooded person. A well-thumbed 1939-40 World's Fair catalogue with a well-built guy leaning forward on his toes about to go off the high platform of the Aquacade interested The Inventor, too. "It makes you think," he said. We thought about that. "He played Tarzan in the movies, you know," said The Inventor. "You used to be a diver," he said. "No more," I said. "You can't do everything. You are a thinker or a healer perhaps." (I the healer?) He'd known me since I was ten. "Go regularly to the library," said The Inventor. "Ten dollars?" I held up the catalogue. Too much, I felt. Yes, the catalogue cost ten dollars. No discount offered, none asked for. (For some reason my uncle was a source occasionally of extra cash.) "Where is your friend Milt today?" Milt was angry because of a claim The Inventor had made for the saliva of an old man he knew the chemical composition of which could help you see better if not cure blindness itself though produced pretty weird sight where people walked up to you like low-flying aircraft and L.A. palm trees which was better than blindness probably. Yet Milt was a guardian of manners. He knew of the China dog. When one day I asked why *wasn't* it for sale, Milt muttered, "Whatsa matter with you?" But The Inventor confessed he'd acquired it in exchange once for — he paused. "In … *China*," I said, not quite knowing and in that instant, an instinct, a picture that receded like a small wave on the beach or a shadow in the corner of your eye, a great thing, though — that you would *do*, but you can't bring it back. What passed between The Inventor and Umo? In reply to one question I could ask The Inventor, many people nowadays, without legal ID, knew how to come and go across national borders. "Even as young as Umo," I said. "He knows his way around," said The Inventor.

Umo came and went at East Hills. He listened to my father "take inventory" on terrorism and health at the end of practice before we changed. The Olympic trials came up, and then, if it was not another evening though Umo was certainly there, a future war my father somehow didn't name but it was not the same as the War on Terror. Everyone had his job to do. He might have been receiving bulletins over and above reading the newspaper as he assigned us, he would do his part somehow.

I hoped for Umo's success. What would that be? Citizenship? To grow up. He was more than grown up probably. What is it we want for others? I said. He said others had to watch his weight. It was a joke. *Secret weapon* — a phrase of his. Later I decided everyone had a secret weapon, and did Umo really mean that? "Your father's secret weapon," he'd said when he'd heard this end of the cell phone conversation at poolside that first day.

Did Umo dive at the Club? Yes, in the separate diving well. Did Dad keep track of him? In his own way, yes. No water partings or geysers for the moment. Someone asked when I would dive again. My father saw it all — who really owned East Hill and by the same token who *they* were. Or were owned *by*, I learned to think. Our secret weapon — but how and when would Umo be used, if ever? — and a distraction always though from what to what? Not ever choosing to be the victim like the rest of us of my father's evil temper (that's all it was), Umo was shouted at in the air the first time, though indirectly: "Get that fat idiot off the board — " Umo already in the air — "in a hurry!" — a zero-difficulty front dive that silenced all sound but a wash of watery echo and the voice of the board stressed and then vibrating, which was time not at all simple for all of us in or out of the water to be alerted to this motion that could if it chose continue.

This talent. The arch high and natural, the legs part of it — not yanked.

Dolphin (!) as I also see him and see him slowed down during the moments of a dive even now with the tortoise side of my brain slice by infinitely small slice, beyond competing. The water lurks always, it is what water does. Cleaned in our city, with eye-burning chlorine (a fair price to pay for our southern California public pools and private) — luminous with its own light given back as a home or density not odorless like some other routine poisons but faintly giving off its promise for Umo leaving our three-meter East Hills board for a laborless entry we almost could not credit, for it seemed so beyond team use, and I was watching both my father and it, for I knew he had had an idea from the beginning of Umo's visits.

My father pointing accusingly at Umo surfacing in the diving pool after that mysterious entry, that pure "front": "How did you do that, boy? It's what I always said before you were born, and you're doing it, it's what I always said before you were born." Umo ducked under. What did the man mean? "Downright distracting," my father said but to himself of course. Why had the astonishing inwash of that entry in the adjacent diving pool all but flattened our waters out here? — stilled them, surprised them? At once, then, to be engulfed by Umo's happy hand-assisted launch up out of the water to stand like a waterfall, then into the lap pool, where he gave us a length of butterfly, which as Umo's go-between at least proved me right in the eyes of the man who had nagged me half-jokingly (which is worse) for months, *Man, you don't know how to compete* ... but I'd brought him a great talent from Asia to be invested in our — or my father's — Olympic future, not buried in the everyday wars of our life. "What do you know today, mister?" he asked. And I told him there was a spit that could cure blindness maybe if you knew how to build it up and I had told my sister who believed me and often one better.

One evening Umo was gone while I was completing my slow/fast drills, though I saw him go. His broad back, his purpose, glimpsed upside down beyond the ceiling like where I was headed as I reached back, stroke after stroke.

6 maybe if it was close by

My father on some instinct had no need to help him, parentless, stateless, but not powerless. Listened, though, to Umo. A brother, we say, and brotherhood, which is harder, like Umo's laugh at brotherhood, when I answered a question he asked. What about your girlfriend, is she your brother? Sure. Your mother? I guess. Your sister? Well, not much, but, no, yeah she is … "You like her," said Umo. Like her? (I must have said something with my face, like, Well yeah, something, and I at least picked it up and answered.) Yes, I do. Maybe she can be my brother, Umo said. Well, I said, she says … "Me, myself, and I." *Me myself and* I? said Umo — he laughed like a shot; and she says our dad's a loaded gun, the thought tumbled out of me, and she says he wants to build us into whatever, and our mother wants — "Is she a brother?" — "wants to keep a united front, you know." " A united front," said Umo. "Yes, that's what she says." That's tough, said Umo, but your real brother — Wait, I said, I recalled one Sunday I and my sister had gone to church with our mother — our brother being busy — and the pastor preached about the woman at the well where she finds Jesus sitting who asks her for a drink of water and she makes problems and he offers *her* water to *truly* quench her thirst and knows she's been with five men which amazes her because how did he know and so on and my sister got my mother mad saying Jesus holds out on her till he springs his secret that he's the prophet people have been talking about and I got in my two cents worth and my sister, with the smallest room in the house, came in again with Jesus competed with the woman on equal terms until he couldn't hold it back any longer, and Mom told Dad. But your *real* brother, Umo persisted, is ... Is ..., I began — Beyond the law, said Umo and laughed, and I wondered what he meant. He was right although my brother was aiming to be a lawyer for a mining or insurance company, I think he had said, and worked out and referred once to his girlfriend's box and never spoke to me much.

What is this box? Umo said. Her, you know, vagina. You call that a box? He does. So when you have to explain something, you find out you knew more than you thought, said Umo. When I came to, I wondered where I'd been but it was only a second or two, I said. Came to what? Umo laughed. Oh, like you've been knocked out and you ... came to myself, Umo. Your brother, he said. And Milt, I said, you know Milt.

Who may have expressed his concern in weeks of silence when I was in the Army passing through deserted settlements apparently, photographing aerosol cans with ribbons at one end, and an archaeological team using noninvasive tricks of finding unexploded munitions, a black lake from a burst pipeline, children plugged into GI earphones in dangerous neighborhoods where I would borrow somebody's unsuspecting laptop and by chance or unsuspected prayer once intercepted word of a team filming GI music-listening habits and pictured Umo back home working the Mexican border.

"Why would you want him as a friend?" my mother had said, "you have homework to do. He needs help. You just have to look at him," she said. We have to. It's true, I said. What did we find to *talk* about? Nothing much, music, his grandfather, wild camels, blood pressure monitoring, family, America, swimming, developing pictures, the exhaust manifold on that truck of his — "Well, there you are, he's not old enough to drive."

"Never seems to get stopped."

"That's worse, but how would you know?"

"Zach would hear about it," my sister called from the other room. "The way I do," she added. "You!" said our mother. "S'what I do for a livin'," said my sister.

There was an *interesting* homelessness in Umo's occupational movements that held you and disturbed you. With a chance for *you* to achieve. What? It was not anything illegal that kept Umo in reserve for my father, my mother retailing to him what I told her of being stopped by his friend Zoose, the state cop; Zoose's new brother-in-law the Hispanic rhythm guitarist, a recent citizen; a recording studio guy in Chula Vista: my father had Umo in his sights and in those of others, his contacts, I know, and should have guessed then. For me, though, it was something I had achieved, this resolve in my father to deal with Umo. Not ask him to compete in time trials. While seeing him some evenings occupy the swimming pool and the smaller adjoining and deeper diving pool, my father saw him also as a traveler among several homes, an alien commuter to be reckoned with, a powerful "body business" to be included without any singling out in talks to the team at pool side, and (once I remember) "of use to us" I was told, but "keep it under your hat." My helmet, one day.

Like his size ("Have a little humility," said my mother) — he should be smaller? — the mass, the sweat of his well-fed ribs and back meat, Umo's truck trips were thought "dirty" by my brother. A phenomenon (and associated with me, my future, not anyone else's, not even Umo's). From my mother, contempt for being orphaned and nothing "done about it." She meant, I believe, *infected* (sort of) by his parents' absence. And a *Mongol-*Manchurian, it had been learned, Mongolian stuck in her mouth — not even quite Chinese, my mother said, who called the police on Umo when Corona phoned from the motel that the white truck with the Baja plates was parked outside, though my father when he got home said he would take care of it: but why? Only because Umo would be useful one day.

Poor boy, with no papers, no family, no good reason to be here floating around, my mother observed, "grandfather a Muslim, they say"; ("His grandfather's dead, Mom") and he gives to beggars when Liz said it's encouraging laziness ("Liz said that to you?" I said.): description shaping rumor and presently from my uncle — was it Fall 2001? — an interest in "identity papers for all citizens," putting us on a wartime footing like Europe in the movies. Reading the paper at the breakfast table, "We're running a check on him," my father said to my mother, meaning Umo. A way to let me know — but what? — though I heard her tell *him my* view on begging as if it was mine and not the minister's. My brother was leaving the room — because I had entered it, I often thought— but paused at the threshold hearing me making a statement he instinctively knew was pointed toward a concept he could get behind: In class once Milt had said that the old Lutherans objected to the monk's oath of poverty because if you vow to remain poor you refuse the chance of a future job, gainful employment, and, key to it all as you find in the parables, profit. "The Lutherans don't put up with any nonsense," said my brother, gone into the hall. Umo kept much information, if not his thoughts, to himself. He couldn't speak sometimes.

Everyone comes to our city sooner or later, my uncle said; they hear about it, it's nice here. A child wrestler he'd heard Umo had been where he came from near the Mongolian border, some city it slipped his mind. Like Sumo in the balancing, the need to keep on your feet, but "nothing like Sumo if you know what I mean."

The truck was in your mind speeding along the I-8 one night, seen one day in City Heights. Umo a big lug who knew exactly, I thought, what he was doing, cheerful, routinely resigned after thirty years in the same job — this fourteen-going-on-fifteen-year-old alien driving a truck. Milt said he'd damn well get a look inside. There was too much talk about Umo, he thought. This proved to be a time when Umo would be gone for days. I imagined him in Mexico sponging (which was true) illegible graffiti off his white truck — those beautiful Baja plates encrusted with seaweed, mud, silvery waste. Where would Umo contribute? An unbelievable swimmer, yet my father hadn't said the word.

He was an underestimated coach, called on to step in and help potential Olympic backstrokers in early Zone meets in 2001 (to my surprise) and 2002. By then, something else was afoot. His love of country well known, I like a foreigner once had asked him what exactly the country was and where would I go to see it? He lowered his eyelids — like, Did I *hate* him? Only that I had known it would drive him nuts and he would not show it (though would), *and* because I had thoughts about it myself and ran them by my sister, which touched her strangely.

"If you have to ask, I can't tell you," he said.

And on the fishing trip when I was ten, I had taken some lame (I guess) pictures of just the roadside at Tortugas Bay and a rusty panel of scrap-iron fence not even the cactuses inside the fence and wished I'd had the buzzing sounds to go with it and had a fleeting thought about a real real close-up so you couldn't tell what it was — this at ten, probably worth encouraging — and the boring foothills by a village named El Arco, some other shots — and my father took the camera away for two days because I was wasting film, but I recall he regarded Baja Mexico as part of the United States and almost was friends with me again when I remembered the fishmonger my mother visited and what he had told her about color-added salmon and hatchery-bred trout which seemed reasonably sad though when I said they could use some fish hatcheries down here in Baja to feed the people but what was the matter, they'd had fish hatcheries in ancient times (I thought), he laughed for once. Took the camera away another day reading my mind about men and women walking the highway — thinking (for myself) who were these people, Americans?

And when we got home I didn't have the camera to show my sister and I thought she was making fun of me when she wasn't and I got her down on the dining room floor and split her wrist rubbing it on the rug and not a whimper out of her, though hysterical giggling, a strong person, my baby sister, and I told her about fish hatcheries in ancient times and then thought of loaves, while I held her down and she waited, and I never took the individual snapshot very seriously after that but the roll turned up partly developed and I remembered I'd meant to give the real real close-up to my teacher Mrs. Stame who was thin as a stem and had given us a poem about a train to read which was hard until you got it and I had thought it was about a shadow but I was wrong.

After practice at East Hill one night (the phone from the Principal's office at my former high school ringing off the hook because my father coached the team there too, supposedly, and blew them off now and then), after optional weigh-in on the old physician's scales with the height rod he had sat us all down on the hard tiles to talk hygiene, diet, bananas and fluids sustaining the electrolytes in the system and preventing cramp; sex as primarily only a matter of releasing tension; and the coming war he spoke about also (standing). Sometimes a nation feels its mission greater than other daily struggles like beating your time for the two hundred, and to submit to that fate now could sharpen the competitive edge for these lesser struggles — let's take inventory and just tend to business, he said. World Series of swimming was an idea of his. The Olympics but more than nations. Silence and some inner, partnering echo of tiles and water stilled the settling echoes of his voice. A war? I thought. A war to end weapons, he had said. Well, we could do that.

It was this I spoke to Umo about when I happened to see him. For he went away and came back you sometimes thought just to start these rumors that few checked on, like news in the newspaper or things you did in place of others. He had been cooped up in a juvenile home in Broadview for a few days, it was said; or he ran errands for a bail bondsman in Chula Vista for three dollars an hour on a good day and then for a sound studio in La Jolla — a Russian who worked there (no, Ukrainian) putting together a music tape for a superintendent of schools' campaign for Assemblyman nomination but Umo said there was a big plan for international recording — even though they found out he didn't have working papers yet rather than fire him as an illegal the Russian saw they could make this kid do pretty well anything. Umo was a supplier in ugly sporting activities in Baja on the Gulf Coast side, my brother heard, some said with his strength an actual participant even at his age; but the rumors like reassuring gossip had a dimension along which they seemed to gather toward a good decision you will make. Though my mother seemed unforgiving when she volunteered that I had "helped" my father even if he was too shy to say so with "all this new business" — that is, that I might thank him for his unexpressed acknowledgment of my help with … what? — his trips, his Sacramento speechwriter contact — news to me. You go your way, however involved you might be with these others — and through things you might have done? — or said? — like the miracle of everyday dealing, as if you knew things in advance like the Man from Nazareth unforgettably profiled in the words of these rumored first-century eyewitness "memos," spreader of new ideas and of himself, plus one prophecy coming home to roost right now as the Administration had hinted.

I kept putting off visiting my old teacher Wick, for there would be time.

Umo caught up with me at the smoothie stand in Old Town, I had my little Olympus Epic around my neck, getting back into it. And I found myself up in the truck cab which smelled of cigarette and paint thinner, chlorine and the car deodorant 2-D Christmas tree hanging from the mirror. I was suddenly going to Baja. (Could I get out?) He pointed at me, my chest; ah, he meant my camera? "Good. Your father taught you. *My* father, he told me how my grandfather wanted to get to Mexico." I already knew his grandfather, he said — well, I nodded, yeah, I felt I did. "You break things down," Umo said, and laughed that laugh. Good old Route 5 looked like we were going straight south. "What are you trucking back and forth?" I asked. "Whatever is needed." "People?" "Not the last time we looked."

"Come on" — Umo a fourteen-year-old immigrant commuter of some maturity or a repeater of phrases he'd heard, his eye on the road. I talked to him, I said my father would ask me a question out of the middle of silent thoughts he's been in all day, you know (?) or they'd been in him, but you didn't have a clue, and out comes this question. Umo said, "Like?" "Like *Why would you go to* any *war?* When *he* was the one in the beginning." "'Or they'd been in *him*'!" Umo said — it was funny— my words — "I like that," he said; "you break things down. It could be OK to go to war," he said. (I'd been phoned by the Army again.) Maybe if it was close by, I said, what about him? "Look at a map sometime, they got a map at your school? They got a big map at that store you go to: find Mongolia."

We passed a police car, restaurants, hardware, where were we going, it was like a plan coming to meet us. Real old jerky Blues on the radio band. Umo pointed to it and smiled. Well, grandfather had gone to Mexico to find the maker of a silver cup, dark and very small, that had fallen out of the bag of a man his grandfather had killed as it happened in a fight that began as a joke. "I got it right here," Umo took his hand off the wheel and clapped his hand to his pocket. "It's the real reasons we look for." His grandfather came first (whom he'd never known — only in his father's stories, the silver cup, those particular letters on the bottom (which maybe were not his name but words, Umo had realized). He had come to Mexico on his grandfather's business that he had made his own. (A twelve-year-old?) Searching for the maker of the cup. Was that him on the bottom? "You sound like my father. 'What the hell do you see in that picture?'" "You mean in the school paper?" Umo said, as if he remembered — "three and a half girls and your father shoved you — once in the school paper, or — " "Umo I never showed you that picture, I never told you!" "You're going to be going to war sooner not later if you don't look out," said Umo, as if he knew. "Well, my father would suddenly say, *Isn't it against the Ten Commandments?* and laugh like a retard, and my sister — "

"Isn't it?"

"Maybe one of them." "Is your father your brother?" "Sure, if he could be." "You talking American?" "Like my sister." "Your sister's your brother sometimes, you said." "A lot."

"I will marry her, " Umo said.

"That'll be the day."

"Right. She will wait, but the day will come."

"Why would she marry you?"

"The sister of my brother."

"She's got other plans." "You go to war for her?" "Sometimes." "You gotta defend yourself," Umo said.

"That's my mother; she's for the war." "Your mother," said Umo, "she's preparing fresh shrimp and getting sore fingers" — such a sharp rememberer, Umo! — "and cooking and taking care of the house, a good Christian —" "You don't know a thing about it," I said wondering at Umo's memory.

"*My* mother was a sheepherder — " "So she left her home?" " — out where desert invading grasslands, Mongol … but wild camels let her come up to them, she was the only one, but that had a bad ending because she learned the medicine herbs they eat and she got arrested."

71

"Not the only thing, Umo." "No not the only thing," he laughed that harsh laugh, really amused at me. His lost grandfather had had in his possession some tortoiseshells with fine lettering on them he had taught himself to do, but what happened to the tortoiseshells … ? Umo, that awful laugh again.

Was I saving him for some loss — even his own — that I didn't ask about his travels or the truck much? He was in Shaanxi. Then he was in Yichang and he mopped deck on a river boat and must have been extremely noticeable. He was in a village helping animals to haul a loaded wagon, but he did not show me his journey out of China or even across the ocean, though it seemed clandestine, a powerful motion, except in certain geographical points, fixed on a map: even the hard seats of a railway train car, tunnels, then jumping off where there was no platform. He had to be just thirteen then. There was a mountain, some foggy mountain at top when you get up there, people like it. (Did he have a bag?) Oh yes, and English book — catalogue, magazine (?) — laughed differently and looked away.

I wondered how Umo had left … where he had grown up. You didn't just leave China. A poor village on a mountain, a wooden pulley over a well creaking, a ranger watching people dynamite fish out of a lake, ermine hunters, the rumored size of a boy slipping through trees, a borrowed bicycle, drumbeats. I felt a miracle next to me: he had taken over his own life at *his* age. And for some reason I said, "But the *women* don't herd the sheep." Umo nodded amazingly but it was not in agreement, his eyes on the road, a state trooper across the intersection waving us over. I couldn't believe what I'd said from the height of my ignorance in the cab of this truck. I wondered what had happened to Umo's mother, or really to Umo. "Listen, your city is far from the coast. How did you get away?" Our truck ran a

red light to remind us of itself. "Listen, my grandfather was — "
Umo braked and pulled over and leaning across me greeted the
state trooper: "Zoose, what's happening?" — the little cop gave
us a look, "Your friend has a license," he said, he was joking. "You
don't even have the permit — " "No, wait, we're talking," Umo
said to Zoose, and to me, "No my grandfather was a policeman
for a while — " "A policeman! I thought he was a miner," said
Zoose. He had a hand on my window ledge. "That's where his
heart was," Umo said; and to me, "He was a magnesium miner."
Umo had some bills in his fist. "He admired Plutarco Calles, the
revolutionary; my grandfather would come to Mexico and be a
miner in Mexico and work with Calles."

"I know you don't have your learner's permit today." Zoose
waved us on. *Arrastras el chasis,* Umo called across to him —
you draggin' your ass.

Umo was sort of known. "Zoose," he said. "When you need
him, you know? He's got a sister. He's a wild man. We tape. She
married a guitar player just got his citizen papers, he's a wild
man too, lead guitar," said Umo. Zoose had a part interest in a
Chevron station.

How it worked, you could ask.

7 a better safelight for the darkroom

The cop was into music, into the war. "Never know what he'll do 'cept let you past."

The grandfather had never lived with them out west in China. (Umo was bummed out thinking.) "How could he? He was dead." Umo took his hands off the wheel and looked at his palms. "He ran into Japanese, they ran into him, find it on the map 1931," Umo seemed to growl. "They got a map for 1931? He died, he liked the Japs, *some* things — I told you — he liked their island, they were smart, you agree? — he was a fighter, he could stand on his hands. Find it on the map. Mukden. But he didn't believe the war. You like this one?"

"We take this guy out," I said. "It's a no-brainer." I might be joking. "Out?" "Throw him out." "You think?" The great Olympic training facility not far from the Mexican border flashed past on our left in the noise of our moaning, downshifted vehicle in need of a ring job. "Olympics," I pointed. I guess I changed the subject but to what? Umo laughed. "'No-brainer,'" he said. "You smart. You know photography. You listen, you break things down. But you are …" "I changed the subject?" I said. "That's what your father said to me," said Umo now. "He did?" "Smart son of a gun." "About me?" "I said me and him, and he turned away, he was gonna shout at somebody — that kid —" Umo meant Milt — "and I asked if you enlist. Not changing subject, Zach."

Beyond friendship, that.

What had Umo said to Dad? I might never know. "First day. He say, 'Where you learn that?' Not front dive but butterfly first day."

"Yeah, butterfly's tough guy stroke," I said, speaking like Umo, who'd changed the subject.

"Yeah, he slapped me here —" Umo took his hand off the wheel to touch his right side like a tender spot, "you saw." "Yeah, the two of you the other side of the pool. He said I —? " "Yeah, how you talk. I tell him you said Jesus, he's our CEO, he meant business, he was a Marine." "Look what they did to him. He was a tough guy they were up against; that's why they crucified him, but he was … proactive," I said — "what did he say?"

"Gonna give me a book to read, for my English." "Your English is killer English, Umo." "But he didn't." "Maybe he will. About an American pilot flying over mountains to help China beat Japanese, I know."

"*God Is My Co-Pilot.* I told him that's a band." Umo shot a burst of laughter at the windshield. Umo and my father met in me maybe. This kid, easily illegal, at home in this vehicle with a sometime shadow coworker, moving what goods who could tell — he had never talked like this… "Hey, he might believe in this war he might not, but …" Umo said something in Chinese, I guess, and I kind of agreed. Umo said, "He has to …" and then, "He say butterfly blind will power. Blind."

A couple of miles ahead a small, bulky gray plane banked around and around at an altitude of maybe three hundred feet, we were close, a repainted Cessna from the Seventies, they had enlarged the cabin of that model I seemed to recall, it would have sat Umo snugly. "Maybe he hates you," Umo laughed that staccato laugh.

"My mom says he tells people things I say, his asshole son."

"You give up diving. You give up photography. 'Killuh English.'" Umo brayed his laugh.

"He didn't like my dumb pictures. My sister figured out a better safelight for the darkroom." "How can picture be dumb?" "Well, my dad said I'm a lousy competitor." "No, your dad likes the war. You do what he says." Came the evil laugh, he was my friend being silly. We had an agreement. What was it? "You be C.O. some day."

Mexico was coming up on us in more than geography. And I thought that during this period I had discovered in my father a new strength (from my point of view). He didn't object to the war policy or controlling the oil, yet what would happen to their country *and* ours? He would call them both idiots, also those close to home he disagreed with. They were not worth talking to. It was the man I had known as swimming coach and father, who seemed to have acquired a different *kind* of reserve, if I only knew what I meant.

"You don't dive no more?" Umo said. I said I would tell him sometime because ... I didn't know why, but I would. We passed a school where some Hispanic children were sword-fighting. And a bicyclist headed the other way on the sidewalk but stopped, and shouting at somebody — or she passed us, it seemed. Umo drove fast but didn't seem in a hurry. We passed a stand with lemons stacked up skewered it looked like on a stick near the beach in Chula Vista, Saint Louis Blues on the radio,. Hear that? I said, the Ethiopian army used that as its battle song. I said this was where I came in I wasn't going on into Baja and I had to get out, and I would take the bus back. "There's something funny going on," Umo began again, braking politely. He needed me for something.

Once you'd decided, he didn't try to change your mind. He stayed with you, though. With *it* or you. The big decision coming up, I thought I might not see him. You might call him kind, but he was not kind. Kindness would be a favor you impose or so it seemed to me, my hand pressing the door handle down, the street a moving belt. I said that I might enlist. Was his politeness a falling-out with me? Strangely, he said to give his best to my sister, whom he'd never met and I awkwardly said my sister wanted to go East to college.

Was he right about my dad? Did Dad keep this noncitizen kid Umo for future use?

The speechwriter had moved on from Sacramento to Washington, DC, my mother advised me, to bigger things if he played his cards right or other people's. I was sitting on the living room floor thinking, and my sister kissed me on the top of my head as she did our dad when he had come home and was being himself — grilling me sometimes. She said, "With him it's the Olympics, not any old *war*, don't sell yourself short." I said if she'd been at poolside and had heard our war called Fate after swimming prac —

My sister was waiting for her boyfriend to honk, not that he had a license, and the two-toned horn outside cuckooed her out the door, his sister was taking them to the movies, and she was gone but had a second thought knocking on the porch window and up close I could almost hear her words like an SOS or see them like a kiss, *He used you.*

Up so close I could almost decode in a ring, an aperture of dark light inside her mouth, what Umo had said to Dad about me that very first day at the pool after the quick, irritating phone call.

Dad had someone's ear (like a business person for a moment cleverly resigned to the nuts and bolts of knowing people); it was a phone call or two you were invited to hear at home his side of. "Thank you, Storm … Well, I don't know about *that*. … We're all in each other's debt, Storm. …Thanks, you keep the faith too." Once, the same Storm asking about a maxillofacial injury he had sustained at the hand of a spokesman for a Christian mortgage concern who took exception to actually perfectly supportive remarks about our Lord's entrepreneurial skills. It was future deals (even just Sacramento-ish) or business and sport "at our level," and some other plan I did and didn't want to know about. Faith in business trips now, their achievement mysterious practically in advance. Sacramento and, I heard, Washington on Olympic business would pay off. Why didn't I want to know? Hadn't his annual Reserve stint come and gone without his taking time off for it? I didn't ask. It was not what I needed to know. I understood that my father had drifted away from something or other. Maybe my mother, who planned a "birthday do." Probably not.

But that name — why, it was "*Storm*" Umo had heard phoning Dad's somehow- not-turned-off cell at the *pool!* *Stom*, Umo said; "Stom"? I asked. *Wind, rain, thunder, lightning, flood,* Umo said the words; was he kidding, and the language game in *his* hands? "Oh *Storm*," I said, and before long had understood it was the man's first name (pool money, I thought, but also the guy who wrote speeches for others). How long ago that phone call? And maybe I with the best will in the world, war-bound, had done the drifting.

I had resolved to enlist. A long-standing impulse, and my secret. I am standing on the beach and my sister's boyfriend has stomped off somewhere, a kid. I am standing behind her, my hands on her shoulders, one hand comes up to touch mine and draws it down an inch or two. Time to go. Do I have the sequence screwed up? Prophetic. Touching her, you see things. It is months later. And I think of sending Umo a shot from the outskirts of an ancient Middle East city, of music was how I thought of it, sand in my eyes that windy day of the future — an Afro-American GI, I imagined the scar down his cheek, earphones in hand, one ear mutilated, listening lost in concentration to "Let There Be Rock"; I would send it to Cheeky for Umo instead in case she knew where he was, and I had a picture in my mind of his license plate: a gray whale's fluke prophetically sinking into the sea. And some rowdy moments at a party, some words we'd had.

I have said Faith. My mother's I might mean, or that we were a family. And her sister's, who with my uncle joins this staggered history from a hopeless angle. They followed Sumo wrestling in its traditional Japanese form as so many American married couples curiously do (was there any other?) . But they paid twelve ninety-nine a month for the Sumo channel as it aired in the border region through an offshore competitor, and they celebrated both the Thursday night bouts during the season in those days and the Sunday night reruns of bouts they remembered in as much detail as a shopkeeper in Sapporo (though how much could there be to remember?) — the chants, the quick side-step and shove, or grabbing the other guy's silk belt, the gravitational scale of budging that reminds one of the consequences of going wrong in small things. My aunt at least shared my mother's uncanny devotion to the War even before it began or had been foretold in the President's dream, and even seemed (though I'm slow on the uptake and probably wrong) to substitute in her normal use of "Him" for Jesus the Chief Executive after a press conference that had devolved into mostly an exchange between the President and one correspondent down on his right in the second row.

Imagine my reaction (and that I kept it to myself, I told my sister) when my uncle had heard of Umo, whom they regarded, sight unseen, as an alien upstart whose underground reputation as a wrestler, whether we're talking bastard Sumo or worse, not yet subsidized by commercial TV in La Jolla and Nueva Tijuana's new Micro Casas on the east side and further south in Guerrero Negro, Las Palomas, and a town with an imported metal church near the Volcano of the Three Virgins, was at the approximate and "Baja" level of cockfighting and human sacrifice. What *was* rumor, where did it come from? My mother, in reply, looked at me as if I might as well drop dead (as she would look at Dad, who had been much struck with my uncle's rumor though they had been discussing my aunt's pistol like the old German model).

A wish that it be so, I thought, in answer to my own question. Like faith, it came to me. Though nothing like why I might enlist. And far from why my father evidently had managed to resign from the Reserve. Why had I almost failed so long ago tenth-grade Math with *my* at least average brain, said my mother. Careless, I said. My sister, kneeling on the porch swing, hand on my shoulder, told me once that when I explained the hare and the tortoise riddle to her she had just gotten her period for the second time and she thought I was a math genius, but then "our two and my two make … I dunno," was what it came down to. And that sister and brother no matter how close don't talk like that.

My father lacked faith in me, she told me like that. We were alone in her room, and she would have shut the door if she'd remembered. I watched her expressive mouth, which knew how to stay closed. It could fix the peculiarness of what she tended to say. Then maybe we held hands like "comrades." We were in her room, the green glinting rock on her bureau, the penknife she would use to sharpen her drawing pencils. Blunt she was though not like Umo, then with a secret unsaid between us if only the future. It wasn't that I should come out of retirement, she said, and dive; but … (did it matter? I thought).

"Every day, " was all I said. My sister knew what I meant. Something I did. Or an aim. An action you just did, that was it. Was it inside the other major major things we were employed in? It was like what I would do in life and out of these little things I had with my sister. And what had she meant, almost soundless from the other side of the porch window, that he had "used" me? I understood her mouth, as when she read to me. *Dad* (she would say) always remembered my asking, Why a half gainer? What was being gained? Advance, retreat, I thought, and the best tactic was both at the same time.

"Oh he speaks of you," she said, as if I didn't live there any more. "A Mr. Nosworthy tried to reach him and asked for *you.*" The caller had called her "dearest" (?). How did he get off doing that? And said they'd "done the best to get the best." This Nosworthy was the Sacramento speechwriter now based in Washington. I know what Milt and my mother thought, and Liz, in her own casual, local way: that I would please my father.

"They don't want you to get a swelled head." "Right," I said. "Swelled head about what?" she said. "Right," I said, "water on the brain." What did he want. It was my father. My sister had faith in me and more, and she asked why I would go, and looked at me. "Maybe oil well fires, rivers, bridges, soldiers, children, desert roads, pontoon bridges," I said. I told her maybe it was route-clearing I wanted to work on, memorizing the location of suspicious trash heaps, scoping garbage piles for buried shells, maybe that was all.

I looked in vain for Umo these weeks running into early November — the war launched months ago without me — Umo gone for all I knew or anchoring a Mexican brigade to that desert front (though the intelligence we were getting you had to put through a strainer, as The Inventor was fond of saying). Why had the man Nosworthy asked for me? As far as I knew he had put my father in touch with the Olympic Committee. So my father lacked faith in me? We know things in the absence of evidence, a housing judge turned television chef and grief counselor was to say to me two years later on the eve of the Hearings, having read it somewhere. And that is faith.

My father's faith was flooded with evidence, and could seem little more than his Olympic ambition. He had paid his dues and had a payoff coming. Or this the speechwriter who put words in the mouth of Chairmen, Governor, even lately Press Secretaries and, I understood, a Vice President assured him. I knew where my father stood: on training, on swimming (what he would say about their work I could tell teammates in ten seconds), "putting it all together," chain of command, athlete's paid expenses, free trade (about which I had learned a thing or two from Umo), Congressional committee hot air, taking the Fifth, will, driver courtesy, his brother-in-law's videocamming and couch-bound spectator Sumo, and so on — so much I knew of him.

My sister knew me. She was moved, I could tell, that I'd asked our dad where really this country that he loved *was* — here, there. She had stopped practicing "Für Elise" and we were on the stairs and she made a sound almost like a laugh and at the top gripped my arm hard, the same fingers that had just been playing the piano: "I have no life but this," she said. Brought me into her room to show me the floor, magazines spilling out of bookcase stacks, Halloween costume catalogues, mail-order out-of-dates, bike trek, worldwide directory of swimming coaches our family sort of was in, me and my dad she said and had once read the entry to me, some of it, a pine incense lingering from yesterday in the room. "Contentment's suburb," I know she said.

Catalogues and all had been stacked on the bottom shelf of her bookcase and she was going to throw some out; but she shut the door and, eye contact with me, shook her head (I knew, at what I'd said to Dad), my little sister, I'm deafened by my ears thumping and I'm two years older, fifteen going on sixteen, and what could I hear? — had she changed her mind about the stack on the floor? Up close a tiny bit taller than she'd been, darkest curly hair in a let-it-grow phase all over the place, and she laid one arm around my neck, cheek upon cheek as if we were dancing (and was saying something), I know, and I heard it out loud — "… to lead it here" — but then forehead to forehead, nose to nose as we sometimes did giggling years ago when we were eight and six, seven and five, but she turned her cheek I think so her nose was along*side* mine and we kissed. Or I kissed her. Not hard either; to get it done. I held her hand, fingers in fingers but someone would be told someday — as when we camped years ago at Coon Hollow three to the tent near the river and held hands across Dad's sleeping-bag feet at the other end of the tent and even rested them on his ankles and she whispered how funny his bony nose stuck up and we saw outside the tent, I realized, to, we thought, animals nearby and to the sky, even all that could happen, and we heard a train, and she remembered a train poem Mrs. Stame had also given her class that I had mentioned.

And I sensed now in her room she had opened her eyes, this very slightly chapped kiss, seconds long, was all there was to it, a smell of wool and concentration I knew again, but I had to give her another if she was doing research getting ready to be kissed by her fourteen-year-old "boyfriend," and how could she remain that strange to me that my genes kicked in? It was almost the same kiss with a blindness to it, a thought, or privileged, hot, casual, and the door handle jarred the quiet, the door flung open upon her curtained room, yet she held with her lips for just a moment my lower lip, my mouth, for one more breath of time, infinitely small, eyes half open, that held, sealed, covered the thought, and my hand moved from her back into the back pocket of her jeans, and I knew she grasped what had happened to me though she hadn't seen me except once or twice through the shower curtain since I was eleven maybe, and my father in the doorway I realized bore a striking resemblance (only as a type) to my sister except that for a moment of extreme and helpless courtesy he didn't know what to do, nothing much to criticize — well I don't know about that! — and we didn't say a word; just couldn't feel bad.

And he saw some catalogue or magazine I guess at his feet and said, "What a mess." And I thought I would like to tell The Inventor what she had said at the top of the stairs.

I was a diver then, I had a birthday. I needed to speak. One night my sister had — this would be right for the Hearings I now see — I gather it all together but it's too good for them, Competition is only the beginning of it … My little sister had one night a kind of old-time sleep-over in *my* room and we compared experiences of looking into the future and touched each other, and then I said what I wanted up against her arm on me and it didn't seem like much because it wasn't clear and she made me laugh about it, that diving, especially the approach and in the soles of my feet, had gotten to be like payment for something. "Two steps forward, one back," my sister lying on her elbow said. The light from the street was bothering her, she said; I failed to volunteer to pull the curtains over the shade, and she got up and left. She had me. What came after or what came before — both and neither in my mind. For a moment I was older. Umo often about things asked what happened *after*. My sister even when she was younger what came *before*.

8 board-shy

One day Umo's employer was on jury duty and we swam at the high school, where diving off the one board you had to look out for swimmers. I tried to give an idea of how my father's corporal punishment views had evolved over the years to Umo—*Tell* me about it, he laughed (his knack with the language) — You? I said — you're too big to … To *shoot*? Behind the legendary Honda mower a rattan rod still stood in a corner of our garage. More talk than much else, abandoned in my case when I was ten following a trip to Mexico, CP (it sounds like resuscitation) couldn't be quite eye-for-an-eye-enough administered, not measurable to the offence, hence —

Umo put his hand over his heart to speak —

Though "Fairness not the Issue," another quaint or really sound principle with my father, I said, like Competitive Instinct. And "fancy-minded," I recalled from my sister's room him calling me, when he looked down at the Coaches Directory and other catalogues strewn on the floor and that was all he said that terrible and innocent time and I said *Even Jesus's family thought he was nuts out in the street when ...* and I'm glad Dad didn't hear the joke, who might be a secret nonbeliever, worse.

Umo rubbed his chest. What happened? He meant the accident. I had hit the board. "Don't want to do that." Thanks, Umo. "Two dives, one crash." "Two at once?" my friend asks — possible for him. "Half gainer too far out; twist too close." "A full twist," Umo said, "you scrape chest." I did not tell him the whole truth, only what was to be seen. Two dives. Two different dives. Like a meet. But practicing the half gainer (?) — coach screaming at me.

It is a great idea, that dive, that forward back dive, looking upward and back like a backstroker, so free and exposed if you don't have to wrench yourself over and back, the great arch still as inertia with a potential for surprise in it, dive within a dive, wheel in a wheel. Wheel? said Umo. When did he scream at you? A half gainer too far out, my feet going over a little on entry; several half gainers, and coach hollering too far OUT, what did I think I was a figurehead? Figurehead? Of an old-time ship ploughing ahead. A woman! "Yeah, too far OUT!" I raised my voice. "Too far out?" said Umo. Well, that's putting it politely. And in the middle of the dive.

"So you came in closer with half gainer."

"No I thought if I'm too far out, I'll try a twist, and I did, because even if degree of diff doesn't get you much points, a full twist, that's ..."

"You never see me do one all by itself. *With best will in world,*" he added, and I heard myself.

Not all by itself, but Umo, the bend, the stretch, arm folded across you then the twist *un*folding it. So this time I went up off the board so high I had an hour up there to play with and this time straight up off the board to show him.

"You father."

I had all the time and it was like I didn't stop rising — "That's right!" — And the turn was like a roll in space, finished with him, I wished my sister could have been there — "Right!" — No, wrong, Umo, wrong, wrong. She took care of me that night.

"Too straight, but your arch."

It might have saved —

"Absolutely — your wrist, your head — "

My face because —

"Your arms are still wide enough to — "

To clear the board so I would have my face, my chin, head —

"You bring your hands together, they break your fall, you hit the bod."

My arch cleared me all but ...

"Ah! Make bod shorter."

"No. Change *him*. Lengthen his fuse."

"Lengthen his fuse, that's good. He shout?" (Umo will not ask further.)

"Yeah. Something. At the top. I yanked it."

Umo rubbed his chest because at the public pool with Liz that other night he had noticed the galactic tread mark still raised on mine, now fading though poisonous under stress. What happened *after*, he wants to know. He doesn't ask what exactly was shouted midair during gainer, during twist, not the whole truth because equal truths substituted are just what he is practiced at. Not that I press him on his travels. Diving didn't get him here. Swimming he had even escaped, I guessed from a mention of the athletic authorities in a city quickly named, it sounded like "Taiwan" or "Tuwain" but it wasn't, it was *-yuan*, perhaps. Alone in the mountains, helping animals haul a wagon, swimming a lake in the dark, fat as a hibernating mouse, spotting the eyes of a tigress following him along the shore, until he reached a network of waterways, rivers, some made, invented, to give you new things to remember to survive.

Umo's body was his mind during the weeks of his trip.

He knows his friend's quite "famous" coach said some things that are not put into evidence, and that is enough, although one day he will talk to Oral the big flippered fool and one night he will talk to Milt the long-armed because Milt was close enough to the diving well at East Lake to hear most of the words but to this day made little of them except Were they about the dives? — and then of course I didn't go to the hospital.

All this I needed now to speak of to Umo. New friend, maybe not close, he nodded about something, did not laugh. Foreigner, Competition, I was saying, my father … Umo nodded as if he had known about … what? "She took care of you after?" How he knew.

And before.

Before you got hurt?

Well, we always talked.

Oh.

Remembered, saw ahead.

Yes, yes.

Loved each other.

Oh.

Umo? I had gone too far. Maybe not.

He could see ahead too. His mother had shown him a leopard in the woods as a beautiful warning, she said, and he had read something in a book — he stopped and was private, and went on — had to get it translated, he said, something of what is expected of sons, you know? (Came out enigmatic, a barrier between us reached, thank God) — and only then understood his mother and could see ahead.

His damn privacy, I was saying — isn't it shyness that's standoffishness? What was that? Umo asked. We call it shy but. (I wanted to ask what he had read in that book. My father private at least through absence.)

We need you, Umo had said at the pool the day of the monster cannonball.

My father had come back from Level-Playing-Field task force brainstorming about the future of No-Competitor-Left-Behind Competition at a retreat in Fort Meade, Maryland. A welcome had been read from the President to the effect that You have the intelligentsia with you always but me you won't always have, my mother reported after Dad had come home and left again. For Fort Meade? I asked. She thought so. Fort Meade stayed with me until it came to me, as I later did not have to tell my sister, she told me. To me, though, our father betrayed no special acquaintance with what was going on in those days. I betrayed little curiosity. Dad was being consulted. He got wind of things early it seemed to me though I was slow to read the papers. His news about capital punishment — that scholars had evidence Jesus with his sharp-honed ploughshare had not consistently opposed it — in fact appeared a month later in an obscure item Milt pointed out that ran in the *Union* supported by a quote not for attribution from someone well placed that there was nothing old-fashioned about Old Testament get-your-own-back grit. Like Christian business, always unfinished, even the Everybody Wins creed my dad had his doubts about. Had drive paid off for him? I didn't know how to compete, he'd said of me at practice. Here comes nothing, I thought, at *last*, but that was it.

And about this time, some months after high school graduation and shortly before I enlisted (where was I? what was I doing? I took the measure of my life marking time, noting that Milt's times had been improving) — my father, a hand on the wheel, driving home from practice as if it were current events a kid hasn't time to keep up on, yet confiding as it half came out some great event, seemed exercised about speculation in water as commodity bought and sold in certain large hauls, the coming thing. And when I wondered if it ought to be on the market when there wasn't enough to go around, Dad retorted that from a farmer's viewpoint it was hardly free (any more than freestyle swimming) or without commercial value, and when I said, doubtless with some measure of defensive irrelevance, that it was salt water inside us, wasn't it? (like tears, and *Jesus wept* and what about … spit?, no, sorry Dad) he was suddenly speaking of the horizontal water wells never in olden times fully mapped by any single hand out among the oil fields of the Holy Land (how did he *know?*) and down toward the Gulf and up into the higher paths of the Euphrates (who had he been talking to?) somehow surviving rocket-propelled grenades (RPGs, you often heard initialed) and serious bombs. Oh they knew we were coming, the old wise guys and prophets in that part of the world, I happened to say.

What was I to gather? I checked out the salt-water-inside-us issue and I was right.

An issue to me where my dad had all this (though minor): from important or unimportant people? from speechwriter and tipster Storm Nosworthy, who once on the phone had acknowledged *my* help? (For a change, I thought. Though how? Through Dad?) I guess I wouldn't ask him to name the source (if he could) but the horizontal wells — did they recall the veins of fluid minerals and water in Earth's body which I had slipped (with a difference) into papers for tenth-grade Science and Global as well (only then to understand what I'd stumbled on) that my Global teacher had praised but over a difference of opinion graded B minus minus, unacceptable to my father at the time but not so bad after all and confirmed by ancient pattern-sources for these so-called wells, influenced in my own way by The Inventor and his cures I had some difficulty in admitting to myself because hadn't I gone him one better?

A country of shallow democratic roots, some said, the Middle East, yet through whose very wells, along these unlikely waterways (networked roughly, yes, horizontal in this unaccustomed scuttlebutt or even confiding to a younger son) a germ or power or proof, or hinted Thing was to be tracked, yet more worrisome or explosive than that. Quite unlike him that he should broach such business to me all but swearing me to secrecy; as if I had partial clearance or might know something through my decision to enlist, of which he didn't speak, having learned I gathered from my sister against my wishes, who had listened in on his end of a phone conversation and reported that "Storm" was "close to the loins of the Administration" (in her own words adopted from Miss Kim at the library). Or it involved me whose brains might be momentarily worth picking, a partner in some event (or device) hard to grasp, intelligently infectious even in its fluid delivery system so incongruous with the desert (though our own coastal city an oasis in a desert *system*). In fact, I did let one "soul" in on this meager lead, though my father (really *because* my father) said some people in the loop feared word would get out as it had of the Middle East "gold rush" for foreign corporations.

What had happened with the Marines? A father question but answered bluntly by me: He didn't really think I was afraid of the Marines?

"Like being board-shy?" he said.

"I'm a backstroker, not Olympic caliber. You're a coach, you can tell."

"And a pretty fair photographer, thanks to me." Maybe the Army needed some action pictures, I prolonged the sparring. Our lights blinked at a car moving very slowly, and my memory stumbled upon my friend Milt, what he had said he'd seen in The Inventor's display case, the Directory of Coaches my dad was in — anything was possible.

9   backstroke a dive itself

Of the Scrolls my father seemed not to know at that time beyond a water passage as unprecedented as some hinted documenting of a weapon-like function. A passage eastward in which I now think he knew I was to participate when my moment came, knowing, unknowing, like two southbound rivers of an almost landlocked state becoming one, if I could put my finger on it. Not originally privy as you might think, as I move from panel to panel of the Hearings listening for history; yet always in *memory* which made less strange what the Scrolls said, we were to learn later and ongoingly through the run-up to the Hearings, documenting in what was left of the Scrolls from two contemporary eye-and-ear witnesses who were there (and interviewed Him) a Jesus even more hands-on and ahead of his time than that shown by the four later hearsay scribes; no member of the board but a radical persuader to clear up and redeem old creeds of employment, gainful enterprise formerly guilt-impeded now prophetically fundamental for, two millenia later, American market values born again each day. Knew how to get things done was what appealed to people in high places.

Always in *what* memory? The day Umo and I spoke to the Marines and I brought him along to East Hill? What did he say to my father who looked across the pool at me? What got transmitted, my resolve? A long-standing impulse, did I say — and what is that? — to enlist? I got something from Umo. I tried to get him started.

In the late fall Dad went fishing in Baja in, we heard, bad weather (and alone, my mother thought) and missed six practices. Not us. We were all there. *We* were there. I recalled Tortugas Bay when I was ten. The roosterfish on a blind strike quite deep trying to run off among the rocks, its blunt body and heavy-ribbed back huge — when we were supposedly hunting for yellowtail. This time he didn't sound like he'd done much fishing. Was it because he went across to the Gulf of California side? Or the water that preoccupied him, fresh in some shape or form — not that he would drink it, not down there, but someone was selling it off to a UK conglomerate to be floated thousands of miles in giant seagoing bags, yet it wasn't water quite in that form that he was evidently thinking about (though perhaps a new slant on electrolytes he was always urging us to replenish with bananas and fluids in case of cramps and exhaustion and in the middle of the night uncomfortable electric leg-nerves) or that he might have learned about the new water material from a contact in Mexico, but anyway, on his return, for the first time he instructed me as if it was mere history or a man-to-man exchange, and seemed to all but swallow his irritation at me. Why alone, Dad? Why did it seem he hadn't really been fishing? And to myself, like an either-or fork in my life, why didn't I speak to him of enlisting for this bizarre war?

I understood my historic distrust.

He wasn't himself. I heard him actually tell our number-three freestyler concerning his "shape" the second day back almost nicely, *I said it was not that bad.*

One Umo-less evening like other swimmers under the eye of our coach — among them Milt three lanes over pissed off at what he had a hunch I was about to do yet perhaps also at the stopwatch unobtrusively thumbed by Coach — this resolve of mine and impulse to enlist found, looking back down at me from the arched ceiling upon this body of mine that shouldered the last two hundred meters of back-and-forth backstroke laps, a map of things drawing him away that I kind of knew about Umo; but with one new space like an absence we shared and in the whole ceiling and surely in no one point — and all this could be just about backstroke, you see, its exposure reaching back for the water yet for the onward end of each lap I had somehow moved my sister Em one night by describing, even if you reach too hard and pull a tendon. Halfway down this topography I placed the metal church that had been designed "by the Eiffel tower man," shipped in pieces to Baja to a town on the Gulf side, though perhaps no less incredible Umo's job to deliver there a load of bottled water, dozens of folding chairs, and, to be assembled, a wrestling platform with mats heavy as lead. On my left, meanwhile, a city that, unlike my uncle's in his rumor about Umo's wrestling, I could name — Tongchuan. Where like a crack in the plaster I could almost make out the path hand-in-hand skating at the annual ice festival, of Umo and his father, a skilled porcelain worker later employed at an industrial ceramic plant making red and white floor bricks side by side with a mysterious American: until Umo's father had apparently disappeared, a Manchu patriot yet somehow of one of the minority tribes and hence earlier a weaver, who years before had carried off from her desert village in Inner Mongolia Umo's mother-to-be who Umo said had been arrested for digging up rhizomes of Goldthread, knowing the old medicines, and this only a few months before the boy had left.

Backstroke another time, I thought, or space — forget that old sweep-hand stopwatch that anyway wasn't timing me at the moment. Breathe the open air of backstroke. Was Umo coming back to East Hill? Was that what I had had to offer? The dive I went up too straight on and so came down too close to the board when I was just sixteen injuring not only my chest but perhaps my heart and making me board-shy drew me this evening to the ceiling, a light up there perhaps, a threshold dividing me; backstroke a dive itself paused exposed to the ceiling with everything paused behind and below from which I must get away. My way of backstroke is to look into the top of my head or with each arched reach quartering left or right trusting my lap to signal itself with a recoiling wash and a "loosening" of the water and over one shoulder or the other the corner further and sooner or closer and later my lap destination always known by some ceiling sign or blemish or crack knowing also how many strokes add up, though distracted once by Milt as he breathed turning a goggled eye at me three lanes across going the other way though I could catch it on the next lap because he'd been experimenting with breathing advised by Coach on alternate sides, to check his roll. My ceiling still there whichever way I went displayed still more Umo lives, which I woke my sister up in the middle of the night (my family almost) to describe and she said, full of sleep, that nothing was "upended," no person, no village, no war, no water, and drifted off, loving me. Two new guys at the recruitment table knew him when I inquired

— yes, he'd been there. And? I said. And? they replied. Wanted to know if the Rock music under the table had been picked for a reason, the new sergeant allowed.

His ever-returning grandfather, the miner near Mukden, admired the Japanese — their culture, their work or at least as a hobbyist the oracle scripts inscribed traditionally upon the curved surfaces of tortoiseshells. And that September night in 1931 he was on the train blown up in fact by the Japanese invader to look like the work of a nearby Chinese garrison. His longing to visit Mexico, grotesque if you know the governing classes there and unspeakable sidewalk misery guttering its bowels, seems fulfilled quite unexpectedly in the map of Umo's arrivals before his thirteenth birthday.

Why should I, looking not back or forward, have plotted these facts upon the East Lake ceiling measured, lap by lap, one evening before my enlistment? One reason was that Umo had stopped showing up. Was it our coach's war talks to the troops, or was it me? That Umo deep in the South passed through once upon a time and survived an unheard-of factory town Teziutlán where they were losing out in exports from Chinese over the water and blue-jean maquiladora closing down — and had found his way up into the highlands from Vera Cruz and Tierra Blanca and, avoiding Mexico City, trekked at thirteen through farmland and chill and rain to the Pacific coast of Mexico would have been already incredible if to him had not accrued the mantle and distance of an Acapulco cliff diver, which I knew from him he never was but felt he could become if need be.

A hundred and thirty feet above the sea at La Quebrada — The Gorge — arms outstretched let him be seen from the hotel he briefly and off the books worked in some capacity at, by freeloader tourists who haven't paid their seven dollars to watch at the cliff, because Umo *could* have done that dive with his talent; instead, watching from way below a diver miss his aim into the twelve-foot-deep, thirty-square-foot rock-bound sea pool, Umo had dived in to rescue this forty-year-old champion who came out with a bloody, shark-size gash along his leg and belly, ripping his white suit. The father, it turned out, of a blind child who made boat models, canoe and outrigger and Bengal flat-bottoms with bamboo mast, one of whose small masterpieces the father had given to Umo, a wanderer who always made a mark where he was or on the move, and once, narrowly quit of China, with nothing to do but "sit on the windlass and sail" on a coastwise Burmese sloop out of Rathedaung built by a Bangladeshi entrepreneur of hard, dark, porous wood from the Chin Hills, though I tried to trace the boat, like Umo's trip, too late to learn more than what I here set down. Umo, a wanderer even the night we all were to meet at Cheeky's to surprise-celebrate it was not clear what — just being alive.

But by then, and that earlier evening of the ceiling, my old friend Milt's lane-rage, the stopwatch, perhaps an absent-mindedness my dad imagined in me from my diving accident and before, I'm not only distracted hauling myself out of the pool as on the far side he's showing Milt the time cupped in his hand, his other on Milt's shoulder in praise, yet then snapping a finger in my direction; I'm also a fool once more thunderstruck by an overlooked fact of my overhead geography: coming from China the Pacific route how in the world would my friend Umo have arrived on the Gulf of Mexico at Vera Cruz?

And with his talent, China would want him.

Maybe diving got him known.

Except it did not matter any more than whether my dad had really gone fishing on the Baja trip or met on business the speechwriter Nosworthy and his 60s Porsche with cocoa-matting on the floor, for the speed of light, my poor teacher tried to persuade us and himself, is constant no matter which way you're going or how fast. And Vera Cruz was up there on the pool ceiling left behind like someone's unknown war as I left that night in a hurry, my face, chest, withered fingers unrinsed of chlorine; the payphone at Adams near the Interchange in my hand to call Liz and her car, yet before she can pick it up, back on the hook because I had won something in my laps of wandering — an absence — my course unfolding secure inside me — Umo or no Umo — though that night my father might wonder for a time what had happened. Though not that I would become smarter or readier for others in my trek. And what he thought of me remained clear, though what? When I was far away my sister — her voice, exact (to me), eccentric — e-mailed the void.

A phone call comes back from the season of my enlistment as if I control the world, two weeks before, in fact; though mustn't it have been earlier? I had been speaking with my uncle about college and the war. He had never risked his life that he knew of. A private person, childless, a weirdly satisfying conversation with a family member considering his looks, round face ladder-like body as if an extension might come into use released, and he had asked if I would go with him to an old black-and-white film about World War II bombers over Europe, and I had said, "Low budget?" half joking but had no intention of going to the movies with him much less in the afternoon. By coincidence we were comparing notes about picture-taking when I took a call though it was about his because he did a lot of family videocam and I didn't even own a digital. I had a little Canon automatic actually in my hand as I took the call and it was a practiced voice on the end of the line said they were an Army agency and was I Zachary? The Army? I said. They understood I was a pretty fair photographer and (my uncle raised his eyebrows and kept them raised) were offering a Specialist assignment should I enlist. I said I was nowhere close to being a pro and had been told so by a member of my family who should know; but it didn't sound like how the recruiters promise you Tahiti — it was praise over the phone and the phone is powerful, and, hanging up, I shook my head as if mystified by my distinction, and my uncle and I went on about college but he was dying of curiosity and I let him be.

Except to say it had been the Army calling. And after my uncle had said I was quite a decent guy (as if that had been in question), I asked him a personal question that all but stopped him: Had he ever been in a fistfight? He had the habit of frowning and smiling at the same time and I thought I had found Christian people doing it a lot, maybe it was me — why, a wedding photographer friend of my mother's who had fulfilled a lifelong dream by going into the firearm business, had a nose like Dad's, high, bony, a pointed tip, look out but ... (Imagined himself a gun, my sister said, I remember her mystifying words, "Vulcan begat me, / Minerva me taught" — a reader at three in the morning? she read me poems as if to my extended body— that one a riddle for some kind of gun.)

10   likes your approach

And so until a critical conversation with a captain about certain shots months later I gave little thought to that phone call (except that it was odd if not improper, mysterious as the clearness of my prior will to enlist, the offer a Specialist benefit I'm prequalified for if I signed a Reserve enlistment package, which at first and because of my uncle's presence I felt no desire to do). I thought of sending my dad a shot from the outskirts of Kut, or of music — that's how I thought of it — an Afro-American GI, scar down his cheek, earphones in hand, listening with his friend to "Let There Be Rock" just after he said it would make his last day worth it and Ghostface Killah rapping about having to pay the rent; I sent photo to Cheeky for Umo in case she knew where he was, along with my long-traveled digital shot a gray whale's fluke subsiding into the sea (his license plate). I recalled the Mexico trip with my father when I was ten, the dumb shots I just shuttered one after the other and the humbling cut I took from him without a peep, though the snaps were not much but something else, it had come to me, sort of true how you can let yourself get distracted in the middle of ... and came back years later during a dive ... because ... it was about waiting and patience with him and to my mind the hidden instant you couldn't ever pose that didn't really exist except in a snapshot was it (?) and even then you couldn't count the time even in memory which was all I thought I had when he took the camera away from me. So there was a positive side.

The week he went to Baja and came back not himself and talked to me, it was of water (yes, yes, what chemical event could move it briefly uphill) and of underground delivery systems they were brainstorming, tricky stuff frankly "if not quite over your head" (but wasn't it me he came to), a thing on the move I felt in there somewhere. *Like* a weapon, were his words. Yet as if I should speak, when what did *I* know, and he was the one. And though it was said to have surfaced in the newspapers like some 4th dimension of information peculiar to half-hidden forces about the time I resolved privately to enlist (despite what my sister had passed on to me though this was from Bea, the Italian wife of the Mexican motel man, Corona, one of my father's Reserve connections), I never came across word of it; not that I read the papers, each day's revelations superseded by the next.

A "weapon" it had been called in government circles you heard in the beginning — why tell me? — and later in an improvised Administration news conference said to be in motion hooked up to a conference call.

A miracle that wound up where it was heading, my dad actually said to a son known for saying blunt stupid things or embracing untenable positions or posing questions.

Mysterious, I accept him, managing somehow to excuse himself outlandishly from the Reserve without ever undermining our morale by letting us in on it though how I got my job is also an interesting question I asked myself at his birthday dinner before I left. Though felt one chance already gone replaced by another coming.

How to find the right person even more than question to ask proved my training no less than hearing for myself and knowing a few people before they vanished, a chaplain at Fort Meade, a sergeant behind the wheel of a car in foreign streets. An office, a captain.

An ochre city not at peace or war outside the window, a parking lot it was well to keep an eye on from time to time, this captain paging gingerly through dozens of prints of what I did best, careful not to touch more than a corner lest some damp contagion reach the thumb and fingertips of his left hand. A captain who traded words with you as if he had some hunch. That the work — the photos, the work now strewn across a desk — claimed some privilege quite other than a camera's light. That my sister once after some months when I had scarcely heard for all her attention to me had wanted to know what had been *said* just before a certain shot was taken — something said in words — wound my slack tighter too.

My father would have liked three white-pyjama'd suspects framed by the open back of a dedicated personnel carrier so they seemed to be on a tilted TV screen. Two Yamaha wheelies spinning off a ramp, I could just hear them, one biker blindfolded. "Jump pay," I said. Two headless kids caught squatting still upright beside an irrigation ditch at Tal Afar. (Non-renewable resources, I muttered.) A one-legged Indirect Fire Specialist with big tits going in for a lay-up hopping as she bounces the basketball, which is also caught in the air ("Woman MOS," I said; captain, "No such thing.") Two left severed ears on the shelf of a bookcase. A Dang Freres ice cream Humvee unloading the day after their Defense contract got canceled when they were discovered to be a French Catholic firm. Seen from the window of an armored vehicle returning for the fourth time I was told to the same village, indigenous trainees field-hockeying a ball around with their Kalashnikovs on a leveled playing field. An old man in a green beret watching fire skating across a river.

"Famous at HQ," said my captain, and telling me that his former North African wife had complained that all this was much more like her part of the world, that particular wartime than all the other wars they were comparing this to. In his look something asking for words looked at the open window and turned to look up at me from what I suddenly understood were these *unwanted* pieces of something or other, weird as the camera itself, though not more surprising than the war. "You have a fan here, from a Reserve brigade, Wisconsin, likes your approach." He looked at the open window. Music ongoing but "Stairway to Heaven," a light in the voice straining to stay alive in the guitars and bass I hadn't heard before.

I could have shared this with the captain and the only hearsay-news news that Umo had a job with a low-budget guy documenting music mostly Metal that American GIs were into over here, but I knew no more than that the cop had told The Inventor who told Milt who told my sister whom he lusted after. You can be psychically connected to a person like this captain even with almost nothing in common. He answered a phone. I heard him say, "They want heads on a plate."

Hanging up, he said, "You've got some radar." Well you had to shoot quick, I said. Right, he said; that kid with his mouth open. See three things at once, have faith in your eye, I said, plotting where I was standing, hoping for I didn't know what.

Kut again. Shoulda seen what was going on on the floor. (My sister had needed to know what happened just before this shot — her trademark question. What trade am I putting her in?)

"Those do-rag graybeards arm-wrestling…" said captain.

"Kut; down at —" I started to tell the captain what he thought he knew already. "— Triple Canopy guy — " he said. (Two guys with a bit of someone under the table, then one reaching for my camera.)

"—Kut," I finished; "well, the security outfit — but he's got the Special Forces patch — and the other one was a friend of my dad's, a total coincidence." "We know him," the captain said; "Reservist." "That's correct, a powerlifter, a salesman — shoulda seen what was going on on the floor," I said, the photographed, the unphotographed; but what had captain revealed? "Piece work, you get used to," said the captain. "Who's we?" I said. "I liked the crane hoisting the billboard into place," he said, the way people say they liked something and don't say why.

"Advertising —"

"— honey?"

"Saudi honey," I said. The captain grinned. (One of three billboard shots where I tried to catch that noose-hole of opportunity, the Occupation said to be over but the privatizers' "laboratory" with several months to go till we had our Constitution, I told my sister and would tell the Competition Hearings.)

"You enlisted …," the captain said curiously. An agreement, I said, but to do what? I asked myself again out loud, always somehow knowing it was in my gentleman's agreement it came to me with Umo. "Let's have some more tank-and-flag shots," my captain said, and wondering exactly what he meant I told him for months I had wondered how much friendly fire I survived. Going where I was told, you know. Was I prepared or being?

Onward — like targeting what I couldn't put my finger on. Days, weeks late my sister had e-mailed love and a misspelling and so glad and sorry of my new friend at Specialist school who had vanished into a building one day we were jogging on the Base but wasn't there a door left ajar? No, he had appeared to be untraceable, I'd replied, though I gave up at first. Older, a Chaplain training for combat photography who, to his peril, might know more than his calling. Underwater photography he had thought he was headed for but they had other plans. "Maybe he went on a retreat," my sister thought, maybe because I was at Fort Meade for those few weeks and she recalled that "retreat" was how Dad termed his eight civilian days spent there, when I had mentioned to her this chaplain at Meade who thanked me for a thought that I personally thought had been his, about finding your real job in another one you'd been pushed into. My sister who even if what she sees isn't yet sees much — that our father once called too much nothing.

I dug up the present.

"Sympathy for the Devil" banging out of someone's CD near the window, I felt my captain wanted me to speak. That field of cukes and tomatoes in the photo could be anywhere. And landlocked green winter wheat along a seam of a river, the Mesopotamian plain nice but kinda flat for a photo, I said, the checkpoint bridge just outside the frame, two guys lying on the ground I couldn't take. "Right," said captain, "you've a fan right here in the office, Specialist from Wisconsin." "Right," I said, "let the chips —" "Something *else* for you now." "— fall …" — we nodded, *where they may* unsaid. "You've got to face the music, " the captain said, as if I did have to. "Your father now. He was in Vietnam. Or …?" "No. His friend …" I began.

For why had the captain said it like that, instead of, *Anybody in your family in …*? Or *Was your father in*? Or — for it was almost as if — I couldn't say it in words, as I told this captain a thing or two about my father's friend who was one of the few guys he would listen to for long. The captain agreed silently. "And he was right," I said. Captain nodded. This exception an older friend in Wisconsin, with a binder full of plastic-sleeved posed-corpse snaps who hunted whitetail deer with legendary skill owing he said to what he had learned along the Cua Viet River in the early 70s. The stealth needed to survive serving in a so-called Studies and Observation Group, to say nothing of his old M-1951 flak vest in case he was shot at by another numbskull out in the woods — too hot to wear in the jungle in the old days, comfortable in hunting season now: so now he would stalk a doe and buck by wading a stream never lifting his feet out of the water — deer didn't associate streams and humans, if you wanted to know. On the ground he adopted a high crawl — hands and knees in waist-high cover, in low you went on your belly like deer scraping under a fence.

Knowledge is power, it breeds respect, my father had told me driving home from practice — respect for deer, my father added of this friend with whom he went along once or twice a year but who did not hunt himself though fished for old ironsnout pike just to get them. It was that other war not properly finished that his friend recalled — "that he's scared now that he wasn't scared then: understand?" said my father wheeling a practically right-angle turn in front of a ghostly oncoming truck into our street, explaining because what was obvious if you have to ask can't be explained to you but he was explaining in case — "And that

he lost time once, time itself — do you understand, Zach? —"
not understanding, himself, how I loved him for that "time"
weirdness — "a dead gook lying face up in the river, minutes
on end, he thought, underwater, and so he moved on" the
way SOG trained for silently, but the VC must have held his
breath, next thing my father's friend heard something, dived
behind a tree, VC winged him, the dead-in-the-water VC up
and firing. "With what?" I said — "he stashed his rifle out of the
water?" "With what, with what? For God's sake, Zach, do you
understand what I'm saying?" "A sound you said, Dad — what
kind of sound?" "What *kind* of — !" My father was angered by
questions he understood as a substitute for something else like
silence or … competitive performance, I actually said now to
the captain, feeling disloyal. "They were stupid questions but
I asked them: *Were flak vests designed to stop bullets?*" "Stupid?"
said the captain. "And you went hunting, Dad, even if you say
you didn't really, and I don't have a big case for the deer if they
want to hang around and get shot.'" The captain laughed. I said,
"The stupid questions are the right ones sometimes." "If you
keep them to yourself," the captain said. "Where I overshoot,"
I said—"You still do, so watch it," he said. It was like *So long*,
which shouldn't have bothered me.

"Your work …" he said, he had been smoking too much
— my "work" had gone largely unnoticed, I had thought,
some not clear enough, the child with his mouth wide open
on teeth and the taste buds only, it was for the files, not the
international wires — "Tell me about it," said the captain.
"— for Intelligence (?)." "Your work is known," the captain
said then. DC came into my head, the War Memorial with all
the names, Lincoln Memorial with his words in stone. Captain
eyed his desk, as if I was leaving. My training at a base near DC

had proved routine, a Chaplain training there to be a highly specialized photographer had asked me why I'd enlisted, and at once dismissing my thought with his, which I interrupted without hearing, they sparked new thoughts in me but what had he said about everyone doing their job? — he had vanished into a building, his heavy midsection supported by long, gangly legs that seemed out of another life, or he was to be cut in two, this deeply intelligent and humorous and divided man, not so divided after all, leaving me unsure if he meant what he said about the division of —

I thought I was dismissed. The captain took in the window and the music running on. "Better not Forward any more pictures" — *to personal correspondents*, he meant. He was coughing fit to die. What did either of us have to offer? His voice gave off an animal-enough sound without inflection. It said I would take a couple days off starting at once to be ready for another assignment.

"You will keep it to yourself."

Plenty of experience in *that* quarter. Keep …? (A weatherwoman I knew personally and had tried to know better had been told the same thing.)

"Scroll Down. Operation Scroll Down." He looked into my face as if I might know already, or something like that. A GI, earphones at the ready, sloped past between me and the window. I would be receiving my orders. It was quite an opportunity, captain said, pulling out a desk drawer as if it was one of the things he had. Some paperwork.

Ready? I thought; what would I do? A hotel near the river had become the stock exchange, maybe it could get blown up along with the sewer (though be it noted that sewage privatization in the war zones had been put on hold, in the sense of retention rather than hands-on). "Your billet, you will keep its location to yourself." My orders would identify me and what I did and announce my appearance in advance. My job, what was it again? Dividing the labor but how? The way you make jobs? The way you halve the distance endlessly?

Could I use the laptop?

"It's down." The captain put down his pen and clasped his hands. Looking at his hands, I missed Milt, who had not answered an e-mail I had sent on someone's laptop down in Khawr. Was it my fault? I would try for a reaction at home when I thought of it.

Opportunity was what I had come here for, I said. Yeah well, said the captain. Opportunity was ineetiative. Try to photograph that, I said. Come on, he said. Had he said too much and knew it and was resigned to something? Well, the assignment ... was an "archaeological site," said the captain, leaning forward in his chair, to at last say perhaps too much. Were there any left? I said. (Which side was I on? captain asked.) Babylon looted, I thought; thirty digs visited by profiteers I'd heard, what *they* took ... A phone rang in the next office — and 8500 treasures, I thought, gone from museums alone kept in some moistly climate-controlled wing of memory like a cropped photo or a fact that would come in handy. The insurgents were living off stolen antiquities, I said. Which side was I on? captain said.

(Had I let Umo go? Those locomotives — the numbers an eight-year-old fat boy wrote down when they passed near where he lived for a while in Shenmu until he was reported.)

The side of the most living and truthful, this history, I think I replied to the captain, so he put his hand on the phone and took it off, searched for a cigarette: "We're a family here," he said, "and I'll see that your thoughts are passed on to those whom they may concern. They're certainly inspiring." What they inspired in him I couldn't tell. Anyway, my assignment … that was all he knew. I said there must be a laptop somewhere if I could borrow it for a quick e- . "Try that one," said captain of the one that was down. "And stay away from any elevators in this city. You were on a swimming team?" he said. "Diver, did I hear?" "Once. Got injured," I said. "Didn't keep you out of our clutches." We thought about it.

Someone arriving at a site — I wondered if they were phasing me out. Dignitary? Scientist? A precarious archaeological operation, I thought, involving … "a weapon" (the captain had reached, I believe to this day through me, a need to speak the word) — " a weapon," he concluded staring into my face as a whole, and I saluted for some reason, hearing quick steps at the door but the person didn't come in — a woman, I felt, from the captain's staring at his coffee mug and eyeing the ceiling.

11   words in the dark

One step back, two steps forward, my sister had said one night in my room, shortly before I'd not volunteered to get up and pull the curtain, the light was bothering her; but *No,* she said really only a few minutes later, twenty minutes, twenty-five, of picking up my loud old clock and chucking it into the steel-mesh waste basket and leaving it there with its loud, old-fashioned marking-time weight — *one step forward two steps back but it's the two back that give you* — it was the doorway of *her* room late the night of the supposedly aborted sleepover, and it was me in the doorway of her room, a scent of what I'd been told was jasmine that her mother had given her strong in all directions. "Yes," she said.

A premonition I would hardly have told the captain how Umo the morning I went for my enlistment physical laughed that harsh Chinese laugh to learn that my dad had managed to resign from the Reserve but had kept it to himself. First glad for my father, Umo then coolly enraged they wouldn't let him go in with me. Finding that my father had finessed the Reserve I saw that it had been precisely at a moment when, from his Club sponsors, all intimations pictured him as a person who knew what was going on. You don't apologize.

I had two pretty good books with me, the captain saw the angle of one digging at the canvas equipment bag but not camera equipment, and when I was leaving he touched the bag for that reason. Books, I said, one from my sister, one from me to myself. Your sister, he said.

Slightly fire damaged, their contents nearly intact, I read them because "experience," whatever Dad meant, "isn't the only best teacher"; or reading is, too, it had come to me and is the best of someone else's all boiled down though one of these was long. Though one short but seemed long. Read it through only when I got home. Ancient but mentioning desert missiles that pass by the guilty and kill the blameless. Feathers that fall no more slowly than cannonballs, death not to be feared though the author didn't persuade me. (Was there a photo missing from the captain's batch of mine?)

The hotel had become also the stock exchange. There had been a pool near the hotel, and there were doors marked Changing Rooms from which it would have been a short run to the waters of the Tigris. There seemed to be no time during the slow three-and-a-half days I waited for the go-ahead, knowing only that I was going somewhere in the neighborhood, and it was my job.

A chance acquaintance, sitting in a street tea parlor under the sunshade canvas of a mail-order lean-to tent, had an e-mail for me from my sister. Umo was with a crew filming American GI's listening to Rock and talking about it. He was somewhere over here. Umo an export? What China has to offer Mexico in exchange for business Mexico has been relieved of. "What an old roly-poly" Umo was, according to my sister's e-mail, and she was "so tired" of the California sun she was moving East. My reply: *Like Dad almost.* Hers: *He don' care what ah do — Apply yourself — Mom buying me clothes every minute — don't know why, but do.*

My sister didn't censor much: *Your soldier there e-mailed asking Was I married? — I said* Not that I know of, *but thought again and added,* Talk not to me.

She would like to hold me and whisper me a joke that what I start in others need no more be mine than streams far as forever from their source. A faithful e-mailer even later when I got out of the service (I thought) and was seeing almost no one and she told me how they had visited a papermaking studio with the big Mixmasters and the felt blankets and cloudy water everywhere and that was the way she did things, from the ground up. Her exact geography in these e-mails of hers, plotting my whereabouts but exactly where is she, in her words? Another retrieved on a poor happy corporal's laptop who couldn't get his earphones or almost his ears to work so rachetting forth was the jam around him (and me) though Stones and Zeppelin-wise.

Again from my sister, this time "some numbers" she promised, and signing herself "Arabiyoun ana Maisoon." What's your sister's *name*? the soldier wanted to know, though he had only to hit Reply to contact her. She changes it all the time, I said. I thought, Is he going to start up something with her? — and she was e-mailing me abroad that our mother had said Dad had told her one night before I left, and in fact did leave before he had a chance to drive me home, that I had come close to equaling the Club record for the 200 backstroke but he didn't get a chance to tell me, I had seemed in a real zone looking up into the sky almost … reaching like … She forgot, my sister said … my mother had forgotten what I'd been reaching like. And

Umo … Javascript or garbage followed yet at the end, *haven't seen Dad over there, have you?* and it wasn't until I got home to California that I learned the other number she had bulleted for me for Umo. Why my father had not taken the opportunity to tell me my 200 time next morning no more needed to be explained (to me at any rate) than his decision (and permission) to quit the Reserve at this time. Because he knew someone — or had something to offer in exchange, it came to me. Yet my days were clear as memory, my parents, the speed of light in its actual presence (and therefore slowness), and the fact that I've never had its constancy (going away or toward) satisfactorily explained to me. A swelled head Dad and Mom would call it. Another e-mail retrieved at Kut asked what had happened just before the photo of the "two headless ones" I'd sent in a wretched mood; a second e-mail, what had happened before *that*? She could always help me. As she had just before I left.

Dad's forty-third birthday evening I was fresh from a friendship-ending debate with Milt. And faced with a scheduling conflict. Almost exactly the same age, we had known each other too long and so could swap words of our fathers' — "let your tool do its work," Milt quoted my dad, and now throughout the forty-five-minute exchange on the way home from The Inventor's during which I laid out vastly more fact than Milt to establish the error of a war that I was joining up for, we found ourselves paused upon a narrow meridian — its gravelly ground advertised for Adoption — a fault line between opposing three-lane streams of rush-hour vehicles that all but drowned my friend out. So I observed him from head to toe with more clarity than regret somehow pairing the seventeen tons of ordnance dropped during the run-up by the President in a no-fly zone, with Milt's higher-pitched Lincoln voice; the

President's unwillingness (like a silhouette heavily backlit) to share intelligence among our allies, with Milt's index finger shaking at me (thumb over the other three), still irritated that I had alleged Jesus had spat into someone's eye; that the ten-foot-high concrete blast walls in the capital separating protected visitors from exposed natives had been acquired from Kurdistan not poured in plentiful local cement, with Milt's huge feet encased in gray Converse; and the Middle East vet once trained as a Ranger in Fort Lewis up in Washington, then trained as a forward observer, now an RPG amputee and devoted hunter in Oregon, who had not liked me and had told us personally that his absolute certainty that there is a Jesus got him through — with Milt's unusually thin, marine neck with its elderly bobbing Adam's apple. So I felt like a swimmer whose shoulders and legs belong to the water on a very good day, with that coast and skim and play of power quite apart from how far you are going as if you had kid fins on, laying down on the dining room table for my sister to wrap it one of The Inventor's envelopes that had cost me twenty dollars I think and added its stake to whatever had made Milt mad — a difference with The Inventor often. Once about sex (which Milt said was just the release of tension, a biological function). Today more likely the news, edited in fact slightly by me as if it had been solo, that I had taken my physical at the ungodly hour of seven that morning. And now The Inventor had summoned us to a party that evening, at an address not his that I imagined I knew. But in the kitchen with my mother and the turkey molé conquistadores I asked that the evening be not about me but Dad, which she thought considerate though considerate of what? (Did I know what the envelope contained? my sister asked. Not really.)

The evening was not well attended. We were missing the

assistant coach at the high school Wick and his wife, and my brother and Liz and Milt. Sinatra singing "Five Minutes More," my mother handed me a platter to carry in from the kitchen. My aunt and uncle came for the fresh local shrimp and turkey molé and spoke cordially of this friend of mine they had yet to meet because a young Mongolian (of all things) Sumo had taken Osaka by storm (they laughed frowning at this), broken taboo by taking prize money with his left hand, being left-handed, but in Japan you don't throw your opponent by yanking him forward by the hair and he'd had to go back to Mongolia until things cooled down. Umo himself, I pointed out, had told me how this Asashōryū glared, but Umo was a diver, he was not into Sumo, in fact I didn't know where he was (I felt my sister smiling on me — the way I had said it).

I hadn't seen him in weeks.

Had I done something? We gather what we can together, and that's it.

My sister made an impromptu speech, wordy for her, in honor of the breadwinner who brings home his loaded gun unfired, and in a moment slightly embarrassing but we didn't quite know why, she remembered wrestling in the living room with brother Zach over a joke and Dad's not breaking it up —

He came upon us wrestling —
Angry on the rug.
Father to us both, he thought
Fight — or sport — or hug.
They dive into their home work —
Espousing not to shirk.
His kids — for all they lack —
Making the path they track.

— and that on the camping trip we had taken with Dad I had seen an indigo bunting on the Bradshaw Trail that wasn't supposed to be there and Dad had said, *But it is,* and with his prompting we had taken another camping trip on our own and learned to make the path you follow even while hearing almost on top of us the aerial gunnery at Chocolate Mountain though we had wound up with all this food tonight, look only at the birthday dude and think of all the different people there in that chair, and someone had said this of James Thurber when he came to dinner.

My father and I didn't bother telling each other what we each knew anyhow — his somehow quitting the Reserve, my more than impending enlistment. His shortness with me, and transferring the beribboned envelope, its own wrapping, unopened from the table to the top of my older brother's straw sombrero he wore on the twenty-nine-dollar-a-weekday golf course on the floor — I felt it in the flush on my face a message in both directions telling me Dad was angry at having, in some original way, used me.

If he had, the phone call a month ago might be paying me off. How was not clear, an assignment the Army might not make good on or I could decline or not enlist.

Yet I was acting for myself. No matter what had been done to get me in. Less enlisting in the Army than enlisting the war in a plan of my own no dumber than other stuff I'd done. Family? East Hill? Math? Love? Getting in my own way, my mother just said when I ran into her in front of the Heartmobile having her picture taken by the butcher, a friend. I had asked my father when he got back from his strangely timed trip if he had checked into Umo's activities on the east coast of Baja. Yes, he said, yes.

Yes? I said.

The kid was quite competent. "Competent!" A reliable shipper and contact person, my father understood, he would come in handy. "And for your information it's a lot to say about anyone, that they're competent." I had missed something and it would come to me. The phone rang. "The envelope," I said.

It was Milt's surprised voice reminding me of The Inventor's party, the scheduling conflict I regretted for my mother and sister's sakes, respectively, the cook and, I sensed then and confirmed late that night in her room, the secret genius of the moment with whom I left the issue of the envelope. Though I picked it up — *Happy Returns* my sister had written on it — and carried it into the hallway.

"Thank you," my father said, his napkin in hand, appearing and taking the envelope from me. I didn't much want to see what was inside right then and neither did he. A wide and brilliant smile in a narrow face — stranger than truth — there was a joke on someone. I said I was enlisting in the Army and had taken a physical this — "It's your decision," my father broke in. "That's what I'm saying, Dad." "If you were in the Reserve you'd be out sooner," he said. "Feet first," I pulled open the somehow heavy front door into the night. I said I thought the President would let me go in good time. "And good luck with your ..." I looked him in the face and didn't flinch at the unknown, a touchy man, enterprising, but why this outlandish hook-up or patron, Storm and with a last name Nosworthy at that?

I heard his interrupting as I ran for a bus that waited. A physical this *morning*?

You cannot fly but your body will sometimes feel spread out, there is so much of it, hand to mouth we say, hand, arm, shoulder, belly, and in the whole body with a little help from our

friends there is not only a future but a gift to see it. I couldn't
have taken my sister, who seemed all the family I had sometimes
when I would lie beside her talking, speaking.

I had signed up knowing that my father weeks since had
quit the Reserve somehow. He himself was surprised, he said, in
moments of humor as soon as I was out the door, I learned; but
at what? At himself that he'd resigned? That his son had enlisted?
The two. "Happy birthday," my sister said all over again across
the table at him upon this last, she told me very late that night
when I came home to tell her about Milt and Umo and the state
cop Zoose and his sister dancing alone because her husband was
in the Army, and the others. Was he surprised that I didn't break
with him? (He'd resigned, because he'd been given leave to. In
return for what?)

My sister and I that night and always in touch, and presently
as fleeting e-mails would remind, tracking me not really. Yet, in
my hopes of some secret employment, this person mine — her
quaint hand on my heart, words on her lips, her words on my
skin now and again, words in the dark touching my words, even
as we heard the footfall outside her door at three in the morning
pause and pass on. Upon which she regretted doing what she'd
done when she had read me my father's entry in the Coaches
Directory so long ago — omitting words, omitting words, her
hand on my chest, perhaps waiting for me to ask, until I didn't
but I had already read them, they didn't matter: you're diving
into the wreck of this war she said that night of my enlistment
when I came home to her, it didn't sound quite like her.

Others think they have plans for you but you keep a
memory of your future free. The dive, its execution some say
an infinite series of instants each bringing you somewhere as if
you were stopped. No borrowed laptop at hand to tell my sister

my orders came where I was billeted and apparently I would have company two mornings later. Meanwhile I waited in my own way. One afternoon I saw into a doorless home, not a rag of a curtain between me and that nearly impenetrable dusk and I was seen by faces, or in their alertness they were willing that I enter, perhaps it was to help the woman lying on a mat dead or sleeping even by spying. With what? A camera? A bow. In a hovel with a rifle bipod lying on a sandal in a corner, a talisman hanging on the wall, other people came in off the street, a gathering just to hear what might be said. Then I had to go. She was dead but her eyelids glued shut, willed, soldered, and I asked to use their e-mail, odd though the welcome seemed, and I asked as I typed myself in what "Arabiyoun ana Maisoon" meant and was told "I am an Arab," and my sister wanted me to know that my 200 time that night of the ceiling had been a personal record.

Another day a boy asked me to come with him, he had American night vision goggles of the type for which replacement parts had run out. Along Haifa Street cavalry were now on foot patrol. One morning two armed men in shorts and t-shirts came running toward me but passed on either side. I photographed an old curved balcony, exposed a whole roll, and a man came out onto the balcony then. He showed his wrists, he was shouting to me, explaining. I thought it was about flex-cuffs so tight he developed gangrene in one hand. A picture of all that? Where was I going during the three-day wait for where I was going? Already there almost, impatient as a bad photographer (recalling, too, the photo of the burned-out trailer missing from what the captain had of mine) I heard of a sound crew taping/recording GIs, I was just missing them.

Rather, a crew filming GIs and their music, word of three guys crossing the desert (a $900 cab ride from Syria!) to capture on videotape the listening habits of our soldiers. Headphones handed to me as friends at school used to, to hear "Raining Blood," and aboard a parked truck where nothing was happening "Little Red Corvette," and "Purple Haze" Jimi walking underwater, and in another set of headphones with this time talk by the numbers. "It's Too Late Now, We Ready," Pastor Troy told it, and I had to ask someone three times if they had seen a big Asian kid in the sound crew till I got the attention of this plugged-in Specialist who said Plenty of Asians, tapping the headphone, grinning, "Weapon of mass instruction," taking it in my stride, shaking his finger like a speaker, when a skinny little guy with rimless glasses said Yes he had "reconized" one of them; he turned away to his laptop. *Recognized?* I said; which one? I thought — but there was action down the avenue and in a warren of alleys, and I was on the run in mid-thought past a shut-down masquf restaurant, Wednesday I remembered the lucky day to eat fired carp guts, or hearing *Nineveh Street* I thought behind me, also someone's question behind me but up ahead Marines, spray-painting "Long live the muj killers" over a rebel sign in Arabic at the entrance to I didn't know what, dived for cover when a shooter moving from window to window opened up again from above. And I thought what "GIs" meant, and how headphones gave you out of mind out of sight. Yet Umo is here, I thought.

And the night before this odd or as I expected then routine assignment — an "archaeological arrival," the captain had said in confidence — why did I feel I had no business here listening as though my life depended on it to the mumbled words of a swarthy redhead from a northern California military police brigade on a table, with a head wound, a bloody bandage all across his eyes, poor guy? — blood under the table.

My sister's lips upon one eyelid, then the other, then the first, dizzying (the touch itself another's touch to call me back beyond the dizziness), my eyes sore from party smoke, I recounted the droll farewell night in a whisper, if anyone here were still awake after The Inventor's '57 Bel Air (never guilty of the sloth on which its owner disagreed with some mysterious "Apostle" who had said sloth violated brotherly love) had picked the worst moment, delivering me at my door, to detonate two blats of backfire in our street.

Though no lights had gone on. Though my sister's face in an upstairs window welcomed me like a wife who'd been sleeping.

12 the stillness between the beginning breakers of his breathing

Who was there? she asked, sixteen and a half years old lying beside me, my shirt half-unbuttoned, a scent blurred and slept-on.

Well, everybody. Three little runaways Cheeky lets stay there; one smokes right along with her. Weed? Course not. Cheeky? It was her place not The Inventor's, out in North Wash. Up the street from him, a bungalow with a blue door, everybody was there.

Everybody? Well, Milt. Of course, he picked the right party to go to. No, he was mad at me. And *me*. You? He thinks we might go out. Milt argued with The Inventor — he was there. Well, the party was *for* him except — Right, it was an enlistment party it turned out. And The Inventor's two nieces and his plumber and the plumber's teacher of some kind, and a Mexican girl, very tall, lives in Chula Vista, husband they let him outa jail to enlist, a music guy worked for a Russian, got into some stuff; and *U*mo, who you haven't — Yes that night on the Interchange — You only saw him — Yeah — And I not since seven — This morning — Yeah — Who you haven't set eyes on, my sister began — Since seven this morning, I said. Your *physical*. I don't know how he knew what time it was, he lined up, they wouldn't let him in. The Mexican girl was a basketball player, she laughed and laughed (such a smile), a friend of Umo's. He thought he was going to enlist this morning. They wouldn't let him in. 'Course they wouldn't, you're a team, said my sister. Did Milt know? He said why would he think they'd let him in, he didn't even have papers, better clean up his act, Milt said. Umo pulled out an old photo ID from Republic of China, Milt snapped it out of his fingers. He never *re*cognized Umo, E said beside me. No, he did, I said. Oh he's a free — Yeah — A mountain in your way. Shoulda gone all the way down to Mexico with him, my sister said. You saw him, I said — Mmhmm, getting up into that — Hey, who was driving — ? On the Interchange — Yeah you saw him climbing into a truck in the middle of traffic. Who was driving?

My baby clucked. She threw the bedclothes back and rolled over on me: *No*body, she said, nobody was driving. Her voice touched my ear, the mouth spread, a finger on my shoulder hours between night and dawn deepened like hope against hope And I told how Umo said, *Give my best to* ... and grinned. Umo did ? That's right. Umo will go where you go, my sister said into my ear, that's the agreement. He's going to marry my sister, he said. Marry your sister? (she coughed against me, laughing) "Milt didn't like it," I said. "*You* didn't." Umo, I murmured. He's luck of some kind, said my sister. Mm hmm, and a friend, but he competes. He'll go where you go. He will? Yeah, a secret weapon. He'll follow you and —

She says in the dark, *I can understand*. You can what? I said. So go to war, you do your job, we'll do ours — words, music, I know she said. And *I have a navy in the west*.

Follow me? I got past the abandoned bathhouse which had served the pool of the hotel which had become the stock exchange, and there around the corner waiting for me (at this hour, when I had no *business* being out, the quick little woman from the Wisconsin Reserve brigade would ball me out in the morning, who had "found something" in my cropped shot of the Reservist arm-wrestling the mercenary in the beret) appeared not the skinny, hungry soldier with glasses who had "recognized" one of the crew filming GIs listening to music, but the black guy *near* him as smart as if he was in some disguise, who had joked about … — the headphones he tapped or music nation coming out of them, whatever — he was waiting for me now and shook his head like you never learn.

I said, "The film crew? Someone familiar?" reminding him. He shook again, "Police?" he doubted me almost. Hey *he* was the one with the side arm, I said. "Asked you before but you didn't hear, man," he said begrudging his grin happy-paranoid recalling the afternoon or Bad Company for all I knew.

"Sorry 'bout that. The Asian kid?" "You looking for him?" "If he's the one." "Plenty a them." "That's what you said this afternoon. And the guy you knew?" "He's *with* one." "With an Asian — the guy you know?" "Knew." "You don't know him now?" He shook his head, something bad, "Real big," he changed the subject. "The Asian kid," I said. "I thought he knew me, how he looked at me." "The guy you used to know? The film crew guy? You knew him …?" "Down around Kut, down there." Yes, I had heard. Kut? It was terrible, I said. "Took me for somebody else." "Your film crew guy?" "No, the Asian kid. I thought he knew me, how he looked at me." "Why would he know you?" "Right." "What did he do?" "He should watch out who he works with, the other guy's wanted." "Real big?" I persisted — "was he like, a teenager?" I said. "Asian kid? Lotta teens. Look at me, I'm older now. No kid left out. They knew about me when I was in ninth grade, nobody told the school withhold my file, no kid left unrecruited, like a track scholarship. You coming from Kut?" "That's it," I said. "How about that." I hung with my questions, there was a problem. "The film crew guy you knew is a civilian …" "Not then." "Shows up *with* the Asian — " " — and not now," my soldier decides to add. "Thought he knew you?" "Nine hundred dollar cab ride with equipment, I heard, like as far as from here to Cleveland." "*Cleve*land?" "*Brook*lyn to Cleveland, sorry. Hey yeah they had a driver, Syrian cop moonlighting, he sat in front with him, the kid, bigger'n …—" My soldier, rewinding, had heard something.

"'Did I have a *sister*?'" he said.

"The Asian kid?"

"I said sure." My soldier snapped his wrist. He heard something. "War child, war child" was what he said — like a not great song — "and 'was my sister my brother?'"

"Said that," I said.

"Right. You could hear worse."

"It's my friend," I said. Soldier snapped his wrist, pumped his thumb. "You going back to Kut?" "How did you know," I joked. "Said he was getting married to his brother's sister, he better watch who he works with, they looking for the other guy." "Who, the guy you used to know?" "Unfinished business," said the soldier clairvoyantly, and was gone, calling back to my "San Diego?" "Naw, Kut" — as if he had been deserted — burning his presence into some act to come that was mine; still taller turning a corner, he had heard me and was gone before I asked if the other guy was his friend. I was left with my thoughts and with tomorrow.

One of Umo's film crew, then, was a serviceman, I thought, though not *now* was a second thought, but why? Not a civilian now *either*, come to think of it. Still in the service but. What *was* he, this known man who might be using as an assistant a very young Asian, and there were three of them and maybe a fourth, a driver (maybe not).

I heard shots clear as kindling branches snapping, and I was certain that it was about my informant that they clustered like deerflies to sting his blood. When would they come after me? The whirr of bicycles in the dark and that double ring of one handlebar bell answering itself, and a third in some code unmistakable to one acquainted with the dark in these no longer bicycled streets curfewed five and a half hours nightly even for women in labor who had to get to the hospital. Locals lacking good radios fired their rifles to let each other know where they were when they patrolled the palm groves and here in town. Someone was coming for me in the morning.

In my room I checked cassettes, battery pack, head, a card in a metal frame attached to the cam that I wrote sequence numbers down on if I had the time; unstrapped my watch and set the alarm. And later couldn't tell if I'd really slept, for in my uncertainty a test would be, Had I dreamt? when the dream this night was just another waking memory and getting up I found a memento on a table and took it back to bed in the dark before I fell asleep toward dawn thinking who they would have the right to arrest back home these days if they wanted. My family?

Milt had snapped up Umo's ID, fingers like a bird. Umo

went for him, not the ID, lifted him up over his head. Cheeky shrieked for the four-bulb ceiling light fixture over the dining table and for the shepherd's pie and roasted birds and a jar of candied ginger and all the food was there on her table and Umo spun Milt like a plank, some poor pro wrestler who didn't get the joke, and Umo nearly falling down laughing his laugh making to lay Milt in Cheeky's thin and veined arms (for I measured with a shock or the beginning of some thought the two years since I'd seen her, by her thinness, who's light as a crust of fire ash, yet also her desire to tell me something — Umo's abandonment of her on his arrival in Vera Cruz, but —), instead laid Milt on the "ancient rug" I'd heard of, a gift from The Inventor, who quickly scribbled in his book a note to himself I assumed — and I needed to ask about a book in his store he wouldn't let me look at (and I thought I gave that surprise envelope to Dad and didn't know what was in it) but Cheeky was saying to me and a chain-smoking little kid gobbling lox-in-a-blanket and the last three buffalo corn dogs and cheese nachos strewn on the table that Umo came in handy at times. (Umo was ... *telling* him something, Em said. He was? I said in the dark — Pretty vigorously ... Mmhmm ... that you would be OK. He's wild, he'll never desert you, we're all family but what's that law they like to forget? It wasn't whether the war was right, he was telling Milt *and* you, it was that you were doing something *in* it.) The war, Milt said. Absolutely, said Umo. I'm just going as a ... I began (but did not say, *picture taker*). See you there, said Umo. He was a little different.

My sister, half asleep, I knew was exposed really to me in all her attention, covers thrown back typically. When I gave up at last and got up, wondering at a fine length of light under the door from the hall, I found an amber glint on her chest of drawers and the little bookcase. "Look, that ol' geode." Next to the old useless "mouth organ" harmonica her grandfather, a farmer we never visited, had sent her, this geode rock the size of an orange — half, in fact (better than a whole, you can see the inside, once upon a time a cavity in a rock vein, like a mold filled up then with crystalline minerals projecting toward the center). And she had dug it up, this craggy sphere in space, and my father had cracked it in two (I must have been eleven) to see the amber, sea-cactus green, violet, yellow icy forms, a mountain six inches across, and worth something.

Take it, she murmured half-dreaming I thought. I ran my fingers over the little bookcase begun in the garage and finished by me for better or worse, the screws countersunk by my father who had left the bookcase unsanded and unfinished one whole winter almost. But, 'member Wiley's Well? my sister murmured.

I did. The geode beds. The campground. They called it "primitive" and it was. My sister made a sound, awake. Brought in our own firewood and toilet paper, she said softly. The feet near her door weren't heard again, though the thin line penciled under the door of light dim from the far end of the second-floor hall didn't cease, and in the near-dark I went and stepped down hard on my keys in the pocket of my pants, sat down on the bed, thought again, found my sister's arm under my neck when I stretched out as if I had never gotten up. "One step forward, one back," she said comfortably. We always went halves, she said, you and me. The three of us in that tent, I said into her hair, and somewhere near there we dug up the geode. Not exactly, I said. No, never exactly, she said. You and I, I said.

Yes.

And Dad, she said … Yes, read the survey map for us with a vertical distance of forty feet between the lines — Yes, when it was almost too dark to see by the fire. And the contours made fingerprints, I said; she turned her face to me. Whorled. Mmhmm. Whorled. Did she speak or did I?

Elevation.

Saddle. That's the hourglass. The dip between two rising — Mmhmm — elevation lines.

Gray for privately owned. Brought our own firewood, water … The haves and the have-nots, he said. Yeah what did he mean?

We heard familiar, heel-hard feet softly seem to pass, cease, pass outside my sister's door, heel, ball of the foot barely sticking to the pine boards.

And the white, she said. That was for rock outcrops *he* said. Right, he did. Open lands, I think; yes, too open for —

Hiding (whispered, giggling) … For hiding a platoon on a single acre it said (I added),… from — Mmm, from planes flying over — a memory in both minds, both heads, mouths. A trek, he called it. You're right. The River. The Colo*rad*o. Yes, a half hour for each mile of dotted lines for trails unless you're climbing and then … He slept between us. (Horse trail, foot trail. Mmhmm.) You and I facing the opposite way from him, talking across (she giggles) … his … shins, his … sleeping-bag feet, 'n we added up the mileage of each stop our father had made: from the gas station to Blythe, from trading post to the Wiley Well turnoff, from the turnoff south to the dirt road past the state prison, from there to Coon Hollow Campground, from there back to Wiley Well — It's Wil*eez*. Until …

We were thinking of another time we'd been talking in bed and God that time when I came out into the hall in my underwear to go to my room, he was standing in the bathroom doorway the light off behind him, and you just knew he was angry as hell. Did she remember? What in particular? she retorts, her tongue softly clicking the syllables. "It was the night before the accident."

"I remember the night *of*," she said, to be a little difficult.

Was he outside her door now this night of the enlistment party — and, now, a second, secret one? She was mine. The mystery of a son's enlistment uncanny on his night when he might just have had a hand in it, the Specialist package, the Army phoning. (An agreement, yes between me and my friend Umo. That I'd enlist. But the agreement went beyond it.) While here, on my sister's dresser, remotely aglint with amber promise, a subterranean mine pocket was what the geode looked like, its own light focused from the threshold's edge.

… till he told us to shut up and go to sleep — and we touched across his sleeping-bag feet, and my little sister whispered, Poor man, and we snickered like paper tearing in the stillness between the beginning breakers of his breathing and held hands more or less all night — and we planted the other half of the "orange" when we moved out in the morning and he said, What're you two — … ? "That's right, I remember, he didn't finish. Oh did he open the — " "One step forward, I bought my first incense sticks at the trading post," the dark intelligent curls falling forward, the face above me, hips, knees, "how couldn't you go way beyond diving?" was what this poetic person, imagining a drive far greater than competitive, her elbows either side of my neck, had said to me the night of my enlistment party, which was continuing into the depths of all I could fathom — "my unpretentious carpenter," was what she said, and whether Dad had opened The Inventor's envelope I'd given him for his birthday remained unknown I thought, where it belonged for a while, though again she said when I left that

I had been to the better party until I had come home and *this* became the best party of all.

Events some of them public only at the Competition Hearings months later: the mere trip from billet to palace e-mailed after I got home to my sister ending with the little Specialist from Wisconsin, my chauffeur, "Out you go," and then something through the closed glass of the passenger-side window her lips like a smooch brought together in a word, "chose," I felt sure. Yet my sister had to know what came *before* that, and so on, message "after" message, clear back to my driver picking me up while once for two weeks I got my sister's mail in reverse order through the Army systems. But I was to learn what I knew already, that they would wish to silence truth by exposing privacy, whoever, one night after I had sent all the stages of the brief trip billet to palace reported like effect followed by cause to my impatient sister (impatient for what? what happened just before and before that), e-mailed me the lot from a merely numbered e-address as if I would want to have it for the record when it was from my beloved wit: though like prophecy shared in a book I carried with me as with its donor my sister then going by the name of "Em" I enlarge upon my memory of the disastrous day, its degree of difficulty, second-guessing my understanding of my father, but no. Run it backwards, I'm here.

My escort coming at 0800. Would I hear my watch alarm? Did I get the function right, the numbers? — one two three four five six seven, if the alarm Set didn't get away into Time itself. I tumbled back into my narrow bed, leaving my little book on the floor and taking my sister's words with me, the geode in my hand, crystals projecting out of time — in love — reversing a dive I once took in one piece — the issue wide open of who would want that War Child soldier I'd just talked to dead in the street. Not that he'd spilled anything of importance to me, not certainly identified the video crew-member whom (*Affirmative*) he did know — the soldier who was and wasn't a soldier, and is anyone blameless (as the book and the actor too says)? Nor had Umo been identified, but.

Taxiing east across the desert hundreds of miles, three of them, four with driver, if they made it past Euphrates River corridor sweeps and past roadblocks on almost half the major roads. Entering perhaps this very city of riddled bridges (three closed of eight), expressway past the park, great mosque dome blue as a Virgin's cloak, blue as a bird, a drained pool right here outside the stock exchange — all to tape GIs glued to their music tapes on the threshold of assaults that classic Rock for all its sound said No to, where Now's neighborhood blasts us off into funkadelic ready-for-anything or *un*ready commitment-is-the-name-of-it action plus just talking for the film crew, making do with the Occupation, living with whatever, with war, what we have to do, our way against theirs, two steps forward, fifty years back in, yo, whatever order, like why'd *you* enlist, Zach? — hey wait a sec, listen to this, an earphone offered.

13   might as well want a dive back

Patient, I had photographed the black soldier, clicked him into some lasting increment, my moment of hidden equilibrium it came to me, a photo in between. I begin then — tell you what happened just before and so on.

7. "This is as far as I go," she said, braking and shifting, and almost laying her hand on my leg, sunlight splitting the dried mud across the windshield from a roadside mortar early this morning, when somebody else had been driving this civilian wreck not a true substitute for a Humvee. What're ya doin? she murmured, feeling me lean and then not. That guy in there by the fountain, I said. She wouldn't know. I knew she wasn't driving me through the great arched gateway. "Wait a minute," I said. "Out you go," she said. "I know that guy from somewhere." She put the car in gear and touched me, put her finger on the back of my hand, Specialist from Wisconsin. "You know more than me. Don't get shot, now, like that Bedouin who was born without eyes just standing by when they shot his cousin who went fishing for the Scrolls." "But, a deserter

were you saying, the film crew, a deserter — ?" I said, stunned to hear "Scrolls." "Yeah. Out you go." "This is the palace," I said, the stone, the fractured minaret, chipped pillars, like my status suddenly in question. "One of them," she said, her braid below the camouflage cap blond and dark-streaked, my driver and fan, my one-way ride: "This is what you're here for." "This is what we're all here for." "That's all I know," she said. "But you remembered ..." (I was pushing.) "Ask the captain," I said. "The captain," she said (who liked her, protected her from E-5 "rapists," but from himself too?). "I wish I knew what we were all here for," she said for some reason. "I hear you," I said, getting myself out, older I felt. "Spread the word." She said something through the glass of the window that brought her lips together, the word "chose" I feel sure, beyond irony. I fingered the micro out the size of a quarter and got, I hoped, a shot of her in profile if I didn't see her again, this fan of my crappy photographs with amazing info, who might have seen what had been cropped not by me from my shot of the arm-wrestlers in Kut, but I didn't think so, she just knew, she had some kind of understanding; but I had to wonder what had become of Umo.

6. Some documents had nearly surfaced at one of the wells networking a region to the west. A desert thief, or enemy, had fished out an eighteen-inch capsule (that was what my driver knew), had opened and tried to read the contents (ancient, what she'd heard — something about scribes and *family think you're crazy,* and *get you off the street,* and *Be a passerby*), and this desert interloper been shot to death, and the documents had been rolled up, slid back in (that was all she knew), and sent on their way at this point of water acceleration identified by an Army engineer as a current, on the basis of what he had heard. That was what my driver knew. It was like fucking to hear this.

She had nothing to do with Operation Scroll Down, she said; she kept it separate, just seeing that I got there. She was taking me a back way, no traffic lights, no stop signs, half the traffic lights were busted, you didn't want to be at those intersections. That shot of the arm-wrestlers at Kut, well it, she said, moved me no end — what had you *said* to them? (Uncanny of her, her mouth, like she knew something of my connection to the weightlifter though he hadn't recognized me from home.) We passed a power plant near a bridge that was open. Didn't we pass a Nineveh Street? "You said something …" "Just as I snapped them. I have to meet someone there I think." "You don't know?" "Get there somewhere." "Kut."

5. "To make sure you get where you're goin' this morning," she said. But she knew me, I felt. They had their plans, she said, and their plans would not change *her* way of … Right, I said, you're — There was a swimming pool in the basement, that was all she knew. You're who you are, I said; now the man who … last night … She didn't know his name, that's all she knew. "Black," I said. A bicyclist in an old flak vest raced us, looked in my window, my driver swerved and hit him almost — no, did — she was a helluva driver, it spoke for itself, she said there weren't any bicyclists any more. "Your right fender." "Armored vehicle, one of ours, friendly heap." She could fix anything, transmission, rings, long as they didn't blow her up. A dog was barking. One dog can make all the difference, she said, she'd seen a dog chewing on a foot. "Now, the black guy…" Found down by the river near the stock exchange, that was all she knew. But this deserter … (?) We'll get you there, she muttered. You're important, she said, for a Reservist. She looked over at me. It … she began …

4. They could think I came in handy if they wanted, it didn't
change my way of doing things, I said, which sounded grand
and I was stretching it probably. She knew what I meant, she
got mad sometimes, she said .... All these people wanted me
here I sometimes thought, I said, and in spite of it, I'd *chosen*
to be, y'know? I could tell that she did. "Wanted you here?"
She stopped herself. "They want you to see what they want
you to see," she said then. All she knew? She took it seriously.
In my travels had I ever been to Wisconsin? she asked. Never,
unfortunately, I said. Never, never. She sort of laughed, said
she'd only been to Florida with her family and it was the wrong
part and the wrong time of year — swerving over to make a
right, and at the far end was the stadium where something had
happened. "You're a photographer." "That all you know?" I said.
We made a pretty hilarious left, they were letting civilian traffic
onto the July 14th Bridge, she said, about the traffic. I saw no
bridge. What was it I'd said before I shot that picture? she said.

3. Well, what was it she had found in the Kut photo? I said,
she'd said she — . Well ... it was the Reservist. What about
him? Well, his eye was like a wild horse, and he's not walleyed.

I said, That wasn't all. Well, he'd just been distracted, said
my driver, pushing me. Well, there was a — There was someone
under the table, wasn't there? said my driver, pushing me. A
local woman out of the frame, under the table tied up, I said.
Was that it? my driver asked. Not entirely tied up, I said —
well, something had just been said, I said. By ...? The Reservist
whose rifle had been ridiculed. But by you? Yes, I asked if they
had seen an Asian kid with a film crew? We'll get you there; I
have a problem with time, you know. I always get there early.
Well, that could be hazardous. Tomorrow even more, she said;
lot of activity Fridays — no, I thought somebody was doing

something to the guy with the eyes under the table, said my driver — If we could just rerun it, I said, wanting some time with her.

2. "Who you hang out with, eh?" I said. "That's all I know," she said. "A deserter who comes back on a civilian job — that's a skid, that's one for the movies," she said. "He came back to his unit?" "His unit!" "Who was hanging out with him?" "Working with him, that's all I know." "The soldier killed last night?" "He wasn't working with him." "A deserter who came back for some job of his own and someone was working with him?" We were going the back way, my driver said, and she had called me a Reservist. Was this why the captain had assigned her to me? I said and I felt she got my meaning better than I did. "I think a friend of mine was doing sound. They ran up a $900 tab in a taxi coming across from I don't know where, three of them and a driver I guess." "Two of them and a driver, until they got to …" A rattle of fire from behind us, she looked over her shoulder, she reached to explore my bicep with the back of her hand. "Hang *out* with a target …," she said, and left her point unfinished.

1. It was the little Specialist from Wisconsin my driver at eight in the morning at the wheel of an olive-drab-repainted though beat-up though sort of camouflaged and evolved Chevy Suburban like what local Guard troops used that should have been recalled new a dozen years ago, appropriated now from some local civilian arm you figured, no Humvee for me, no mine-resistant vehicle and she said we would hurry up so I could wait at the other end and get set up. Let's not get beyond ourselves, I said, recalling my sister's way of — That was some photo, my driver said. I got in and we were gone before I could haul the door shut that was down to the bare metal. I took a

look at her and she had the kind of nice looks that she would turn and check you out while she was driving or knew you. "Last night," I said, and stared at the windshield. "Last night was someone else's turn," she said. I looked at her leaning forward at the wheel, small but compact. I asked what about the soldier. "We lost a man. That's all I know. You hang out with a target, you're one."

"What he told me I already figured out," I said, knowing what she meant — *not you but someone else* because *of you* — yet I understood more than I figured she could know — that Umo was here somewhere and with the wrong people; "but that soldier," I went on, needing to know, unlike this fine woman who kept saying that was all she knew with each new thing she yielded up, "the film crew guy that he recognized as a deserter wouldn't be after *him*; a buddy?" I could feel my driver's contempt coming at me and, in my ignorant neck and eyelids, almost a longtime affection in this woman. She leaned back and raised her chin. "That was some picture." Down in Kut? Yes, that was …pretty wild. (She was thinking about her day ahead and me, I believe.) The arm-wrestlers? What was it she had found in it? I asked; the captain said you —

"The captain, the captain," she dropped one hand into her lap as if we had stopped — for she was a rebel in there somewhere — "it's the others," she said. "The finish line keeps moving," she said. "And then there's the fobbits, the ones who never get off the base. Well you know, you're a Reservist the captain said."

I wish I had those words back, my mother said, having told my brother it didn't matter what he did with his life, long as he liked it. *Back*? What her spouse would not say after demolishing the cub reporter from the paper who could have done him some good or a loan officer, been abrupt even with the man he cultivated known as Storm (once, by his Christian name Nosworthy in my hearing in those days, and once since), the speechwriter frequently on the phone trolling for input. *Don't bring* him *into it*, my father said over the phone, my sister said, and told me I was meant. She could tell from his face hanging up that he had gone too far and intimate momentarily with his daughter if he could have embraced her nature — how had he received the Coaches Directory with the data about him plus a little comment? But words Dad wanted back? Maybe just the *time* they took up. Both he and my mother, as if for her, time was family, in the way of beginnings, yet then she came to understand there was my sister and I.

Might as well want a dive back, what degree of difficulty to do it in reverse?

History spilled in front of others at the party by Milt — words he evidently knew by heart that had once upon a time distracted me in the middle of a dive but when I asked if he knew what they meant he could not say. And Umo the same night who said that he would marry my sister, she could read faces, I asked why she would have any interest in him and he could not say. Milt was after her but she said how could she go out with a guy whose father's eyebrows converged diagonally like that? — there was something else there. Yet never could I offend Liz whatever I said, who was after me to get back into diving who's so seemingly alive up close you close your eyes. Those steps along the board alone and decided, the hop to land on two feet, back straight up and down, legs bending with the board, or, if a back dive of some variety, the private step and balancing pivot so different from the swimmer's lap turn. There, though, a dive, too, like your sea lion reaching its aquarium wall and heading elsewhere. Come to think — because I did, about to pass down among the depths of the palace — I myself would slow-motion a dive in reverse on occasion from a few feet above the entry water back up to the midair peak where things changed and took shape — with my eleventh-grade "relativity" teacher we fondly called him, assistant swimming coach at the high school, Wick, who thought of many things often at once, I learned, doctored once with his math — but more likely redo it from the beginning in my head or some regrettable remark to Umo who in an expansive mood might associate himself with me as if I were someone and when I left that night I presented with the old, once opened, once resealed birthday envelope I had purchased from The Inventor for the same price as the World's Fair catalogue I'd passed on to my sister, who was interested in Tarzan and bayou snakes — "a tighter breathing …Zero at the bone," and in an e-mail that anybody could read said our mother had "salvaged" The Inventor's envelope I'd given to Dad.

Distant music, Palestinian pop. And here was the disused fountain and the man with the nose was gone, as I turned from the departing car, and facing me in his absence through its open gateway the dull and dangerous palace, official, pale, and square. Loitering personnel cued from me got inside in a hurry — not only uniformed, for it came to me with their scuffing steps and scattered fire rattling somewhere and an explosion and then one closer — and mortars — as I made my way to the pillared steps, microcam in shirt pocket — that my driver meant by "others" *civilians* (my short-lived driver, beloved maybe): and at the steps on impulse, hearing like a social escort more fire not even totally unfriendly, I stretched out a hand to touch a limestone pillar's fine spiral of fluting and a chipped crest, and something in my arm punished me in the act or stung a muscle or tendon stretched or sharply questioned. And I passed inside and was directed to a stairway and led down by a beat-up-looking man who, in the sudden abyss of the entry in his black T-shirt apparently Special Forces, I mistook for the one at the fountain when my car had pulled in.

Each downward step of marble or inlaid mahogany stair my boots like feet felt grit on, tracked inside from the city, each lintel-post and arch, each turn sealing me in, and each shadow coming up to meet me demanding protection or a now-and-then faintly vibrating all-bets-off plunge, a salt of humid reek ahead stirred by bodies using it, a clubby steam and memory of last month's chlorine from some mosaic wash of light I knew pooling and dissolving us, and, someway nasty (why not, as my guide vanished ahead), a climax somehow disreputable of plan yet stubbornly mine beyond all plans of those who might have set me up as if I were not anyone;

and that bad guy I had seen from the car window I suddenly now in his absence knew — yet how could I? — I had been summoning him for months only by voice and name and suspicion and honest, doubt-dreaded, phone-fantasized face, broad but very *thin* shoulders I had thought, and was right:

but the face (of course of course) I in fact recalled looking up at from the waters I was working during an afternoon practice months ago at East Hill, the astute circumference of it, yet its parts disturbingly independent, the long upper lip, strong buck teeth, goatee, hair parted old-fashioned in the middle, the gross lucidity, though, of (of course!) the bluish nose now focusing everything with its swerve and parallel force broken since then but not seen by me broken till now. For this had to be the nose and cheek bone rezoned by the angry mortgage lender (who after all found himself in basic agreement with them) who had flown off the handle a moment at remarks updating Jesus's enterprise skills lighting a friendly fire under you, beliefs which Storm had attributed to an associate, though this was apparently before the Scrolls arrived, which contained this stunner in the recorded interview as if Storm had had advance word, information enlarged in the fragmented Scrolls derived seemingly, though, from the associate later reported as *two* contemporary persons:

all this that had been crystallized in an absence now erased as he stood before me, an atrium and indoor garden suite behind him luminous of dwarf palms, giant virginsbreath (I now know), bird of paradise at a glance with the spiked orange blooms. Aromatic wood somewhere, his words a double dream, "Storm Nosworthy, Zach, so glad to intersect after all this time working together, Fort Meade ..." (a rueful pucker of the strange mouth) shaking my hand, holding the other one then too sliding up past my elbows to hold my arms, pinching one; I thought (and *working* together? — a shmooze, yet startling too) (and black, short-sleeve guayabera just like vertically embroidered shirts Umo and his cop friend Zoose and Zoose's new brother-in-law, the musician, had on in a snapshot with Zoose's sister at her wedding in Laguna Salada more than a year ago?): "You smelled the cedar coming down. Look up, we've redone the ceiling, it's one of the special things about the place we wanted to restore. Though ours is Himalayan cedar, true cedar, though it will doubtless be called cedar of Lebanon. Had it shipped direct by an appeals court justice's law partner who has a second home in Tibet. He left a small branchlet and its couple of leaves still growing from the end of one plank as you can see in the far corner up there like a signature smelling of rosemary. I feel like Solomon. We're so indebted to you, Zach, for what you're doing."

"'*We*'?" I said — "'*restore*,' '*Tibet*' — 'working together,' you said — and Fort Meade —" "Didn't work out." "It didn't?" I led him on, he didn't mean my Specialist studies but something else. This one of God's creatures was rubbing his hands together and then on his white cotton, distinctly local pants, saying he felt like Solomon. "Solomon?"

"The war effort! Your father, and that whole good family I've heard like the good background noise over the phone, siblings real close — you have a *sis*ter," came then the words all by themselves topped, then, by "nice work if you can get it" (so I could have soiled my palm swiping that broken nose back into line in that somehow familiar face, eyelids thick folds, eyes small or remote). "Where'd you get *that*?" I murmured, chilled by a risk of memories above a springboard, Dad's shouts, the law of pool tiles, the laws of slowing down very nearly grasped by Wick who, doctoring your thought, tried to pass them on for me to apply. "We've done our best, *out*done ourselves, to shoot Operation Scroll Down, get someone whose photographs ..." Storm shook his head, agog, mouth open, drool-ready, twisted (expressive but of what? a change of subject?). "Done our best to *get* the best." (*I* wasn't in competition with — I hear you, he said, hey I'd given him an idea.) (He me.) "And kept it in the family. Your dad's ideas, well I confess I wondered if they could all be his, they were so ...as if we didn't know."

Storm Nosworthy, smiling once twice three times, a dark, burnt-looking rim inside his lower lip. He did something to his pants, which now showed faint smudges. (What were they? Had he been gardening?) "Great springboard for the Operation — maybe it *is* the Operation, Zach. And keeping it to yourself. You won't be forgotten." (Operation Scroll Down, I thought he meant.) "As your father asked you to" — (*to be forgotten?*)

"Nobody even in the loop knows *ev*erything — but he will get what *he* wants, the Committee will see to that, what a competitive … hey competitive with his son, why not? And the diving? *That* whole story, you've gone deeper than diving, how does that grab you? Leave the board to someone — … you know what I'm saying. Another better way. You have to look ahead. You have a sister. You have a former …teacher you — (?)"

Storm came close up, a breath of mildew, and between dread and some partnership I recalled Dad had spoken of Umo as someone who would be of use to "us," and I should keep it "under my cap" even from Umo, he knew what friends we were. (*If* we were, Dad'd added in that way of his, probing, remote.) Of use as a swimmer? I thought, a diver? whatever, was he a team person? — all I wanted now with Storm in my face was to get where I was going to do the job I'd been sent to do, yet no — was this the real job, to be valued by a person like this somehow? Turning, thirsty, I felt that sting again maybe like the nip of a snake where Storm had thumbed my arm, clasped me, his fingers pinching underneath, though this adder had a chemical on his breath, and I started to mention that odd remark of my father's after his trip, stopped myself, started again, "There was that trip to Baja," I said, "when he had a meeting — with you, I believe …" For on his return Dad had called Umo "competent" and I had missed something he'd said that would come to me and now seemed sinister if I could recall it. What they learned of Umo in Mexico — little more, I'd bet, than his immigration status.

Storm had my hand again, my name in his mouth implicates me, "You're right, Zach, faith in the system— even over friendship, other priorities, risk by association, you know what

I'm saying — silence is golden. You're up to this, it's already part yours, we wanted to be able to get you outa here in a hurry if we had to, so the captain probably mentioned your enlistment got switched to Reserve — finish the job I always say." Up to *what*, did Storm Nosworthy mean? Videotape, but stills too? Some historical thing arriving — getting unearthed, or plucked in a rush from these waters somewhere below me. Storm had nerve. A vast horizontal well system? Ancient. To impact the war (though it was said to be sort of over).

No contingency plan — this is it: Storm's words a spinning, flip-sided guarantee of reward and/or punishment (in the frowning smile of a faith-based relative, a punitive *reward* comes back; but a *Reserve* enlistment?) — I experience Storm's hand moist and distinctly sticky, local candies maybe, until I can bow and, processing these words of his *hang out with a target*, you're *one*, and *proceed down to the pool and wait there for your* … — turn away then behind me, distantly, a soft snap of the fingers I thought as I saw a figure appear ahead of me and something else from Storm almost to himself (*what's this …?*) … the indoor garden there behind Storm, the dwarf olive, my thirst, several violet and orange and, I think, indigo, pink, and bulbous plants, in a gold pot a dwarf tree too small for Jonah to have retired under — "You need a drink, Zach" (Storm toasted me with an empty hand) — a silent tortoise, a bird's shadow near the skylight in this land that seemed to Storm though not exactly *our* land a new frontier to build having been torn down, a small volume of Kipling with a half-empty, sordid drink on it he hands me, a family crest on the glass — "*What's this on the* … ?" (on the what? — I hear fingers snap as distinctly as the neck of a hanged culprit — "our family Virginia 18th century and before that Cornwall, Devon" —) — stairs rejoining me down past ceramic alcoves, a mouth-watering recipe of pots on the stove and ovens roasting as a door opens somewhere for a second, as my palace escort appeared once more in the shadows on this flight of stairs taking me past a rose-colored room and the elbows, butts, a momentarily one-legged foot of a man and another of a woman or two stepping into or out of something I thought, another door flings open below upon the warp of voices and pool waters, closing again. Till I am there, and a steel door with deadbolts and a lever-handle I jiggle must yield more stairs, but I'm guided away from it to the two swinging portals into the pool area that I push following perhaps my guide who I have the feeling now is not ahead but behind me and more gone from me than even he knows, for I would not tell him what I enlisted for.

14 a necessity like water

Humidity stood and unfolded toward you like the music agitating distantly under the pool itself and you could blink away a cloud transfiguring your upward sight. Though, having on the way downstairs passed in his digs a very ghost of a sometime Administration speechwriter "on the way up," I was not here to film a ceiling mosaicked blue green crimson with river birds and one great-lobed ear, an esoteric oblong drawn in or on it, anciently listening downward upon this forty-meter-or-so pool, saffron and gray of water, a roped-off, only somewhat deeper section for the diving board where a bald man with a moustache treaded water.

Plus shower rooms; swimsuited civilian and military mixing nakedly (how did I know one from the other?), soldiers in fatigues; and this sketchy guy somehow, a large face I knew I would act on if I could just recall his job, his deep chin stonier for his short stature, eyebrows so thick and angularly peaked they didn't need the small, recessed eyes beneath, a man bronzed on neck and forearms contemplating both the busy pool and this big woman guard in camo fatigues one-handing at her side a more or less automatic weapon I wasn't familiar with with an awkward-looking outside sling swivel; yet also aware, I knew, of me, this stocky, quick civilian I half-remembered, tense, factoring me into the scene his blistered lips saying to the woman what I must hear while wondering all at once why he was here and why would our people consign the Scrolls to underground waterways, why not fax them home?

Why would the enemy target them, was it envy of this newly documented Jesus reportedly confirming in actual interview the Enterprise Conference's bold person-to-person Win-Win interaction two thousand years later? I try to honor my own ignorance — about people and what they mean. One forthright Syriac phrase in the transcript of the apparently prevailingly Aramaic-language interview with some Edessian dialectal colorings reportedly literally translated "succeed succeed," a seed of EC's "there are only winners if the market plan is followed"; another Syriac term, literally "bird market peace" reportedly meaning "seller's niche" supposedly echoes our own venerable "flight plan" or "Christian game plan" which was a surprise to me in my ignorance if I believed my old hunch — or my struggling teacher's, really, the assistant swimming coach at the high school — that Jesus must have been pretty left-wing. Where *were* the Scrolls coming from, some Holy Land? An oasis where David I have heard escaped Saul? Further north where winter rains once clothed the Mesopotamian plain in verdure? Or where Euphrates attains its height in the mountains? And if this new, not secondhand profile of the Master chief executor of the miracles — saved virtually live in talk by an early first-century Roman with a genius for history, makes the Vatican like a man suddenly bald or worse feel challenged, will the new

Pope still judge weapons of mass subtraction the lesser evil to cloning's multiplier?

Old Milt's kind of question, irked at The Inventor's envelopes, and at my "rage" to see — *See?* — the war which through my other so young Asian friend turned from seeing almost to another sense, as I subsequently tried to show at the Hearings though less for a theme of Competition synonymous among our people with freedom (to buy, for example, a fragrant candle called His Essence that smells like Jesus, his robes, in Psalm 45) than toward another of our senses I will call Understanding first sketched in samples of my sister's way of speaking or relation to me though nothing I could do justice to at the Hearings from which I become less connected while realizing that, not bluff or dynamic enough, I no longer knew if I was an emerging professional in the field of sports psychology, or had fallen into Errorism, a humorous but not all that humorous term in the field, which is a branch of sports medicine, and meaning an overprecise differing with somebody (and if they won't pass you the ball and you're the open man, it may affect your shooting eventually). And then my sister's voice so clear inside me it might have been messaging asking how "old Milt" had called me on the carpet about my enlistment for it had never been principally a birthday party for The Inventor. Only trying to make a contribution to just about every panel of the Hearings on Competition when it came to it eventually and say what I saw to show myself months later what I saved even to describe for others what went down when my friend, as I have already said, all but miraculously appeared.

Sports psychology out on a limb beyond its parent trunk sports medicine if I am in the right field even, led on and on from friend *and* foe by the equivalent of what you get along the upper wall of castles in old Damascus and Mesopotamia, those projecting galleries supported by arches with holes in the floor which came in handy for pouring boiling oil, water, or blood upon competitors below if you can make the time it came to me to say, finding at last the one person around — in the doorway of the next-to-last panel room of the Hearings — who understood thoughts of that kind probably because it was her kind of thinking, my sister.

Thoughts in an "up" moment at poolside leaving me exposed so to Storm's associate (yes) this deep-chinned KPMG accountant UK transplant to California I once saw through my swim goggles at East Hill checking their investment — though now as time, broken-down or not, ran out (shudderingly, I believe) through the palace building, witnessing an event that was and was not my job, I heard again the stupidly familiar words "*Come in handy*" this man before me now said to the plain vanilla Specialist he may in fact have fancied, meaning surely her old automatic rifle (of course of course — his words like memory itself) a Chinese SKS way-out-of-date post-World-War-II and trade-prohibited under U.S. law I'd caught a much better equipped contract-civilian on film ridiculing — the words felt in my chest an interruption of my heart waking the old surface scar bringing back my father's prediction *Come in handy* of my friend Umo, and that they'd bring back the Draft, it was only fair, hearing like never before my name called from above, near where an almost invisible trap-hinged section of the ceiling's mosaicked giant ear had snapped shut again too quick for me:

for there was Umo, compelled to be there, I could tell, arrived on that diving board notorious for penalties suffered by divers who fell short of excellence, yet in all his foreign flesh free

— and "going," as we say in our public pools back home or ask of somebody who stands up there on the high board too long (*You goin'?*): (but a dive multiplying all your damned questions into some moving, unanswerable statement, yet Umo here for me somehow)

and not here, I felt, for the same job as me:

yet for a job, solo probably — for where's his crew, where's the deserter? — for something has happened: and on the board still a boy, overflowing yet not surplus, still bound somewhere, diving it came to me for me at the same time as Get outa his way, a life weapon in himself. My throat would not sing out his name to him — he might have been Montezuma — I heard some familiar Rock 'n Roll distantly below the pool yet somewhere central like a comfort level or taped home; mental yet sustaining like a wheel and on message, and as Umo (to these folk *what,* by these waters? — a not sufficiently developed or identifiable alien presence in the camouflage shorts, a local who doesn't belong here — did my job give me these words? — troublemaker rising up — how'd he get in, through the ceiling?) — hailing this sweating, dumbfounded Army cameraman in boots on the wet tiles — "Zach!" — who aims his handy beat-up company-issue camcorder quickly from the hip and too low for Godsake unthinking reaching his other hand into his pocket:

registering behind me the double cluck of a different chamber readying (because it wasn't the big blonde but the woman, small and dark, whose smell of jasmine soap, so bizarrely distinct from the gun oil and the gleaming slide and interlock of her newly rerustproofed M4 there and a hint of burn, I knew from the bedroom across the hall from mine at home) so I seriously doubted that this was my Operation Scroll Down job, handy as I might be:

for I suspected under these waters beside which I found myself, under the great tray or vessel of the pool itself, another level down or two, ran what I had been sent for to shoot — to witness, that is — where a branch of the vast desert well system passed by for the palace-builder's onetime use and now for ours that we might deliver safely cradled the truly New capsule testimony to our Man and faith in what we were doing here and "next door" with benefits for all, or down there just some sewerside den.

I would not shout out I thought to Umo, he had made his stately approach and had given his trust to a strange diving board and I wouldn't have my friend — targeted? —distracted as I had once been, yet found fixed in my throat dread or a power thrust into it of plural cry or covenant the silent question from my eyes and mouth *Why're you here?* — virtual Hey Momma somewhere recalled song that my sister or (that was it!) *Umo* would have understood, hearing in this split delay or vocal two-note chord already, before Umo had launched his upward, arms-flung-outward trip like a vanishing crane white above its black flight feathers from some depleted tundra bog in the far north, the stab of the accountant's voice at me, "Hey you're bleeding." Words come just in time to be part of what I couldn't say quite, or only hear, the *come in handy* my father had summed up Umo in — and knew what had stung my arm arriving at the palace and reaching to touch the pillar's fluting, and presently what I had seen on Storm's pants and felt of impossibly even myself in his sticky palm.

And hearing in my head, arm, throat, fingers of my left hand that had drawn the tiny camera from my shirt pocket so that I was double-taking after first bringing my left hand to my chest then out again, Umo's participation in a moment I didn't grasp (except as I guessed they had promised him some corner of citizenship) and never taking my eyes off Umo calling to him only in my *mind,* my *mind,* to slow down, pause, in midair so we could talk, I stepped back flinging my other arm that was holding the clunky Army-issue videocam back around behind me half-knowing what I would strike and hearing as if I had detonated it the explosion from the M4 fired by the small dark Specialist its aim deflected because it's a free country and you can always try — and in the corner of my eye aware only afterward of the accountant falling shot; for the dive I had never seen Umo or anyone try — from its surge and peak and sudden all but yanked and independent half twist and the surprises that followed it called up from the depths the gross counterpart of its own folding and unfolding and fall to be all but met by a concussion from below the diving well, bursting, bulging like a huge toilet flush or great bubble of oil from the diving well, bombed definitely from below as Umo was to have entered the water feetfirst, his joined legs, feet, and pointed toes all one, and a flying splinter of shrapnel like a shuttering split second tore a piece of his shoulder, expansion beneath and all around us as he would have made his entry into the vanishing water, yet the diving well section of the pool gave way, not inward at first — a gulp of force drawing up a gush under pressure, a bulbous blossoming water sucked where it came from yet at its ashen, pinkish rim for a split second not moving until following the first souvenirs of tile, cement, chrome, and human material, a leg and foot (the bald man who'd been floating in the well perhaps), and my friend's vanishing form, the pool water largely draining out into the disaster area where Heavy Metal music resumed, never having ceased, spinning, coming up like what my friend and his team had come here to tape

GIs listening to most of them and talking about this badly served-up war the wages of which were regularly paid out of experience to guys and women in sums of money quite modest because experience is almost beyond price, being a necessity like water, though what the terrorists had been after I had to figure was not swimmers or palace but the arriving Scrolls, and had a second explosion boosted the first or aftershocked it or was it still the first?

And the poolside faces and their bodies all so contingent, looking like bearing weapons's the job in itself, turn this way and that shepherding nowhere in particular the rest, who might just be the voices all around in the still watery areas of alarm thickened by risk falling at you and away like speeds through some darkness of the noise, new to me in a threatened building. Denizens crowded about the near side of the pit left by the blast, my wrist was wrenched and the camcorder that I had put another notch in when I struck the rifle behind me like a backstroker in a busy lane was gone from my hand. I turned and went after the guard behind me but the big woman standing in the accountant's watering blood steered me with her rifle another way, I was not to follow the small woman in oversize combats who at the swinging doors turned, rifle stock braced against her ribs her finger ready, my Army cam in her other hand, startled understanding across her cheeks: "Nobody on the high board after 1300 hours," she said, she was backing, half not believing what she was doing, through the doors into the stairwell where a crush just visible not coming in or out nor loitering ascended from below — she said something else about the diving board.

Where I overshot is where I still am, he and I. Thought where is he now? A dive divided. Yet they could have their plan and that company camera I guess set to auto-iris whatever they figured was in it. My job blown but not by me, still mine even my own I hoped to do if I could find my way. The gray pool a current with a sideways wash evacuating toward the pit opened by the blast, I am addressed by a swimmer standing up to his shins as if the associate of Nosworthy up here curled on the tiles undone by his own blood didn't exist, asking me what I had thought of the dive — "was it not two or three combined?"

"Always," I think I said.

"Quite the diver."

"A brave diver," I said, so stunned.

"He want you to veedeotape."

"No, he wanted citizenship."

"Citizen!" The man vaulted onto the tiles, built like a wrestler with lethal eyes and looked like some Russian soldiers I had photographed at an airfield in the south in Wasit playing soccer and dolls with little kids; physical, broad-faced, he had the blond brush cut, small ears close to the head, and the blunt blue eyes. "Dey will take you for enemy combatant if you hang out with wrong people. Hang *out* with a target … " his shoulders shrugged forward, you know what I'm saying was what he meant.

"What?" I said forgetting even to turn away from him. What had the guard making off with my videocam called back to me: something "diving board" and "nothing happened."

The man bobbed his jaw at the smoking pit, what had been the diving well. Human sound loomed up from somewhere below. "I think he had no choice," said the man. "Think what you like," I said.

"He was competitor to the end," said the man. "He's my friend," I said. "He's a great diver."

"Nothing break his concentration. Unless his own death."
The man laughed. "He was your friend."

"Is."

He looked past me with his lingering hair-trigger alertness,
this civilian adviser or reconstruction hustler, as I took him to
be, on the margins. "Go see what's left of him," the man said,
then thought better of it: "That dive," he said.

Three point something, high degree of difficulty, I was
saying from somewhere in myself, a wish to be accurate, self-
important ——

"A simple dive but den a tweest … and den —"

"— but tuck *then* layout then *pike* before entry — he's
known for his entry."

"You know this stuff," the man shifted tactics. "So tell me,
under this kinda deal could *you* …?"

"I damn near killed my — "

"This kinda pressure —"

"— killed myself once," I said.

The man squinted. "Your*self*?"

"Oh I let it happen."

"Ah well …"

I heard the killer contempt, yet I was on my way, I was
stricken and needed to get to my job but speak words.

"Somebody …," I began.

"Een meedair," said the Russian softly with a Russian
clairvoyance quite poisonous.

"Yeah. Somebody shouted."

"Een meedair," the Russian said.

" That's right."

" A dive, a diver. My sympaty."

I dropped the mini into my shirt pocket and freed my hands, supposing that the soldier who had been pointing her rifle at me and had used it as a prod that had originally brought me to the edge of the pool, was behind me and my best way was through the pool, yet free of the videocam the woman in oversize combats had taken with film inside but had said what about the diving board?

"Like lights going out," said the Russian, almost a memory, but Russian. "You are upset now, what you have seen, you are crazy, I think you are involved." Nearer my age than he had appeared, "He was *my* friend too; it can drive you nuts," he said dramatically. "And then?" I said.

"You should have that seen to," he said; "you came in here with that." He laughed, it was the dark wet stain where my arm stuck to my upper sleeve. He thought I had put two and two together about him, something he had done.

He was quick only.

He turned away toward the changing rooms. "We better get outa here," he said.

I squatted supporting myself on my hand and jumped into the shallows and a tremor seemed to spread from my footfall upon the rust-streaked bottom and was my nerves claiming territory. Over there in what was left of the diving area, they were trying to clear the fools away from the great rupture in the floor that had carried the drain down with it. "You're done," the blonde said, meaning my job, I thought, and the muzzle-sight at the end of her rifle barrel came my way from above as if it would target me sideways and the barrel struck the camera in my shirt pocket hardly bigger than a coin, I felt it clear across my chest scar. I kept my hands off her rifle, walked through it, and kept going.

CANNONBALL

The Russian said wait a minute, he was the fool who makes a practice of not being one. I had seen him from a car, a truck, yes maybe my one trip in an armored vehicle he was standing in the sun watching, listening somewhere. I stepped over the safety rope of small black-and-white buoys slack in the shallows and into the diving well, remembering him now with headphones. A bathing suit. California. "Hey you're the Russian."

161

15   Heard of you

He came after me along the tiles at the edge of the pool. I made my way down the mostly drained warp of what had been the diving well floor, catching traction on split, broken grouting, slipping on the downward break, getting almost the hang of it, a ship, a section of deck, disaster. The Russian followed along at his level: "Hey. I am Ukrainian!" he shouted. He was trotting around the pool to the far side of the demolition area. "Ukrainian, not Russian! — Ukrainian." "All the same," I called across, heard a siren above.

I pulled a bather away from the edge — I might be Security, I waved several bathers back, an elderly Arab couple with small knapsacks, this wasn't a public pool. Close to the pit I would see for myself. Groans from below, clamor, rooms shifting and things piled and after-concussion and structural undulation abhorrently underfoot. I had thought there had been a second explosion as well. I would more than see what it was, it was what I could do for Umo, if I believed such truths, this rebel bombing, this accident, this the two of us coinciding and far away a steady thump of Rock 'n Roll going down.

Someone in a bathing suit got hold of my bad arm, I lost my footing like a skater, now it was this nearly naked fellow who held *me* up, and then I had a sight that almost drew me far down in the smoke and structure though mysterious of what I seemed to hear — yet a visible glint of waters burning like sewers you just know are sewers and then gone from view as wreckage of darkness or raft of rubble slid across below, and under my feet and down there a yelling, a sieve of words even howled but only a few clear — "… up behind," a bosun's order, reached me, and two voices I almost recognized, or one voice in trouble, struggling, so you thought "not with the men" wasn't the real words.

The Russian shouting …

But I would get down to where I should have been all alone.

"Why they shout at you when you dive? " he demanded to know. In midair, he meant. Why did he know something? Why would Umo tell him? He was directly across the pit from me now, past the diving board ladder and above the destroyed diving pool. "Ukraine," he shouted. "When?" I said ("Last year! Always!") — my passing interest involuntary, like future turning these tiles into the bread of his own life and schemes to be pursued as sheep follow the provider, and, papers, green card, everything in hand he won't forget, for he needed a deal to get here and will deal again. What would he do? — a "Russian," after all. But he would come no further, his no one-way ride. He was talking at me, stopping for new tremors I took to be a sign damage was ongoing like aftershock. Had the insurgents overshot? Where were they? Oblivion?

"The dive, eet began like swan. He tweested halfway to face board and then doble somersault. Layout and tuck was amazing thing." Russian had missed Umo's last pike.

The warped slope of tile shivered sideways, and the woman who had fallen again and I were pulled back. They had caught on to me, that I was not Security. I slipped, I fell.

"He was your friend, he was my friend," I heard the Russian say, the link itself alert with lurking shifts, motive, plausible profit. "Changsta, they call him." I crawled, lunged with a bloody palm now down to the lip of the pit that was peeled, burned like shit, jagged and the drained peach color of fat tissue exposed by cutting. "He bothered you," I got out.

But then where I kneeled came to life, it got me to my feet like aftershocks homegrown, bad arm out for balance. It was the Russian calling: "What they shouted?" he had to know; and then "You have a seester" and then, "Was *hees* idea —" said on a surge of the same old music from below — "to film here." I had it: La Jolla, Chula Vista — the truth like a friend's staggering indiscretion or the jump when something comes to you — for that was who this was: Umo's *boss*! the sound engineer — no, an assistant sound engineer, this Russian who had dared mention my sister, recalling her radiance recalling so vividly *my* Umo at La Jolla leaning on the fender of a truck watching paragliding as if the sun itself was buoyant: but if like Umo the Russian is traveling with that third member of the documentary recording team a deserter who would be viewed as an enemy combatant caught out after curfew, why hang here?

"He was not *my* bloody friend — hey what deed it meant," demanded the voice, "what they shouted at you?"

My grandfather, whom I'd met only once came to mind (why was that?) like grass growing under my feet. I was stressed, the Ukrainian said he was from somewhere, it sounded like "Chernobyl" but not "Chernobyl" with its meaty knell, coal mines, Kiev train line worker, Chevron nearly, Chervonoarmiyska!

And now down there below pool level, the voice stricken, oh, stricken, squalling, "Lift it," I tipped, for I will do my job, into also Umo's blabbing and am gone — *someone headed somewhere else gone into the water forever* — my sister's thought remembering all by itself my chest-treasured heart, and California, and Umo's two-and-a-half entry tuck-accelerated that time when the lights went (though back on in a second) one summer night — though, falling now toward the flickering sewer below and an extreme voice I was quite certain known to me, I jumped.

And no time to check my plunge or midair a gap someone else forms into named unknowns:

for Time — so little between fall and water — all but ignored me, slow-on-the-uptake, a pale panel came up to skim me and raw studs wrenched askew and steel I-beam end and four- by- eight ply split torqued velocity at you between instants of a life you could call failed yet met — by me, my jump, my fall, my shadow of uncanniness, its reeling plane, sparks pouring upward through me, my bond waiting someplace, my *job* after *all*, which you may still stumble on in this other that they stick you with, on the take, I will tell the Hearings later:

already months before explained at low ebb to a military new I hoped friend listener that only by some stretch or perverse aim had I joined up, or from my father's example or his thinking impulse self-serving first, or, by some torqued reasoning, my *fam*ily (?) —

But, *No*, unh-unh, my listener disagreed, your *job* — yet then ("No no") *I* disagreed with my*self*, interrupting with what I maybe knew *he* was going to say — a man of God as it happened and for a moment leaving his voice in my thought and prevailing, "No, unh-unh, negative negative, it was just where you felt … —"

" —forced —" I began, "coerced" —

"Drafted!" the Chaplain had croaked —

Well yeah but —

— 'zackly —

— my *own* way —

— 'zackly —

— choose for my —

—'zackly — like these (he caught his breath, recalled by me mortally, exactly, months later as I fell, knowing vacantly in a vacant fate of my own the voice down in the pit) — these damned *Scrolls* that he'd been assigned to (?) just when he put in for … underwater training for crying out tears which was why he was here at Meade if you want the plain —

— my*self*, I finished, adding some dumb thought about camera being an eye but a … a … a fucking shield, no, casement window — no excuse for not speaking — word.

We were two exercisers then, like another pair we passed when he remarked, puffing, that only this morning he'd been told never to exercise outside on the avenues here at Fort Meade except with a coworker, like a spotter in the weight room. And here we slowed to a walk down a Base avenue, still at a great rate all elbows and hips, and my companion looking around stopped and we looked at each other and reacted, almost laughing, the Chaplain thick as a bear in the torso with the long, lonely legs headed (he told me) for a monster simulation tank and I, much younger, who'd fallen into step with him when we converged and we had struck up a conversation about lab facilities at Meade and photography the old box and about seeing all that was really crowded into, well, things and how one guy has a certain take and they appropriate it and use it and it's not what the guy had in mind at all, he said. Chaplain was no genius, *he* said, but he'd seen a few things and told his trainers what they didn't like to hear. Meade had chilled one then, looking ahead, the Chaplain had said, if I heard right as if it was more than him.

And his take on my enlistment threw me (but my companion for these few minutes is a Chaplain after all which deserves respect even from an outranked know-nothing), while I defended my act and running or speed-walking all the time I would not recall all I said about what you had to do and what you discovered — he listened, he reminded me of my sister. But did he talk: and he had seen some terrible things, yet en route now at the end of it to the *desert* for crying out tears where they were shipping him to do battle-stress counseling. He believed he was some contingency plan of theirs (Underwater photography, I said, making sense of what he said) — "A swimmer," he said of me nodding. He was holding it together, he was looking away from me at a building we had come near. "You got no idea what's holding me together," he said, hearing my thought — and, yeah, he could tell I was a swimmer, he said — needing the *water*, or (he laughed) it needing you. More on that, he said. His voice was together, his eyelids, cheekbones, mouth were, too, and yet he did not preach and was not the type and he was taking me somewhere, it occurred to me.

— people come back from ... he looked at me ... The dead? I said, exhilarated maybe on Base oxygen — can you *do* that?

He touched me, we were jogging again — Or abuse, he said, winded, it improves your character — or *not* come back, if you want to know.

No?

I put him in mind of a problem with (he lowered his voice) with Jesus (?). "To my mind Jesus didn't have one particular pal, though my candidate was" (my running partner lowered his voice) "Lazarus," he'd become convinced of it, and the women at Bethany, never mind, and Martha's sister Mary gave Jesus a head-rub with special oil we should get the name of again, and the miracle wasn't raising anybody from (the Chaplain's voice barely audible, where was he headed?) the grave, but was the friendship y'see between Jesus and Lazarus. But they doubled Lazarus for more exposure, the two Gospels split it into two guys, beggar with the sores and the rich man named something, and the second one the friend he brought to life, and put the second a week before the Jerusalem wind-down and added a dipperful of magic and, groaning as he approached the tomb, Jesus's I mean dark (make no mistake) discomfort about bringing Lazarus back — resurrecting him, I mean — and thanking God for granting the miracle of this guy four days dead staggering out of the cave in his stinking sheet, a painting shows someone holding his or her nose, Jesus already knowing what would happen next week in Jerusalem. So they doubled Lazarus and wrote him into a miracle in John but it was nothing like that — which is decades after the … ("Oh well," I said) And now, "What's the rush?" he said, for we had clocked some personal mileage it turned out, and you had come back from the dead but in actual fact had just gotten healthy with a little help from your friends.

Nor did he bring up the Scrolls again, a polite soul, until—
but did I know of the two Crimean War photos and one of them
was said to have been staged and fake? An English photographer
name of Fenton clip-clopping along the Valley of the Shadow of
Death mid-1850s with his assistant and his traveling darkroom
like a Gypsy caravan at the risk of Russian cannon fire, and
two photographs the road was clear in one though there were
cannonballs in the ditch and in the other, the exact same place,
balls were littering the road like shot-put shot.

Then as we approached a long brick structure that a Navy
Captain and a civilian, African-American, in a double-breasted
pinstripe suit were vigorously motioning *us*, I thought, into
— but it was him ("Brother against brother's the message," he
muttered) — "Scrolls," he said, breathless, "on faith as killer
weaponry these guys sight unseen," and he thanked me for
what I'd said about … about coercion and your real job, it was
prophetic —

— for what, Chaplain? I slipped in.

— you will see, he said — that you found it after all *within*
the job you were *forced* to do and had even been set up to play
a not very creditable part in —

(had I meant that? said that? guess so)

— it gave him a lift, he said, in the midst of (nodding toward
the two men waiting at the building) all this profit and loss,
and your origins and your aim should be two quite different …
"well, you know what I'm saying." Though the "within-the-job"
brainstorm had come *not from me but from him*, I would have
sworn, though I gave him the benefit of the doubt, he meant
well. Stealing a look at the men waiting for him, he didn't look
like a minister, he said he had not much faith in these classified
Scrolls and if he had a minute, if the CEO were not watching

his every move and the Navy Seal who was some kind of … —
he thought he knew why they were classified.

Well, I'm not dead yet, were his words under his breath. *A
disposable life*, he said.

His voice itself held you that would not lay down the law: and
that is what I said as he made his way, loose-limbed, disjointedly
hip-heavy, to the meaningless building, its exterior, some species
of lab, and didn't look around but shook his head, as the two
figures consulted at the door looking perhaps beyond him but
he had said he would see me again or would recommend me,
yet was he doing so well himself? Long after this my sister read
me some lines about Lazarus and I said there were two of them
that had been doubled up from the real one, and it rang a bell
for her, I think, and I told her out of my ignorance where I'd
got it.

If it doesn't move throw a coat of primer on it, Bosun First
on a Coast Guard weather ship out of San Diego liked to tell
his guys, and this was a moment to move. I was gone down the
street of that invented town of Fort Meade at near quickstep, yet
my own surveillance in the absence of the minicam somehow
implanted so in the back of my head that I might have been
jogging backwards as my own brother after graduation before
he discovered golf had been seen to do on our high school track
feeling the cinders fly up against his calf muscles keeping track
where he'd been, I guess. In my confusion and fear at seeing
some of the truth, I was putting distance between me and the
men ushering, I gathered (as if I would never see him again),
my Chaplain down to a simulation tank greater (it came to me)
in area than the visible extent of the seemingly aboveboard of
the brick building so long, so low that its structure pursued me
which only now months later, my knees aching from my fall,

my left arm sore and throbbing, came back to be understood, yet with a thought of building itself, hearing a voice so weak.

"Lift it up behind": the voice so slight and near it might be little more, the memory of a throat and chest — voice, but left hanging in the burning damp dripping down and up if I could trust my eyes and skin, a gust came up from the rank current of the active well if you could read it. Thrown onto my hands and knees, sparks flowing outward from a dismal corner like welders who'd left work going. My left arm athrob with whatever was to be done, I reared up reaching for balance as the surface tilted back, a strip of interior shielding, ceiling become floor I realized and more to come down — was it my brain I was in? — posts angled adrift like the destroyed national bank I had been sent to shoot weeks since, yet in the twilight shambles singed, rumbling, stinking still, and tilting adrift on current here as well as below dealing errant blows by some pitch of afterblast from above *and* below, the voice fainter — "Leave me be" — a constant like a binnacle compass to balance amid the wreckage its own survival if more the words to vouchsafe than the speaker, so *they* were more my job than he — his "up behind" (my Bosun mentor's command well remembered from a bad day south of Point Loma but instantly taking up slack for a couple of belaying pins made it better for me) and "team got out" (Chaplain groaned tellingly) — "c'mon, you're the brawn I'm ...," again familiar from possibly the wreck of my life, where I must have said, "Hang on, I'll get to you," running like time between instants a driving force encountering isolated individuals — the snarling security guard who had hauled me back from the edge by my bloody sleeve; before that, the totally tanned, slight woman in almost nothing who gripped my bad arm when I rescued her from the edge; the soldier who struck me in the chest with her rifle; the Russian who would barely admit he'd found talent in Umo, as I had hoped my father would, while the intrepid wham of the music might be his doing lasering now and then down to some shredded rock rush like fit-to-be-tied mandolin; the quick little lance corporal whose rifle I had reached back unerringly to whack from one aim to another; and before that the late accountant telling me I'm bleeding, whose "Come in handy" meant the big blonde's Chinese gun not at all that use of Umo my father had mysteriously meant so many months ago — what they figured Umo could do for them in a pinch now a photo op for his distracted friend Zach and a now repossessed Army camera; and further back, my powerful though almost imaginary escort down the dark, onyx-figured stairs, and Storm and my driver I could not now stop for, for in this double floor below the pool reeking of fire and toilets, metal welds, and probably skin, the speaker had become a pale face, but from the neck down a sheet or partition of steel or panel or plane, poor person, and he's calling, Lift it up *behind* I honestly didn't know why for honesty penciled into the plans of others was mine too, and the face's words faint as memory *Not dead yet* became "Your job now," for it was the man I had run into (and with) at Fort Meade months before, and "slab" was what he said, though how I would move it I …

A Chaplain I recalled who, about to complete underwater photography training preparatory to being sent to use it in this very desert, had said that I had given him "a lift" — I — and even now at death's distracted door if not slammed *by* it offering terminal help more even than asking it, "Your old mole," which meant God knows what, the creature working in the dark though his eyes were there above the neck-high steel sheet (or slab) wide open — and unseeing, I thought, though hearing *why you should rush here like this*, like a laugh somewhere between us.

Distant but breathing, soughing in his gullet like night tide at Chula Vista, telling me something, he was alive.

Of use, it came to me. Like me. Of use, as your employers like to think, even beyond being alive, and his face had not fallen apart.

"Team got out." "The team?" I said. "Got out." "Our team," I said. "Got out." "But not you?" Above us my name was shouted, shouted twice. "The only team," said the man trapped before me. I got hold of a corner of the steel and was able to lift it an inch, this steel ceiling shield, if that. It wasn't going anywhere. I tried again. "The only team here," I said. "Zackly," came the reply with breath alone. "Just add water." Was he losing me? Mentioning his old yellow camera. *Fenton*, I think he said—he'd never fake a picture. The cannonballs were there and then they weren't. Great photo... I could hardly hear him. "But the explosions," I said with my whole body, and I slid the steel shield away from his neck.

"Teamwork," said my mole as if he were smiling, the voice scarcely there; "like the ..." "The Scrolls ..." I began. "Zackly." "Operation ..." "Zackly." "Scroll Down." "Zackly," the word's breath only exhaled in the darkness, a will working across crippled membranes of stillness, yet against the imperiling sounds from above. "Bomb went off, guy came down like a shot." That was the teamwork the voice, this partner of mine, had meant. And I realized with the surge of memorial sewer below us, the one we later learned had recently been named after our leader, that you may live beyond yourself in what may be heard still. "That was a diver," I said.

"Feet first." "Where did he hit?" "Hit me," were the words. "Him?" I tried to follow.

"It."

Was that it for the explosions? Was my man dying on me? I was smart, I see. Where Umo *should* have hit, had moved and hit this man instead. And Umo passed right through. "You know him," he said. "I do." "They'll get him. It's not your job." Unthinking arms flung out, brought in — Umo, that series of instants I had hoped to grasp, was each one lessening but not truly interrupting the distance to entry, calculus of friend to friend? — who and what had I tried to postpone, my borderline-high-blood-pressure brother at age fifteen gone below into a mysterious pattern of horizontal wells or into a branch of a capital sewer composting anything at all, meaning or revenge, into the waste of Zach's state.

Two ways out of here, I said: up, or down. But his words knew me.

Try again, I heard from my Chaplain witness photographer partner, fellow soldier. So I put my back and shoulder into it, my hands, my heart. But I couldn't bypass my bad arm, which had grown a weight, a tight implant thing not pendulous but like a muscle uselessly on its own. How I slid the unthinkable steel sheet away — I had help from the floor or ground tilting under me and thought the palace was coming down, the job further mangled by the second explosion — what job? were they after the infidel Scrolls alone? — if a second explosion was what it'd been. You don't need to compromise your own palace where bunkers, soundproof practice range, interrogation chambers, a major pool, multiple sound systems, a private mosque, and a rumored internal boating moat speak for themselves. I had to lower the steel plate again but couldn't and, pivoting the damn thing like a plane to shift away from, stepped on the man's ankle and was dizzy when space tilted I recall, my job or a new demanding plane finding *me* or some tide along the sewer, and I could see the rest of him now, he'd emerged from that stinking sandwich of a cave in the wet half-light subtle like him, and I think I heaved the steel all more-than-two-hundred-pounds of it against a stanchion-pillar beyond him bearing its fair share of the building's structure now in question. He was almost a friend. I could hear him thinking, *Seals ... 'nterrogation,* and then *Like this ... only* opp-*osite?*

Truth, you knew. And if it could be known curious enough to be someone's loss or gain. From the clamor above I heard my name.

"That's you?" asked the man watching me who was the man I had met at Fort Meade and liked, now revealed bare above the waist where his wet-suit torso had been peeled down, his black short leggings and some closed-heel fins that had been bent over by the awful weight, bloody at the knees, his ankles crushed, his chest changed, heaving on one side, a strip of duct tape along a rib as if to hold something in, one ankle already waterlogged-looking. The jabbering voices from the ruptured overhead must be getting ready to act, no need to ask where they had come up with my name, someone always knows you. I yelled for a medical evac.

This man not yet disposed of — what he had said of Umo.

Dislodged cement around me and light from below: *"You,"* I said.

"Got what they needed."

"With a bomb?"

"... Scrolls." Was it his long legs that replied whisperingly unmuscled, free of the upper body, and it might have been reflected or that I had counseled *him*: "What they needed," he said. "Who?" "Not what was meant." "Meant," I said, his breathless sounds like someone, like The Inventor, and losing me. "By the other one," I'm sure he said and sure he meant me to hear or to know.

In the stillness which now counted waters still further below I gave a shout, I yelled, yelled for help, my voice broke. Had the pool been cleared? The palace? For where had the noise above us gone to? Where does noise? No archaeology crew down here in the pit; but they'd been here. Now I thought of the crush outside the pool doors coming not from the pool but up from below. Great as this floor, I felt it a Between forgotten between decks of a ship, storage space, steerage. This man telling of an interrogation — not here. A story tired. I didn't like the silence. "One of the invited," he said. Between us a submerged tranquility, and he had given me pieces of a story... of suspects, of persons, back home a woman questioned and more than questioned, a Sister, he called her, but I knew what he meant, a piece of her. Pieces of time, time itself desperate. A story, I guess. I was approaching what I had apparently wanted. "And who was the other one?"

The Chaplain laughed in pain. "Bladder," he groaned, and then, "Take one Jesus, add two..." He tried to twist, to turn to me, the left leg didn't come with him. "The Seal captain knew," he said. Seals again. "Hates me, ignorant." The *Navy* Seals! Was that it? He twisted up toward me hearing my thought, I would swear. "Heard of you." "Me?" I said. The leg looked detached, and now free of the steel lid weighing on him he was worn out. "You'll know what to do." "Who's 'the other one'?" "You you'll ... you know."

I saw myself speaking, and to my sister (who often knew how things came about but needed more and wanted to know what happened "just *before*"; whereas Umo, it struck me, what happened "*after* that") and The Inventor and that loose survival family and how they talked and, that first time years ago, Inventor mentioning the new City pool, and then that I had seen Umo dive. "Who is this other one?" I said.

"… One who had the ideas," the man on his back half-blind said into the rankness of this wrecked day and curiously abandoned double floor. "For the Scrolls?" I murmured. I was hearing steps above and over at one end.

"Zackly. Not *them*, not the ones who will … I *see* … use it, who don't see any other way to use it."

"It?" I asked him, my body hurting though tightly fastened to my twisting hopes.

You, I thought he said, or *Use;* for I hung on his words exposed to what there was of them — and I could swear I'd heard "no other way" before, also in a subtle voice. *Thee alone to …* I must have heard now from my friend — or *to thee alone.* Pieces of a story he had coughed up, people interrogating a person. A woman. In California. A Navy Seal herself. Nearly naked. But presently he was out under the desert waiting at an intersection of the well system like a hungry ironsnout, it came to me, that Wisconsin water wolf the northern pike — the yellow marine camera his long before Fort Meade — an MMII he'd bought with his own money, bayonet mount, weights that kept him under, bearing on his back forty minutes (minus) of compressed air, and the capsule swimming into view like a silver spinner, and the dark thing reaching from above, arm, hand caught on film as it snatched the Scrolls capsule from fingers that might understand them but after that where come to rest, except that days later he was in the awful waters that crossed below the bed of the Tigris very near here, and it was last night?

Below?

Yes, the well bed, though entered through sewers. *Take me with you.* The capsule like a map case had swung toward him, and he had caught it, this photo-witness but of what? "Show you," he said. *Take me with you*, seemed to follow, aloud or in me already I should be able to say.

But next thing he was down here below the pool, assigned below as I had been assigned above.

And the blast? An afterblast seemingly too. Where was everybody? he said and answered himself: Gone upstairs with his old yalla camera commandeered by — ("Yours, too?" I said. "Ah," he breathed and understood. It came as a reassurance to him that they had taken mine as well. But an imperative to resist. "As above," I thought he said, "so below," the words seemed to help him to say them, I hadn't heard those words before, it breathed hope, it couldn't be true.) "Where was … ?" He turned to catch, I imagine to see almost the steps coming down the stairs, to be where he was, alone as a spar on a beach. (*Heard of you,* he'd said. Heard of *me*?) "See, they forgot something," the breathed words are life. Neither of us could wait. "Got my eyes put out," I distinctly heard — this man who'd been my fellow photographer once — "hates *me* but … likes my Lazarus." "Can you tell me who?" "Take me with you," the Chaplain said. I heard the memorial sewer like a canal or moving well below us getting used perhaps to me.

16   Best friend you never had

The Scrolls damaged, had the home team saved what they needed? What did they need? But they had been the only team, I thought. Why did I doubt the other side's hand here, they were the terrorists. Causes of the war. Christian soldiers right flank harch.

I must know — or would need to someday soon. I crouched by the half-destroyed Chaplain, and my knees were sore, bleeding inside my pants legs, and my arm half-dead, my fingers cut by steel, my back sending and receiving. Damp steel, killings rankly near and palace stone I had to keep blinder than I myself and leave here with what I had which was not pictures. A need to live, not kill. The Chaplain had recognized the name called from the clamor above.

And I — that person — saw for the first time in the gloaming his hand, thumb and two fingers pinching a paper.

And felt my mini in my shirt pocket and could just see the blood that tried to brim past his lip. "I hear you," he said, hearing the steps now slowly descending off to my right, their exact concussions received at the base of my spine in fact through the raw sore or agony there telling me of my body and my comrade's, for would I go without him and was he already gone?

 For what would his absence, dead or alive, tell those slowly making their way down the stairs at the far end of this floor? At stake, as I guessed, the Scrolls, or an attack on them, and on Why We Were Here.

 Some of this I would not say, months later in a crowded Panel room remembering faint, dark, kindest words *You'll know what to do*, which, when I quoted them in the dark to my sister not long after I had been ferried — "spirited," she called it — home, she hugged me, wanting nonetheless more from me; and at Day 2 of the Hearings on Competition I was careful not to recall what had come next from this man who had known names, mine and another he could not quite get it out or — it cost him too much life to — what this "other one" had "meant," that wasn't what the Scroll people "needed," for who or what this "other one" was I wouldn't have wished to say in public in my home city.

 And two guys were standing at the back of the Panel room (as these people will), a white and a black, whom I didn't at first recognize in combat fatigues. And in my account as an involved photographer of the explosion (my palace pool fiasco perhaps, I'd say to the room) and water running out, I found myself seeing my listeners for myself and recalling a man below the palace pool who was dying of voicelessness, but on the point of learning what exposing myself might in turn expose I kept the scrap of withered paper rescued from between his index and thumb scrupulously to myself.

 A flashbulb went off in the Hearings room next to another camera person training a videocam as if the Chaplain-photographer's story were not his but mine though only my witness to his words seeming to mean that oddly only one team, our own, had been anywhere near the explosion the film of which at least at pool level had been shown at the end of Day 1 with Umo's dive interrupted by the blow at the guard's rifle and resumed in one swing for some reason to seize priority, get ahead of the competition, a first for me though I did not add that I had been relieved of it and its videocam on the spot. A scholar had been cut off asking for documentation from the Aramaic of the Scrolls' condensing Lazarus "back into one man not miraculously resurrected but — "

Tapped for an early second-day Panel I am introduced to seventy fellow citizens (you assume) some with copies of the Scrolls now published and we say packaged in English. But although it is not about them I am to speak, I am introduced as the Army photographer who bore witness to the attempt upon the Scrolls. At not quite twenty-one barely in the workforce studying sports psychology, I am asked here to speak of swimming or diving, and the knack or business of winning, and I find myself in free-fall reverie about backstroke: To not hear other voices or any voices; the body tempo of looking over your shoulder; relief at barely seeing where you were going (*laughter*) so you trust whatever it is, water, length of the pool (*You*, murmurs a neighbor), the ceiling, I tell them, let me tell you about the ceiling — (*laughter*), hearing myself and remembering what Umo heard sometimes in how I might easily speak or curiously or was it helplessly strike a note.

The literature says to set performance rather than outcome goals, I told my people. You know that where an athlete using a larger *outcome* goal fails to achieve it for reasons outside his control, this can generate enthusiasm-loss, failure feelings, be dispiriting — even for a full twist I had nailed a hundred times, it only took once ignoring the immediate unknown to fail; therefore always they say (and I think of a photographer's backlight headaches so you set your exposure for the subject), set performance goals within that … that … I was about to say Unknown but found myself saying Known, and saw frowns among the listeners but not only. My shoulders and back as a backstroker I didn't have the words for it once but even now shadowed by shoulder blade and rotator cuff muscles that arise from it, a bond between shoulder and back — and hands — and your lap flip … how you do it, forgetting something or other, the finish, the time, because … I'd had a friend who was good at this concentration, and he was going off a high board and I had called out to him, couldn't help it though was it only in my mind? — because *he'd* called out to *me* from up there —

"*Why* did he?" someone suddenly asked — Oh in this packed room of necessary unasked and necessarily unformed questions asked, thanks for this one at least — the voice familiar from our city, the face (not noticed by me till then, as I tried to continue) Wick, who of course would be here, old assistant father-coach and calculus messenger.

"— his concentration —" I said confused, yet was I?

"So you —" a woman cut in, softly, hard to hear —

"unreal … ancient," why did I add, "*I* wasn't in the air or anything" — it was to Wick not the woman, who was on me now persisting, "… after that footage of the diver like they were bombing *him* that we were shown yesterday, you add this hearsay of some maimed underwater Chaplain witnessing the explosion all by himself, to insinuate that no insurgents were even there when the blast nearly erased these — denied us these these priceless — " the woman all but inaudible, and boring, yet kind of electrifying — a question about her — her powerful hands — and next to her a face I'd known for years under the Padres blue baseball cap worn pulled down over her abundant pinned-up hair and her brow and her large Mediterranean or India Indian eyes, until I cut in to remind not only the patriot who had been simmering I realized but also this great roomful of accredited participants (one soon to be challenged), that I had been stressing where I'd been ordered to take up position my*self* — at pool level where not the detonation below but the impact for crying out tears —

"*Why* did he call out to you?" my old mentor Wick asked again — called out, in fact.

"— these unique Scrolls — "

"Unique, ma'am!" I challenged her, ignoring Wick — "they bear out what we've been told for a hundred years, for crying out tears" (I was guessing) "so it's a relief to find the prophet in his own words, one on one — "

"More than a prophet, thank you," one hand reaching straight up above her shoulder like an athlete but in what sport I could tell no more than the scale of the hand if a scale can be gauged not by size but by strength, or was she recalling my backstroke words?

"— A pro," I said, "a pro, blessed with initiative, not opposed to win-win — hey, the vineyards and fruits sold off by the servants while the master was away wasn't just a story in Mark, it really happened. Again, an *eco*nomist this Jesus almost creative, sensible — American!" I said, "and if you have to shoot those people — the lesson is you don't leave your land to be worked by just anybody — walking on water is something else."

Faces nodding here and there. I got a leader's rush, what that would be like. My heart sank. What did I mean? The two men standing at the back, the white and the black, had their eye on me. They stepped out for a moment. They had come here looking. They could do what they liked as they saw it or within their thinking. "You don't have to wonder why Matthew, what, forty, forty-five years later, didn't have room for this stuff they found in the Scrolls — 'Blessed are they who come to market for they take the trouble to know who they're dealing with'" — I held out my palm, oppressed also by the Chaplain's interrogation story, fragments kept to myself brimming with ire now this swimming pool unmentioned here thus far underneath it his half-destroyed story gathering in me again as with my sister one night when I told her most of it but not all, my instinct warned me not to voice — and what did I sound like? an attitude … I yielded to the Moderator, who was in a state. The two men were back.

And my emerging job found itself in some use value I put them to as if I were not in the middle of something else.

Yet I sat down, faithful to this question, *Why* did he? Forthright participant I'm faithful to the evidence I gave this second morning. My voice now known, we listened to a very foreign man in dark glasses who spoke of fifteen languages heard in this city now and (he smiled) refugees from the war so changing demographics that (another smile) some neighborhoods are like an electrocardiogram of international conflict — a smile, a sweep of the hand, this expert who went on now to laud digital imaging used to tease out this ancient text, its often crushed fragments of characters not seen for nearly 2000 years, thus its fine touch "beggars description." We learned how the wider use of this process had spurred investment in that war-torn country (and our own); how the technology had enhanced medical diagnosis and fine-tuned miraculously our satellite pictures.

And what a super-(light-)sensitive digital camera could restore for the archaeological team, the ink itself reflecting light at one point in the spectrum while the blackened background reflects with a wavelength only a millionth of a meter different. Meanwhile, the room — "What a friend we have in Jesus," does it think?

But I was coming to that question *Why did he call out to you?* It had come to me because I could not stop for it.

Just like that asked about a friend *by* one.

Dead or alive, comes back, *me take you with* — my friend just scarcely known pieces of himself — *you'll know* — *what to do*: with such words a thread of blood drawn down from the mouth like a seam in the chin which barely moved: "Last words I am — without, my friend — they will gainsay ..." — which drew a bubble of pale puddingy and purple and iron-rusty mucous out of him to relieve him like the words and let him go. Was he gone? Unsaid is he in me, like not absence but overload, and why the Scrolls were classified he'd promised to tell, and maybe could still — a laugh when you counted the leaks to the press — a furtive friendship dashed — was it *Take me with you, dead or alive,* he'd said? I balled the curiously durable papyrus from his thumb and index finger and ripped the duct tape from his belly and tearing a narrow strip of it taped the paper into my ear.

The blast and what seemed like its after-companion in overkilling must have done for Umo or the pieces of him which my videocam they'd confiscated shooting from the hip I had imagined would show us. Unlike the Scrolls, I thought, bereft.

What in the end had I to do with them or the war? The Scrolls! Compact and to the point, they have issues, American, they are questioned in the open market, welcomed, unstuffy.

A seamless whole even from what I find uneasily familiar in the clips flooding my sleep. Their seeming completeness a drug for this inspector of paper trails if not a recorder of deeds — a phone ringing and ceasing in the night someone could help me to answer (and it is my brother I would speak of — and they would *have* me speak — though in closed session, in private — and not of those last days, the music project, deserter, dive, explosion, fiasco; and not of these businesslike thoughts scrolled-down to your hopelessly interrupted level, but whatever might call them into question).

That this "Interview" as the Scrolls are called (though another equivalent from the Syriac is thought more apt) should so seamlessly all but blot out that palace day, the bombing of our American Scrolls not quite shredded as they arrived by well and met almost their match and the deaths assembling in my thought faces wrought there. CPA curled in his own blood, that hairy back palely humbled by its bronzed and wasted neck to let you forget he had done business with my father at East Hill. What business? Would it matter? Chaplain, crushed by his steel coverlet, like a cruel plane compressing him, real, remembered, living to the end, his fists clamped in the rigor of his character so the scrap of scroll got torn in two, lucky to make it out — of whom my sister, who knew a little about paper, said when, one day, or rather night, I gave my dank, cordite-reeking account, "Best friend you never had" — so much of her in those words. To be what she means. Where sound goes less to her than what music leaves — a chill corroborating what? His people I would contact. Somehow I waited, picturing falsely to myself the Chaplain given last rites and left where he was, yet gently asking who was the Other one I had mentioned the Chaplain mentioning weakly at the end — "they" had got what they wanted, which wasn't what "the Other" had "meant" ... what did that mean? She was always mine and she knew the Chaplain through me and may have known even then, the night I in my way told her, that he was not deserted by me. The sewer told its tale, it waited for us.

He was in that plane that I hope I didn't pretend with him, though building secretly and in the account I gave my sister leaving out (and always the father I never thought of!) for secrecy's sake and for mine where the Chaplain might be. To my *Two ways out, up or down*, he had replied, *Try again*. A third exit? I'd take the Down. The stairs now putting unfriendly feet through their paces sounded an overlapping pitch of two people coming down, two at least. I did not hear the steps. The steps resumed, slow. I snapped a string of shots with my remaining camera if it was working, though mini which is somehow good. My bad arm dead but strong, the peeled-down wet suit caught on a corner of steel and stretching till the body of my friend jumped as the rubber came loose, I had hold of him through it and I let myself down through the ruptured floor and was hanging from a ledge above the well and its foul surge that recalled where these waters had been. I let go, spreading one arm out to break my fall, and broke the dark surface, and he came down on top of me, and I could see beneath its rush of displaced bubbles for a second, as I and the Chaplain were borne away in possibly Umo's traceless wake if he'd ever trust me again (though why should he in the first place?). The thought, so immersed in the wicked stench as to be part of it and hardly noticeable to itself, had dumped me some not even wilderness place or beach of delay, I had done my time, it was said, but I didn't believe. I thought for myself if I could find words that had found me, it was at first to be an adviser or the water itself had been what I'd sought by enlisting. For above the tunnel's subtle roar like a calling or added intelligence or an angry sleep like toxin in the water searing my bad arm for me it was my long-nosed father I envisioned — never to be listened to again I would trust. Though what would I have to show for this? I had slipped the camera into my shirt pocket now immersed like some deed in an awful dream to drown in.

Seamless someone called them when they came out and I didn't read them. Was the California season, the Spring, too long? What was I waiting for? So soon after I came home alone, my father by turns in Colorado Springs to do with Olympics I was told, and DC, in a desk job treated by my mother like a sacrifice made in time of war that I would rather not know about yet not as I don't know about the Scrolls.

17   a nation that would one day

Something sad I did not put my finger on as if I were hearing thoughts of my own in someone else, so that the hand I saw scrupulous evidence of in my small living room on my return one evening — an article I'd clipped and underlined in red about an archaeologist found dead in Mexico, my ballpoint, however, not standing in the crusty old mug where I'd left it but lain across the magazine page, and clothes hangers in the bedroom closet now spaced evenly. It might have been my doing but wasn't. A lower kitchen drawer open containing cardboard boxes of Hefty Easy Flaps, and stiff old sponges and clear plastic wrap and the Ziplocs I had purchased at a midnight 7/11 on the way back from the war. Let them come. Like a joke played on me by Liz and I thought I would ring her but she was married to an older Navy guy and lived in Oceanside. I read Thoreau in bits to get the idea —the watchman fox, the self-appointed inspector of rainstorms, the molasses, the telegraph, the briefness of the Walden time a badge I guess of depth — and thought of myself and my threatening secrets and a few works I was putting off reading for fear everything was in them, a short poem, a long play, and that most people under surveillance wouldn't come *up* with much to keep the watchers significantly interested (though we our*selves* are of interest, it all over again puzzled me to think, with my cowardice strengthening my thought, rebuilding that palace like a temple of faces). How sincerely had I befriended Umo, lived as a soldier let alone as a son?

What is a bond? A seam, a divide; a suturing a doctor in me closes up the divide *with*. Some part I myself will take, familiar now (or perhaps only later, or too late) in what of the Scrolls I gathered from the news. This contemporary talker, this real walking-around Jesus, all business, interested in certain new, connecting ovens (something like Shoshone) either recently invented, it seemed, or sketched on First Century tablets. The idea to divide labor and multiply product, and I gather in the Scroll interview cheered on by his own remarks and coworkers to apparently call family itself into question, not surprising when I thought about it remembering now the picture of Shoshone ovens and how E and I were caught planning a trip out there by Dad whatever else we imagined about that way of life (and said in his hearing).

The Korean woman I would see at the high school track told me she did not believe in these Scrolls, she did not know why. (Faith, I said. We warmed to each other for a moment. I've seen nobody lately but my sister, I thought.) Yet the Roman interviewer's Jesus had smart things to say about sight-restoring spit, I'd heard, and it was this coupled with a note in the *Union* (and then a magazine) about the death of a member of the Scrolls archaeology team while vacationing at a remote coastal point near Acapulco that moved me to read a few pages at the bookstore. This saliva precipitated from mustard, myrrh, oregano, and another unknown herb of the Galilean desert growing near one great geographical bend of the horizontal wells allegedly one might have to swallow and regurgitate but here could be the truth behind the miracle in Saint Mark, itself written long after Jesus and not from eyewitness, the Korean woman told me — pausing suddenly surprised at herself. For then, resuming stretching, she said Mark was the Gospel written soonest after the Death on the Cross (a generation, more than that), which took my mind off Bea's not turning up for help with the vault box. One surprise of the interview, which seemed right and even familiar, was that this "chemically special" spit might be grown in each individual's body and salt-multiplied and one day without dependence on others or, as our own Administration put it, the government doing it for you. Self-reliance was how Ralph Waldo Emerson had put it — a good Christian thought, I learned in the Hearings, it came up the second day I recall, a healing expert from Colorado Springs. "A sound apple produces seed," he said, and self-reliance made you a sound apple, I think was the point, though self was unclear to me but only when I thought about it. Self-reliant, OK, did that mean don't count on these other people you grew up with? Who supposedly raised you — from the ground or from the dead? There should be a Complete Idiot's Guide to it — self-reliance.

Sad still what you heard about the Scrolls. *How so?* as onetime friend Milt would put it, echoing his father — and those same words a poet politely challenging our own leader in Washington when he had called it an honor to have one leg of the well system named for him. I had spent time alone burdened by my knowledge, the swiftness of my release, waiting to hear from my father if only to ignore him; read so much "ancient history" (as I called it introduced by my sister to her librarian friends) in seven, eight months (happening not to call anybody though one day saw from a pedestrian overpass looking up at me from eighty feet below the Russian at some typical business that brought him to the University), my eyesight erratic or perhaps just deferring to undoubted experience between the lines of my reading, that, asked here to these Hearings by a University big shot friendly with my librarians (and less friendly faces) as if to get me out for a few days, my sister listening to me a lot, I tried to think I might have been overlooked as Scroll-implicated. They had just recently appeared, were they the reason for these Hearings, "postwar" so-called? I had other reading, limitless to do and afterward to have, though I had absorbed some sound of the Scrolls in the paper, on TV, a remark dropped by a stranger. This dialect Syriac for *Blessed* was *valuable,* I learned. Thus, "valuable are the peacemakers" — but how could Luke, reporting long afterward Jesus's *Do violence to no man*, have overlooked the practical survivor's "Blessed are they who come to market" creed of the Scrolls' firsthand Jesus?

The Inventor might have known. He always had an opinion in that black Dravidian attention of his face, and he knew Parsee, Urdu, Syriac, I understood, and knew Kufic script and could read also the Leader's alleged script in between the Red and the Black of that national flag or he had the dictionaries to back it up.

Had I been party to the fate of Umo? For that matter, to the death of the Scrolls archaeology team member by drowning in Bahia Petacalco? — himself just let go by the agency that had sent him to the Middle East in the first place. It hung in memory supported by all the lack of information about the case, for he had been not only in the forefront of radiocarbon dating in samples drilled in standing trees but an amateur ad-lib tap dancer, and then I thought I could hear him behind us one late night when my sister was with me (and said she saw me better in the dark), his measured, archaeologist's voice, his knowledge of what had happened, or his steps, for hadn't he been one pair of steps descending the stairs when I had dropped into the well waters just in time bearing the heavy and welcome and secretly light burden of my late friend but also in my stunned chest and like a signal on my chest scar, it seemed, the great absence of the other friend who'd gone before us like a Third Way I'd missed by taking the Second Down even with a second body half coming apart I'd never told a soul of?

Transmitted like a message swiftly home, I'd been since then almost everywhere in my studies, more than alone, ahead of myself (and thus already seen) and long ago, my life its homeless chips and shavings scattered by a gleam in me which might have been Umo's whereabouts.

Or my promise to myself to find my Scroll scrap's absence from the text of the little book now making its way worldwide; for if the scrap's text was there then the book's full text had been in government hands before the notorious capsules set sail. My gleam might have been Umo's friendship, his questions recollected — *what were Cliff Notes?* he had wanted to know, almost surprising to me he didn't.

Or might have been my sister who had first seen the scrap of Scroll by slipping her hand into my pants pocket and drawing out the Ziploc and knew who I'd got the scrap from but not what I had done for him, and I believe borrowed an early copy of the Book of the Scrolls from the library — it seemed familiar, she didn't quite know why, she knew her poetry but not the Gospels I now proudly knew meant to most people only the four "synoptic" whereas there were several other Gospels — but wasn't this Jesus sort of acting out?

"He gave you this?"

" … "

"How did *he* get it?" she persisted. "After the explosion it must have been." "Where the bomb went off?" "Below the pool, yes." "Why did he?" "Why? Because we were friends." "And why was that?" "We just were." "On such short acquaintance." (My sister loved me.) "Well, he credited me with figuring out what our real job is, the one time we had met at Fort Meade months before like I told you, though I thought —" "Yes, there's always another, isn't there," said my sister. "Though I thought he was the one who'd come up with what it — what our real job is, that —" "*Is?*" "— that you found it *within* the job you were …" " — *forced?*" "Yeah." "To do? … Zach?" It seemed to be my sister and I. "You could say he gave the scrap to me but you could say I took it from him. That was all I could do." "That was enough," my sister said. "It was?" It was us and it was also me.

Wick! our science teacher and/or math, true to us, our assistant swim coach, our true coach at school — why hadn't I visited him these last months back? Just didn't.

Wick, I thought, sitting back down because the Moderator was in a state wondering what I believed or was about to say, and hearing Moderator's stomach like a thunderclap homing on lunch break. *Wick,* I thought, and his question what did Umo call out to me?

So the heck with the Moderator, I stood up and acknowledged Wick: "What we hear, forget all that little stuff about digital imaging we can't even see without digital. For godsake hear the human voice. What we hear. You ask why that diver …" — the Moderator in a shake of his fist had received a signal and would not object — the answer to Wick, to what? … some complicity of mine in Umo's appearing and vanishing, and it came to me like a sting in the chest or I was terribly slow, the Chaplain, his disorganized body nowhere in evidence when the steps on the stairs turned into perhaps two members of the archaeology team if not two armed guards, or in a still better universe one guard and one archaeologist. *Wick,* I thought. High school once inside a time, Wick, young, who cared about us almost too much — fellow seekers — equals, family, if we could pick our way through his downhill parentheses chalked on the board and Log over Log, and these *arrows* you had to *do* things with, add, multiply, depending if an event was a succession of steps or several happening independently and at the same time (same time) (same time) — my eyes choked my throat — all his unknowns that left us with these clarities you didn't quite get but believed in like stunts, just math, came back to me, like a stopwatch he described depending on the color of the light particle which could shrink or turn. Very cool stuff: Was it over our heads? Why was Umo here in this unsettling memory who never went to our school? Wick ringing my father at East Hill, the job that mattered — whereas to Umo one day that we talked it was high school that interested him. Not that it was my father's real job, though he could show his interest in my classes there in his own way.

"Why?" I gave my old teacher back his question — "Why'd he call out to *me*?" But looking as we do elsewhere, blinking at the hand back of the room raised at the end of a camouflage uniform sleeve, we need the Moderator a too broad, too blond decently worried hedge manager who'd made a noise while the camo fatigue uniform man I would not forget went ahead anyway in the gathering stillness of the Panel room a killer I would guess, with a question more like an answer: "Timing in sports performance and business profit may affect concentration and vice versa, wouldn't you say?"

"Say?" I said, for we knew we knew each other from Fort Meade — I'm this raw trainee hustling away down the Base avenue with eyes in the back of his head, and then thousands of miles east the Chaplain marooned at the Scrolls explosion. Camo combats, this was still that Navy Captain — famous classified Seal — his words no less a weapon jump-started me straight through the event like timing it in advance, so I could see back, thing by thing, and time less the matter than the smell of his interrogator's eye stuck with gluey infection behind its lens and thrown by this need of me (or something I had) — or it was the treacherous breath of water, scent of cement walks at Meade, friendship and shouts and necessarily induced war labor gathered into a formula gone into words and they had never forgotten me (or my sister whom they had phoned and I thought I knew what she was to me if I didn't think about it, like where did sound go, we once looked into) and what I must know, nor could I forget the Chaplain's interrogation material I'd so far censored wisely — why had he told it? — and lunch break was coming and after lunch, the Moderator asked us to believe, a distinguished visitor from DC would be welcoming us — though we were already here — like a Mystery Guest you get to meet if you're a major donor.

In the communal stir of sitters getting up on signals from their stomachs and hunger primarily for change of almost any sort or lunch, the Moderator thanked me for my contribution to the Panel and to the war effort. But I recognized my original questioner and was heard to say (aside to the audience), "You're consulted as some kind of expert when probably you're an expert in something else —" (*laughter*) " — in this weird profit-stricken country like —" (*laughter*).

"Like *what?*" spoke a hoarse, lost voice at the back, "like some ancient *nation*, man? I hear you but you don't, you don't, you don't you know mean it with all your — "

"— one great war-torn …," I said to the lost voice, uneasy both of us at its words to me, and where was he coming from? — when closer at hand to my old mentor Wick I said, "Diver called out because I'm his friend, I should know why he's up on the diving board because …"

"And can you cite a recent example of your friend's 'ancient' concentration?" the Seals captain in combats at the back interrupts, and, short of something else I knew but did not yet retrieve about white captain and black agency partner, I realized they wanted Umo.

But not him to be talked of publicly.

And seeing that moderation in all things made my uncle an extremist, I heard through time a living catalogue, as if I had been coached but had coached myself (and my own catalogue), of Umo and his take on my family …

— odd about my sister ("Your family," he called her whom he hadn't met); and about my uncle ("He could be a cop where I come from; they frown, it's murder"); still stranger, "Stom," whose phone chat with my father at the far end of the pool Umo had witnessed ("He has a secret weapon you better get to know"); and Zoose, whom Umo did know — whose brother-in-law was not spoken of any more, the guitar player who had deserted — "Zoose thinks twice before he backs anyone for citizen"); and Umo on my own father (lost and found now in a desk job and its decisions) — ("Thinks he gonna make the Olympics"— that sudden Chinese laugh — "a' least he taught you photography"); or, and why come to think of it now, Umo sort of on science ("Look out window. Zebra fish can grow a new heart, you know"). He described his mother's singing once upon a time: it was the double-toned throat-singing technique common to her part of the world — thought to interrupt fertility — "I was her only, but she's gone, you get arrested you're gone, well maybe." "*You're* gone, Umo" —

— why had I said that? Gone from home and family. It would have been good to talk to Umo about competing, young as he was. Why? It was like living. It was one thing within another thing. Yet at barely fifteen, to claim my sister as his bride, he got a snub from me and then nearly fractured Milt's skull as a joke who had shared with him the shout (its words, anyway) that killed my dive and nearly me maybe, though Milt merely a messenger of words he still didn't get. Regrets but not for Umo that night at Cheeky's before my enlistment, which others but not Umo might think I had been enticed into, whereas it was into knowledge of them, against which (as if it were The Man) they weren't quite now ready to enlist me among the missing in action.

Know, or tell, just enough. My instinct strong to call the strangely, in-pieces told, interrogation account (if and when I would tell it) his — which it was — but keep him, his fate, his Jesus even, his body, out of my account — while Moderator knew to defer to captain now if he could: but some meaningless force of discussion took a turn and I waited mine, narrowed to the face of the Fort Meade captain in his combats who had just spoken, yet in all this my once and, it came to me, still somehow science teacher Wick's loose, wide-eyed face whom Umo knew of and of course had something surprising to say about this man he had never met so you would not have guessed how Umo lived.

Was it Umo they wanted, however?

I read Mormons and Puritans, the accounts they say firsthand, their freedom yours for the having would you but live as they lived in their villages. I read histories of farming, of water and war, success and musculature, herbal stimulants, a brochure for caregivers, tools, the tools of tools, cities, even the gig of a Zen city, and what some person in the asylum of a library stack helped me find, not the painting I was looking for by rocky Giotto the Chaplain had told me about but Saint Zeno it turned out arising resurrected I think from a tomb in Verona in a little b-and-w print in a book and three people holding their noses; or out on a dock a guy in a wet suit trying to tell me something in broken English and Spanish and German about the harbor in the old days or, marooned in a Hawaiian bar on Fifth, what a woman told me to read or, fucked-up in a bus stop waiting room, a guy I knew in high school claiming Kerouac had written a book at one fool sitting indivisible it seemed or one sheet of paper.

Emerson's "American Scholar" beyond me except that action might be subordinate, yet in his "Circles" the lowest prudence being the highest, and (which I admitted I didn't get — but to whom?) "Self-Reliance"; building materials texts — iron, concrete, steel, wood and their joinings — nests made by birds of the air and caves by the ancient shore, Frederick Douglass and his oxen, Covey's *7 Habits* especially Win-Win — soil, weather — my father's own seldom named father a Connecticut farmer, or used-to-be, wherever he was or whatever now — I, like a convict, reading up on law terms for self-defense I knew I'd need, a word bobbing slowly past me glommed onto (*debauched, sanguine*) — no word from my father, a memory or two to forget: Camus, he said, for we were reading Camus senior year, Camus. For Camus swimming was all but sacred, if anything could be, said my father. I said I knew what he meant. He exploded at my lameness I guess: Had I missed the point? An overturned bucket I might seem: science in the face of my father. Old newspapers in the library a year or two ago. Yet there came across at midnight Chaplain's words *as above so below* again and I switched them around, having thought he meant pool level and our own; took notes, and one night if a terrible thought hadn't come to me when my sister was examining the welt-scar, raised high, hard, purple-and-orange on my tricep in no time by the toxic waters that had borne me to safety, nearly told my sister about rescuing his body, because she said, "The underwater photographer, he was dead when you took the piece of Scroll from him, was that it?"

All this reading at midnight somehow drew closer and closer together medicines for sports psychology to which I had come like a migrant seeing the California light, I could always discuss with my mother, and wet behind the ears like a seer to his calling it seemed, one afternoon soon after being automatically mustered out into the Reserve driving a balky old car to meet my sister at her part-time intern job, who should I see but Bea, her friend, at the high school track unwisely all by herself hardly get off the ground hanging on her striped vault pole swinging hopelessly into it, braid hanging down; and I drove around the block to check her out again and she was making her approach like a jouster, her knees driving high, she was leaning back a little and brave and something missing to my eye, only as she brought her pole down for the plant anxious lest she miss her aim at the box (as she glanced over angrily like a confidence between us not quite knowing me) her end caught in the ground and her motion lifted her a good six feet and the carbon catapult gave a little, not enough to whip her upward — there's no bar — so I almost ran down the bicyclist in the street in front of me bald, very active. Because I could help Bea.

And now, wearing her baseball cap and a Hearings badge that entitled her to the Lunch Buffet, why was she here?

Slow on the uptake, my father would joke. Umo's new word, too. The "i" word "ironic."

Zach doesn't need to be fast, he knows a better way to get there, my sister said. Yet in the dead literally of night leaning so close to me her breast itself listening to what she may have guessed was not just what came before but screened what followed, still something I had attained to get back with a story so awful albeit drawn together by her presence and a story from the Chaplain she measured as if it were all of *me* coming to meet *her*: "You mean she was contained inside a capsule until she couldn't breathe because she wouldn't —" "Wouldn't cooperate, give them what they wanted — " " — under questioning, a Seal woman — ?" my sister not even persisted, only was patient to get what she could: somewhere in California under a cavernously deep indoor pool all what my dying man recalled and it coming to a head for him and now for me, the nearly naked woman I pictured for my sister in the dark of our bed couldn't come up with the goods, what it was like to be sealed inside a glass tube until she couldn't breathe and suffocating get shot upward plungered through a trap opening the full pressure of the pool above down upon the escape valve risking her neck at the top of the tube automatically suddenly uncapped if she bent her head even an inch — I cut short my tale of the concussion of pressure released from above upon that perfect fit of an opening where, smothering, she waited to be shot upward — "… neck snapped — ask your friends if they'd give you a job at that pool, ask my friend another ordinary photographer a witness to all this" — where, in this valve function, the pool pressure above upon the stressed subject equals the pressure back up at you from a water surface to equal which one would have to dive from a height of one hundred eighty-four and a half feet a no-hands "sailor's dive" and she was a Seal herself (not combat-billeted but Explosives Ordnance Disposal — I spelled it out), nor sworn to secrecy regarding Jesus revelations she knew nothing of — in question certain Scroll Down leaks they were investigating: "When did your Chaplain tell you this?" my sister asked, wondering respectfully and seductively about the rest of the story.

What I missed.

Though not the promotion, my talent to fit into all but the buoyant war commercials the almost not even evil reconnoiterings contaminant as they were airborne of the supposed person Storm Nosworthy, government employed but exactly where? — my fit even into the faith long untimid embracing our real business of everyday dollars and cents, nickels and dimes, what it took to build whatever. And friendly/unfriendly fire you or your government would take for your initiative extending even to a good old Crusade, cost benefit decently absorbed but don't take us for granted. Specialist at large for the Army thousands of miles from here in desert places hot as Utah, and, lately, flattened as Texas, and across our vast intelligence grid ancient cities, streets of wheels, inclined planes and stones, earphones, shouts, city eyes and noses, near-revelation if I wanted while I was there, in danger and reserves of danger I could hardly think of except in that bared and unknown place the job I didn't deserve; yet, then, did like some inherited Reserve obligation: to just miss the actual arrival of the Scrolls but be part of it or the scenario Storm Nosworthy had figured. Yet why me? Who was I? Acquainted with the diver.

And who was he, gone without a trace? Wholly Umo, I knew. The Russian knew. Nosworthy with his closed circuits and face must know. The question lurked here and there in the run-up to the Hearings, once nameless in a mention of the explosion in the Sunday *Union* Arts section noted by my sister whom I told in confidence, after she'd replied to a phone call about (she thought) Umo that — she had thought quickly and said, No, he'd "gone back." Her way of not giving in to the voice, deeply politely in charge in her ear, her very mouth — her aching back, she reported to me, black, like the actor who does the commercials Biblical, an agency presence supreme and felt by her to be a threat like all isolated voices. Though to what? her brother? his reputation? we laughed). Gone *back*! I could love her for that, the impulse (and not to hang up) — back to China? Mexico? The family alley in lower Mongolia (though Umo without any folks to speak of)? The Middle East without me? (I feared for her car.)

Then, *Dead,* she had thought and nearly said but didn't, she told me (and asked if I would come by and see Mom — See Dad? I said — He won't be there) — but thought the black man's rich, searching voice had uncannily believed the unsaid thought (thus can smarts outsmart the smart if he is a killer for the mad can read minds). "Anyone see him passing through?" "He's probably where he belongs." "Underwater photographer (?), doubling as?" said the caller like he's reading off an alphabetized — *Doubling*? I said to my sister. Yes, that was his word. (The Chaplain's word.) "No, that's another friend," Em had said.

"Passing through?" "By water?" she had answered question with question. "Over *there*, then." For the voice, clearly the executive civilian from the Fort Meade run, was not without intelligence in his intimacy, his phone style we agreed, his phony-phone-phone, Em called it. "Here or there," she countered. He: "You're giving me double talk, honey … not smart, nobody raised Lazarus from the dead he just had an influential friend improved his health," said the voice. Had she said too much? Why Lazarus? The black man had rung off. "Did I …?" "You're you," I said. "I got the idea it wasn't Umo he was after." "You were right." It came to me that she wasn't scared so much as — "Am I promiscuous?" "Discriminating," I said, pulling back on the thought that she would after all go East to work as she'd said she would, yet she was writing some things down, no matter where she was, "something high-handed," she called it, and I could feel when she gave me a hard, uncanny neck rub pausing over some tendon nerve at either side like roots of a tree or a vein of all of me or resistance in me to not the war so much as Dad's silence or, running back up her own long arms, a between-times or between-people grief in her. Loaded for him at last and Sierras would answer she said, though these government people might get onto friends of hers that had nothing to do with her brother.

I had not told her how I had swum the sewer.

I would not speak for anybody but ran into Mom on purpose at the Farmer's Market, her full face peering into mine over her shopping which I helped her carry. *We have to strike out on our own*, she said in the kitchen. Afraid to ask about me, vague when I said I was reading, bizarrely showing me the house if there was anything I wanted, her and my father's bedroom with the framed picture of her looking like me under the lamp on my father's side of the bed. She pulled out drawers of handkerchiefs and socks and showed me The Inventor's envelope its wrinkles much flattened. I ran a finger over it, and felt my mother's hand on my shoulder. *I saved it. It had some food for thought.*

I safeguarded the Scroll scrap, would hardly tell my self where.

In these later months, our economy booming, or bombing, people showing signs of getting behind these historic Scrolls, I had thought what to do (for others would always want to tell me first). Bea would never make it as a vaulter, she thought. She would phone me. Blamed no one. Knew I'd "been there," she said. Had become vault-box-shy lowering her pole. I told her what the optimal performance literature said; had my own view, we could talk some time … she an older woman practically, very experienced from how she appreciated something about me, my "nerve," she said, she could listen, she paused — tops on her list, she said off phone a moment, "you with E-m, amazing, like …."

It was sad that The Inventor had been threatened with the termination of his green card though he was not a Muslim, and two windows had been broken and an almost invisible break-in, Milt had told my sister, had cost The Inventor nothing of value, though I heard his syncopated voice in this information and knew there was more to it — perhaps just time. I tried every way to reach Nosworthy, I had the captain's name but no reply, I would not ask my father but he was out of the country, I heard. I wanted to know who had ordered Umo shot coming up off the palace diving board.

Still wondering, in these beige Panel rooms, Why the delivery by water? Why the secrecy of Operation Scroll Down — and if my own damaged scrap was real, why had not the full text (in a species of Syriac) been photocopied before being launched along the well system? (Not easy in the field? What would The Inventor think? I didn't call.) Before I had left for Fort Meade news of Scrolls had been leaked to the press I now learned, if slantingly or randomly, never verbatim. If you picked up on this news slotted to an inside page, found interviewed in his own voice (called "Jesu" at least once in the TV news clip) this contemporary living legend rougher, more go-ahead than the Gospel Jesus (Mark or Luke, I would have said for had I ever much read them, hearing them quoted? Though more like the controlling scene-stealer in the woman-at-the-well story in the John Gospel. Though in John, I learned, he sometimes goes off the point or doesn't answer the question — like an exec at a shareholders meeting — "Thanks for the interview," Em said inimitably.); down to the translated words of the Scrolls at first not much challenged that at one point foretold implicitly a *nation* that one day would spread the news of popular rule, profit both in spirit and talent ledger, and what amounted uncannily to R & D we now say, knowing much is expected of us. Apart from all this I persisted in believing that of me some other "much" was asked.

18   this shifting equation

Only now did I realize that the woman who looked like my driver, early that palace day and astonishingly that night where I came out along the canal, who on Day 2 of these much publicized Hearings had belittled my sports psychology training while noting my well-regarded photos of the war only to call the "fascinating" handheld dive footage "accidental," had put her finger on what might well be guessed from my witness of the injured photographer. That however common the insurgents' theft of their own antiquities and the enemy's desire to appropriate a find on its own home ground like the Scrolls, a weapon additionally in the war of ideas against the green and ancient life of an Islam fundamentally uncompetitive and without a future in the region, there had *been* no insurgents that day below the pool, no team but our own archaeologist and his Occupation specialists; so the explosion might have been set off by us.

One scrap of its damage I kept Ziploc'd. I took it to bed with me, showed it only to my sister, mapping its meaning and privately some small gap in our national, published text that it would fill — when one morning she asked me what had happened to the man who'd given me the scrap besides that he'd died and I said he hadn't really given it to me I'd ripped it out of his hand (assuming she would only ask what had happened before that and not after) — against a day when, expected to speak about competitive swimming at the Hearings, my chest scar from the dive accident, like a poisoned lash or (I knowing little more than English) a translation key like the Ziploc warming in my pocket, my leg, my suspect heart, all signaled what I must do.

That onetime dive timed like the blast from below that Storm Nosworthy you knew had monitored upstairs — my friend competing (though for what?), coming to the rescue somehow (though in the film now to be devoured the dive multiplied to fragments might have *caused* the explosion) — would sometimes at night divorce itself from the diver. To talk to someone. Even my mother. Ah, a mistake to single out one, though in our family it had been for me my sister. And still — and more and more — my sister read my body and my mind, as she had lately on her own I learned been developing a practice (apparently now approaching vocational status) of no less than, and (as she would say to me) no more than, reading faces, which she had always done, like picking up heat and chill from people. To talk to a former teacher about the dive's four-dimensional volume, it came to me, in-air shifts like layers, the entry feetfirst like all even-numbered flips, to gather the parts. While Umo's body, with all its sleek surplus simplified and beyond the exploding pool, carried away, as the Chaplain, whom there wasn't time to talk to about it (about my friend, or if this *was* friendship), had inadvertently imagined for me not blown to bits. Yet for viewers at the Hearings, how to put Umo back together, this casualty of mine faceless and on my confiscated film torn apart by motion?

I was burning oil the day I tried to track down the Russian in Chula and had to leave the car at a Chevron station when Dean Moriarty would just take somebody's and drive it to Denver and bring back a better one. And I remembered "the Other," who the Chaplain had said had "meant" something "they" had misused. And then the Chaplain's mingled words, *They'll get him. It's not your job.* My job, I recall his interest in it with time running away on his life which yet ran into mine — his last kindness, split-second view of Umo plummeting by feetfirst to vanish in style, my friend, forgotten, irrelevant his entry splashless or at the last an unseen cannonball impacting whatever — a well, many wells, steel, and then flushed down a sewer.

In the privacy of what I came to think could be my Chaplain's Third Way Out — some of this up on my elbow looking down at her, some confided in the dark to my sister — I had put together my footage, the pool debacle it recalled, and my exit from the region that afternoon and night by swift water, foot, car, sky, sometimes an escort but with barely a trace it seemed — with, escorted or not, no fingerprint check or ID asked for by earphoned perimeter guards plugged in to their music, to say nothing of the imperiled camera in my breast pocket or the strip of duct tape across my ear that I'd forgotten, or at the outset my right hand that ruddered me along the well canal hearing a shout, meaningless, a call, a violent sluice, my eyes stung inward swimming. And still in stunned exit mode back at a night post exchange more like a 7/11 where I bought toothbrush, toothpaste, something to put them in, with money I'd forgotten, laundered in the well, and was looked at strangely though it was California where for that matter I was to be notified of "Active/Inactive Reserve" status, modest per diem a surprise and college tuition as needed, no questions asked, and one bleak dawn (though she had said I was better) leaving my obscure apartment my sister on my arm and catching like a snapshot eyes in a parked VW down the block, I realized that my late Chaplain had described the interrogation of the Navy Seal woman because it was his job to pass it on. What outsiders know of you is much and shallow or little and profound. The Russian knew about the shout in midair. From Umo it must have been. Why would Umo tell that? Anyone will say things. Nothing else to say. Silence within their words potential. But the word "sister" struck me in the mouth of the Russian and of Storm.

Not quite as American folk will talk at an open-ended Lunch Buffet if given half a chance about vacation condo time shares, the hours your liver transplant took, or neither (1) *hiding* your talents nor (2) showing them *off*, or about growing a small consulting business unfazed by practices and especially drawbacks, unpleasant surprises, possible draw-downs in your region and field, to say nothing of replacement knees, or even No pain, no gain on the way to market — the secret cradle of democracy as Middle East was cradle of so much else, which might be a gathering risk for me exposed at Lunch that second day. Yet in the jaundiced eye I cast on the Scrolls I was hearing something else: some of it made sense, as when this Jesus, now occasionally called the American Jesus, takes it way further than Saint Mark's a half century I'd recently learned after the time of the real Jesus, who is reported there as telling his men, Peter and the others, to check out what they've gained leaving father, mother, wife, kids, brothers, sisters behind and becoming disciples, but in the earlier *in*terview urging in person that we virtually disown our family, to put them behind us if we were to be successful (talking to the Roman of course interviewer since identified as an out-of-favor nephew of Herod the Great). Whereas in Umo's case (and it had become one, for he was wanted), leaving had been forced on him — not just here but on another continent a mysterious journey away from the sea, as I had plotted those orphan points like an interminable delay, then toward the sea, confirming him in his self-reliance and in family, mine possibly, at a time when I really must leave, and among reasons given us to do things — somebody's words, a job, going to war, duty, the character of a friend, even uncorking a pretty great dive off a springboard (or a cliff, I'd had rumors of a month ago) — I find that different reason I understood the Chinese authorities who were a factor in this shifting equation had basically dismissed, to do the thing for its own sake almost, and this might not come to you under the yoke of family.

I thought I would go ask The Inventor if this could be so, bounce it off him. Was it to return something? I had phoned once since his break-in, I'd been home and he had abruptly had someone on the other line and never called me back. I had kept an eye out for Umo's truck. Once I tried to look up the Russian. What was done was done.

Why would I visit The Inventor now? Word passed along the Lunch Buffet that we were plenary this afternoon and a surprise guest would welcome us.

My teacher and coach spoke up at my elbow: "He called out to you because you would know what he was doing up there, is that it?"

"Wick," I said, turning to find him not at my elbow but a distance unclear and here were others circling nearer with their plates, one in combats I now recognized from months ago wearing then mufti (that unlikely word The Inventor taught me, speaking of empire); "Wick" — I reached with my free hand clutching napkin and fork — "And did you?" Wick said. "Wick." For he had skipped the warm greeting you expect after so many months and I lowered my voice. "What?" I said. The GI music-listening project, people Umo had been with, both of us set up, but the real job inside it that you stumble on. "A deserter?" said my friend as if my voice were a form of subdued dishonesty; "someone they were looking for?" "Wick" — he had picked up some fool need in me the last thing you show if you're … "he had no choice — " "You think?" "They knew who he was with and he had something to lose even though they must have told him he was showing up for a photo op, his friend Zach filming at a pool in a palace basement."

Who I saw gathering near gave me pause, but better, I could tell Wick knew pool, palace, the days, the vectors, rates of change, more assured than I'd seen him, and kept his distance with attention I would not fault: it was his respect for a marked person who would speak, I'd missed him, his obscure life.

"He was always competitive," I said. "You never met, you never saw this — "

"Not quite true, I saw you guys on the corner, he saw me looking out the window, I'd swear he did — " "— and there was something else," I said.

Not quite true, Wick's words — Umo bobbing his head, cocky — a window of memory open and shut — Wick speaking above the smaller voice behind me (like a meaning), the woman in the kerchief from which at the back fell a blond and dark-streaked braid like my driver's the day of the palace: "You said," she said in such a low almost inaudible angry voice,

" 'this profit-stricken country' — well you made fun of that poor GI who wanted to know — " "The captain?" I pointed out the steel-haired observer in fatigues. " —about timing and concentration, he was only asking — "

"Stating," I said, recalling the nights of my life, my driver appearing again, my driver's offer of first aid, her boat hook, the piece of black rubber wet suit clutched in my hand that was not mine.

"Needing to know."

"That's his job," I said. "To put it nicely. Like Navy Seals, sunning themselves, barking, slipping into the water to swim so magically." (I was about to make a mistake.) "He gets paid for extracting information." (I was guessing and I had guessed right.)

"And you're a six-month graduate of the war well what's so bad about profit you're cashing in on with a camera they taught you how to use —" "He is?" "That's what she said," I said. "Oh but of course but he was in the service," said a man with a briefcase on a shoulder strap who enjoyed revelations. "Still is …" said a knowledgeable older woman. "He's what?" I heard Wick and Bea say. "The shots of the …," a familiar hoarse voice tried to say, "of the headless kids sitting bolt upright." A woman in a maroon blazer took him by the arm and spoke to him, pointing to his badge and more than pointing and somehow he did not retort. He had a frog in his throat; while a woman in surgical scrubs asked if anyone had seen the color photo they'd turned into a poster of GIs at night driving green and orange golf balls off the back porch of the Visitors Bureau hotel into a lake. "Doused in chemicals," I heard Wick say, and the nurse in scrubs, "Lake full of good-eating carp." "Fed on American garbage, " I said, "dozens in there, huge, rabid," the photographer telling you what you were looking at but wasn't in the pic.

The two men in camos inched up, a shadow passed across the long lunchtime buffet, was it the freshly renovated acoustic ceiling already discolored here and there? "Still cannon fodder, the war's not done," I said to Wick, who, though I turned away, knew I wanted to stay, "A/I they classified me if anybody wants to know exactly," I said to my teacher, my father's indispensable assistant, my friend I believed like the shadow that had come down and was within.

I had seen Storm Nosworthy. First time in eight months, the face as I read it told me I needed to get the scrap of scroll Ziploc'd in my pocket into English. I banked away along the "Spaghetti Springtime," the blue marlin it said on a photo ID flagged into one once airborne chunk, a substantial brussels-sprout-type tree stuck over, instead, with jumbo olives and it said live anchovies, and over there shrimp spring-rolled with orange sections, and further along raw cauliflorets embedded in vegetable ice.

Behind me following me, "The new world is messy, someone's got to clean it up," I'd heard it before, this woman's anger overdone: What would she have of me? — her intelligent eyes, lips, hands but who was I? — people listening for anything interesting — surely she quoted someone. Her seatmate Bea close at hand, something in Bea's attention to the woman. While at the far end of the thirty-foot buffet hovering prophetically, the oval exaggeration of a face not quite containing its parts like deeds that won't go away and shorn of its goatee now but moustached heavily like a Turk, the rezoned nose at such a slant it might have been in motion and independently was, with that swerve or parallel if I could track it, discuss it, with Wick —

one eye arrowing the windows, another the dwarf palm layout
and veteran wheelchair contingent I had spoken with (to try to
tell one guy in particular where I was coming from), surveying
the spread, the field of conferees, my first sighting of Storm
since the palace day who had probably arranged for Umo to
be blown to pieces, and attending Storm the sweet-breathed
Law Dean long-skirted, menuing the food for him when she
saw me, my work here gathering in and expanding determined
to ignore the Seals captain and his African-American *superior*
I thought (within earshot a moment ago as they had not been
at Meade dressed for that occasion, respectively, in uniform
with four gold stripes on the jacket cuff and a lethally tailored
suit like exact plans for my Chaplain's coming participation in
Operation Scroll Down), two thugs you look for again only to
find seeing you.

The woman might have forgotten these men or have drifted
in from a contiguous building: "Get out of the way if you can't
lend a hand — God you and your swimming pool pictures," her
voice rose — her brother in a military police brigade, she went
on, and "at least that shot of the mobile lab."

"What war did you go to, girl? I thought I knew you, who
you *working* for, honey?" — it was the body and voice of Bea,
bicyclist, pole-vaulter; admirer of my reputation, my sister, my
stupid nerve, my learning, my driving— " who you?" "Thanks,
Bea" — "How do you parse these — ?" — "Fact is, I'm on my
way to a translator." "Wow! You're not here this affie?" from
this admirer also of my small apartment she had only heard
of — I said I'd be right back — Bea even, I felt, in a suspicion
of lust, admiring a narrow escape I had never broached with
her yet hearing in Bea's eyes though in fact from the troubled
woman near us *My brother, my brother, that's who,* in a voice

hurt, hooded, overdone — she had mentioned a mobile bio-lab shot by, it seemed, me? *My brother*, I thought, what had my example done for Umo?

It was Storm Nosworthy, the bright shadow spreading here. The past past, where was my videocam? It was the Army's. Nosworthy frowned and smirked to all and sundry, conscious but of what. With Bea near, I would at last ask what circuit besides mere monitors he had had at his fingertips in contact with not only pool but detonation site, counting down; yet, bursting in me in the life *and* death of it — stirred by the support of this hot older woman nearby — was that *brother, brother* voice the "Get-out-of-the-*way*" woman? — and the virtual presence of my most absent or despised father, the interrogation account I had put together from the Chaplain's words for my sister one night, sounds, breath, the fume of urine and broken bowel on seared steel and gathered fairly truly of the Seal woman's agony how long ago, not long, with California sprinklers trained along hot water ducts to throw up steam to shroud the hapless subject of the interrogation, the low-overhead communicating rooms located somewhere in California under a Crater-Lake-deep indoor pool all what my dying man recalled and it coming to a head for him and now for me recalling the containment inside the capsule of the apparently uncooperative Seal woman, just a glimpse coming out of me like justice and anger — "Ask *him* about water," I had to answer my attacker at my elbow almost again who's quoting Dylan for crying out tears; ask the Seal woman, I thought, who couldn't come up with the goods what it was like to be sealed inside a glass tube sworn to secrecy regarding Jesus revelations she knew nothing of — in question certain Scroll Down leaks they were investigating.

And I — why had I leaked even a word or two, a picture almost, of the interrogation story, some of it, in anger at this person whose kerchief you might like to tear off and in character even to the astringent soap smell of her perspiration. It would be of interest to the captain and the, it came to me the Chaplain had called the black man, CEO. A loaded gun, maybe, that poor, ill-fated Seal trained in EOD.

Why *had* the Chaplain told me?

And why had I spoken this morning to the angry woman at the Hearings as I had? Was my part to be provoked by these people? By history in the making embracing how belief in competition, as someone in a Goals workshop yesterday had said (and found it cool to have said), can eclipse competition itself in the name of faith in your own business or the promotion of these Scrolls that might put paid, as the British said, to our war (though it was said to be over) or eclipse it in importance?

19   like a Third way

Still, my leg, the scrap of Scroll Ziploc'd in my pocket against it, knew what was important. Attempting to leave, pressing this damp half-hand of a celebrity, I knew, like the mutual and distance-embracing future I and my self-reliant sister at curious moments shared, that Nosworthy on message addressing the afternoon session might find himself amended. Not that my real job would come to me in time, but had *already*. At war — in Kut, I thought, and in other unfinished business, and half-drowning with, in the custody of my hand, the body of the man with whom like a Third Way this very thing had been broached, *Your job* — grasped, too, in the words of the kerchiefed woman against an almost twenty-one-year-old profiteering sports psychologist, sometime contractor's assistant, photographer, like a rightness inside her grosser or even pained and personal attempt at meaning; wondering now more than grasping, and calculating in baffling yet infinitely encompassing increments a distance from my father so unthinkably out of touch and his own up-or-down plan for himself in which I had been dragooned to function under fire, wait a minute, maybe it was true! (the Law Dean bearing down on me, her calculated scent only to be brushed past now by me for the business at hand like the initially by her announced "smorgasbord of topics the Hearings would offer" which was proving to be a broad umbrella for Operation Scroll Down, or what Storm Nosworthy for the Administration had planned to air, introduce, expound, and take possession of and validate the existence of, it came to me like the end of the war growing a new crop of enterprise) was it not possibly true, as a recent TV-interview citing from the Scrolls came to me like a familiar and sister-associated teasing memory of my own, that this first-century "Jesu" could really have envisioned as a practical enterprise to feed the hungry a natural fish hatchery with water captured from Lake Galilee?

"Umo," I said, "the diver," Storm reaching for my hand again, "There's another, Zach —" "Why did you have him shot — with his gifts?" "The guard had her orders. Poor timing, Zach." Still, Storm liked that I could ascribe that kind of act to him, whatever he said. "It was perfect timing," I said, finding something in my words. "Not for him, Zach." "With his gifts, what could have come to him, so young ... " "Posthumous," the hand on my elbow, I think. "Posthumous?" I said. "Posthumous *citizenship*?" I said. "Great idea, Zach." (A person passed through me, or so it seemed; a gathering — my sister, Umo, the Chaplain, some lost father let him stay lost, all or none of these, gift and burden.) "Another?" you said. Another what?" "You were hit, Zach; we gotta do somethin' about that too. Too bad what happened to my number cruncher — no purple heart for him." "Well, you know why I was there for *him*," I said. "To document whatever happened." "Lucky I had more than that camera." "Sister thought we were after the diver. Sister — "

"Kind of a lost cause, you know." (Did I mean Umo or Em? It was worth that moment, speaking with the ring of instinct.) "She'll think twice about who we're after," Storm fired a grin at you.

"She doesn't."

"We know who she thinks about."

"Wait for me," I said.

"And nice work if you can get it." Storm fingered his nose like a deaf signal, traced his lopsided mouth, pinched and long, his low, face-mask-wide brow, the center part in his scalp hair, this man I was trying to turn from. "We know all about her talents …," the face said then.

"Who's we?" I had the Canon out of my jacket. "Wait, Storm" — flashing it with equal depth of field by chance to read both his face like a fucking keyhole and way back in the room as if I had known all the time that she was working for them the woman in the kerchief with a plate of lunch pass the two men in camo fatigues; and as she blatantly ignored it, caught the captain's polite smile expressly acknowledging this supposedly eccentric lady and obviously hiding his appreciation of what she had gotten out of me, under a ceiling of new acoustic panels stained by an intricate coastline of leaks.

"She's in our sights, that job back East (?)," Storm let me know, "that application (?) …" — Storm was on the case, taking even *care* of us, yet in himself a field of experience full of the smell and plot of the real canal encircling delivery of waste and memory to be lived with not squashed like a locust or further eviscerated and maimed like a Kilimanjaro lion or a medicinal Mongolian rat — "yeah, that application — we can get in her way, bro, whatever."

"Wait for me," I said, thinking there should be laws for this, would genius and legislation just be at odds? What could that face tell me I didn't know, but what had I just said, or heard? East Coast in my sister's mind a while now, college, a marginal research slot — but news of her from that man turned it weird as if he would harm her, she hadn't seen that face, but he thought he knew about us. It could only have been from one person but Dad would never in so many words have told Storm of a closeness Dad didn't grasp himself as the heroic intimacy it was unless Storm, in his inexperience, had put unknowns together out of my father's mouth and, fingering them, had finessed into insight some sexual case. I'm gone, hearing behind me the soft finger snap recalled from that palace lair alerting someone to keep an eye on me on the way down yet someone else following unbidden but not quick enough; the finger snap recalled the pale kilim newly signed with spots of healthy blood, recalled a job still to do beyond this errand that made the scrap of untranslated scroll heat like an aura its faithful Ziploc in my pants pocket.

Diving past the elevator door closing I would figure how to reach The Inventor without leaving a trace in Coronado; envisioning vehicles, drivers, my driver from the palace almost — sighting of all people my mother's butcher a fellow communicant at her church idling in his minivan at the traffic light. He it was, then, who drove me twenty blocks to a bus stop he did not question; he pointed out the red, blue, and silver Heartmobile trailer (why?), said he'd heard I was back how did I like it it was different over there he guessed — his elbow out the window, his thick, pink and purple hand restoring a Camel to his teeth. I could see myself going back — I said this to some shepherd sympathy in him for a Reserve who, pretty slow on the uptake, he could not know was puzzling out whether the woman driver weeks ago I'd never expected to see again who'd fished me out and given me a fresh shirt had seen another bodily form moving under the surface or — half an hour before? — a great meaty shoulder gashed, peeled back by initial shrapnel sail by but free at least of the shot that found Storm's CPA on the pool tiles. So, as I freed myself from the butcher's front seat, thanking him with a surprise in my eyes for what had come to me and for his own loaded life as well before me in his long, narrow face and his competent, even savage, and for the moment helpless, hands and a curious glint in the left earlobe, and wondering if the Heartmobile nurse had weighed Umo; who should I see — or what — but a white truck (smaller than I remembered), blurred graffiti on its flanks, Baja plate, elbow out the driver's window, though too bony, too dark to be Umo's.

I thought about that elbow boarding my bus, my silenced devotion to Umo, his life our life I took apart, just now the free Heartmobile, the Sprint cell, a pack of Camels in the well in the butcher's front seat with a blue ballpoint just like one in our kitchen, for I would have to phone my mother.

It might have come to me like an envelope from within the house, it came to me ringing the bell feeling almost followed by what I sought though I would not look away except up the street to some memory of Cheeky's garden now overgrown like a field the stalks and weeds all but guarding her low, warped porch. Here at The Inventor's the shades drawn against the sun, one window boarded but fresh paint slick as the painter's hand on the purple and saffron front door, no peephole blessing this place, store shut but waiting and my job to know this like the Ziploc I carried in my pocket and not even under my pillow at night as my sister knew turning the pages, cross-legged on the bed, fresh from her shower, reading to me from the clipped, planed, carpentered sentences of her book, a loaded gun, ours I felt, bound in our heroic intimacy that must change.

I saw who they were after and it was not Umo. I rang again.

It was the underwater photographer they were after, the Chaplain.

I was satisfied that he had died in front of me and I had done for him what he had asked. So his body had not been found at the scene of the explosion. He had evidently not turned up in the water filtration plant downrange either, where two heads had been found, or riding memorial sewer currents or resurrected to tell (or be guaranteed not to) his story another day. His candor, plus the detached wet-suit sleeve — its animal toughness — that I had found still in my hand upon being boat-hooked like a miracle in upon the slimy rungs of an iron ladder where the well roof opened briefly to a luminous, late, and gathering sky, persuaded me again my Chaplain was dead. (Others were not persuaded.)

And the job we had somehow agreed was your real job. Not Up again (to the drained pool). Or even Down (into the rapid well currents). But something in the Third Way (even of Umo's feetfirst dive I think I muttered of) persuaded me also. Muttering, vomiting the memorial waters, slipping on the rungs, feeling the lower dissolve as a foot found the next up, transferring the rubber sleeve onto my driver's boat hook. And I understood that the Chaplain had given me the account of the Seal interrogation, or its cruel end, because he had been there. And both his death and living persuaded me, and the scrap of Scroll torn from his hand — not the Scrolls, but the scrap, or, more, its tornness — yes. So in a way he was still among us.

My finger on the bell about to ring again. The street never quite empty behind me, the greenish bronze god head of the door handle, turning, passes a glint across my eye as if to open, while inches above it the tumbler within yields to the other hand.

Inventor? Only our name for him, two kids fairly color-blind for California. After so long away — since my enlistment party — where do I begin? With questions about the break-in? The "nothing of value" taken, my sister had heard from Milt. News of my continuing war. The lease at risk, Cheeky's, we had heard too. And a green card.

My scrap of papyrus, fingered and rubbed curiously by my sister, had become a necessity today. The translation, so strangely delayed by me, I needed now and wouldn't get for free. My visit was for its own sake, though, like old times. A drab two-story wood and stucco house where, if I hadn't already heard of that briefly historic pool, I had been advised by The Inventor to show up for its opening. Not the first time told to go do what I'm probably going to anyway. But I forgot promptly that I'd heard it here. (I was doing it.) Yet later didn't wonder why. Because The Inventor, with his envelopes that made Milt mad, knew things — *Be a passerby*, his contrarian view of the disliked Samaritan story, in my birthday envelope the day I had taken Umo to East Lake — and was interested in my chest wound and how it came there — and in my roundabout humor; knew Umo before I did, and in some way that I accepted without expecting to have explained, had been expecting Umo before he had arrived in this part of the world. Perhaps a time had come when I would naturally have asked about these things, as I would have asked this black Indian treasure-house collector and poor sorcerer who his people were and what he thought he was doing here in this war-torn country, but that moment was when, against my suspicion of my father and his part in this, I had enlisted accepting a Specialist deal not even Umo knew of, much less this night-faced, genteel but life-and-death-eyed India Indian with a sharpness or kindness he could seem to save for two eleven-year-year-olds who over their formative years would blow some cash they almost didn't have in his store by the time one of them had a bad pool accident soon after which an extraordinary or fugitive diver materialized first on a high board and then in my acquaintance and my disturbed loyalties who could at once promote *me* to my *father* who never took advantage as I had hoped of my introducing Umo to East Hill as a prodigy who could help him nor would grasp the real job I stumbled on because some foresight not all mine had planned to.

Yet what came back to me now in this deserted noontime street, inspecting The Inventor's colorless, sandblasted or epoxy-patched Bel Air parked two feet from the curb and hearing his front door, was Umo's *We need you*, that day. Said once across a corner of a grandly opened pool, what did it mean? — distant and personal like the lock tumbler and weathered bronze handle right here of this freshly painted front door which now sticks a little as it gives:

— untrusting as Umo, who hid his distrust in humor, or was it *of* (Stom's "secret weapon you better get to know" — well, what or who was that? my sister lite?) and gifts of friendship — that palpable drive south, or a snapshot: yet hid his untrustingness also in true trust asking who was meant by "brother," and telling *me* his grandfather's plan to come and work in the mineral mines, sign up with Plutarco Calles. Calles? The revolutionary leader (though I have learned now always to ask exactly what revolution) who wanted to keep church and the government from teaming up, and became a somewhat ill-fated President of Mexico; "while" Umo busily sought a place for himself, U.S. citizenship in fact from authorities who now presumed him dead. The day of the explosion, he had by quite some minutes, twenty or thirty, preceded me like a shot, a condemned in unfree fall, the aftershock-shifting plates like trap or shutters parting for him miraculously. And I hadn't known where I was going — up, down, a third way, delaying the plunge, taping the scroll scrap into my ear hearing steps and the waters almost beside me. And a difference now in the steps of three people, one pair softer, like a voice not to miss. And chaotically thinking I would ask my oracle about Umo's "secret weapon you better get to know" if I made it out of here, why I let myself down into the well-stream current dragging the body of my new friend over the brink so it came down on top of me and took what from me? Above and at once behind us the people by now arriving downstairs searching for the photographer, the waters' rush and wish, density and stench too great for us to hear them calling.

For *us*, I say.

For The Inventor's door opening had twisted my own story round to see instead of a stretcher for a medevac carried out of the stairwell like a companionway into the still heaving wreckage of that lower floor below the palace pool, a surveillance monitor totaled, two or three of them — shredded — down by where the blast had detonated and the Chaplain had been crushed, and the need of somebody's eyes to see for themselves if not finish the job.

The pitted door gashed, gnawed-looking, but so freshly painted in half, saffron above, purple below, the soft oak itself in an instant had shown me how the door would be opened. Swiftly by The Inventor or not at all. Dead bolt snapped open-and-shut first as a test by Milt. A little kid in there might look up at the door and call out or fling it open; a bigger one would have yanked without first turning the knob — all people are different sometimes for their own sake at best (the *war* said — though like History, it could be made to say anything, or nothing, which was harder perhaps in truth.) And my sister, it occurred to me, would sometimes peer out the far corner of our living room window slantwise. All these openers, upon opening, would take a good look at you. But the ravaged one who opens to me now already talking a flood of hope that I had come because I was expected, and recollecting "*last* time," and having begun talking already, it seems, a few minutes ago, like an experienced poor tramp on a moving train who jumps off sideways and hits the ground running, was Cheeky, her old brown forehead spotted more than ever and now scabbed as if she might change her skin or might be stuck with it.

"Vera *Cruz* remember — I didn't get to tell you, because Umo had to swing Milt around my ceiling. They were upset with you, and you have the snapshot I took of him coming down the gangway because he told me you did, such a big roly-poly boy, such a small suitcase over his shoulder, what shoulders — and that was the last I saw of him for two months. Some welcome. And I got sick in Vera Cruz but not a bad place to be sick and I went bass fishing with this." Cheeky touched her forehead and her bare arm. "Made the best of it before I took the train home, went fishing with a former Miss Costa Rica who was on vacation from her job at the national park studying the mantled howler monkeys and their strange family turnovers — "

"I tould harr not to go," called The Inventor from the far room.

"He had no papers!" Cheeky screamed like I didn't know what, meaning Umo, I assumed.

"You knew that?" I said.

"And here they broke in," said The Inventor, changing to the current subject, "took my envelopes — forrteen shoe*box*esful." His laughter unseen, edgy, Cheeky's by contrast agreed, transmitting with her brown fingers on my arm all but family memory extending me hither and yon. "Fourteen!" I said to a man who believed in words coming out of nowhere — that could be a good thing. "He had no papers," Cheeky calls back.

"And now you have brought me something from the War," the voice continues learned in the blinds-drawn shadows. "To translate," I called out. "And he's wounded, you know," said Cheeky — "his shoulder — " "He knows." "We need you. What's this?" Through my sleeve she felt my hard, gristly scar like a sinew growth. Were they mad at me? you had to wonder. Hard times ("We need you"), news of The Inventor's green card to be reapplied for unexpectedly, Cheeky's lease, her runaways moved on, and *Umo* —

But the man, nearer now, still unseen, interrupts. Hearings have begun? Can something be done, about the War, the terrorist governments in the driver's seat, the people being nickel-and-dimed, the Cabinet, the money, when what are they about?

"He dreamt you were there," Cheeky confided to me. (Where? I thought.) She a starved little horse of an extreme Southern California human. Beyond her, the long tables empty now, the glassed-in display cases of this nomad imagination-for-sale-or-browsing ("no problem") crammed even fuller and anchored-down-looking, my God, a shadowy light as from water waiting for company and sound. And in the other direction, from which I'd come, beyond the boarded-up window an outdoor whirring sound, a sidewalk, a car door somewhere, a footfall, someone passing in the brightness, and I had to show what I came for.

The Ziploc out, Syriac characters rippling with the page and almond-dye letters (or were they just ancient black-ink-faded) with angular arms like minute megaphones, backward *r*'s, an authority instinct with care, beauty, faint water stain as if, now that I'm about to hand it over, I had never really looked at it.

Why am I speaking about Umo to this couple who I know are reluctant to comment (the woman touching me, the man as yet unseen — who are they to me)? What am I up to? Is it the Scrolls, my part in them, which even if bizarre, as I sometimes guess, won't matter? Consulting another oracle, a childhood sanctuary of the miscellaneous? Is it friendship? Umo's résumé?

For he had divided his time between Baja and here and every point between, a catalogue of jobs if you wanted to know about jobs not for illegal kids but an infinitely resourceful soul who came in handy anywhere from here south able to turn always Between into a possible home. No end to it. Though his music job in the war zone I leave out, partnering an enemy combatant. The Inventor at last — he stands in the inner doorway, his face of a dye darkly material and fierce.

Cheeky is so upset, "He said he's glad to be thought dead," she says.

"How does he know he is?" I said, so religiously almost relieved to be learning it for the first time for certain, hearing the front door sticking. I knew someone, I was telling these vivid people, who was dead but thought not to be, I said; whereas Umo … Umo was pretty noticeable, wasn't he? Was it he who'd painted the front door? I asked, holding out the Ziploc yet turning from The Inventor to find, standing inside the front door having pushed it shut, my sister, who took my breath away.

20 make time free

A stranger to this house I was certain.

But not to the Ziploc she saw our irritated host take from my hand. She was dressed for her job, her dark hair tied back, her eyes bluer even than her shirt, her collar white, her black slacks tailored to her hips, cell phone at her waist, and some new partnership prophetically between us like a mysterious ultimatum quite beyond your control.

"I saw him dive twice, I never met him," said my sister, "and somewhere in between I saw him hop into a truck on the interchange with cars streaming by, and he was glad to be alive," said E-m. "And so were we. He acted out, sort of ... for us, for my brother ... he acted *for* us (?)." "No, no," I said — how could she speak? "He met *you*," said Cheeky. "It's always possible," said my sister.

" — spek lak he did. Lak he knew you and Zach ... ye'fathuh."

"We knew of you, Sister," said The Inventor. He had a lamp turned on with a green-glass shade, he was staring at the piece of Scroll and would not quite be able to give her the once-over. "I have read your envelopes, some of them, and seen how they affect those close to me. I have seen your car drive up in the middle of the night," my sister said, "and heard it."

"'I have no life but this,'" said The Inventor, "I have harrd your brother say the seem." "It's so," said E-m, The Inventor's theme uncanny or was it familiar through my sister? "Bottom lines I re*cog*nize but not just before," said The Inventor. "I will be back in a matter of minutes." He flapped the scrap of thin, stiff paper. "You don't know how some fool might use your words, your ideas, your thought, your cut-up memory, philosophy, family, your gift, your shit," said The Inventor, leaving the room. My sister looked about her and at me. Cheeky limped over to open a sliding glass display-case front.

"What are you doing *here*?" I said. She had a job, and looked like it. And she'd never been invited in the days of my friendship with Milt, and had had a previous engagement, Dad's birthday, the night of The Inventor's party (though held at Cheeky's) celebrating my enlistment from all appearances. Why would she come here? She was uninclined to, she wasn't much of a collector and would have had no reason to visit The Inventor while I was gone and none now — she was so intelligent, it occurred to me. This so obvious a reason it was disturbing. She'd had to come here.

"The girl has her own reasons for visiting," Cheeky said. "Have I told you how that big boy took me in his arms when we met at the dock and thanked me for coming and gave me a book, but not a book book, ... this — " she took out of the display case a catalogue big as a phone book, and slid the glass front out and down again, she was moved. "His own person," she said. She wasn't about to hold forth. She seemed to embrace what was coming. An old person listening. What for?

"Your place" — E-m nodded quickly (so unlike her). For the story E-m told now wasn't as she and I ever ever would speak to each other, like a clock telling time, boring almost, chitchat, going through the motions, and something was up to me: what was it like, a controlling person, which my sister did not know how to be, yet we were used to being surrounded by them.

"Mom phoned my cell, she thought I was at work. There's a break-in at your place. Stud called her. He dropped you off at the bus, she thought it would be the 41, but I figured out why —you were coming here and caught a ride with Stud in the middle of traffic (?) — He said, How's it going? Ask me tonight, you said, tomorrow, next month if I'm here, Mom said, you were in a rush. And Bea phoned."

And, and, *but when did she phone?* I said mouthing the words — this was all jumbled, not even at our typical slant — it was up to me to calculate, and Cheeky, understanding that it was between the two of us which is not what you do when you invite yourself into someone else's place, said "Break-ins" so softly that she seemed to want to speak only to us and it had its effect — "and phone calls. Only way to stop what's going on is not to live anywhere. I'm going to have a pyre in the back yard here when I die; and I'm easy I don't care if it's quite soon." My sister said she would like to see that. "What took you to my place?" I said, strangely for I was OK with it, more than OK. "Bea briefed you on the Hearings?" I seemed to change the subject. My sister looked at me, she put everything into it. "She sort of went on about it, how you handled those people. 'Nice work,' she said." "Storm Nosworthy's words," I said changing the subject for she was jealous. "Him again?" said my sister —

my father's daughter, I understood — "didn't we have enough of him? What did he mean?" "Us. The old Sinatra song. *You*, really. 'Nice work if you can get it' 's all I remember. He's got a …" "He came clear across the country for this?" "No. But we'll find out this afternoon."

"Well, *there's* a job I won't get." "If what?" I said. Cheeky held the catalogue up. We heard The Inventor at work in the other room. The envelope room among other things. Was my hearing newly acute over my disappointment the last months with photography if not sight itself?

"I don't *know* what." She must keep on behind me, my amazing girl for this historical moment if I could put it together (but *what* job?). "If he's not afraid of you, what you know," I said, and I saw the warped, mobile face she would read when she met Storm (very soon I saw), as, just last night, I heard her draped in a towel read to me, "My Tools took Human —Faces — / The Bench, where we had toiled —/ Against the Man — persuaded — "

— where "Against" also means *anticipating*, and "Bench" itself did the persuading, it came to us;

and hearing The Inventor muttering like a priest I saw Storm's eye gravitate to hairs on a toilet seat, stained underwear on a threshold, damp, dark towel reaching across a tossed family comforter my mother had given me; yet I seem to have foreseen that it wasn't our intimacy Storm cared to use against us but my knowledge he must keep inactive though not me.

"You went to my place?" At the office was where she was when her friend Bea phoned. "Collect some a my things," she almost couldn't say it.

"Were they there?" Gather together things. Books, closet, laundry, bathroom, notebook on the kitchen windowsill, necklace on the bedroom rug, God knows what else incriminating on the dark green comforter she had given me — "a green bed," she called it, though she'd left me her incense holder, gift of a neighbor child made in ceramics class. "Oh *we* have that!" my sister took the American Coaches Directory from Cheeky. Ours I had seen last in her room at home, on the floor, and long before that heard what I'd heard, and left it at that.

"She said —"

"Beatrice?"

"Yes, quite a story you told."

"Part of it."

"She told me. From that photographer, our Chaplain, my God, it made me realize — " "Passing it on." "So they need to silence him?" "I said too much." "But he's dead." "Between you and me." My sister alone for a moment, was this why she'd come? or to use all this? For what? to set out at last? to leave? I knew what she was thinking.

"And he took me in his arms," said Cheeky, "and hugged me and gave me this very book he'd brought all the way with him thousands of miles and risked his life taking and I was to take charge of it, from Mexico he wanted to travel light, and here it is." ("And 'the Other'? all that?" murmured my sister, for I took her hand: "If I only knew who it was.")

The Inventor was back among us. He said: "I will show you what I have written down and I will read it out loud, it is yours, but, but … " — he was deeply surprised, almost quieted — "I have made … " He had penned the words on an oblong brown paper panel torn from a Ralphs grocery bag in letters still smaller than those of the Scroll scrap. It was late. What did I owe my sister, him, anyone? " … I have made a discovery!" he said. "But here is your own private and perrssonal scroull, you and yours," The Inventor said, who seemed moved or leaving

something out in advance, his voice urgent, disturbed, honored.
"Listen," he said:

" ' — always inspiring' [it begins," he said, "(where
someone tore the paper) — he means, 'Be'—'Be
inspiring'] 'but make yourself like firewood or water
scarce, commodity-wise' [that's what it says] 'though
present' ['on call'(?)]. 'And when you are mobbed, and
the Jerusalem scribes try to get hold of you but first
your family try to detain you out there in the street
because they think you are crazy' — ['beside yourself'
is closerr] — 'to your hearers you will say, "Who are
my real mother and brothers?" and answer, "Those
who do the will of God, and have the Godspeed gift,"
but in another place next day, "A house divided within
itself is a bed of ferment where enterprise can thrive,"
and without warning you appear somewhere else near
a barren fig tree for which you prescribe a particular
transplant, or another day ask, "Why baptism if you do
not understand water?" Or elsewhere if you imagine a
water that quenches thirst once and for all for a woman
just like a sister who you know has taken several lovers
and she thinks you are a prophet to know such a thing
about her, you as a storyteller in your own story this
time keep your identity secret from this mere Samaritan
woman whom you compete with on equal terms until
the moment when you can't hold it back any longer and
it will be a stunner until … when they write about you,
you will seem to have said all these things in one day, and
you can foresee a tool invented many years hence, to put
pictures side by side better than talk.'

"But the last part," The Inventor looked up to see E-m, "where the Man from Nazareth speaks about the woman's cohabiting sex *part*narrs, is not in the Scrolls they have published." The Inventor turned upon me eyes glitteringly darker and because foreign now all the closer to me his young friend. "I know it for a fact. Can your papyrus be authentic?"

The phone went. We heard it like a voice, a face, a reply, something right in the neighborhood. Should he answer it?

What did I owe him, please?

With the hand that held the Scroll scrap and the grocery-bag brown paper translation, our host pointed to the Coaches Directory (*Big as a phone book*, Milt had said): "It's yours. Take it. It is bad luck. We help them, then one day they don't confide any more. Therein is why Umo came here to…" (I took both pieces of paper out of The Inventor's hand as he turned away distracted.) " … to our part of the world," he added. "His place is marked." The phone call might be about us, I thought; *for* us. "Be back," The Inventor said politely, going to take it.

What were they willing to do to protect the Scrolls? Was it from higher up? A height from which nothing real is felt? Unreal becomes real when it hits you.

I hugged Cheeky, her feelings, her bones; and what was left of her was what I smelled, garlic and orange and bread, her well-used skin, the coffee churning in her stomach that had passed through her mouth — and the frankness of her grip, the earth of weeds and iron. "We're outa here," I said.

Who was the one who was dead but was thought to be living? I heard her ask, as I got the door open. She was holding the Directory against her. My brain is in the street, my hand on E-m's arm, I see that I will go back to the war.

My Specialist driver tells the tale of her car parked down the street. She had checked on it every little while. Stood back from the office window, smelling the captain somewhere. She was parked at an angle between a mud-matte Humvee and an old truck with double-plated steel siding a local pickup could never have supported, welded at Camp Warhorse up in Baqubah forty miles from here. The captain calls her. Three boys stop to look at the Chevy, her old Suburban, and the boy at the hood glances up uncannily at her window and the other two lay hands on the doors and the driver's door gives way (she can hear it even from here — and I want to know what the captain called her) and the boy is inside in a second leaning across the front seat, and the whole car blows and the boy at the hood is tossed against a wall fifteen feet back from the curb and the boy at the passenger door is aflame and not going anywhere, slowed down he looks darkly absorbed in the material of the car. She steps forward to the window (had he flipped the ignition even?). The captain wanders in and watches with her. His smoky hand on her shoulder, she resists a gentle pressure encouraging her to lean back. Did she have anything in the glove? The trunk, the back? — he might be asking something else. Is he kidding? "Do you not understand those boys didn't do it? They only tripped a wire (but where?). Car was waiting for me to open the door and get in, me. Who would do that?" "No one. It's the car," said the man who had procured it and will procure a better one but thinks about it. Has she only one name?

A story to tell my sister one day — it won't have happened yet; though if about to, here to her beloved Honda, foreseen too catastrophically late — fuse wrapped into exhaust manifold is one way, drive around for a while let the charge warm up; though you can trip a car bomb with a phone and Em's cell sounds the first notes of the Fifth Symphony then caller hangs up as she thumbs Speaker — her notebook half under my foot, clothes and books in back, bicycle seat and half-empty suitcase in the trunk.

My sister said: "So he was dead, the Chaplain."

She knew that, I said.

"How come *they* didn't? They're trying to silence a witness to the explosion — no, two explosions, you said — … Zach? — the second" (she thought a second) "… like a corroborating witness (!) — but all this time he's dead somewhere (?). Why wasn't he found?" My sister, looking through the windshield, eyeing the rearview, would answer for herself: "Because you took him with you. You were friends because you said you'd take him with you."

Other way round, I said, I — Alive *or* dead, she said. I said I hardly knew why I hadn't told her. Not the first time, she said.

The fewer who knew the better, but tell her of all the people in the universe, I hardly knew why I couldn't when I was getting us into the water his body coming apart almost before I could haul him across the floor to the edge so when I dropped into the water he came down on top of my head.

It didn't matter, Em said. "On top of you?" She's amused, almost not there with me for once. I could feel the abyss, was it above or was it below? It's hard enough to make it in alone without somebody else unloading on you … and your ear all taped. She wanted to kiss, I knew. She slowed and turned and I leaned and kissed her at a slant and her mouth was moist and tasted of nothing but her.

Unloading? It sounded like something else. I hadn't wanted her to see me lugging a body and then losing the body. "Water," I said, "wait a sec —" — someone's voice *in* you survives their death — " 'Water makes many Beds,' " I began. Em went on, "'For those averse to sleep — Its awful chamber open stands …'" Her mood again, her agenda today. I wondered how well I'd done at the Hearings.

"It was good of you, Zach."

Beethoven's Fifth false-alarming again, Who's that? she murmured, and may have forgotten to ask what became of my cargo, my saved dead man, my attempted cross-chest carry, for she made a zigzag of residential blocks, she enjoyed it, a new route. The car was a mess inside, but she could drive, the tiny white scar on her right wrist came into view. Passed a couple of Craftsman houses. "I won't miss it; everyone wants to live here." She might drive East or sell the car. We passed the bus. "You won't sell your Honda," I said. What were we talking about? Were we putting off getting downtown or finding the way there? The Hearings, I said. I thought they went well for me but maybe not.

I was thinking out loud, Em too, driving, and together we're more prophetic it comes to me (and from the future) yet never again quite the couple. A trade-off, and we passed a playground with ceramic figures you entered and looked out of the eyes and mouths of — like Tarot, Em said (specific reference like her poets always with her — someone who'd actually built such things) — and then, "We temples build with human faces," which made sense; we passed a school and a woman in shirtsleeves was leaning way out a window, and in a residential street a horse, a good sturdy quarter horse, a long cowboy sitting him, they seemed not to move and yet were headed in the other direction from us, the man's hands resting the reins on a snakehead pommel and I in this weird profit-stricken country like a great war-torn … body, I had said to the lost voice at the back of the Hearings room and what had he said? — that I didn't quite mean it with all my something or other I didn't get back to him; we passed a dumpster of rubble and fill and old painted planks and bare-ticking pillows and pure garbage waiting for pickup, and in our conversation maybe Em glad to have the windshield to keep her eyes looking through and the rearview: "The fresh paint 'n all, Umo's gotta be somewhere." "Inventor's hanging on." "How does he live?" "Hard to see how they're plugged in."

"There he is again," my sister said as if it were nothing new. I twisted to look back. The rearview did not lie. The Inventor's old coupé ran a stop sign and just missed a car crossing like clockwork. When she'd said, "Who's that?" she hadn't meant the cell phone riff. "Em?" My sister wanted to deposit me and get back to her office, perhaps. "He wants to give us that Directory of Coaches and we have a copy at home," she said. The Bel Air, though a loose-slung affair, was handling well, there is nothing to say that Hindus drive poorly, but I could see the driver's fierce eyes. I said we didn't know what he wanted when we were leaving, that call had come in.

"We have to get you back to the Hearings." My sister slowed to pass a California Highway Patrol officer sitting on his parked motorcycle waiting. Did I remember the ten-dollar envelope I bought myself for my birthday that time? Em said.

I remembered showing it to her, resealing it, and giving it to Umo at the enlistment party. Did I remember what it said? I remembered a year or two previous citing it to Dad when Mom was calling the United States the Good Samaritan. Be a passerby, the envelope had said — or rather, its contents — the first line, and it only made him mad when he learned it came from a Gospel but not a well-known one, not that I'd read it.

The cop had not pulled The Inventor over. His inspection had lapsed. The whole envelope was like that: You can't think except in conflict with the Other but stopping to help someone isn't the way and we are being told to feel things we don't and it might be a relief when a favorite uncle dies suddenly, like existence itself, and visiting the elderly might have nothing to do with one's real feelings. This had come up in the Scrolls, my sister had said. Between the lines there was another Jesus who conceived of the earned leisure of a successful person as a disquiet blessing the useless and the tiny, which, like the stone in the road, reality passes by. I'm putting into words what's pretty dumb but I can sort of see it.

"So …" I said, "this translation in my pocket, y'think Jesus ever … —?" "He had a mission statement." "The 'house divided' (?) — sounds familiar like a fucked-up family's a good thing not a bad thing (?) because it —"

"— gees up your — "

"Unh huh, initiative yeah (and not even very fucked-up), you think Christ ever said anything like that?"

"The first part of your … *papyrus*? — your piece of paper, your scrap, it's in the book: I remember it from the library. So they didn't need — " "They didn't need it — " "For the book they had their Scrolls down already, their Scrolls," my sister pushed forward her lips, dwelling on the word.

"And the explosion," I said, as my sister put her hand on my knee, "it probably didn't make any difference — "

"— they had what they needed — "

"— wait: 'they got what they *needed*,' the Chaplain said. Does that mean, from the explosion?" Scraps and glimpses to weigh like a fool, my life, not papyrus which would disintegrate but parchment, animal, but my scrap manufactured to look old, it came to me.

"God you remember. But didn't the Chaplain say also, '*Not* what was meant by the *other* one'? 'cause honey you told me." "I must have." "There's that 'other' again," said my sister; "well, he said a lot for a guy who was dying." "I don't see that." She took a right turn at a stop sign, both hands on the wheel, was she going to the Hearings?

Honey? Em would never call me *Honey*. It didn't sound right. We had slowed and the Bel Air was behind us, the full anatomy of The Inventor's old Bel Air drummed wild syncopation around the moan of an engine soon to drop its tailpipe, the message radiating at greater speed than our own forward motion. My sister asked if I was going back to the war. How she knew, I had no idea. She like Umo didn't think of changing my mind, she was cruising an edge of family feeling and calculation and something she wasn't telling me, well she was in the workforce. Yet could there be anything too much to talk about with her, the strongest person in our growing-up home when she chose. I persist in finding my job. What if she's way ahead of me? It is gathering *my* "things" together on my free time. Something awful here, as she swings the wheel and the front wheels turn and turn and then turn back and we're south-west bound and I'm telling her how Wick seemed at the Hearings, Bea too, and the odd memories in the Scrolls, though I've not read the book, forcing on me action yet asking a presentiment, a shadow to cast in order to be in.

Yet like following the path we are making, it is gathering now Em's things and future and other durable goods like the Scroll scrap. Down a canyon in Little Picacho once where we could still hear the Chocolate Mountain aerial gunnery range, we went the wrong way we thought and passed a tortoise carcass on the way down and photographed a wild horse we thought on the opposite ridge that didn't turn up on the print. A turning point for us the canyon path we made more than followed, followed only by making, we agreed, a future, an apex for us, knowing we couldn't live forever in the tent and tossed a burning coal into the stream little more than cool and damp sand like what Indians we once visited plant their beans in. Make time free, it came to me, for we were in reverse at the same time that we were heading into the Hearings feetfirst, and a teacher Wick and Umo as if I owed it to him to find him, and with any luck an inexcusable father or the deserter, Zoose's guitar-playing brother-in-law whose whereabouts I had little interest in now; or a Scrolls archaeology team member whose steps were among those I'd heard on the stairs coming to check the blast site for signs of life or witness, who had met with foul play while vacationing at a remote coastal point near Acapulco — all gathered together by me in motion beside my sister so as at once to make free time.

21　where he takes the plunge

Though I would have to say that's where we were going, the Hearings, and I would have to make my sister come and find out what Storm Nosworthy had in mind; he had his value over time.

But if Storm's people harmed her, her name, her faith in herself, a hair of her, the Scrolls would be exposed by me in at least their circumstances and called into question, minor as maybe they'll prove — and for Storm they were a special project he'd organized, his claim on whatever, for he got even the Intelligence people tracking for him and had found out about us even more than was worth finding out. Why? We'd know how to give him a good time. What if we had a Biblical child? she had murmured. I know what night. A Biblical what? I said — no, I meant *what* kind of ...? We were well along. It was intelligent, like the tent night when E and I held hands, fingers really, across our father's feet but tonight I had a hand on M's belly, recently now she was in writing "M," which, said, was "Em" (between us). Would that be a lucky child? I said.

Depends which Bible you keep. Keep? I never threw one away, she said but not only the self-proclaimed holy kind. I wondered what I had done.

And so did the man who was waiting at the end of the hall on the bathroom threshold with only the darkness of the medicine cabinet mirror behind him, it was war as I left her door faintly ajar — yes, her door was open — and crossed to my room and when I locked the door I was free or had a breather from it, but two hours later I woke up in my room thinking and alive and I had to piss and I pissed into a collie dog coffee mug and two old tumblers that I found in my room rather than walk the hall. And lived with my sister's intelligence when I said, This kid wouldn't be like the one in the Bible that his father took him out and sacrificed him. No, she said, another night, at the last minute his father didn't after all. It was a story. Last minute. What good is that? What can you expect? The Old Testament is old? Old news. Out of date, Christians like to think. Pretty primitive, black-and-white, low-budget. It was slanted, her joking, from way back. It could be anxious a little (like asking if something had happened today as if that would explain tonight). (I said "primitive" was a good word for her.) Whereas the *New* Testament would never sacrifice anyone like that... Are you kidding? I said. *Now* look, she whispered, having me in her grasp.

Wheels out of line, chassis swaying, The Inventor overtaking, we let him, God. We pulled over and he to the opposite curb, the street broadening as we did so. We were late. Posters way up ahead — FINISH THE JOB — IF YOU GOT A JOB GIVE IT TO A BUSY MAN — JESUS ALL THE WAY — JESUS KNOWS THEY'RE RUNNING ON EMPTY — JESUS AND CO INVEST IN REALITY — FROM BURNING

BUSH TO FREE ELECTIONS — two corners further south, the blue-and-white helmets of the California Highway Patrol here at the edge of downtown and parked motorcycles leaning next to squad cars. The posters meant really *finish the finishing, end the ending* — well, I hoped it was still going when I got back to the Middle East if only to finish my business not making any sacrifices for anybody. Pretend Arabic script I was able to make out, perhaps as a veteran, said, "Train them to take care of their shit so we can generate some wind to farm." Though it was then, recalling I had hoped those wretched waters might jolt my friend to life, whose name I still didn't know — and at the Lunch Buffet a wheelchair sergeant who had suffered some spinal nerve dissolution only many months after he had worked with a team that, up to their neck in the Euphrates, had cut the detonation wires in April 2003 to save a major bridge from blowing — that I heard Em's cell, after her V for Victory deaf Beethoven man's ringtone, announcing on Speaker the speaker I'd been expecting.

While our Inventor hastening across the road brought us the "bad luck" Coaches Directory he'd wrested from Cheeky's bosom, whom he didn't like to leave alone, warning us as he came stumbling toward us that the calls we had missed meant trouble (and two whirring bicycles nearly sideswiped him before, behind — man, woman, hybrids going possibly nowhere so in some endlessly final slowness of delay Time itself it almost came to me, the great interrupter, gathered all the motion it marked), while with his strange ear our dedicated Inventor by turns quick and occasionally deaf to what was uncool told us the new seeds promised if we recollected in the Scrolls that could "grow on fucking rock" and send "ears to heaven" (it was said) might all be "Fascist listening *dev*ices" of which the *re*pellent voice on his home phone seeking us was a purr*fect* instance. Realizing as he came across to us that that very voice addressed us now on Em's speakerphone, The Inventor was especially irked when by now Em had shouted back across me that we had our own copy she'd already told Cheeky — though No, he said, *she* doesn't need it she — Cheeky of *all* of us should (I said), God, man, it's Umo, Vera *Cruz* — !

"No, I will tell to you it is right heerre the page he marked —"

No no please, Em said, as Inventor reached our side safely, we *knew* the place. Which was strictly true only of her, my little sister who once upon a day, knowing I, the angry one (I thought), had no need to touch the Directory much less read the entry on that southern California swimming coach, had with one slip, a stumble, summed up for me: so the brief résumé that named East Hill (its local swim club area Imperial in the western zone of USA Swimming) and his background and the gist of his methods, let slip the reference to the son who it was hoped could... (it gave Em pause) ... "could double as diver slash swimmer" — her pause, like so much in her reading and speech for the brother always infinitely worth attending to like her other body or a thought poised to spring, an omission not so much right then in the entry but a few words on so that, as she would do when she was sight-reading at the piano, she was reading a little ahead as well, "Page one fifty-three," she said to The Inventor, a special number for me, she said (and then I thought *he* muttered — like an achievement till now kept to himself — Indeed *I* once translated that number into *Chi*nese).

Blackly outraged is The Inventor now by the phone voice its Speaker message that they're glad we're almost there they're waiting patiently for what will keynote the Scrolls as ongoing war strategy but more a calculus of the aftermath; where today we "add what only one person, Zach, can give to amplify our sense of where these Scrolls are *coming* from, Zach, as if in the broad view historically we 'outsourced' for bottom line *your* veteran contribyoosh —"

Mine now? was I over-hearing, alerted, bummed, shocked, awed only at some toxic effrontery to be explained — *my* contribution? Says who?

— "so pivotal" to this project of "…pandemic democracy" — confided without a whiff of irony by the onetime Sacramento speechwriter, as, overheard now, The Inventor pounded the roof of our Honda lamenting the loss of those "forrteen shoe*box*es" of envelopes yet now to my ear alarmingly even heart-sinkingly regretting just moments ago an "indiscretion by Cheeky surrendarred to that warped and viperous voice" when it phoned seeking *us*, her parting question *Then who was the one who was dead but thought to be* living? —

— my true job nonetheless gathering with Cheeky's true charity and hope, against sirens heard converging on us, their hood emblems pointed unknowing toward the future and what Storm Nosworthy and his team foregrounding the Seals captain and the agency "CEO" who had phoned Em would do to safeguard the Scrolls for the War's sake where my job might be to safeguard the *threat TO* all this of a dead witness's potential afterlife, my Chaplain — *best friend you never had*, my Em had called him.

"Why did we buy your envelopes without seeing what was inside?"

"You were good fellows. You knew."

"Well, Milt got mad at them."

"Ah yes, I tould him to get in touch with his — "

"— 'close to the loins of the Administration' is all Milt let me see, and a name — where did you get that?" I asked The Inventor — "Em you remember Sacramento?"

"It is ulluways researrch of an eclectic —"

"— No no, no, Milt grabbed it back. But it was what I *didn't* get to see, so who *was* this eclectic source?" "Ah, it may have been Umo?" "You mean it was?"

It was like the stones that when you took them to throw at someone they reversed to igneous and burst into fire in your hand according to Milt's father, but the envelope had said, *Make your sibling the apple of your eye* and Milt didn't have a sibling, furthermore it spoke against fathers, he said.

"And you did not only buy," said The Inventor, preoccupied perhaps by the indiscretion he had admitted on behalf of Cheeky and forgetful of the Coaches Directory he held like a catalogue at his side, and looking in back as if he might ask for a lift, "I *gave* you two envelopes for your *diving* wound: the Goldthread to crush into a poultice — "

"You had a hole in your heart," my sister said. "You were looking right through it," I said.

"I knew what you were thinking, I heard the words through the hole —" "Yes you have the gift when you are together," The Inventor began. "— you were thinking you couldn't breathe."

" — and the *other* envelope I gave with the worrds — " "But you *sold* him two others," said Em, she was my fortune, my beauty coldly knowing more than me, and she tapped the heel of her pedal foot on the floor, the sirens two blocks away; but had The Inventor ever seen us together before today? "It is good to get worrds from out of nowhere, a tradeoff," said The Inventor, the cell phone streamed its Fifth Symphony tune into his mood and made him laugh — "The number Beet*hov*en put aside most fre*quent*ly and took up ah-gain of all his — !"

"Out of nowhere? Words from *some*one don't come out of nowhere," said my sister. (That envelope, it was the one I'd given Dad, the day, the night, of two enlistment parties, sight unseen.) "Your Leader it is said never opens en*vel*opes except when it's a memorial awarrd," said The Inventor, "our trip has more than one cause, and I traveled to find the oceanographer's handmade aeroplane but also to *re*plenish the Goldthread which I *fore*saw we would need."

I flipped my wrist to show him the time. "The Hearings," I tapped his fine fingers. "They were *cut*-rate," said The Inventor, and let go of the window edge, "hey, a steal at ten dollars for the last you bought and more pers*o*nalized than you …" He lifted the Directory as if to heave it past me into the backseat. "I tould that scoundrel on the phone only that yes I was competent in the Eddessian Syriac you had just given me to render." Em's foot on the pedal left The Inventor standing alone in this street of two-story homes, me with the translation and what it meant. Squad cars passed us in a line. (Maybe ten dollars, maybe twenty, I thought.)

I looked back and five cops were gathered about the Bel Air, which was a spectacle in itself, and from the driver's side, even at this distance of three long blocks it was the Coaches Directory being unloaded (but who to? — for in it what might you track to what happened before all this?). You don't go around with an expired tag in a car like that if you don't want to be just another immigrant.

It got thick with downtown traffic now. Something had happened. Was it this morning's revisiting of the explosion now thought to be ours?

"The green ink and his fine hand," said my sister, chauffeuring me, but on the move I could tell. That would be the Veins envelope — I knew what she was thinking, though we were not speaking, for the moment. *You*, I heard her think, but now she said, "You never went to the hospital. He wouldn't take you there; then you wouldn't go. I tried to bathe your chest. I thought it was broken. You couldn't breathe, that's all. You spent the night in my bed. Mom came in. She felt it but couldn't speak, except. 'For cryin' out ...' she said, 'Where does it hurt?' she said. Your hand was on me."

A cadre of reverse-collared clergy stood waiting near the Center, and a crowd, or majority, waited massed near them, steadfast and American.

"You were talking, it woke me up, you had your hand on me. That was OK. Four in the morning it was plenty dark. I see you then. You weren't talking in your sleep. You told me the half gainer again, so free, that forward back dive, looking upward and back like a backstroker but impaled by trust — which way are you going? — dive within a dive — and Dad shouting to you, *Closer, closer* or worse. So the next time you answered with a twist, and came too close, which is not close but ... the body is bombarded from without and within, that book said."

We came into the intersection where Stud the butcher had picked me up. My sister and I, however, were recalling a child who came within a hair of being sacrificed. "Milt said Dad shouted at you when you went up for the full twist too." "Well it was an interruption," I said, "whatever he said."

"I know pretty much what."

A state trooper laid his glove on the hood. I'd seen him one day walking up a sidewalk on Golden Hill I'd swear. Em braked and laid her hand on me, I'd been thrown forward in my cross-chest harness. It was not the moment to kill or even sideswipe a cop, and out of nowhere there was someone else outside like, of all the traffic surrounding us, a shadow that she would face more or less face to face, us plus this third person. "What became of him?" she said, for though we were both thinking of Dad and between us she could mean that too, she meant my Chaplain-photographer who I prayed had had an easy burial. My palace driver, who delivered me before and collected me after, divides *her* loyalties — *that's all* she *knows* — and she'll get another car out of Cap. I'm there again. But on another job. I feel it like a river moving.

A wicked undercurrent dragged athwart the well rush a track not mine, and he was gone. One ripped-away sleeve of my friend's wet suit I was left with.

"You could have told me." (Em swam well enough but without that undisplaced delight in the water; it was in a couple of poems she read me, but.)

"What would *you* have done? — I lost someone's body."

"Well," she said (so close), "you were friends, because … but you were friends — "

:be*cause* — the word so close to another word Em was about to say and maybe no more than *"just* because"— (friends with the Chaplain only because I would *do* something for him? — yet Em continuing) " — because you told him what our job is, the *real* job found inside the coercion —" (had I told *Em*, emailed her, the job found *within* the job you were *forced* to do and had even been set up to play an ugly part in?) the cause, the before like the after, becoming *"just* because," collapsed to an instant as suspended as a dive above its remembering, or my despairing trip in reverse back up that dive's tunnel to the top, where the twist has already begun, bearing words fired from an observer enraged who stops you because you stopped him, and yet an instant suspended for an hour at a time (and she would read to me when I came back from the palace war and I'd drift forward on a line to another car I imagined on its way to Kut with a fan of mine to finish what a photograph had started, win back something, answer more than her original question (driving me to the palace) *what had just happened before the picture?* so that (seeing her not as before in reverse, 7,6,5,4,3,2,1) I glimpsed her in future in a fairly late-model car-replacement finagled by our captain (now a major — so relieved to be not just an Army captain any more); when after, yes, a two-hundred-and-thirty-mile trip north to the border where the possible division of the country was visibly an issue, we would now return south, Livia her name though called Livy by the captain and by me, and go to Kut I had virtually known in advance, she and I, approaching a roadblock and forced to pick up an armed passenger …) —

— when the lock behind Em clucked because she had touched the back door release and, the door open, into the warm day of her car (which she had once wanted me to think of as ours) came a face she'd heard in the old days on our home phone more than once, and for a moment she was quivering and chill, seeing in the rearview like a tiltable screen the man whose presence, function, *use* that we must face I knew now not just for all else he was and likely the murderer of my friend Umo even though Umo *I* knew lived (to jump one afternoon cannonball, then dive; then, like a Third way of gathered understanding, that wartime palace dive which as a double somersault also like a jump went in feetfirst), but a Storm voice that praised me for "ideas" or "other" of mine mysterious for he'd received them prompted some way that I hadn't grasped because even bad people have second sight and hear things:

I have a driver with orders from above and we are entering Kut where I have unfinished business that will show itself to me only when I get there. The Chaplain's voice is waiting but not the Chaplain. I see powerlifting equipment; brand new squat benches, but see no more, though am seen.

And joining now our very track close in in traffic convening for the afternoon session like he'd been listening in or had bonded (giving us however not more stability as Wick once explained chem but less — and a scent — but of the three of us, now? — some mustard-sweet gum from the incense tree, less myrrh than frankincense it might have been named), Storm it was who settled down on hangersful of colored shirts and rested an elbow on a plump laundry bag (pronounced it a nice little car), though Umo was in my thought and not Storm's real aim, the car rolling now I'd swear sliding half-sideways on a surface influenced by our slippery and pointing-out passenger. And with a word or two from him how to get where we needed to get and pointing out for some reason suggestively the trolley station— though as "your fans, Zach and *others* upstairs," didn't know, "your friend Umo has been reported near Acapulco, a false sighting we think — for why would someone want us to think him alive, Zach, after we've agreed on *post*humous citizenship in principle? Another great idea from Zach! (Are these your things, E-m?)" — the letters pronounced separately like an in-the-know interviewer.

"Posthumous — ?" she slipped through a red light, attending only to cars. "Your dear brother's — " "What if he isn't — ?" "— darling idea still."

"Guaranteed?" I said.

"Dead *or* alive." Storm getting into it exactly but always overdoing it, it would get him killed (I saw, I saw it, was he in an Iraq mess hall? — lauding the Scrolls? — or was that me, another tour of duty up ahead?). "In return for what?" I said, my sister murmuring agreement.

"He had borderline high blood pressure. Heartmobile told us; though where exactly he did die matters less and less ... even if not known to you the friend he followed halfway round the world — now, your dad —"

"You have nothing to do with my father."

"He trusted me. Did he you? But we —" My sister squeezed my hand, then needed hers to steer. "He thinks the world of you, Zach, but he does not put his best foot forward, but — "

"He has a birthday coming up," Em said, I felt in my legs and actually in hers that she wanted me to take the bait, ask what the deal had been, she had her elbow up on the edge of the window, which she never did, and she heard what maybe I didn't in this man's words.

"— we will see," Storm said ominously, again the sweet odor, surer than sight or sound; "the world being at stake, the bleeding needing to be stopped, I'm sure you on my case and I on yours can find common ground for tradeoffs to safeguard for the time being ... your sister ... her job ... college applications, what not — am I sitting on your underwear back here, Em? — and, to be frank, Zach, Dad's future. You two, you, you," the man seemed to stammer, "who find each other and a matrix ready-made, the clouds burst, the stream flows, it is them, it is original, and then comes the matrix ready-made which turns them into ..."

A basement garage Em had driven us down into must prove to be connected with the Conference Center. Why does he call you *Zach* all the time? she muttered under her breath, and You're quite generous (I know why). She pulled the ignition key.

"What could you *do*?" she said over her shoulder, getting out of the car. What I had learned I would have to use. I felt that Wick was close now and someone else up there I would need.

"If we can agree about the explosion …," Storm walking across the subbasement concrete floor rising on the balls of his feet, led the way into a brushed stainless steel elevator big enough to lift a car. "That it happened?" I said. He turned to the buttons, wheeling about, now, so the evidence of his recreated and horrendous face of slants seemed to belong to him no more than a parallel field. "That we don't know who *did* it." "Not the actual ones." "Though we'll find them — "

"If we haven't already," I said.

"— be they after the Scrolls or their leader himself who there was a story going around of the *palace* detainment unit housing him when in fact we've had him locked up safe and sound elsewhere for months. *As* we will find the Chaplain-pho*tog*rapher," said the face Em read, its talk, the finger on the Up button.

I said they might.

"You don't seem to know his name though you met at Fort Meade." "Lucky for me." "We fucking arranged it," Storm Nosworthy said. The confiding (and cursing) of a fool, a killer. Em near me at once all but inside me but in the new way, her "you" voice had ceased in my head for the moment, for steps approached along the echoing floor of the great garage — with luck there would be another break coming — and Storm got the door to close. "We don't know how he swung this, for all I know you may have described it to your sister-love whom I would have known from her pictures" — Storm's smile thick, warped, richly working — "the dove's eyes, no, too blue, a Celtic queen sold to a King of the Nile, what says the Song? 'my sister, my spouse,' and where I was sitting in her backseat the smell of her laundry was as the smell of Lebanon."

I was the killer now.

The elevator lifted almost at a slant and slowly and like a cabin of secure space that stalled when its computer received calls from a higher and lower floor simultaneously sometimes, Storm warned. The smile again, now quick spasm of a public asshole's fitful show, punctuating the tradeoff to be agreed to: "The palace explosion I trust we can call a mystery? In return for … Not that I'd expect you two *chums* would need much cajoling … (?)."

The huge elevator cut off and my sister leaned on me. Storm Nosworthy clear across the elevator floor from us jabbed the buttons — Is it us? she breathed — brother-sister …?

What could he *know*?

The break-in. Your place.

The bed … the bathroom?

What could anyone know?

Think.

"West Coast contractors," Storm said, hitting the whole button panel. "You saw the acoustic ceiling above the buffet, the recessed lighting?" "Over the farmed blue marlin," I said, seeing that coastline-stained, that darkening map. Water damage, worse than water, Storm, I thought. "Care about two ado*lesc*ents?" my sister whispered, meaning What was there to *know* and nobody did anyway. "One person," I murmured. Em snapped her fingers and the elevator was on its way. "Would he?" she said.

"We outsourced the blue marlin farm," Storm said remembering. A brown business envelope in his jacket pocket, he had it out now. "We know we know … that he crawled some fifteen feet or was dragged because … because … because we tracked DNA from the main urine deposit and and through skin scrapings, waste products, fabric. To where he takes the plunge." ("A friend," Em muttered.) "What was that?" "A devoted friend," I said. "Yet a three-hundred-pound steel plate was found to have his traces on its underside —" ("For friendship's sake?") "— and how he could have got out from under it — crushed when it fell on him …" ("Not his face, though," Em whispered.)

"Two'na half maybe. Three, never," I said. Storm hasn't missed my meaning. "Your devoted friend?" "His." "Ah, his." Storm alive as not before. "You would … " "Do anything to bring him back." "Somewhere, along that metropolitan well network that we're setting to rights, he exists (as we need to address spills right here of untreated sewage, Storm purred), and how he got away from the blast site we can guess, Zach, until we know more— " Em slid her arm through mine again — along a leg of that sewer named after the President I recalled— a sewer I'd described to Em, water part of what contained it inspiring me when she would kindle her incense, turn out the lights, ask what came "just *before* that" as if not what comes now.

22 the already strange distance

But now, "His *nose*," she whispers, "the blue *spots,*" she whispers, "it means 'Im*pris*onment,'" she read the face across the elevator car, my arm knew each finger that gripped it, we heard now a hubbub coming our way. And the other wide door at right angles to the door we'd come in slid back leaving us face to face with a mob in the lobby going to the same place as us and struck silent as we came into view. First, though, or almost first, the Seals captain and his ramrod teammate "CEO" in combats waving back a hundred others who could wait or take the other elevator, but clearly a two-man escort for the sixth passenger making this trip to the Conference level.

Was it my frog-in-the-throat questioner? It was.

In the long white spiritual garment and no badge showing. And Em greeted him ("*Hus*ky," she said), the very one who before they'd cautioned him this morning had told me I didn't "mean" what I said, but we had been uneasy and close and I'd cut him off; and my "profit-stricken country" and more than that "one great war-torn body" meant also the globe I suppose, glib with parallels ungrasped and the facts we collect on the job from the voices we hear, yet left me taxed for what I might have said. To Umo, my sister, my father, Milt, the accredited conferees, Marine recruiters on a no-kid's-butt-left-behind watch, War Child snapping his wrist by the hotel turned stock exchange.

And now against this crowd balked by the spaces of the multiuse elevator closing on their faces, accreditation badges somehow not to be seen on their lapels, pullovers, shirt pockets, breasts, ID lockets, though there in their free faces *Entitled* (but to what?) — "Get 'em outa the building," captain said ("Done," said CEO, his idea practically ... "This Hearing!") — it was jealousy in me not envy of Husky, and even as my sister unsure of what she had entered into gripped my arm, and captain and " CEO," his cell phone out so quick it might have been up his sleeve, took up formation along the wall opposite us with this peaceable, curiously significant person in front, I must gather what was going on even in an elevator and against this operator Storm to be undone I believed but dangerous to Em, who had met a friend of hers who seemed to be in custody and hardly acknowledged me though he had something remarkable in him to say and would say it.

"Your people," I said. "My people?" "Come on, that woman working with captain and the black guy acting the wacko?"

Though now Storm points at my chest.

Tradeoff time, he means. A brown business envelope in hand, Storm Nosworthy will cross this room that rose toward our Hearings floor, target what he will use, and, doomed, it came to me, can't know how my father's birthday envelope divides me between what random hurt Em hints it held and what really I'd paid twenty dollars for (or *was* it ten?), Earth Veins you make your own running universally through each of us, rift and river, a hole in the head, a half-completed dive to heal, yet quite parentless (if you could prove it, Em once said); how Umo pronounced him — "Stom's secret weapon you better get to know." The humoring muscle of distrust an orphan doubt no less trusting me, asking what meant "brother," describing grandfather's plan to come to Mexico, work the mineral mines, sign up with Plutarco Calles, live right; the secret weapon, though, Umo, how do you figure that? The brown envelope, always about to be drawn out for me, delayed, I can feel it, that voice to nail down our understanding *quid pro quo* as, on the other cheek, Storm's face shouts our very History *et habeas corpus silentem* — beside us (for I was right, he *has* come across to us) he speaks in confidence from his own, base Faith — Umo dead, Chaplain alive (yet Umo come thousands of miles to hook up with *me* — do I understand that trip, those Umo miles? — while the other guy lives again in a scrolled-down monitoring of those dark and memorial waters) the Scrolls Storm's *baby* (!), for holistic proof rests beneath ineetiative, ineetiative beneath democracy, and what shall it profit us near term if we lose the Near and Middle East? — this giant lift inching up retarded by what's left in return for what was always there; Wick's morning-after calculus healing more wounds than my dive, more pitfalls than an elevator's division between waiting silence and, with two adjacent doors, a need to speak before time runs out.

To me a friend and mere miracle, the Chaplain on the other hand matters so much to Storm he'll flush him even from extinction along old sewerways. Just one of many you'll silence who might explain the explosion uncharitably for the Administration, for us. He had the Vice President's ear.

"Citizenship for Silence," Storm speaks what is in his pocket — "more than a fair trade, kids, and clear as anything" — then (smile grim as a clock face): "*Post*humous Citizenship *now*, your idea, Zach, deeded whether 'deceased *or* living,' I think we can certainly put in writing, with a No Rescind rider guaranteed by some pretty amazing signatures faxed from DC an hour ago." (The smile weird as words.) "In return *for* ... " the hand gesture suggestive. "Not much to ask from someone and you really are someone, you *two*."

"Em," said her friend Husky in the white kurta (and in custody to all appearances), "Em?" "What could you do to us anyway?" my sister said, in the ceremonial advance of the elevator. "What did *we* do but be a family of two somewhere?" my sister said, Storm staring at the shared and to-be-revered floor as if he saw it moving. Then to me, "Silence —" he began (my sister by my cheek muttering, "Dead or *living* 'posthumous'?")

"This soldier, Em (?)" said her friend — "said, 'You can call me Captain.' 'n' *I'm* OK with it. It's my first commandment right to honor my own ignorance." "Husky," Em said. They seemed to laugh. (I was on my own and could tell Husky kind of respected me.) "Tryin' a recruit me, Em." Elevator moaned. "For what, Husky?" softly. "Cap'n said, 'Djou read the Scrolls?' Not rilly." (The Seals captain in camo combats gripped the hungry shoulder of the man in spiritual dress, breathless too.) " 'Well, it's not two Lazarus but one,' did I know that? 'And *he* ditn' *need* to come back, right? — 'cause *he* never died in the *first* place — and Jesus was best *friends* with him,' and did I read the Scrolls? and I said, 'Not rilly; did you?' "

"Silence agreed on here and now," Storm commenced, his eyes narrowing the floor — but it was also the exchange with Husky. "'n y'know what *Cap'n* said?" said Husky.

The captain spun Husky around to face him, muttering, "Squeeze you out like a sponge."

"Said, 'Ditn' *have* to read it! Had it from the horse's mouth,'" Husky said over his shoulder to Em, to me too I was certain, a friendly exchange once jogging with an even then fugitive friend fellow photographer and Chaplain all but resurrected in me now, Lazarus, yes, between me and the Chaplain! The envelope drawn forth for my hand, I have it still, a document, next week when we'll be on a last junket to locate Umo, Em and I before I leave, tell him the good news — while Storm rapid-fired terms of the deal in intimate undertone now: Explosion unquestioned, it is what it is; authenticity of Scrolls unquestioned; and by same token no leak to media describing a relationship between major principal Zachary and sister (since "*certain* Family Values sat not well with the national community that had gotten behind the war, the Scrolls, this Christian President"). The elevator door strained — perhaps against its newness, for the unit was undeniably masking-tape new — and gave way at last upon more light than people where I'd been at noon, and now Storm thought he would charm the Dean tilting his head, finishing with me, he thought — the brown envelope mine now — or sort of addressing both of us: "For backup we got a fantastic film record of the bombing the Scrolls heinously survived, if fragmentarily, to be distributed for spiritual export crediting a cameraman of genius (which brings us to another quick trip for you, Zach, if it's OK)" — the good news I felt in my blood.

Heinously surviving (?) … to recall, I half recalled, and less than half understood, this same man's *forgotten*! (that palace day): *You won't be* forgotten … *as your father asked you to.* I slipped the envelope into my jacket pocket, and drew out by its torn feel one of two small sheets already there, hearing between us faintly the best of Storm last — unreally weird, yet … yes, Zach, family values, yes, that Storm could just eat up if it was only him himself ("though unlike you I never had so to speak a sibling"). A small sound of … was it pain from my sister, ecstasy? and for my ear only, *This citizenship, you know,* she hissed while I to her, "That 'carpenter' one about the 'unpretending time' being our 'plane,'" I said from the book she had given me the first time around, chagrined to recall so little of it and almost like Lincoln's someone else's words at that for some new farewell.

Interrupted now by her friend Husky, a perverse call for help, "Guy's so ugly you gotta wonder, but in this country that's still a person," Lazarus and the horse's mouth rose up in me like foresight *and* memory and in return for what I'm half losing, was that it?

"You had that badge?" I said. CEO followed us.

I waved The Inventor's notepaper as Storm made to go for the Dean, shaking his head at his wristwatch, like We're here, we're here — the two limbs of the little notebook of her cell phone open, a look on her face, What a *work*horse! Storm's body language complimenting her, but —

"Check out the hand, Storm, half an hour old," I waved the paper, the entrance to the great abandoned buffet lounge before me, a smell of seven-grain and spiced turkey or was it liver; mayo and melon slices in the sun, the yolky paprika'd statement of rank leftover deviled eggs and cold fish — and over by the windows stood Wick unmoving. "Check out the words here, Storm, at the beginning, right? — 'n'here at the end (?)" — Scroll words Storm would know, wouldn't he? — they came from parchment saved from the blast and in safekeeping eight months ago in my ear and subsequently in pocket, bed, glove compartment, love, but as I hardly had to tell him, so precisely between us, though we were drawing a small audience, "because you already had it — the whole thing — this wasn't needed, this scrap from the bomb," the text like all the other revelations to see the light of day in English had already been in hand somewhere else, "your explosion that day pure show, your palace — " I peered at Storm. A smell from his face now of stale cardamom seeds, leaf extract, dead tortoise, and a couple of on-the-run lunchtime shots of Jim Beam I realized I'd smelt in the car told me he knew what I had here in my hand but had never seen it.

But, the car! I thought.

I turned, my sister was with me and I told her and her hand dived into her bag and held it up, the remote-entry fob — the car left unlocked — her things, her plans (CEO was instantly on his cell) — our distance new, gathering prophetic and unknown upon me — losing one Em, gaining what? CEO watching, behind me, the Law Dean's futile call, I sensed a scattering of the accredited not yet adjourned to the Conference room though the afternoon had more than come, CEO gone, and — "This citizenship Umo's getting, living *or* dead" … my dearest sister entering from our already strange distance tells me what I had already realized, "'Posthumous' even if citizen's *alive*? Isn't that what it means?" she asks beautifully; and "In return for what, Zach? — you don't owe him."

The acoustic ceilings, a clarity or known future that turned their stains to coastlines intricate with nested corruption, the bay and the sea sky out the windows, and a familiar but now unfurled figure, the woman who had attacked me to make me give something away I thought, closing on Wick, who's looking out the window absently, for a moment a ghost.

And remembering him so long ago seen by Umo — of course! — from a distance leaning out the classroom window and I must not ask but tell Wick — the dive I have slowed down as if I could divide it endlessly from its end — my job now nearer somewhere between my sister's "before" and Umo's "after" and another trip vouchsafed only to her for its own sake — and knew better than my own my sister's breath close behind, and my name in Storm's diseased throat:

"You for*get*, Zach you for*get*—" a connection coming with Storm Nosworthy, who would see no way for himself but through me.

I hailed Wick, and for a moment hadn't recognized the blond-streaked hair of the woman whose kerchief not now in evidence had formerly seemed a token of some American religion even Muslim though I'd assumed she was working with Cap'n and "CEO," but now Storm's voice gathered so in me the scent of virginsbreath and of my blood on his hand and some gross praise given in his cedared atrium in advance of my video-to-come, flights of stairs below, documenting my friend Umo's scheduled shooting, that, turning, I registered Storm's rage or madness only in its synched succession of grins that twitched some screaming code way inside the man somehow presiding in the words that reasoned firm as a priest's invoking *habeas corpus*, or villain's, tight as a lawyer's or parent's, glad as a politician's, modest as an athlete's, sanguine as generals' used to be, mysterious as a friend's or a false friend's, a doomed dominance and resource — these out-loud words pretty fast for Em and me but no, now out of nowhere breathtakingly like coup, like collapse, betraying here —

— like a blow to the chest —

— *Stom's secret weapon*! — "You forget *your* part in this — "
— my sister trying to hear, to hear some complicity alleged with
this ugly person — "the family that thought he was crazy and
wanted to get hold of him mobbed in the street get him outa
there, whom he disowned to go his own way — this leading
Man from Nazareth 'a more hands-on Jesus,' (?) don't you of
all people recall? Not without friends, yet said, Be a passerby
minding your business, but a virtual CEO, Zach? Your word,
we have it on good authority, Zach — " "Zach?" Em says, an
artist it comes to me who can put things together — "and that
family, embarrassed, prudent, of *Jesu's*" —

— of course of course but ... kill his own chances, to trap
me? Storm? —

— when I had by now a way if not a job, my own and no
one else's.

My roads not that remote, a couple of roads, a war apart at
the same time sitting in two vehicles beside two future drivers
I hear Storm still, meant for me his words: Civilians run this
man's war.

And Jesus seeing profit ahead, your guy and mine, Zach,
medicinal saliva and wind (the future of, respectively) you
remember your own ... *mem*ory, was *that* it for godsake? linked
ovens, this Jesus one-on-one live — fighter and economist,
private entrepreneurials, food-fasting and possibly fast-fooding,
sensible take on capital punishment *when appropriate*, a very
early, matching-grant Jesus where if you're not willing to work
forget about it, sloth violates brotherly love, an *American* Jesus
— what you said or are said to have said on the connecting
ovens from you to your sister to your father, who was persuaded
your fancy thoughts were redeemed by this Jesus's view that you
don't beg if you can turn to, and against giving alms, he meant

business, Zach, he had capitalized on what he had going for him, Christ had a job to do.

Em keeps watch but over *what*? — me at that slant of hers, getting it all in one short thought possibly, half-heard, the Scrolls ascribed to her brother, was that it? (Even to *her* through our *father* if she heard?) when the rest, or all I knew, *she* knew: 1) the arrival deep in the palace covered above by 2) a friend's dive, 3) disaster, 4) a cockeyed photographic record, while below 5) a questionable explosion to cover 6) a questionable project (to please an officially Christian government?) followed by 7) a deathly well current and now 8) back home uneasy phone calls and at least two break-ins:

but what can Em be processing now? We're equals (all but) and our father beyond his Reserve against mine cannot be much more of a father for her now than some use of me unknown to her but drifting in upon me — and almost not to be believed, his help, his confounded desire bringing him near some imaginary influence through this speechwriter from Sacramento Storm Nosworthy. But the root of the wind is water, I hear (from my sister, reading aloud). I was driving somewhere in two cars, true American, here in Calif, and back at the war, it was quite real.

The Law Dean touched Em's wrist smiling toothily but grew impatient; alerted, startled (even she), to hear the volume almost in rhyme of voices arriving from the lobby, she turned gracefully to direct the crowd debouching from the elevators down the broad, decisive hall at the end a plenary roomful of folding chairs, those who wait, those in profile who talk to their neighbor, something just to be here, surveying the wreckage of lunch.

Forget I had, / the things I'd said — home from the war, my sleep flooded by some of them. Undeniably said. How meant?

Husky himself had asked this morning if and how I'd meant
what I'd said, and once long ago Umo too; for Em and I had
our joint angle of saying — and now my things had passed into
Storm's listening system through my father, and not only — for
in the elevator the Seal thug captain and my bothersome but this
morning friendly critic Husky jazzing the real not dead-and-
alive Lazarus getting a strange reaction in Storm's eyes, brought
back a friend jogging, gasping, crediting me with reminding
him of what I must now think he had passed on in anger to the
men waiting to train and perhaps question him that day.

Storm's voice and by contagion mine had reached a terrible
hush like silence or unavoidable corruption or like the thought
they rested on, and Wick, who had heard no more of what was
happening than the others, approached now from the windows
and near him the woman from this morning who looked so like
my palace driver, and from the direction of the elevators and the
hallway, the Law Dean, angry as she could be, who would draw
us toward the plenary session where the afternoon Hearings,
if not Storm Nosworthy's welcome fresh from Washington,
promised to go deep.

I a source for the Scrolls.

I said, "If it's all from me suppose I go in there and say so."

"There exist reasons not to. Your friend the diver's citizenship.
Your sister," said the man grasping my arm as he had the day
I was shot. "To say nothing of your father — your name as a
photographer. And quite apart from their *not* being, as you put
it, *all* from you, many think the Scrolls in their own way are
true. Isn't it what we're about?"

I had heard right. And here was Wick, and behind him the
troubled person who hated me beyond even her call of duty as
a coworker with white captain, black CEO, and whose brother

—unless I was way off— served in an MP brigade. My sister hadn't moved from where the Law Dean had left her, her hand in her bag, while Storm was saying we go on faith in everything *else* ... (?) "And the favor we ask of you, it would put a seal on all of this, Zach, a Presidential Seal of course but my seal my friend — the photographer of the Scrolls' arrival, and my word! what a twist your survival that day — your enlistment bumped into the Reserve as you know, and — " ("What's the deal," I said bending confidentially close to his shoulder but Storm now like a show-off sharing some personal phone call or his half anyway for anyone within range) " — look, activating you we cut you a second tour, short form, go where you like, you got fans over there who you know will liaison a... a *deal?* — like — " Storm pointed to the hall — "the twist! People in there who can't wait to hear you." Speak, he meant, of that dive at the Hearings today — Storm tapped me on the chest, my scar, the wound (if only my deluded father, working somewhere, probably in Colorado Springs, for USA Swimming, could be here!), "if I'd only been in time downstairs to see your entry into the well that palace day!" — the *deeffayronce* between me and Storm — and "liaison"? What meant liaison? — for like the future when it was only the past it came to me why he, as his eyes, their weather of prescience now dilated, wanted me back at the war, and he might not, like Em, have known that it had already been in my plans almost for its own sake.

His, flooded by the clang that came down upon us now repeatedly final of the building evacuation alarm that caused people to look around them, inconvenient as an air raid rounding more responsibly with each strike of the clapper, a blame for its own sake — Storm's plans were overtaken utterly awash judging from his eyes, larger suddenly and you might have thought less unready for the great hands of the woman otherwise slight-looking crying, "*Deal!*" reaching over her head then down upon him not me, fists that being all about themselves and their fighting, tuck-position fingers riveted you wielding a hell of an iron bar it seemed but holding nothing. Well apart at the top; at impact together. Yet it was more the consuming clangor of the alarm set off near the brain that for Storm did away with the moment. This was only apparently so remote from any school fire drill alarm for Wick to line his "people" up (most not unhappy to be interrupted) and walk them to the third-floor stairs (when the alarm had gone off the day after my accident just as Wick had begun an account of calculus cure, though hardly thrown off his stride as Storm, his weather eye out for a tornado, surely seemed to have been).

For this present charge, this bell of sound was like the chaos or comfort it saved you from and it was this in those eyes of a man who'd indirectly murdered or meant to two friends of mine hardly countenancing the woman's blow I and somebody else and Wick tried partly in vain to deflect, that told you Storm's mind, if he ever in fact had read a page of the volume of stories on his onyx table in the palace, was too quick to hold a thought. And the thighs and belly too slow, the damage control shallow, sweeping; his a body that had sought always maybe a face to go with it, unfold from it, yet one afternoon a modest blunder touting Jesu's idea for a gray mullet and dogtooth grouper hatchery in a great pond drawn off from the Galilean Lake had got himself slugged by a Christian lender from McLean, Virginia, Storm sustaining the damage you saw, the face he had gained (appropriately in the lobby of the Willard Hotel in DC).

If not the bewildered eye barely flicked at the furious woman but penetrating the bell timeless for all its sequence, term, and alarm where it came from who knew, and what it meant, as we at once began to learn from the black officer I had been calling "CEO" absent some minutes but back to break his news first to my sister; since it was her car cordoned off.

Storm's eyes shocked in their irises by plans put off or worse — no more than that, no less. And by interruption, not fear. And not at all by blame which bewilderment at a thing shouted had once caused in me lifting off a springboard. My sister did not turn to me or the wide eyes of Husky at large looking for a friend, soon that afternoon to be found in my voice in the Hearings room, yet I found a look in her mouth and cheeks and hair cruelly alert as if she'd had her pocket picked by the man who had threatened her over the phone, all thrown into the days following. And I looked back at Storm — he at me, as he could, his bloody temple, the ripped fold at the corner of his mouth; but his eyes, the meat of his eyes — but really the moment *in* them waiting for a bandage, even as the emerging multitude facing another delay would stir, do something, get out of that plenary space or exit the building by emergency stair. Up and down and back again captain and CEO in their combats boarded the major elevator bound for the lobby to screen would-be attendees, reduce them to manageable numbers, just a job, less for Hearings' sake than to remind us who was in charge; and there was the garage.

23 like nobody in world

A Heartland, if memory serves, almost unidentifiable but spotted by me thousands of miles away as a make of trailer seen in Chula V, the exterior door blown out, though, and the toasted styrofoam like bread, like tissue sandwiched between the weather-side thin steel plate and the inner-side vinyl. A raw hole in the steel where the dead bolt had been once lockable if useless against an intruder. A blown-out window aperture where just the framed head of a bald child of nine or ten had quit grinning as I shot, later to be framed out by the Intelligence processor as not germane to prove this mobile home a bio-facility.

My driver recalls what she knew of me, listens for what she's been told to listen for, watch for, this second time around. (Not "get you there" this time, but.) Expecting we'd first go south — to Kut! — but here we are, just over forty miles north of Camp Warhorse where they weld steel sides onto small and medium trucks that can support them, and memory serves to oblong a space of weeds and empty ground where the trailer once sat. It trusts my smart Specialist from Wisconsin to see the boy's face I describe in words, just where the hairline began scarcely fourteen months ago, hear him ask in English are you coming into his house, and hear as a joke, one is pretty sure, his *Don't get too close.* His village abandoned by its residents who were hardly that, having been forcibly moved in under the old regime.

No pictures so far? No pictures by the Photographer of the Scrolls? If only of their arrival by water, it is said. Like me, leaving and arriving, *after* and *before* merging like a war victim's real life, accepting her boat hook, her dumbfoundingly being there (for let your tool do the work according to our father's handy nostrum out in the garage), and a dry shirt and pants. Speechless that late afternoon and untrusting but not dead; speaking, if memory serves, only of Umo's feetfirst dive, of home, the two bloated books in my bag, and the color of winter wheat; and water, what it could do: she might have learned nothing of the jobs I did deep down in the palace though she remembered me.

Memory trusts her knowledge of anthrax, wells, hoopoe nests of olive-colored eggs, she knows also how they improvised claymore mines, knows the road, has a toolbox in back; memory trusts also her interest in, two day's drive at our pace north from here past checkpoints, a bridge by a river from which we could see a field of green winter wheat I had once photographed, she recalled. Because I had told her on the way to the airfield for my flight home the night of the palace bomb, I beginning to smell, drying out, alive and smelling not only of that, the fresh shirt she had given me reeking of cigarettes I had not smoked. Her who had boat-hooked me out of that rank well rush. Needing a wash dreadfully — and the boots and decomposing socks she remembers and actually told people. That I stank? No that there was a nice feeling, almost a confiding, without any. What people? Don't recall, she lies. (For what she told got back maybe clear to the top.) You were tired. Something about a third way — another route? But you didn't know where we were going.

But memory trusts her impression of the northern Mesopotamian plain. U.S. contractor skipping status reports blowing millions on a pipeline intersection under the Tigris without doing the geology first. The division possible of the country up here as a result of this war, at the highest levels in DC thought a great idea. The depth of the water by our little bridge here, her eye a lead line, the current surprising, close. And a body passing, she thought (or the back of a T-shirt inhabited *by* it; or *only* a T-shirt? asks her companion) about which we argued as if about something between us, she hadn't seen the head. Two people alone contain so much. And how was it, being home? she said, and was I not taking pictures this tour? What I had to say about an experimental bridge back home, 450-foot footbridge made of composite carbon-and-glass materials so far twenty times dearer than steel and concrete construction but a tenth the weight — her interest sort of in these things for their own sake, as is her right as a citizen. Or in me. Can you be interested in a bridge as an end in itself? A person yes, though maybe not. And one punctual star we saw above the desert near the bridge and the asphalt plant, and two cars that had pulled in near us.

One night near a city known now for danger, I pointed out a campfire a mile off the road. Did she have any brothers and sisters? Three bros. They were not serving. The campfire? she persisted. Oh just I recalled a campfire that we had approached along the lip of a canyon once in California near the Arizona border and I spoke of it since it was her I happened to be with.

We? said my driver. Me?

"When you were driving me to the palace, you would say that was all you knew, yet it wasn't and you kept adding things and you still would say, That's all I know."

We had time to laugh about it now, she touched me. She checked the oil. The car had been acquired secondhand, thirdhand.

How I evacuated the palace my way. That's life. I didn't even know her name.

How outside the gate she said, This's far as I go. What she had said to me through the window when I left her sandblasted half-camouflaged Suburban to go into the palace. It looked like "chose," her lips meant *you chose to be here.*

That's right, that's right, Livy said.

Her names. Livia to her mother, Olivia to Grampa, Liv to one brother, Olive to the humorous one, Livy to another, O to her father who later calls her Livy, who tells others, *She's never wrong.* As a compliment.

"You enlisted," I said.

Well, trust her on dogs. Where she comes from, hunting, but. (And dog love.) But? Well, here it's son of a dog, *ibn il kalb.* Thought to be filthy, should you touch them you shed your clothes.

Man's best friend.

She gave me a look. She's smug, a little. They should talk to a friend of mine who grew up eating dog. That's right, that's right, she … I had *asked* her once (?), she said (I'm a little astounded) — on the way to the palace (?) about an Asian kid unnamed working with (?) … Film crew, mmhmm —

South, she replies.

The splendid *dive*, though, the lost diver, the palace trashed (a *bank* now?) —

That explosion, she said, people who vanished.

Stuff of legend now, Livy, the selling of the Scrolls.

What a mess when she enlisted, she said (knows I'm interested). Never wrong? I suggest. When Dad's old Saab started making a godawful noise I told him it was the diaphragm on the servo system operating the automatic clutch. No one else got it right.

The captain now. The job she is doing for — the major, excuse me — *Is* it for him? This trip, this tour for (we don't quite talk about) the photographer. "That campfire," she shifts gears. It's night. Somehow, as I try to tell her in a blaring, acrid café full of soldiers my job within the job she comprehends, she pouts with insight, desire, she's compact, hair unfurled, she knows that there is a job within the other job often. I have not called it the Third Way, but she is not unfamiliar with it. The winter wheat, and in the lower corner of my shot from the river a couple looking opposite directions, together. The Bedouin born without eyes. A bald child's shaved-head hairline. Narrow escapes she knows of, amazing reappearances. Life. Her brothers, father, uncle hunting in the snow out of season — for her it's walking in the woods, that's all, she goes along. Farmers' early warning systems at best, the dogs.

The café noisy, the crowd of men aware of us.

My move. What's next? Time can be itself tonight, shifted into new places, reassembling, like power between people.

Though *selugi,* she continues: hunting dog (?), after one of the successors to Alexander's empire, Seleucus in the South. And south is where she is inclined to head, how about it? She had several good harmonicas in the back of the car, all different keys in their red and white Marine Band boxes and protected in a backpack with her things. The major, now, I said. His irritation at her assignment to keep the photographer monitored I know that came down like major's promotion from higher up — and something more. He got her her car replacement, I said, she was lucky.

Me? she touched my wrist. (I hadn't thought what I was saying.) You know about all that. She taps my knuckle as I finish my drink and go to get up (we're going).

No, I ... — how'm I going to explain what I'd pictured, driving with Em from The Inventor's into the Center, the car bomb with Livy's name on it, boys, windowpane shivering, odor of cigarettes on the man's fingers. "I must have heard," I said, holding the door for her.

"No, I don't believe so." She smiles up at me in the dark, the outtake of breath from her nostrils, walking to our billet. Sometimes two people were better than one, she said. That campfire you approached (?), she said.

The person had vanished, I said. (We've double-checked the car, and taken the backpack with the harmonicas and her things.)

You have a sister, I recall.

I had never mentioned any sister. So Livy's been briefed. (Who by? Does this come under briefing? Trickle-down intelligence.) I had hopes for her, and clear as many running feet in a ruined schoolyard a block away sounded distinct from the Metal Rock massing objective at a distance and distinct from, close by, the indigenous instrumental we had been told was about a murdered Palestinian child — it came to me that they were after maybe the Chaplain (Storm Nosworthy's baby still at large) yet even Storm didn't matter now at a distance except as someone associated with my father, and I asked Livy why she'd enlisted and she said she would dredge that up for me sometime, she was no prize package and —

Dredge? I'd brace myself. Perhaps so, she said.

Interested in her, but not without doubt, I told her something of a story inspired as the Russian in Chula V, the teller, had himself been inspired when, before shipping out again, I had come by the sound studio one day (bearing gifts in case).

A story the Russian for all his affable suspicion could not know had filled in my own: that the "water" archaeologist, the specialist, on the Scrolls team — who, that day of the palace, getting a brainstorm, was the one whose steps with a guard I had heard descending as I was making my getaway — and a third person trying to keep up — heard just as I dropped into the well current, like a casual death by elimination, Why I Enlisted opening unexpected reasons then as I sank and swam, some dredged-up remains of which from the virtual sky Livy herself had boat-hooked further down — this specialist, said the Russian on his own track, had got himself killed: what you get for a Mexico vacation but almost certainly had been investigating fallout from Scrolls explosion, the Russian had it on good authority ("eef you recall our conversation" — as if *that* had been what we'd talked about on the intensely inescapable tiles of a pool!). An archaeologist of water itself, said the Russian, holding forth a bit for present company but with a savor of intelligence — for who knows what "vahter" brings with it from where it was to where it will go, "he tell me heemself" — and where eez division between what-has-been and what-weel-be? — "a shout in the meedle of the air, eh," the Russian adds (not lost on me): and water archaeologist had been drawn to the foundations of this palace as a sinkhole for the net of horizontal wells "like secret map across land before even Scrolls were found."

Inspired by suspicion to tempt me to betray he didn't quite know what — by delusions of tactics perhaps, the Russian had himself betrayed more than he knew: for the archaeology team-member whose steps coming down I'd heard along with those of guard and third party, was none other than the ill-fated specialist written up in the magazine I had underlined who'd been independently tracing someone not to be identified to Livy *I* knew, a friend (I thought now *two* friends, Umo and the Chaplain) —

nor, for safety's sake, even the person with whom I stood my ground listening to the foreign sound engineer play the authority, interrupting himself to go and dive into his earphones, adjust a dial, keep us waiting, and come back — and something else that all but came to me, about the archaeologist getting a brainstorm at that moment after the explosion *and* after a soldier the Russian had talked with had just jumped down into the void.

But the Russian, a dark and gravitational or sinkhole or routine imagination but without real character, could never quite put real things together — my reluctance to learn he was not Russian but Ukraine; my vanishing down the bomb rupture in the palace diving well after the water; and the object of that archaeologist's search then and later, what he might have said publicly and to Storm who might not want an actual Lazarus on his hands; then, home again in California weeks later, from his path one morning when he had some typically Russian or Ukrainian business I figured at the University looking up to see *me* observing him from the famous footbridge high above; our host only now in his place of work in Chula V recognizing the dark-haired girl close up who had been with me at the rail, her legs, her look, and recalling the "meedair shout," yet that the archaeologist, with that profound specialty had been seeking not me but an underwater photographer (and Navy Chaplain) had entered the Russian's brain no further than I had permitted it into my midnight story to Livy inspired by suddenly guessing her particular mission assigned by some headless HQ, though the Russian was much taken with my sister who had come with me to Chula V, for each to each a goodbye errand. What was hers? "Lucky your little war is done with," he said.

He had lifted the earphones off and stared at a computer screen. So we had just stopped by? he went on, secretly alert. "Our Umo doesn't work here any more," he said, and laughed at his joke. Found something better, I said. Long tables, mixers, swivel chairs, screwdrivers, window into another room. I had something for Umo, I said. Em at the far end, the Russian let the phone ring, cagey, his back very straight, physically strong. Everyone has an instinct. "He's prob'ly dying somewhere, I mean diving," said the Russian, making a joke. "Nothing throws *heem* off."

My gift would not be posthumous I felt sure. My sister had a good look around; returning to our end she might have been thinking of renting the place. She picked up a screwdriver, a big one with a black rubber handle, looked at it, a Phillips-head; looked at me, pouted. Russian measured the distance to Em's humor, her eyes, her breasts, her hips, in a dress today, so it was in self-defense that he plotted the positions of everything here, equipment, speakers, job clipboards hanging, the sound of the phone. "He deed what I told him. Good working relationship." And? "He told me things."

"Yeah?" said Em. The Russian thought something was up, I

thought of the deserter, the way Umo had been used, even of my father for an instant, whom I did not think of.

"Why he came here in first place. His trucking: where he went. He kept that wreck running. Music. The cops. Why he came here."

"Why did he come here?" said my sister. Russian found this amusing. "Some t*rr*ash he read in a book. He gotta get some papers. That's where you came in, right?" the Russian grinned at me narrowly. "He lied about age, no?" "What book?" my sister said.

"A nine-thousand-mile job with you guys and he doesn't have papers?" I said.

In the eyes contempt beaming for an illegal trying to survive. "Papers we deescussed."

"And the deserter?" I signaled Em, we were going. She picked up an invoice off a stack of cartons.

"Discussed many things. Mexico, drugs, music, Chula Vista, you and your vahter," the Russian seemed to ignore my question. "Lied about his age?" "Both ways, up, down," was the reply. "*Well*," the Russian said then, sagely ... "talked about *you*," he said, "and *you*," flicking his eyes at Em. "And your vahter when he shouted meedair."

My sister frowned at me and my life. "Milt," I said — with a gesture, we were going — *Milt* had told Umo, why would either friend speak to others of it? "It was the half gainer," said the Russian as if he knew. "So what you bring?" he asked me.

Em flapped the invoice. "Whadda ya got there?" said the man.

Why had Em come along? It was my next-to-last week, I was going back, a brief tour. Yet what my dearest only sister thought she owed me for — and astonished by my intervening at the previous afternoon's Hearings when CEO and captain thought they were hustling Husky away at the end of the day and discovered they were not going to do that and stood publicly warned in front of a hundred willing Americans — for who was this brother of hers? — it was, I believed, no more than that I knew where somebody was that especially Storm wanted to catch up with. *And* Em came along today guessing it wouldn't be Umo but the Russian I would run into, and said later when she'd looked down from the bridge at him looking up that he had the unafraid forehead of a killer — "a life you could miss without a misery." Also she came along to Chula V because her car liked the road and she liked to drive; and she believed something was going to get said.

The person I loved, but more. "*My tools took human faces,*" her poet had said in my sister's voice reading to me the night of the accident having sought to protect, bathe, soothe, heal, use a bloody abrasion wound dividing my heart nearly, and painfully imperceptibly kissing the raging tissues and opening her book — had she a headache building in her temples? — which became my homework for a Wick quiz I wouldn't miss the next unbreathable morning then miraculously foregone by him for this new calculus he would glimpse for us of narrowing down from your position to some instant speed if it ever could exist while also narrowing down even more magically and for me that hour from speed to speed to where you are, for the assistant coach knew where I was. Between what has been and what will be, that horrendous crash dive to be rethought — though paused as gravity rushing through you isn't?

"Mul*tee*ple half gainers!" the Russian pounded a table. "Coach yelling, 'Too far out, meedle of the air, too far out!'"

"Umo wasn't *there,*" said Em, letting the invoice fall sailing onto

barely a corner of the long table. ("*Milt*," I said.) "Somebody
tawled him, that's all. And so you quit half gainer and went up
for tweest," said the Russian dryly.

"And then?" I said, wondering if Umo had grasped what
Milt could not.

"I would haf killed him," said the Russian, creature of eerie
attention and arrested imagination, his accent distinctly correct
this time. "Your father?" I said. We turned back at the door.

"Never had one. Let us say first cousin," our man grinned,
"what does it matter, it's done." "What's done?" "But could it
have been meedair, to cause such an accident? No, I think it
was as you hopped and landed on board before leaving it that
he shouded." What the Russian saw in my face — a standoff
between us. "Umo had sympaty — whatever happen with *his*
vahter — those border Chinese working all over the place.
Eemigrant mentality." The Russian said *father* like he said *water*.

Was he on a green card? I asked — I'm half out the door
holding it for Em, who weighs a step, because he is not done with
us, *he* thinks: "You did not follow his coaching. He was testing
you." "Your cousin," Em said, "was it a him?" "But so what," the
Russian said, "some asshole shouts, 'Go fuck yourself,' so what
if you crash? You see I remember the words 'Go fuck yourself all
night, be your *own* fucking vahter.'"

Em is about to shift into Drive, he's out here rapping at
my window and I run it down. "He sayed you understand half
gainer like nobody in world." "Who?" "Inertial, I forget — it
doesn't matter. Tweest also, but." I had brought something (?),
the Russian asked ... for Umo?

News, I said. His citizenship. It had come through.

Bending to the window, stunned, "Maybe I see him," the
Ukraine sound engineer said rather slowly. I thought he would

reach in or go grab a tire iron. He shouted at us as we turned into the road north, "Feegurehead woman" the words my father's on my half gainer virtually. Someone just like Cheeky came out of the 7/11 with a newspaper and a pink bottle of Snapple with a straw sticking out of it. "Cheeky," I said, pointing. Em understood and didn't look.

"So was that all?" She was shaken and lit a cigarette. Or I lit it for her. I knew what it was, and it was not Umo or the Russian. I remember talking for a couple of miles. It was stupider the truer it was, because she was thinking about her father, what to do about him. I talked about him maybe setting myself up with such fluent indifference. Yet then, "What was the trashy book that was why Umo came here?" I thought she knew but was thinking of us, our father, our family.

24   your real job

Maybe the only way you get to do your real job is when you're set up by outsiders who use you but they don't know what they're doing, I know I said, finding it as easy to talk as if I and Em on a sunny day in California had been marketers around an oval table, and simple for me in words to be indifferent or unforgiving, wherever he was, in Washington at some desk liaison job that would get him what he wanted in swimming, or in Colorado Springs, or back here for a short weekend with our mother, who said, We're a good people — which he would say of an individual and without the *a* — of the CPA with the long jaw, "He's good people," as if he came with a group; or of Wick, who covered for Dad. So the Russian and the other one used Umo, and Storm used them in order to use me after Dad thought he was using Storm who used Dad to use me and even Em — "even you" — *through* me … I caught the smell of aloes and jasmine from her knees apparently — But the music video project, she said, watching the road, her cell in her lap, where did that begin? — "And look at them all, where it all got them," I said.

A Well of Lebanon spa closed I remember, a fountain elsewhere for the moment, for none of this smart, gathered indictment and story was of interest to the person next to me. It was as if we were not getting anywhere, because the opposite was true, which later I grasped as the real job, receding into itself as we overtook it. Static on the radio, so many littler and littler things, her bike seat stolen from the trunk in the parking garage before she could get down there, anger in her eye when I noticed sweat on her upper lip, a bubble at the top of the windshield where a grain of gravel had been spun up by a passing truck — did she want some fruit we drove by (?) and her mouth pouting in concentration upon less and less, erasing a dimple, meant she might have to pull over and have a laugh, which didn't mean we would never get back for we were not hopeless about all the tiny things adding up. ("Did he think Storm would get me into Yale?" I joked but it was no more true to what it came to me was "the real job" than my little string of people using people.) And somewhere in all of this she asked like a fact what we had done to drive him away — We were always wrong, I said — No we were always right, Em said, angry with herself almost indifferent to me. And I was able to say that we had made use of him to his surprise.

How? I in a silence I occupied could feel her ask; and at me from the north-bright windshield came the unjust *Why do you persecute me?* war he would wage on us now and again, but my answer to her: "to have our life."

What had happened to precipitate Dad's diving-accident words Em had never asked, nor why they threw me off, an experienced performer. You can't know, for one thing, no more than why people have the voices they do. Em not one of those women's voices, squeezed, pinched, all-business, and/or going on about nothing, soliciting (but it's their job) on the phone, talking in line in a public place to another woman, a store, finding a friend to exchange emergency insights with at the same pace and with same vocal cord and nasal quick talk. European women and even African didn't sound like this, not Polish, not even Mexican. My sister, though, was almost a singer in speech or a natural actress, sly or guttural too when I think of what she could say, and with a stagy range she kept for me.

So I remember summing up, in the car-quiet, a danger-corrupted year or two, leaving out the Scrolls mostly, but what was to be done about our father, too.

While swelling in my own voice I felt Em's in my chest that always seemed to have returned from a droll surprise and disappointment to become her own surprise and overdrive — "'I have a Navy in the West,'" (!) quoted from our poet in an e-mail intercepted I believe by Intelligence and Storm — and subtlety riding alongside my voice now with gift, anger, mouth, riding north also in her car in which, since it had not blown up, though someone had Remoted her trunk open in the parking garage the other day of my reeling, remarkable, but perhaps irrelevant analysis of the full twist in the afternoon to the plenary Competition Hearings (and taken her bike seat), she was on the move away from home and by some route not yet valued away from her brother who would be also far away and with other wheels.

All of which, not just the sound guy's quote from Dad, was turning over in Em's mind when she said, "Was that all?" and I said I was going back for a second tour.

My driver driving me sometimes to distraction thank God complained at our slow progress south. For we would stop often, in mixed towns around the capital. But look, it was she who'd made al Kut our southeast destination if not beyond, where I had said I had unfinished business which she I knew took to mean someone they thought I would lead them to. Hey, from here a hundred fifty miles dead south along the watercourse you would see its vandalized gates and dilapidated, dam-like barriers, she told me, called barrages to level the flow, and one of the embattled if not poorer oil fields near where she had seen twenty of our own oil tanker trucks lined up single-file — near Nassiriya, a few flat-roofed yellow-mud houses left here somewhere once the silver worker we kept an eye on who followed a religion of John the Baptist and Shem and the Mandaean Enos but one day died of burns inflicted by Sunni visitors with his own instruments — though all this made less and less difference to me. I was happy to have her to talk to, be with, she was good — we were both happy about that, we talked fast and it was warm and sexy, her beret in her lap. She said No it was I who had said Kut, I had unfinished business, yet had never, she added, told her on the way to the palace or since —

"That turned-around morning —"

— what I had said before I shot that picture.

"It moved you, Livy —"

That wasn't all.

"You said the picture moved you no end ...."

The Reservist —

"Powerlifter, friend of my *father's* — salesman, my father didn't — one of *those* friends — in the picture arm-wrestling with the do-rag Triple Canopy construction mercenary, I told your beloved boss — "

Going a little far with Livy didn't stop her: "It was him like a wild horse, the eyes — someone under the table too, cropped out of the picture, a woman tied up *you* said," my driver, my companion, I better believe her, Livy said, because remembering what happened she was never wrong. Well, I didn't want to be the first to give her negative feedback. No, all Dad meant was telling him and her brothers not to believe a neighbor that if you're wading in a stream deer won't notice you.

I said one reason obviously she enlisted was a talent —

She agreed but —

— a talent for Intelligence, I finished my thought, she picked up something *I'd* said, That turned-*around* morning? (Oh now she saw, it was just the way things went at the pool. I said No it was something else before that, the drive to the palace, for she had reminded me of seeing things in reverse as if to rerun them.) Meanwhile, if I was right, her assignment made less and less difference to me, a cushy slot compared to most women, leaving us with the mysterious real job like exactly where we were and where we were coming from, my sister's one step forward two back or diagonal or a relief so I very nearly told Livy the job within the job idea my Chaplain credited *me* with — long dead, my underwater friend and no matter what they'd told her to watch for she was never going to see me in contact with him, I very nearly told her, but … nor could I explain that flash turnaround so arriving at palace came first, leaving from hotel in repainted Chevy Suburban last.

Did she recall me asking about an Asian kid with a film crew? Asking, yes. I had gotten him his citizenship even though they thought he was dead. Livy drove. What kind of citizenship was that? Maybe it brings you back to life, I said.

An American soldier in the road wanted something. There's more to it, I said.

We stopped for him. He had his headphones on. Where was he going? It was the drive-bys, four in Kut last week. We gave him a cigarette he didn't want. He took some crackers and a newspaper we unloaded on him. He just wanted to talk. He was interested in Livy, talking across me. He said the Secretary of War had announced that you could make a claymore out of office supplies, some tape, some toner, talc, pepper, a straw he almost forgot, he listed them. Did we know that a palace was being renovated for a bank? I said it was a branch of the Euphrates. Drive-bys worried him, what it was was you're the target but they're moving. He was nodding at us. He didn't want a lift. We left him standing there, his headphones, what was he listening to? — the Base newspaper under his arm. He didn't belong out on the road, Livy said, she knew him. His unit anyway. Which wasn't Kut. One reason she enlisted she was good with people, I said. We arrived at a roadblock. Was that it? she said, was that — ? *Most* people, I added.

—was that all?

It wasn't a reason in itself, but maybe it was, I said. A dusty militiaman in a T-shirt got in back with a rifle and heaved a sigh.

Well, the Russian's story, she wanted to get that straight. Archaeologist of ... (?).

Livy, I said.

Of *water,* Livy said. She seemed to ignore the guy in back. And he had discovered the well intersection under the palace — (?)

The intersection of the whole — .

— before the Scrolls — ? Livy was armed. She sniffed, she kept an eye in the mirror, what was the militiaman sitting on?

A hundred yards off the road a hooded man was rifle-butting three it looked like men on the ground. One, with a wine cask for a belly, got up like a snowboarder who's been having balance problems, and was shot. "Why don't you do something about that?" I said to the militiaman. "What you have in trawnk?" he said. His automatic rifle had a taped-together ammunition clip. He opened his door. He said that we were not moving, Livy braked and he got out, leaving the door open, and walked up ahead.

"He discovered it before the Scrolls were even *found*?" Livy finished her question, her fingers on the door handle.

"If they *were* found." "What else could they be?" I got out and shut the rear door. Words came to me and I said them, that my sister had once read out loud: "'Dust is the only Secret — / Death, the only ...'" "Get inside," said my driver. "'... the only One / You cannot — '"

"Please." "'You cannot find out all about / In his "native town."'"

"Thanks. What else could they be? I think we're moving."

"Made up, I guess. And he was — this archaeologist was," I said, "liquidated. In Mexico (?)." She'd thought I would take a picture.

I was telling this woman who might be pumping me that what didn't get written up was the day that she'd delivered me when the Scrolls were supposed to come in by water and the bomb went off and the Scrolls were salvaged, most of it, and a half hour later —

Livy's window caught a blow from a rifle butt and the militiaman with the moustache was back just as the two cars ahead of us and the truck ahead of them took off and we with them and on my side out off the road a hundred yards the fat man who'd been shot in the leg was beating someone on the ground with a rifle butt and our militiaman running up stopped and lifted his musket — "Friendly fire, step on it" — but something, a cigarette, hit him from a car window, and he acted like it was a dog of a wasp at him, and I knew Liv had heard the words I'd come up with. "What did I say? — good with people." She thought about it.

Her boss phoned all afternoon, she knew it was him, where there's a will there's a way, we were talking till two in the morning, I debriefed on recent events. The mobile gave up, and there was nothing left of our candles, one after the other, the flame shadowing her blond and dark hair as if her hair were the light, and I debriefed on the Competition Hearings back home, my talk on diving — the Twist, what you actually did, the time factor, competing not against but (in this slippery way recalling by chance the gray-haired square-shouldered man over on my left as my old girlfriend Liz's Navy now retired husband) … One more candle then, a special one I thought found at the bottom of Livy's bag and only when it was down to nothing she said it was in honor of us and her uncle in Australia had sent it to her on her enlistment a year ago it was one of the sixteen-thousand-plus candles a minister had organized along the median of his town in the mountains to remember the civilian dead swept under the carpet in this unconscionable war and this candle had been blown out by the wind and rescued by her uncle, all they had was paper guards, no hurricane sleeves.

I had tossed a live coal from the campfire into the stream where we were camping once in a canyon, I was telling her when the mobile rang. I thought she better answer it. She explained what I wrongly (why should I have?) told her she didn't need to — what a mess at home with her enlistment, and family friends were worse. Vietnam-vet banker, hotel administration prof, mortgage broker, working mom attorneys, sporting goods equipment, all these tough guys in the neighborhood trashing the war — like, shoulda got out before we got in — and their legendary high school math teacher Ms. Mansfield, still unretired, hey younger programmers, though a *much* younger coach from Romania backed the war — nuke thaim if we need to, on'y keeding —

Gymnastics, I said.

Howdjou know that? she said. I said I had a brother making an insurance run at mid six figures before he hits twenty-five, irony is it's the worst risk he could take with his life.

That campfire sounded nice, she could see it, the stream, the canyon, no canyons like that in Wisconsin. She was a good camper.

I held her for a long time, like reflections flickering on the walls. Our campfire, I said. Here thirty miles north of al Kut vehicles weighing down the asphalt all night, a billet for us at a faithful old base someone said the Under Secretary of Defense was going to pay a flyby visit to.

She's the one at home Dad said was never wrong. 'cause she looked up to him. Did I know Livy at all? Yes, going to sleep dissolved, thinking of sixteen thousand candles, talking softly as if anyone would hear us. Waking up, hungry —

But the Russian …

We weren't done with him.

And the archaeologist.

Went back down to take another look.

At the blast area, yeah. Good idea. Livy looking down at me, propped on her elbow.

"He heard I was down there …"

"Oh the Russian!" "Ukrainian." "Like a big wrestler?" "Not that big." "We know him."

There it was again, the GI music-listening project, my friend coming in (as my father guaranteed) "handy" to dive with such originality it had been ignored at a moment when they wanted me at poolside. Dad could have swatted Storm like a fat, stumbling fly though he was not fat or hit like a bug with his windshield on a hot and threatening day, couldn't he?— upstairs with brownish blood on his pants brownish and blurred and a monitor screen above the virginsbreath and the little volume of large short stories, and I had told the Russian's little story like him to tempt a listener but this one wouldn't betray her assignment, which I knew was to use me to pick up the track of the Chaplain. "They're supposed to be so warm," I said, as her mobile rang. "Not him." "No." "No," she pursed her lips, "he never fooled me." "How come you're never wrong?" "Never volunteer anything. Wait till they ask."

25   out

"That's all it was," I at last replied. My sister tossed her cigarette, we'd come a couple of miles up the highway. She put three fingers to her temple. "It was on his mind," she said. "Mostly his," I said, thinking the night before the dive, when I almost fainted in my boxers seeing him at the other end in the bathroom doorway, and looked once and went in my room and never lost it, and we sort of shook our heads about it now in the car, spinning our wheels. "I remember," she said.

"Because I told you in the morning." "I remember everything," Em's voice was husky and droll. "I wish I remembered everything you read to me, but I kind of do," I said. "I remember what I didn't," she said.

The Directory on the floor, catalogues strewn among books, brochures, Summer programs, I didn't know what. And Dad coming in on the kiss that didn't end. "Not easy for him."

The Coaches Directory entry. I'd forgotten how she censored it. "He doesn't like writing. But there it is. Résumé, nothing to it. Methods, goals — 'no secrets,' 'industrious,' 'punctual.'

Mom said how he agonized late-night. Then you — the son 'who'" — her pause (she was "E" then) like everything equal, gripping, ready to move, and present in her speech and reading always for the brother infinitely worth attending to — "'who, it was ruefully doubted could ever have it in him to double as diver slash swimmer on the East Hill 'Imperial' team West Zone USA Swimming affiliate.'" An omission — (Wait, she said under her breath) — hard to exactly recall as if it was not so much right then in the entry on page 153 but a few words on so that, as she would do when she sight-read a hymn, a Sousa march, the Haydn, or "I Thought About You" (where I now added a personal campfire to the standard's stream, train, cars parked, and that A flat 13 chord Em showed me that comes after "you," just *before* you hit the going-away G9 again), she was reading a little ahead at the same time. Like a dive, I had thought filled to the brim with the life and apparent slowness of a full twist finding myself at the top standing in front of the plenary session following not a hard act to follow erstwhile speechwriter Storm's proxy welcome from the Chief Executive ("that we are one American family in healthy competition brother and sister") and describing at Storm's behest the full twist wondering what had happened to Em though relieved to learn her car was OK in the parking garage.

"That birthday envelope I wrapped."

What was in it, Dad had held it up to the light, *money?* Held like a slide above the dinner table after I'd gone to the other party which turned out to be an enlistment party. It was not a poem, he was sure (though he never understood that I would learn to write, or how), and definitely not drugs (a hint of humor, warmth). Maybe some artwork? or words of wisdom (?) — or a will! Em had provided the blue ribbon, which Dad had been loath to disturb. "*Happy Returns*" was in her high, round hand. "It was like a fortune," she said to me both hands on the wheel, "somebody just wrote it with no one specific in mind but it didn't come out that way."

I took our mess hall trays away when Livy answered her ringtone, tilting her head as if she were taking the call while out walking, and I felt her waving a hand behind me to keep me there at the long table (near two friendly men in fatigues with, as it happened, the telltale cross on the collar). I didn't like whatever was being said at the other end of her cell, but not because the major would want her back at headquarters.

I stopped opposite the Chaplains, noticing a copy of the Scrolls propped open with a mug and a knife between two breakfast trays. What did they think of it? The elder said, Thought-provoking even if it's not quite from that time. Either it is or it's made-up, said his friend. From what? said the first. You think He knew anything about fish hatcheries? said the other. Wind energy, said the elder, oh shoot, the Apostle Thomas said some of that stuff a century or two later — India he got to. Further, said the other. It is what it is, said the elder to me like a whatchamacallit — benediction. Shoptalk they cut off abruptly, smiling and shaking hands after I had put down my two trays. The Chaplains had a look at Livy leaning into her cell but slanting a friendly look our way.

Her cell did not make her seem between. And in the car presently her absent boss seemed more the proxy than she relaying what she knew wouldn't surprise me but the trip was scrubbed and we had to turn around but she'd told him the car was heating up and we might need another day. She had left something out, I knew, sealed in a fond female act just as she had made our time a gift. And as we drove I marked her being "thoughtful" (my mother's word if you were being quiet and she had to know why). Like increments of delay, intelligent breath, this thoughtfulness — hope, control — touched by me she was — nothing too wrong between us if she could only privately plan. "Oh I'm no prize package," Livy said coming along what she said was Highway 27 toward a bridge.

We were suddenly enveloped in dust from truck traffic congestion and the desert and we ran up the windows and we kissed each other: Was it true I had said at those Hearings in California that the President should get the No-*Bid* Peace Prize? I nodded skeptically. Where'd she hear that? She tapped her cell and put us in gear. I said I had taken a hit or two and came out better on a particular dive I had explained the competitive fine points of, though was that even it? — I had taken a hit or two. Livy said I had to protect myself, where was my camera? — and it came to me that the major might not be my friend.

We weren't turning back the way we'd come, but wherever you are things go on behind your back and the real job of your life comes in pieces wherever you think you're going, to be at the war or opposing it or answering a stranger or at a bridge.

I had a hunch they'd decided my Chaplain underwater photographer was dead. I figured that was the good news.

His torn scrap of Scroll snatched by me supposedly lost from a master that had been part-destroyed on arrival in the depths of the palace yet present in the eventual book, argued an explosion not by insurgents but by the purveyors of the book whose master text in the custody of Administration scholars (and in the absence of the underwater photographer's voice and witness) had gone largely unchallenged.

And would go unchallenged, except for me, armed with the scrap that could now be harmless without me. Yet who but a crank would put down the appeal of these so-called Scrolls, this small commodity?

Another historical Jesus you might say sold by authority to an inspired people. American Jesus. Humbled but blessed by the term outlook for a democracy of those who are motivated. It was one thing that hadn't quite come up with Livy — the Scrolls. The Cross found a whole new world of meaning when the Chief Executive with his unique distance on the issues of our time calls for the supreme sacrifice from some of our families. God's Lottery. Jesu's Casino.

I was moved to have told Livy how I plucked a coal from the campfire and tossed it into the stream we found along the floor of the canyon, how it hissed meeting its reflection; like recalling what Em read me. Like a member of the family, Livy kept on about little things — that other lonely campfire in extreme southeastern California that my sister and I had approached over the ridge of a canyon in search of water which, in talk, spread to another fire that had flickered on the horizon of my dive talk to the Competition Hearings people, I who might not know how to compete. One dark summer night swimming out to the neighbor's float and leaving our suits on the old planks and skinny-diving into the bare and waiting lake. The arc, the entry, my sister's fear of the unknown depth at Pyramid scooting up almost as her head met the water — who swam pretty well, with a quick long stroke or a short, bent-elbowed stroke but not quite with my feeling for the water.

How the dive itself wants, yes, to outwit the water below yet never maybe get there, be it a two-and-a-half tuck or a half twist or, as I'll show, full, I told the Hearings people, though Em wasn't there yet.

And to Livy, back at the war a month later, that campfire down the lake shore six summers ago noticed only upon arriving at the float, for we saw then beyond this cove to a point on the next, minute, darting flames, and gathered there savage faces you only saw when you got this far from shore — a shoreline, the Earth, *others*; yet not to Livy us diving, emerging on the canvas edge of the float, my sister on her knees, her arms, her flickering body observing the darkness of the lake; then my patented backflip, then Em jumping in, hand-in-hand the two of us, treading water, her fingers on my shoulders, remembering things said at dinner, snickering, swallowing water, giggling, when subtly there were flashlights on our shore here forty yards away prowling our rocks bobbing and stopping; one lifting across the water, finding us before we went briefly under and beyond us the swimsuits left on the clammy planks, her gleaming white, my dark, her legs now around me, giggling low, her whisper the lake naked on us, *Let's swim in and make a run for the towel,* the second flashlight in our eyes, was it the dinner guest's?

(*Bliss*, I remembered.) "Bliss, understand me, bliss — up, out off the board, exposed," I said to the Hearings the almost endlessly delayed afternoon after we were done with the evacuation alarm, and Storm, walking wounded, bandaged and God knows what under the bandage, had given the executive welcome clear from DC (and still no Em) — thinking what do I do now? — Scrolls, Umo, Dad, future, a going-back verbal agreement with the unspeakable Storm; but *Bliss*, Em — "you have basically three axis variants," I went on, maybe being in myself jumping hand-in-hand off the float, what I was thinking to break down. "First, the fore-and-aft axis of your body remains constant and you turn forward or backward, spin, whatever.

Second variant, body axis itself turns, as in twist, half and full; and the old fore-and-aft of number one becomes just the dive's own axis but where *is* that dive? And third" — I saw Husky, Wick, Bea, a square-shouldered, gray-haired, clean military sort younger than he looked whom I had met (if I could only remember — and so it *seemed* important — and are all these faces accredited?); and CEO and captain and between them the woman who resembled Livy who had attacked Storm a scant hour and a half ago; who, at the back, his job done, slipping out, grinning through a gauze and adhesive creation that looked like what was left of a bandage covering his whole face, Storm himself, but where was Em? gone in the car? — "number three," I said, "'Bliss,' I'll say, joining the first two in the slipperiest of all so you forget ... you forget ... how exposed you are further out — and who's watching or competing *against* you which is in your mind (excuse me) but you ..." "'Happy Returns' for Godsake," the light changed, she was a good driver — we're not giggling in the water about a dinner guest, or in a Bureau of Land Management zone we think trudging toward that other campfire beyond the canyon ridge, or in her room, reading out loud. "He had it coming, I don't say he didn't, but you, you still don't know what was in The Inventor's envelope."

"'Food for thought,' Mom said."

I hear myself not joking quite but doubled. And Em easing her pedal recalling, half-reciting, *"absentee slash parent we knew of you and beg to doubt,'"* from The Inventor's envelope (the fifth in my life by my count), *"proud father has it in his absence'* something something *'to be both here and not'* (wait, honey" — the endearment word from her odd again or, maybe like me, she's in two places) — *"'tiger and fish ... enigma'* (I think) *'For'* (what was it, Zach? didn't you tell *me* some of this?) *'right*

words will do more than all a parent' (I forget) *'deeds away by'* yes!
something something and ... *'rue the day thinker slash dreamer
doubles the single vein* — ' well 'absentee' is clear enough — hey,
who knows what he means?" — Em made a sound — "he's
right here with us, our Inventor — some of it's familiar though
I swear, 'rue the day' and 'slash' spelled out, I ask you!"

"Is it us he means or — " (just words now out in the car
—) I recalled whatever — it was not only board-shy and Dad's
breathing but my own small wave receding down the beach like
a great thing to see I nearly held onto — the envelope not quite
so anonymous after all a cooked fortune revealed on the anvil
of our aims to be annealed not by dumping cold water but by
long ruminating, I said to my sister. Not funny. Our wheels
spinning. "You may laugh," she said — we passed a stand with
lemons stacked on skewers and I remembered getting out of
Umo's truck having had enough — "but it's *my* father, not
just yours." "He tried to do too much probably," I said. I had
imagined he would be present for my Hearings talk on diving.

Instead Em. Come in haste, there she'd been at the back in
time for Husky's loud words with me and CEO and captain
appearing front and back to grab an arm to remove him, when I
was the one (and another person's gesture I took in but recalled
only later). For what Husky did to speak up they were right
enough to try to get him out of there, as my own admonitory
interdiction to CEO and captain proved a signal hit for the
majority of the assembled accredited. And our military presence
hadn't gone unremarked even among such a loyal citizenry and,
now on hand at the back, my own latecomer sister trying to
think things through still had a car to drive me to Chula Vista a
week later gathering my resources.

"See, it's heating up," Livy said, she'd been wondering about my California campfire just beyond the canyon ridge, in fair flame though mysteriously deserted, but she meant the car now. We approached the bridge in low gear. "That's what you told your ..." A smile between us — *boss*, I meant. "In case," she says. "You must have known," I said. "What I know is ..." "Well, you're never wrong." "That campfire above the canyon? when you were looking for water late at night?"

"Bliss."

"Bliss?"

"' ... *the plaything of the child,*' Livy — '*The secret of the man*' — yeah that's it — ' *The sacred stealth of Boy and Girl / Rebuke it if we can,*' it comes right back."

"I wouldn't know," said Livy; "that campfire, though, was your father."

"We found two gallons of water but left them," I said, stunned, not exactly agreeing.

But now exposed by the bridge, oncoming.

Improvised by our own Corps of Engineers, a floating bridge, if we speak of the foundations laid across the river for a modest span to handle fifty thousand of us a day. You would hardly know what lay below arriving on foot. No vast perspective of six miles of Seattle concrete pontoons, and, once on, not the vibration of a suspension bridge, the constant flood beneath. Yet like why you enlisted, a swirling voice transmitted from the river and the structure to our feet having left the car to walk for the sake of it.

I was exposed. It was ahead always. It was base and banal news whatever the major had phoned in.

Through the burden of vehicle sound Livy heard the cries

ahead and looked at me. She said, "That photographer? They gave up on him. I believe he was a Chaplain."

News, I thought. "Lost in action maybe," Livy said, eyeing me.

No link to our trip, of course. Her assignment, her men. "Where is the *cam*era?" A shout, a shriek coming up from below. "And that Nosworthy?" — her voice behind me now — "with the face?"

From the barrier I could see a sturdy child in the water swung overwhelmingly by the surging tracks of river that came together there. He hung on to some projection he could just reach with one hand below the roll of currents, it might be trying to pull him lower. The cries not his. I ran ahead and found a way down. Not a high bridge but a serious crossing. Below me two women on the ledge of a pontoon a dozen feet above the water seemed unable to move turning back and forth calling for help, calling to the children — there were two children in the water. It seemed like one. The women, their heads covered, found themselves trapped by need, not their own risk.

On the ladder I heard Livy call. She couldn't leave the car.

I looked up at her. I had stopped for a second. "Stay," she said. She meant don't come back up. What would I do, climb back up the ladder to see if my father was the one who'd caught up with Storm? Never in the world, and I do not forgive him even for not being the one who trained the flashlight on two naked kids racing for a beach towel that comes into view, huge and yellow draped over a rock, but figure he was behind the government's almost unprecedentedly turning Umo down, finding *his* decision unacceptable when, just before I left, he had reportedly declined our offer of citizenship. Umo's value as an Olympic prospect? China's part in this.

A paint job on a door may be a job with some exchange value to split your heart between here and there — what did Umo owe The Inventor?

I have the time of others to work with, more than they know, and another father though this old mole died but not to me, and a faint ringtone is neither here nor there but like family to be gathered in and understood in its time: look at a half twist on tape, rerun it, the arch all but inertial, at the top the head-tilt leading the way for the shoulder and its extended arm to bank into what becomes a back dive, an axis that was always there, timeless, and you're unbeatable you know then, but what (I ask the Hearings) is this half or full twist like? — it's that you have no competitors, they're another zone. This was my Chinese diver's secret the day of the palace, his dive a jump — feet*first*, as they describe how the Reservist gets mustered out of this war — (*laughter somewhere*) — his twist and the three different positions his somersaults assumed capturing time itself and with it, better still, an understanding better than any dive. Which must be like my real job. To see the ground coming up, and from a long angle winter wheat growing out of it. Be the Bedouin born without eyes or a bald child's shaved-head hairline, or a tongueless.

And what gives me, through having worked my way down to semiretired Reserve photographer reportedly of the Scrolls' landfall, eighteen-inch capsule turning and aiming, turning some more, along the currents of the great system of wells restless as undulating rooms I hear my sister reading when we think of water, the right to hold forth on competitive full twist or answer if the President should be on the short list for the Peace Prize? At least I do not dream of training on the job as CEO of the nation having owned a chain of prisons or laundry slash dry cleaning establishments or a baseball team or for a thousand days read the Tao in a public place to learn how to do nothing, or studied how to be a photo op against strong backlight.

"Yes?" I said, the crowded Hearings room still before me, the hand raised now Husky's: "That's it," he says, "that's it. '*Yes*,' you said, *Yes*," getting to his feet managing to tip his chair into someone's lap — "I said it this morning, or I didn't say it, or I did," Husky calls — while, edging down the aisle as if he would do something or, now in the row behind, hand Husky a mike, CE*O* broad-shouldered — while at the back who but my sister comes into view, Husky's *her* friend —"the kid with his tongue cut out, Zach," Husky unaware of CEO, the stillness embarrassed, souls having to cope with intelligence, Christian doubtless or fascinated, and still adrift in their own seamless interruption, mortal, knowing, shy, American, Husky though trying: "Feel like I know you, Zach. Photos I wasn't meant to see — headless kids, that blindfolded wheelie going off the ramp at the Base — *you* know what you did — down by al Kut, was it? And the one-legged Specialist coming in for her layup, and someone tied up under a table biting somebody, blood on her leg, on the floor, the Wildcat of Kut, was it sex you cropped outa that shot, take a mouthful to tell what's going on there." CEO with *captain* behind him reaches through the row. "And you're smart here and we all get the point but do we? Like 'profit-*stricken*' country, and it's funny, it's called for, but listen —"

Captain stepping on the overturned chair in the row behind and almost falling collars Husky; CEO stepping over bodies to pull Husky by the arm back toward the aisle, who finds himself if not the word, "The trouble is you're ..." —

Umo, my brother I will call him, who agreed that this Jesus must have meant business and capitalized on what he had going for him, asked if I really believed all that about proactive and gave me a look — did I believe all that? "'Course not, but — " and Umo said, "You're so ..." and found not the word but the moment.

Wind like another gravity slashed the crests and put the boy under again and rung by rung foot by foot I found a place to be hit by wind, dust, river, my own weight. The women at the other end of the ledge see what they see — that I have no rope, but a hand, a foot, to reach with, a foreigner here. Will I go in? The boy's face comes up, it knows it has lost the other. I will reach a whole level lower than the women's and crouch and find a concrete ledge to grip now half underwater for my hands and crawl out at right angles where I'm in range, it might be easy then. I miss my footing and hit my shin slipping down two rungs. It is only river wind but the current lifts even the cross-troughs, the surge rises at us on another scale, and the boy is cold, holding on and beaten. The women are speaking possibly to me, or silent. The time I have is no one's and I remember nothing, but it is in me.

Wick thinks it was good, very good, my choice words dispatching the military timed so well, public, how they just let that guy go. "Better get outa town, Zach."

Bea and the gray-haired retired Navy, who must be Liz's husband, and others crowd me now as another speaker on algebra olympiads and middle-school mathletes is announced and we might get away in one piece, yet Wick, with an always loosely assembled face of planes and a sag from the pure eyes, and I are here. Wick so glad I had rethought that old dive. You saved my life, Wick. Thanks, he says, but — it took him back, insisting now on some "fact of the matter" for I must pay for praising him.

My sister's disappeared on me, and I'm hearing Wick out. A window is thrown up on that terrible morning after the dive unbreathable, my whole self limping like the aged, left at the door by E to my teacher who'd heard.

Not very artistic, I said. You sleep? he asked. Back to the drawing board, I said almost voiceless. No, Wick didn't think so. Not able to ease into my desk, I find a chair at the back. What was the test gonna prove, Mr. Wicklow, a girl asked. It is what it is, was the answer. Our formative years, I said from the back, and got a nonlaugh. You finish building your house, Mr. Wick? Milt asked. Wick shakes his head, Not really — it's a job (the wife, the kids, money). Now at the board he's drawing posts like pillars. An infinite house, I say, an effort for me; an infinite ... Wick goes and throws up the window and I felt the frame collide in my carved, beating chest. Rethink it, Zach, rethink it, he had turned to me reserved, decisive. At the back of the room I looked up from my throbbing chest recalling I had offered to help him and his wife with the —

Rethink, hear? He was writing letters, fractions, on the board under the temple of his unfinished house.

So he bagged the quiz inspired he tells me now by me, and, barely holding a pencil, I wrote down stuff we hadn't had and hearing him demand to know what instantaneous motion was in a dive from point to point of the arc, then instantaneous position from time and a little more time, I grasped only that he had run the two tricks of what he called calculus together and, while the class writes frantically from board to page glad no gravity quiz today, I'm left with some infinite division of my failed full twist and a promise that I could remeasure it or myself, having made it to class really to measure how this high school swim-coach assistant to my dad might measure, move, assist me in what he now at the Competition Hearings called *my* doing. What *I'd* said.

Derived I couldn't take time or have mind to show spilled out from my sister reading with a headache the night before for me some space-time carpentered and planed self-building by a poet's unpretending time.

"You gotta go," Wick said, one eye on the math Olympics coach talking up front, and it's only after I'm in the elevator, angry Em had left, with according to Wick "ironic" the word the Hippy, like Umo long ago and to be sought out this coming week in Chula V, meant for me — "though that's how we grasp time, and Zach… and — " (everyone stopping for everyone else yet in motion) Wick thanking me for saving *his* life that morning of the canceled test — it got his *house* finished! — Zach? — and I with the smell of my sister's sheets winding along the ventricles of my hopes, soothing my terrible chest — Zach?

I had seen somewhere in my head the Honda's taillight and license plate disappearing out the basement garage ramp, trunk unlocked, which left me in a position not so miserable as in time not now endless but still to be gathered up in thought.

An instinct not to stick around, who were we, staring at someone else's water shadowed by their campfire? Our pathmaking along a different route back into the hidden dark of our chill canyon carries barely with us the evening light surveyed behind along the ridge and time that rushes subtly down around the horizon. A giant paintbrush so-called, ragged and growing up three inches off the dry ravine toward us living off underground relations, weeds — who knew what? — now blooms scarlet under the flashlight, it wasn't supposed to be there. Pathfinding we're as long as it took to find at the bottom our coals distant under their ash beside the stream our undrinkable BLM stream and the taut flank of our two-man tent and inside our half-zipped-together sleeping bags, a sweatshirt, a toothbrush, restless, ungathered, and there over the rampart of this canyon, just one of several canyons, that stranger's fire, the gallon jugs, three waters but what had we to swap for such a steal? — not even an underage beer.

I bear it in me on my hands and knees to the end of the concrete ledge and hear nothing but the river water and wind and trucks on the bridge up behind me and over my shoulder catch sight of four or five watchers on the bridge and so as not to lose my place and the boy, I lie in the shifting depth of water on the concrete ledge, the small of my back balanced on the end, extending my legs, my boots as far as I can and further for the boy to bring his other hand this way, and then I bring my legs together to give him more to get hold of: one hand and now, something in his open mouth and eyes, reading my foot, the other hand letting go of the submerged projection I figure he'd sunk his claw anchor onto, and I feel his weight in my stomach and push with my hands against the raw sides of the ledge to bring us in toward the other ledge, a two-person dive in reverse but almost too slow exchanging what we bring to each other.

A great thing you would do that fell away even as your question in mid-word turned to statement. And it was not you but the black-skinned man from the West on a bench aware of maybe being watched who wrote the last words rendering into Chinese the page of the English-language Directory the great boy, who figures in the plans of the local sports authority, has improperly borrowed because the city and state of the entry on page 153 and "Olympic" and the year numbers and some shadow of bond extended as if you knew the language if you'd find it in you persuaded him that he must have someone who doesn't know him tell what it is in Chinese. The man looks up, a traveler, irritable and taking a chance he can't name, and hands the little translation to the boy who takes it from him almost rudely like news, reads what is there, and reaches into his shoulder bag, so different in scale from him. He peels off layers of tissue from the small porcelain object, a China dog. The man can't accept it. Not a gift, the boy retorts. Made by his father who is not here. In exchange for translation — these Chinese words. It is something great the boy has found to do, this exchange, one thing for another. All right, he'll keep it for him, the man says. The boy laughs. His father made hundreds like it once. But this comes from you, the man replies. They look around them for it is not safe. It is noon, and the Directory is returned to the boy's bag. The two examine each other. The transaction is done. What is it they trust?

JOSEPH MCELROY is the author of nine novels, a novella, and a volume of short fiction. A volume of his essays, *Exponential*, has been published in Italy and in expanded form will be forthcoming as an e-book from Dzanc. Three short plays are forthcoming. He received the Award in Literature from the American Academy of Arts and Letters and fellowships from the Guggenheim, Rockefeller, and D.H. Lawrence Foundations, twice from Ingram Merrill and twice from the National Endowment for the Arts. He has taught at numerous universities. McElroy was born in Brooklyn, New York, in 1930. He was educated at Williams College and Columbia University.